Praise for the novels of Heather Graham

"Graham expertly blends a chilling history of the mansion's former residents with eerie phenomena, once again demonstrating why she stands at the top of the romantic suspense category."
—*Publishers Weekly* on *Phantom Evil,* starred review

"An incredible storyteller."
—*Los Angeles Daily News*

"A fast-paced and suspenseful read that will give readers chills while keeping them guessing until the end."
—*RT Book Reviews* on *Ghost Moon*

"If you like mixing a bit of the creepy with a dash of sinister and spine-chilling reading with your romance, be sure to read Heather Graham's latest.... Graham does a great job of blending just a bit of paranormal with real, human evil."
—*Miami Herald* on *Unhallowed Ground*

"The paranormal elements are integral to the unrelentingly suspenseful plot, the characters are likable, the romance convincing, and, in the wake of Hurricane Katrina, Graham's atmospheric depiction of a lost city is especially poignant."
—*Booklist* on *Ghost Walk*

"Graham's rich, balanced thriller sizzles with equal parts suspense, romance and the paranormal— all of it nail-biting."
—*Publishers Weekly* on *The Vision*

"Mystery, sex, paranormal events. What's not to love?"
—*Kirkus Reviews* on *The Death Dealer*

Also by HEATHER GRAHAM

* * * * *

Look for Heather Graham's next novel
An Angel for Christmas

HEATHER GRAHAM

THE EVIL INSIDE

MIRA®

ISBN-13: 978-1-61793-191-8

THE EVIL INSIDE

Printed in U.S.A.

For Lisa Manetti, Corinne De Winter,
Brent Chapman, Juan Roca, Dennis Pozzessere,
Jason Pozzessere, Dennis Cummins, and all our
group, and the amazing scares and laughs
we all shared at the Lizzie Borden House.
(And thanks to the house's beautiful current owner!)

In memory of my in-laws,
Angelina Mero and Alphonso Pozzessere;
I can't think of Massachusetts without
thinking about them, and smiling.

And in memory of Alice Pozzessere Crosbie and
"Uncle Buppy," and for the Crosbie clan,
Steven, Ginger, Linda, Tommy, Billy,
and Mary, and their families.

And for the great, diverse state of Massachusetts.
Especially Gloucester, and Hammond Castle,
where Derek and Zhenia had
the most beautiful wedding ever.

Prologue

The boy stood naked in the middle of the road.

Sam Hall's headlights caught him there, frozen in position, like a deer. He was covered in something slick, and it dripped down his flesh. It looked reddish, like blood, as if the kid had run off the set of a horror movie after being drenched in buckets of the stuff.

Sam slammed his foot on the brake pedal, grateful for once that his years with Mahon, Mero and Malone had given him the ability to afford the new Jaguar with the stop-on-a-dime brakes.

Even then, the car pulled to a halt just inches before the boy.

Swearing softly beneath his breath and puzzled beyond measure, Sam jumped out of the car. "Hey, what the hell are you doing there, son?"

The boy didn't move, didn't seem to realize that he'd nearly been roadkill. He just shook as he stood there. Summer had recently turned to fall, and the air had a sharp nip, typical for Massachusetts at this time of year. Tree-laden tracts lined the road; the old oaks seemed to bend and moan with the breeze, while multicolored leaves danced on the road and swept around the scene as if they, too, were deeply disturbed.

The boy didn't acknowledge Sam or look at him.

Again Sam swore softly. There was obviously something really wrong, though this kid couldn't have been injured severely and still be able to stand as he was.

He couldn't have lost that amount of blood and still be conscious.

Was it really blood...couldn't be.

Either way, Sam couldn't leave him in the middle of the road.

He looked at the new Jag he really loved, with the leather seats he also loved, and walked around to his trunk and found the beach blanket he'd picked up on his recent drive to the Florida Keys. It was sandy, but it would warm the kid.

He returned quickly, but the kid hadn't run off, much less moved. "Are you hurt?" he asked quietly.

He received no response.

"Here, here, you're going to have to get into my car," Sam said, approaching the boy with the blanket. "We'll get you to a hospital."

Sam wrapped the blanket around him. "Sorry about the sand," he said.

The kid looked to be somewhere between fifteen and seventeen, but underdeveloped. He was painfully thin. His eyes were huge and brown in the lean contours of his face. His chest was devoid of hair, so most of the blood had slid down his chest.

The temperature seemed to be around forty degrees

Fahrenheit. It wasn't freezing, but the kid shouldn't be exposed to this long.

Sam intended to get him into the car. And yet, as he stood there, trying to be compassionate while saving his wool coat from the sticky red substance that looked like blood, he suddenly froze.

It didn't just look like blood—it *was* blood.

Denial rushed through his mind.

But it was blood, no denying it.

Pig's blood, cow's blood…hell, *rabbit's* blood.

But something told Sam that it was not.

He drew the blanket off the boy and turned him around, seeking an injury that might have caused that amount of blood.

But he didn't find any. If he had, the boy wouldn't have been standing upright. He wouldn't have been breathing. He'd have been dead from a wound like that.

He'd already wrapped the blanket around the kid. No undoing that.

And if he could, would he leave the kid there shivering with nothing?

Still standing in front of the boy, who didn't even reach up to hold the blanket in place, he fumbled in his pocket for his cell phone and hit 911. An operator with a droning voice asked him what his emergency was.

"My name is Samuel Hall. I was driving into Salem when I nearly hit a young man in the road. He's covered in blood. It doesn't appear to be his blood, but I can't be certain that he isn't injured. He's standing on his own, and doesn't seem in any way to be too weak to do so, but he's nonresponsive. He may be in shock. Can you get someone out here—fast?" He looked around and quickly gave his position as best he could. Hell, it was a quiet backwoods road. He'd opted to take IA north from Boston, but had turned off early. The dark, quiet road through the trees had seemed a soothing path for his first visit home in a long time.

"Stay calm now, Mr. Hall," the operator told him. "I'll have a car out to your position immediately. Patrolmen are in the vicinity. It won't be long. You're sure the young man isn't bleeding? If so, you must stanch the flow of blood. Stay calm. Are you doing all right?"

He hesitated for the fraction of a second, staring at the phone, his mind racing. He thought of the horrors he had witnessed in the military, and he thought of the crime-scene photos he'd studied as a criminal attorney.

"Ma'am," he said, his voice even and strong, "I'm about as calm as a dead Quaker. But you need to get someone out here fast. I'm going to suggest you send an investigator, because I have a feeling this might be human blood, and I don't want to compromise any more evidence than I already have by putting my blanket around the boy."

"Of course, sir. Please remain on the line. And do your best to remain calm."

"If you tell me to remain calm one more time, I'm going to implode and become consumed by spontaneous combustion—"

"There's already a car on the way. Sir, you just have to remain calm. This is Salem, Massachusetts, sir, and we are moving into the Halloween season now, you know. You may be the victim of prank. Now, stay on the line, and remain calm, Mr. Hall." She gasped suddenly, her well-learned rhetoric failing her for a moment. "Oh, you're *the* Sam Hall—"

He heard the sound of a siren then. "They're here" is all he said. "Thanks." He hit the end icon on his phone.

A patrol car pulled up on the road in front of him, and the glare of its lights met and mingled with the Jag's headlights, almost blinding him for a minute. Two uniformed officers exited from either side of the car, guns in position.

"He's not armed!" Sam called. "He's—he's in shock. He needs medical attention."

"An ambulance is on the way," the driver called out. "And Detective Alden. I radioed him on my way out."

Alden? He wondered if it was his old friend John. Puritan names still abounded here, and John Alden and he had been on the football team together. John had always wanted to be a cop, a detective, actually. He must have worked his way up through the ranks.

The patrolmen walked forward, slowly holstering their guns as they saw that the shaking youth carried no weapon and that Sam seemed nonthreatening, as well.

"Patrolman Nathan Brewster," one said, introducing himself. "And my partner, Robert Bishop."

Sam nodded. "Samuel Hall," he said, but the patrolmen were just staring at the boy. They glanced at each other uneasily.

"Yeah, yeah, Detective Alden is on his way. Any minute now," Brewster said, almost as an afterthought.

"What's going on?" Sam asked. The two were behaving curiously. They had holstered their weapons but appeared ready to spring for them again at any second.

Neither touched the boy. Neither spoke to him. The kid was shaking harder and harder, despite the blanket Sam had set around his shoulders. Neither did the boy make any attempt to hold the blanket to his bony frame.

Again, the two exchanged glances. "We're not really at liberty to say, sir."

"Fine, well, I think we have to get him into a heated car, or he'll die of exposure pretty soon," Sam said. True or not, he couldn't bear watching the shocked youth stare wide-eyed at nothing and shake anymore.

But before the patrolmen were compelled to respond, the sound of sirens suddenly seemed to grow to an alarming pitch. First on the scene was an unmarked car. A grim, solid-looking man of about fifty in a worn woolen coat and plaid sweater exited the driver's side of the car and strode quickly toward them.

Plainclothes cop. Detective, Sam thought. He hoped it was John.

And it was.

But unlike the others, he didn't pull a weapon. He hurried forward, passing between the patrolmen and Sam and the youth. He didn't look at Sam, but at the boy, and his expression wasn't authoritarian or harsh, but sad.

"Malachi," he said. "Good God, Malachi, you've done it now."

"Excuse me. He's shivering. He's freezing. He's in shock. John? It's Sam—Sam Hall."

John Alden turned and looked at Sam.

"Sam!"

"I was on my way to the folks' place. I nearly hit the boy. He was just standing there, in the road. Covered in blood."

"Sam," Alden repeated.

He looked as if he was about to say *good to see you* or something to that effect, but in the road with a blood-splattered boy, it just wasn't appropriate.

"John, this kid needs help. I think he's in shock," Sam repeated.

John Alden nodded and indicated, with the cast of his head, the ambulance that had arrived. "Yeah, he'll get medical attention. And he's in shock, you say? He should be. He just hacked his family to death."

1

Lexington House.

There it stood, on a cliff by the water. It might have been a postcard or a movie poster, and it was as eerie as ever—a facade that graced the darkest horror movie. Its paint was chipping, the exterior was gray and it had been weathered through the centuries by icy winds ripping in off the Atlantic Ocean. The ground-floor windows seemed like black eyes; the second-floor windows might have been startled brows, half covered by the eaves of the roof.

Oddly enough, Lexington House had always remained in private hands. From its builder—the Puritan Eli Lexington—to its recent owner—the now deceased Abraham Smith—it had always found a new buyer after each and every one of its tragedies. People had once known its early history, of course, but that had been lost amid the witchcraft trials that scarred American history and continued to fascinate the social sciences. And when Mr. and Mrs. Braden had been brutally murdered two centuries later, in the 1890s, the world knew that their son had been guilty of the crime. But the legal system had worked for the killer this time, and he'd been ac- quitted. He and his sister had promptly sold the house to another private party. Eighty years later it had become a bed-and-breakfast, and then it had been purchased by Abraham Smith, who had longed for the property on its little cliff, segregated from all but a few neighbors.

One of whom had been murdered last week.

And now today...

Jenna Duffy had heard about nothing but the Lex- ington House on the radio since she'd started for Salem from Boston this morning. Uncle Jamie had called her days before, begging that she come to Salem and speak with him. Peculiar timing.

She'd pulled to the side of the road and parked to stare at the place.

A patrol car sat near the house; crime-scene tape cordoned off the entire house. There were no onlook- ers, though. The house was at a little distance from the historic section of town, where most visitors strolled through the Old Burial Ground, visited the House of the Seven Gables or sought out history at any one of the witch museums or the Peabody Essex Museum. And since it was October and Halloween was approaching, the real-life contemporary tragedy would fuel the ghost stories that were already being told around town.

She stared at the house awhile longer, wondering about its history. What happened at Lexington House would prove to be another horrible case of mental in- stability or greed, and as much as she longed to actu- ally see the property that brought about such gruesome tragedy, she had a meeting with her uncle. She glanced at her watch and pulled back onto the road. With Halloween tourists clogging the city, it might take her time to get where she was going.

Somehow she was still early.

She parked her car at the Hawthorne Hotel's parking lot, and wandered across the street to the common.

Autumn leaves, beautiful in their warm orange, magenta and yellow colorings, rustled beneath Jenna's feet as she strolled. Before her and around her, the leaves swirled and lifted inches into the air as the breeze picked them up and whimsically tossed them about.

She heard the laughter of schoolchildren as they made their way through Salem Common, heading home but not too quickly. Autumn was certainly one of the most beautiful seasons in New England, and schoolchildren, raised with all the colors as they may have been, still loved to stop and lift the leaves, toss them about and roll in them.

Jenna had loved Salem since she'd first come to the States and her parents had chosen nearby Boston, Massachusetts, as the place to begin their new lives. They had come up here weekends, in the summers and for the Halloween festivity, and also for the fall leaves and to see Uncle Jamie.

But this was a difficult visit. She was about to meet Uncle Jamie at the Hawthorne Hotel, and she was worried about him. He'd been so anxious when he'd asked her to come. He was asking her in a professional capacity, but he didn't want her bringing "your *team*" or "your *unit*" or "the *official* group" with which she worked, not yet.

As she walked across the common, her attention was

drawn back to the children. A group of five- to seven-year-olds were holding hands, running in a circle and playing a game.

She froze as she heard them reciting the old rhyme repeated not just in this area, but around the country.

Oh, Lexington, he loved his wife,
So much he kept her near.
Close as his sons, dear as his life;
He chopped her up;
He axed them, too,
and then he kept them here.
Duck, duck, wife!
Duck, duck, life!
You're it!

Jenna felt as if ice water had suddenly been injected in her veins—the old ditty now seemed to be words of mockery and cruelty. A young woman, who had been standing with another group of parents watching over small children and a group of older teens who had gathered in the park, rushed forward. She caught hold of the little boy's arms, spun him around and shook a finger at him, reprimanding him.

Another of the mothers came hurrying over to her, her voice carrying in the cool air. "Cindy, don't be so hard on them! They don't…know. We used to say that rhyme all the time when we were kids."

"Samantha, I know, it's just that…now? Now, with what's happened again? It's that house! That horrible house, and that boy… He used to go to school with *our* kids."

"But, it's over now, Cindy. It's over. They have the boy in custody."

Other parents began calling out sharply to their children. The two women herded the children toward the group of parents. A tall man in the group said something sharply to the teens, words that Jenna couldn't quite hear, and they disbanded, as well. The conversation they all exchanged became whispers. The families and the unattached teens began to drift away, as if none of them wanted the reality of the situation.

The great seafaring days of Salem were in the past. The city survived on tourism, and most of it wasn't because of the autumn leaves. Salem had been the site of the infamous Salem Witch Trials—and it had also been the site of two horrendous and savage murdering sprees.

And, now, a third.

Tragic incidences of human ignorance and brutality in the past were one thing; bloodletting in the present was quite another, especially with the town anticipating the season's mammoth number of visitors. The income generated by the holiday alone could sustain many a shopkeeper and inn through the brutal New England winter to follow.

Of course, for Uncle Jamie, the recent tragedy would not be in any way fiscal but personal. She knew Jamie and loved him dearly, because he was a man who took the troubles of others to heart. This was often to his own detriment, but that was Jamie.

From her vantage spot, she could see the Salem Witch Museum with its English Gothic facade across the street on North Washington Square—the point where she always told friends to begin their exploration of the city. In a comparatively short presentation, the museum did a fine job of explaining the climate of the city during the days of the infamous trials. The statue of Roger Conant, town founder, stood proud before her as well, larger than life, his heavy cape appearing to blow in the same breeze that tossed the leaves about.

The residences and businesses surrounding the common were decked out for fall. Pumpkins and black cats adorned windows and lawns, while skeletons and, naturally, witches dangled from branches. Some people were more into the traditional concept of fall itself, and they had decorated with scarecrows, feathered turkeys and cornucopias. The image of the city of Salem she saw as she stood in the common was that of old New England, family and festivity, tinged with the strange pleasant warmth of the coming of fall.

She glanced at her watch again. It was time to go and meet Uncle Jamie; she suddenly realized she had been dreading the meeting, and she didn't even know why.

Sam poured himself a second cup of coffee and looked around the house, trying to concentrate on its details and trying to make up his mind. He didn't like wondering what the hell he was going to do about the house, but it was better than thinking about the bizarre and tragic circumstances under which he had finally made it home.

He didn't need to get involved—he wasn't staying here. He'd already taken a nice long leave of absence, and it was time to go back to work. But, then, he mused, maybe he shouldn't. He'd not only saved his client from prison, but he'd proved beyond a doubt that the man not only deserved to be declared innocent, but *was,* in fact, innocent. And he was still a bit worn down from all the effort.

Sam had really stepped on every rung of the ladder on his way to becoming a renowned attorney. He'd worked in the D.A.'s office following college and the military. He'd worked as an investigator as well before joining his first small firm, because his boss had needed an investigator more than another attorney in the office. He'd learned the ropes from Colin Blake, Esquire, and he'd come to terms with a sad truth: a defense attorney was still required to give his best effort in a legal defense, even if he thought his client was guilty as all hell. He'd learned to make the cops and the prosecutors suffer, but discovered he didn't much like that side of the business. Still, despite that, he wasn't sure he could ever go back to being a prosecutor. It wasn't the money. Well, it was *about* money. Often. It was sometimes about the money it took to put together a great team of defense attorneys. He'd seen a young woman sent to prison for years, convicted of the murder of her newborn. He'd seen a rich young man walk on drug charges, and a poor one sent up fifteen years for the same offense. He understood the law; he didn't understand why the slow wheels of Congress took so long to correct the inequities that were to be found in so many instances. He was violently opposed to the death penalty, always afraid that somewhere, sometime, it would send an innocent person to his or her death, and yet he understood the desire others felt to see it utilized. Too many drug lords, murderers and rapists made it back onto the street.

But last night...

Something about the kid he'd come upon in the street was still tugging at his heartstrings.

The kid, according to police, had axed his family to death.

There was no doubt that Malachi Smith's father, mother, grandmother and great-uncle had been murdered, and horribly so. Jumping on the internet that morning, he'd seen that the news regarding the killings had gone global. Abraham Smith, sixty-two, Beth Smith, fifty-nine, Abigail Smith, eighty-three, and Thomas Smith, eighty-seven, had all died from exsanguination—Beth, Abigail and Thomas all receiving at least eight blows from a honed ax, Abraham over twenty. The previous week, a neighbor, Mr. Earnest Covington, had been found hacked to death on his parlor floor. Six months earlier, a Salem native living in nearby Andover had been found murdered in his barn. Police had been following leads and now suspected that the cases were related.

Indisputable evidence indicated that the youngest son of the Smith family, Malachi, was the killer. The police had the young man in custody, and he remained under guard in isolation at a correctional facility hospital.

The Smiths were the current owners of Lexington House, famed for its bloody reputation. The family had adhered to strict fundamentalist teachings, being members of the Old Meeting House in Beverly, Massachusetts. This was a strange connection of sorts with the

original murders in the place. In the midst of the witchcraft trials, Eli Lexington had murdered his family with
an ax. He'd been imprisoned with the nearly two hundred arrested for witchcraft at the time. Then he disappeared. There were no records of his fate after prison.

Then, in the late eighteen hundreds, Mr. and Mrs.
Braden had been killed in the house, as well. A his-
torical parallel of the Menendez case? From the books,
movies and court records that had come down through
time, it appeared that a disgruntled son had killed his
parents for the money. And, of course, similar cases had
been suspected elsewhere. The Braden case was similar,
too, to the Lizzie Borden murders. Both Lizzie and the
Braden boy had been acquitted, but nobody doubted
that each of them had murdered their families.

Just like today's case.

Sam told himself over and over to get the hell away
from his computer. He was *not* involved.

But he was.

He'd found the kid in the road.

And, he'd grown up in Salem. He could still remember
being a school kid, and the rhyme every school kid in
the area had learned. *Oh, Lexington, he loved his wife...*

A good attorney, of course—even a hack—would
go for an insanity plea. The kid had grown up in what
everyone in the area termed a haunted house—*a really
haunted house*—which, in a city like Salem, was saying
something.

Any attorney could defend the boy. It was too easy.

He forced himself to leave the computer screen and
walk around the house.

His parents had been dead for nearly two years; he'd returned for the funeral, and he hadn't been back since. The house, however, was in excellent shape. His father, until his death, had seen to it that no electrical wires frayed, that the heating system was state-of-the-art and that every board that even seemed slightly damaged was replaced. His father's friend and contractor, Jimmy Chu, had kept the house in good repair during the two years. His dad had come from old Puritan stock, and he'd considered it an honor to care for the home that his parents had owned, just as his grandparents before them did. It wasn't one of the oldest houses in the area, but it ranked right in there with many of the homes surviving from the turn of the eighteenth century all the way into the twenty-first.

He smiled suddenly, shaking his head and taking a sip of the coffee he still held, untouched. "Darn you, Dad. You knew that I won't be able to sell the damned thing!"

A house—in a city in which he no longer lived—was a pain in the ass, no matter what. He guessed that his father had always figured he'd come home one day.

Well, he'd managed to, but on the wrong damned day. He dropped his head. He didn't want to be involved with a legal situation here.

But he couldn't blink without seeing in his mind's eye the blank brown eyes of the naked boy covered in blood and shaking on the road.

"Jenna!" Uncle Jamie drew her to him, giving her a warm and emphatic hug.

She hugged him in turn. She loved Jamie. She loved her family in general. Despite their long history of warfare, the Irish were an exceptionally warm, passionate and profuse people. They were full of magical tales, and they seldom felt obliged to refrain from speaking their minds.

"Uncle Jamie!" she said.

He pulled her away for a moment, holding her at arm's length to study her. Jamie had brilliant green eyes and graying auburn hair. He was her mother's younger brother, and had always had a mischievous side to him, making him very popular among children. He was so devout that he'd nearly gone into the priesthood, but had decided at the last minute that he didn't really have the calling. He'd attended medical school and become a psychiatrist instead.

"You look good, my girl, aye, that you do! Pretty thing, you always were. Beautiful eyes, green like Eire, and hair like fire—you got my sister's temper to go with it, eh?" Her own accent had become little more than a hint of a different place, but she had come to the States when she'd been a young teen. Jamie had been a grown man.

"Mum's temper isn't that bad, Uncle Jamie. She's a lot like you—opinionated."

He grinned. "Come over here, I've a booth for us," he told her. He slipped an arm through hers, leading her toward a corner booth. "Lovely, lovely, isn't it? I've always loved this city. You have the Wiccans with their wonderful shops—and their Wiccan gossip and squabbles, of course! You've got the immigrants and the old Puritan families, and all of them getting along—and not. But fall here is the most wonderful season in the world—everyone loving life and creating cornucopias and carving out pumpkins."

"Yes, I love it here, too, Uncle Jamie."

He looked around and motioned to the waitress. "What will you have, niece?"

She was surprised to feel a sudden chill. Jamie was hedging, and he usually just spoke plainly. It was unusual that he'd dawdle by ordering like this, but she decided she'd let him talk at his own speed. "Something warm," she replied.

"An Irish coffee?" he suggested.

"Why not?" she said.

Their waitress was wearing a cute, short-skirted pirate costume. Jamie asked to make sure that the bartender used Jameson Irish whiskey, and that they didn't go putting a wallop of "white stuff"—whipped cream—on either drink. The waitress smiled. "Jamie, you order the same thing every time you come in."

"So I do," Jamie told her, grinning. "But, still, a man's got to be careful when he orders his drink."

Laughing and shaking her head, the waitress moved on with a swish of her short skirt.

"They do get into Halloween early, don't they," Jenna murmured.

"Well, you know the whole pumpkin-carving thing is Irish, of course," Jamie said.

"I know, Uncle Jamie..." she said to the familiar information, knowing it wouldn't stop him. She thanked the waitress as she delivered their drinks. Jamie didn't seem to notice.

"It all came from Stingy Jack," Jamie said, studying his cup, and speaking to himself more than her.

"A myth about a man named Stingy Jack," Jenna reminded him.

He waved a hand in the air.

"The devil invited old Jack to have a drink with him, and Jack, he wasn't about to pay for the drinks, but then neither was he about to turn one down. So, our Jack, he tells the devil that he must turn himself into a handful of coins to pay for the drink. But, thirsty though he was, Jack was a clever boy, and put the coins in his pocket, around his silver cross, and the devil, next to that cross, couldn't turn himself back into the devil, not next to the holy relic! Finally, though, Jack let the devil return to his old self—long as he didn't bother Jack for a year and a day—and would not claim his soul if he should die. There are stories of Jack playing a few other tricks on the devil over his lifetime. Eventually, of course, he did die. And when he did, the Good Lord would not let him into Heaven, and the devil could not claim his soul, and so he was sent into the dark of the night with only a burning lump of coal to light his way. Well, Jack found a pumpkin, carved it out, and carried it about endlessly through the darkness of the night. And so he was called Jack of the Lantern, and finally, Jack-o'-Lantern." He paused to take a gulp.

"It's not a bad tradition—especially for those who scoop out the pumpkin and make pie and then carve the pumpkin to burn with an eerie—or happy!—face throughout the night," he finished.

"Pumpkin pie *is* delightful," Jenna said, leaning

toward him and touching his hand. "But I'm pretty sure this story isn't why I'm here, Uncle Jamie. Talk to me. Why did you want me here? I'm delighted to see you, you know that. But you called me and said that you needed me."

Jamie nodded, running his fingers over the varnished wood of the table. "It may be too late," he said softly. Then he looked up at her. "They think they have him dead to rights. They say that the blood of those he murdered was all over him, and that his fingerprints were on the ax. But he didn't do it, Jenna. He didn't do it."

She frowned. He was talking now, but he was beginning in the middle.

"You asked me here…about the murders that occurred? But…the family was just killed last night. You called me two days ago."

Jamie shook his head. "I called you about two murders that had happened earlier—and then last night occurred…and now they have the boy…and I just don't believe he did it. He'll be railroaded into a mental hospital for the rest of his life—but he's not crazy! People started saying that it was the house—that it's Lexington House, and that he lived there and started killing because he was listening to ghosts. Thing is, I know that by what seems like *obvious* evidence he looks guilty as all hell, but that's only what it *looks like*. He didn't do it."

She shook her head. "All right, back up. You called me because of the two previous murders. The radio mentioned those on the way up here, too, but only bits and pieces and suppositions. I don't really know details. Tell me about them."

"Six months ago, a farmer in Andover, Peter Andres, was killed in his barn—with a scythe. The police had no suspects—the scythe was in the barn, but there were no fingerprints other than those of Andres. Everyone was baffled. Andres was known as an affable man. But the rumor mill got started—the rhyme about Lexington House doesn't tell it all. In the nineteenth century, a scythe was supposedly used on the Braden father before he was given the final blows by the ax. So, the police started looking at people with an interest in Lexington House, and then at Lexington House itself. Malachi was always the subject of some rumor or other—he's a strange lad. But he tells me that he prays, and he believes deeply in God and in Heaven."

"Many killers find Jesus," Jenna said softly. "How did you know all this about him?"

Jamie shook his head. "They find Jesus in *prison*— Malachi has always had him." He sighed. "The boy came to me three years ago. His parents brought him to me—they were forced to, by children's services, after a few incidents at school."

"Like what—he attacked other children? Threw rocks at birds…set cats on fire?"

"No, no. Nothing of the like. He was teased, beaten and bullied by other boys. He just sat there when they hurt him and said that God was his protector and that Jesus would turn the other cheek."

"And then?"

"Soon after, the parents decided to take him out of school, but because of another incident, a really strange incident. And that's when children's services ordered that he see a psychiatrist—me."

"So how long have you been seeing him?" she asked.

"If you'd asked the parents? He was my patient for a year. Social services paid me for a year. But I've seen him ever since—more as a friend than a patient. It all began about three years ago, when his parents pulled him out of school. Thing was, in his own way, he was happy to come see me. Musical instruments, other than the voice, were a sin in his house. But he's something of a genius with the piano. At my house, he could play."

"What was the incident that caused social services to step in?" Jenna asked.

"He looked at a boy," Jamie said.

"Looked at him?" Jenna repeated, puzzled.

Jamie nodded. "The boy was throwing food from his lunch tray at Malachi. Malachi looked at him, and this other boy froze—and then he picked up his tray and beat himself over the head with it so hard that he had a concussion. He was hysterical and told the doctors that Malachi had forced him to do it—with his eyes."

Jenna leaned back, staring at Jamie, frowning. "Wait—this other kid said that Malachi looked at him, and made him beat himself silly?"

Jamie nodded.

Jenna shook her head. "Why—that's preposterous. Especially here. It's like the girls crying *Witch! Witch! Witch!* and causing the unjust deaths of twenty people and the incarceration of nearly two hundred more. I'd thought we'd learned some lessons…"

Jamie sighed. "He was better off out of school. The

thing is, I think that Malachi desperately wanted to be normal. He was malnourished, and he was raised to think that just about everything in the world was evil, an idea browbeaten into him by a fanatical father. He never lost his temper—the other kids couldn't goad him to act. And that made them mad. He's the most peace-loving individual I've ever met. When the neighbor, Earnest Covington, was killed, one of the boys who he'd been with at school went to the police and told them that Malachi had come running out of the house. They brought Malachi in for questioning, but Mrs. Sedge at the grocery store, said that Malachi had been in the meat section at the time, choosing dinner cuts for his mother—she never left the house—so he was off the hook. But, then, last night... well, Malachi was found drenched in his family's blood, standing naked in the road."

Jenna put her hand on her uncle's. "Uncle Jamie, you have a friendship with this boy...but, if he was found covered in his family's blood...?"

"Jenna, I need you to find out the truth about that house," he said with resolution.

"Uncle Jamie—"

"We can't let the system take this boy. We have to somehow make it work for him now—now that he has a chance."

"A chance?"

"His parents are gone now," Jamie said quietly. He looked toward the ceiling. "God forgive me!" he murmured and crossed himself. He looked at Jenna solemnly. "You know I'm a religious man, right, Jenna?"

Surprised by the sudden question, she arched a brow

to him. "Well, you were *almost* a priest.… I didn't figure that meant you'd turned away completely but—sorry! No, I know that you still love the church."

He nodded. "I'm disappointed in the way human beings interpret religion at times, and God knows I loathe the horrible things done daily in the name of God and religion. But you don't go throwing the baby out with the bathwater, you know?"

"Jamie, you're losing me again."

"They were—fanatics," Jamie said. "I don't even know exactly what belief they adhered to, but it was with a vengeance. There was hell to pay when that boy didn't learn his Bible verses or when he couldn't recite huge tracts of the Bible."

"He was abused?"

"Not physically—they weren't beatings, or even severe spankings. Parents often tap the hands of little ones—to stop them touching a stove top, a light socket… No, the abuse was mental and, well, I do suppose physical in a way. No food could be eaten without the father's blessing.…"

Jamie stopped speaking for a minute.

"You can't imagine the peace in that boy's eyes at times. He doesn't do evil things because of the ghosts in a house, and he doesn't do evil things because his father was a religious zealot who turned everything to sin. I don't believe he does evil things at all—especially not murder. If ever anyone has been touched by the hand of *God,* I think it's that boy. And you have to help me save him. Maybe it's my mission in life, I don't really know. But I'm begging you. You have to get into that house, and you have to speak with Malachi."

"And how am I going to interfere when he's now in the hands of the police?"

Jamie looked past her and lowered his voice. "Well, with a wee bit of help from the Lord, I think I can convince his defense attorney that he needs your assistance."

She turned to see what had drawn Jamie's attention. It was a man, tall and broad shouldered. The coat he had worn into the bar was excellently cut, and he moved like someone accustomed to custom-tailored clothing. His face was strongly molded with a classic masculine line. His hair was neatly cut and combed, just slightly awry from the breeze. She thought that she recognized him, but she didn't know why she should have.

"Who is he?" she whispered.

"Samuel Anthony Hall, attorney-at-law."

She almost laughed aloud. She knew why she recognized him—she'd recently seen his name and picture all over the internet. The world had wanted his last client to fry for the heinous murder of his pregnant fiancée. The prosecution had DNA evidence that the two had engaged in intercourse the day of the murder, but Hall had proved that one of his client's enemies had killed the woman—a revenge killing. She couldn't remember the details, but the client had loose mob ties and the case had received major press attention.

"Actually, you've met him before, you know," Jamie said.

"I have?" Jenna looked at her uncle.

"You knew his parents, Betty and Connor. They were friends of mine, and they were friends of your folks, as well. You've been in his home. Maybe only once or twice—you were here when you were a young teenager and he was home from law school. He was supposed to be watching over you and a few of your friends. Silly, giggling girls. He thought you all were torture."

"Wow. Can't wait to meet him again, though I think I do remember his folks. They were very nice people."

"They were."

She studied Sam. He had the bearing of a man in charge—and a fighter. Or a bulldog.

"Samuel Hall," she mused, turning back to her uncle, slightly amused. "That's not the kind of attorney the state acquires when you haven't the resources to hire your own. And I'm assuming all the money Malachi might have will be in probate. And unless you've changed your ways—working for the state most of the time for almost nothing—you can't afford him. And even if our entire family was to put in our life savings, we still couldn't afford him. He was said to have made several hundred thousand—just off his last case."

"Yes, he can command a high fee," Jamie murmured.

"Too high," Jenna told him softly.

"He's going to do it pro bono," Jamie said.

She stared at him with surprise.

He grinned. "All right, so he doesn't know it yet." He leaned forward. "And, dear niece, if you don't mind, please give him one of your best smiles and your sweetest Irish charm."

2

"Sam!"

Sam Hall turned to see that Jamie O'Neill was hailing him from one of the booths. O'Neill wasn't alone. He was with a stunning young redheaded woman who had craned her neck to look at him. She was studying him intently, her forehead furrowed with a frown.

He thought at first that she was vaguely familiar, and then he remembered her.

She had changed.

He couldn't quite recall her name, but he remembered her being a guest at his house once, and that she—and half a dozen other giggling girls—had turned his house upside down right when he'd been studying. But his mother had loved to host the neighborhood girls, not having had a daughter of her own.

Before, she had been an adolescent. Now, she had a lean, perfectly sculpted face and large, beautiful eyes. Her hair was the red of a sunset, deep and shimmering and—with its swaying, long cut—sensual. She appeared grave as she looked at him and, again, something stirred in his memory; maybe he'd seen her somewhere—or a likeness of her—since she'd become an adult. She was O'Neill's niece, of course. And her parents, Irish-turned-Bostonian, had been friends with his folks.

"Sam, please! Come and join us," Jamie called.

He'd ordered a scotch and soda. Drink in hand, he walked to the booth. He liked the old-timer. O'Neill was a rare man. He possessed complete integrity at all costs. An immigrant, he'd put himself through eight years of school to achieve his degree in psychiatry. He lived modestly in an old wooden house, and he still probably took on more patients through the pittance granted him by the state than any other person imaginable. Sam had heard a rumor that Jamie had gone through a seminary but then opted to live a life outside the Catholic church.

But when he really looked at the grave look on Jamie's face, he felt a strange tension shoot through his muscles.

Jamie wasn't calling him over just to say hello. He wanted something from him.

Sam wished he'd never come into the bar.

"Sam, do you remember my niece, Jenna Duffy? Jenna, Sam, Sam Hall."

Jenna Duffy offered him a long, elegant hand. He was surprised that, when he took it, her handshake was strong.

"We've met, so I've been told," she said. He found himself fascinated with her eyes. They were so green. Deep viridian, like a forest.

"I have a vague memory myself," he said.

"Sam, sit, please—if you have the time?" Jamie asked.

He was tempted to say that he had a pressing engagement. Hell, he'd gone to law school and, sometimes, in a courtroom, he realized that it had almost been an education in lying like wildfire while never quite telling an untruth. It was all a complete oxymoron, really.

"You're on a leave, aren't you? Kind of an extended leave?" Jamie asked him, before he could compose some kind of half truth.

"It's not exactly a leave, since I choose my own cases, but, yeah, I've basically taken some time. I'm just deciding what to do with my parents' home," he replied.

He slid into the seat next to Jenna Duffy. He noted her perfume—it was nice, light, underlying. Subtle. It didn't bang him on the head. No, this was the kind of scent that slipped beneath your skin, and you wondered later why it was still hauntingly in the air.

"You're not going to sell your parents' house, are you?" Jamie sounded shocked.

"I've considered it."

"They loved that place," Jamie reminded him.

Jenna was just listening to their conversation, offering no opinion.

"They're gone," Sam said. He shook his head. "I just don't really have a chance to get up here all that often anymore."

"It's a thirty-minute ride," Jamie said. "And it's—it's so wonderful and historic."

"So is Boston," Sam said.

"Ah, but nothing holds a place in the annals of American—and human!—history as does Salem," Jamie said.

"You're trying to shame me, Jamie O'Neill," Sam said. He smiled slowly.

Jamie waved a hand in the air. "It's not as if you need the money."

Ouch. That one hurt, just a little bit.

"Jamie, you didn't call me over here to give me a guilt complex about my parents' house..." Sam said.

Jamie looked hurt. "Young man—"

"Yes, you would have said hello—you would have asked about my life. But what's going on? I know you. And that Irish charm. You're a devious bastard, really." Then he looked at Jenna and murmured, "Sorry."

"Oh, I don't disagree," she told him.

"So?"

"You found Malachi Smith in the road last night," Jamie said quietly.

Sam tensed immediately. The incident had been disturbing on so many levels. He couldn't forget the way that the boy had been shaking.

He stared back at Jamie. "I did."

"I don't believe that he did it," Jamie said.

Sam winced, staring down at his drink. He rubbed his thumb over the sweat on his glass. "Look, Jamie, I feel sorry for that kid. Really sorry for him. I've been watching the news all morning. His life must have been hell. But I saw him. He was covered in blood. How else did he become covered in blood if he wasn't the one who did it?"

"Ah, come on, you're a defense attorney!" Jamie said. "It's obvious."

"I'm missing obvious," Sam said drily. *No, not really. There was just this odd feeling. Why get involved any more than he already was? The horror he'd felt when he'd come upon the boy bathed in blood, in the middle of the road...*

"I think," Jenna said, "that it's possible that Malachi Smith came home to find his family butchered, and that he tried to wake them up, or perhaps wrap them in his arms, and therefore became covered in the blood."

"He was naked," Sam said flatly.

"Right. He became horrified by the amount of blood all around him, all over his clothing, and tried to strip it off—but there was so much of it, it was impossible," Jenna said.

He looked at her. "And you believe this?" he asked pointedly.

"I didn't grow up here—I was always a visitor—I never knew Malachi Smith or his family. I heard the rumors about them, and, naturally, everyone in the area knows about Lexington House. Well, it's the kind of legend that gets around everywhere, I suppose. I can't tell you about Malachi Smith—not the way that Uncle Jamie can. Jamie treated the boy. But I think that's the kind of possibility my uncle might have in mind. And I myself suppose it's possible. We'd have to know what Malachi has to say."

Sam stared at her for a long moment. Her eyes were enigmatic, so deep and mesmerizing a green. If he remembered correctly, she'd been something of a wiseass kid.

"Sam, they are your roots," Jamie said.

He laughed. "My roots? Lexington House is not part of my roots—I barely knew the Smiths. Again, and please, listen to me, Jamie, I understand how you feel.

I'm sorry for the boy. But, I don't like staying here too long—you wind up tangled in the history of the place, shopping for incense, herbs and tarot cards—and hating the Puritans. Religious freedom? Hell, they kicked everyone else out. Witchcraft? Spectral evidence…it's no wonder we have religious nuts like the Smiths moving in. And I like our modern Wiccans—do no harm and all that. But I'm not into chanting and worshipping mother earth, either. I seem to get too wrapped up when I'm here—I'm like you. I want to argue the ridiculous legal system of the past, and I find myself wondering sometimes if it does affect any insanity that goes on in the present. Maybe it's in the air, maybe it's in the grass and maybe people just really want to hurt one another. Maybe they can't *not* buy into all the hype of this place."

He stopped speaking. He was surprised at his own bitterness. He had never hated Salem. It was his home. The Peabody Essex Museum was an amazing place. People still tried hard to figure out just what had gone on, and how to improve the world in the future, to learn how to stop the ugliness of prejudice and hatred. Actually, he loved Salem itself. He loved many of the people. Maybe it was just him; maybe he still wanted to understand what could never be truly comprehended in the world they lived in now. But people *tried*. Tried to preserve the past to improve the present and the future.

And yet a whacked-out son of a bitch like Abraham Smith had moved in, tortured his son in a like manner to the rigid principles practiced long ago, and he'd never forget the way the kid had looked in the middle of the road, shaking, his eyes huge and terrified, blood drip-

ping off his naked body…and he couldn't help but feel that the father's method of raising the son had something to do with all that death.

Jamie was nonplussed by his speech. Jenna just looked at him with those beautiful green eyes that seemed to rip into the soul.

He sighed deeply. "You want me to defend the boy. It should be an open-and-shut case. There's just no way that a prosecutor would ever get a jury to believe that the boy was mentally competent when he committed the act."

"No!" Jamie said firmly. "I want you to prove that the boy didn't do it."

Sam groaned softly.

"Isn't that your specialty?" Jamie asked him. "Proving your client's innocence—and in so doing, finding the real killer?"

"Jamie, I'd like to help, but in this case—"

"I know we don't pay as well as the mob…" Jamie cut in.

"Oh, low blow, Jamie. Not fair. I've worked pro bono many times." He sighed deeply. "You don't just want me to defend Malachi Smith—you want me to find a killer. I haven't lived here in years—I wouldn't even begin to know where to look. And I'm an attorney—"

"You keep up with your private investigator's license," Jamie pointed out.

"We could be talking a conflict of interest in this situation," Sam said, "if I'm defending him *and* investigating the case."

Jamie smiled serenely. "Nope. It's perfectly legal for

you to hold and use your P.I. license while you practice law. And you know it. That's not an excuse—you've just come off a case in which you managed to do both. Any time whatsoever you're afraid of a conflict of interest, you send someone else out. You use your mind and your license when you need them. Send others out to do the work you've decided needs to be done."

"*What* others?" Sam asked, aggravated.

"Jenna," Jamie said, smiling then like the Cheshire cat.

"Your *niece?*"

"Jenna," Jamie repeated. "My niece is part of a special unit of the FBI."

Sam stared at the redheaded woman at his side. FBI? *Special Unit?*

"I'm not here officially," she said quickly.

"Of course not, you'd have to be invited in, and Detective John Alden is certain that he doesn't need help, that he has his murderer," Sam said, looking at her. "What kind of a special unit?"

"Jenna's team was instrumental in solving some of the most high-profile cases in the country," Jamie said proudly. "The recent Ripper murders in New York? That was her team. And all that trouble down in Louisiana with the death of a senator's wife—them again."

Sam stared at her, memories stirring in his mind. He remembered now. In the news they'd been called the Krewe of Hunters, and they had a phenomenal success rate. But they were known to be…special, all right. *They looked for paranormal occurrences. And what better place than Salem?*

He didn't mean to be so rude; he took his eyes off Jenna when he spoke. "The ghost of old Eli Lexington caused Malachi Smith to murder his family? No, wait, he wouldn't be innocent then. The ghost killed the family himself!"

"In my experience," she said evenly, "a ghost has never killed anyone."

"Kill someone? *Ghosts don't even*—" But he cut himself short.

Ass, he told himself. *She was being even-keeled. He was looking like a superior fool.*

"I'm sorry, Jamie, I'm not sure how we can possibly solve this thing, really. The kid was covered in blood. John Alden has arrested him."

"So," Jamie said, smiling, "that should get you going! It's too easy—way too easy—to take that line of defense. You should step up to the plate quickly. Please, Sam! Come on—they'll give him some kid fresh out of school as his public defender. Doesn't this interest you?"

"It is quite a challenge," Jenna said.

Sam groaned. "How about I sleep on it?"

"Evidence is growing cold," Jamie told him.

Jenna smiled suddenly, looking at him. "You're going to do it, and you know you're going to do it."

"Oh? Out of the kindness of my heart?" Sam asked.

"Maybe," she said. "More likely, because it is such a challenge. If you pull this off, you'll be known not just as an incredible attorney, but as a miracle worker."

Sam stood, not sure why the meeting with Jamie

O'Neill and his niece had seemed to set him so off balance.

Could he do it? Yes. He didn't need money. Was it an intriguing challenge? Maybe—and maybe it was more likely that the kid had done it.

"I'll let you know in the morning," he said, and walked away from the table. Then he headed back. "Look, I don't think you know how much is involved here. Besides the filing, the briefs…paperwork you can't even *begin* to imagine. And then, yes, investigating this? When the police think that they have their man? Not to mention the fact that you don't have a plausible alternate suspect. In fact, none of us has a clue."

For a moment he saw something in Jenna's eyes that agreed with him, and he wondered if Jamie hadn't managed to challenge his niece into this, as well. But just as quickly as the glint appeared, it vanished. Now, when she stared up at him, her eyes seemed as sharp as her tone. "Two other people were murdered and no arrests were made. With no real evidence, it's being quietly assumed that Malachi Smith murdered those other men, as well. He hasn't been charged with those murders, and I don't believe that they have a plan to charge him with them because they do have conflicting evidence where Peter Andres and Earnest Covington are concerned. So, in fact, you won't be going against the police if you are to claim to primarily be looking at those two incidents. There are plenty of places to start, Mr. Hall. Who were the other victims? What enemies might they have had? And what about the church Malachi Smith was involved with? It certainly had to be out of the ordinary."

"And you're going to investigate all this?" he asked her.

She smiled serenely. "I do have friends, Mr. Hall."

"Ah, yes, team members."

"I'll remind you that most of the cases we solve are at first thought to be almost impossible," Jenna said.

He couldn't decide what was really going on in her mind, her voice remained so even, and she maintained such an unruffled calm. He couldn't help but goad her on.

"Funny—I thought the NYPD had something to do with that last one!"

"The point is, Mr. Hall, no one is asking you to do all the work. I'm not a lawyer, but I do know how to work my way around legend and superstition, and the head of my team is one of the foremost behavioral scientists in the country. We can help you."

"And the police are just going to let you snoop around?" he asked.

"You, as the defense attorney, will demand that leeway be given in your investigation—for the benefit of your client, of course," Jenna said impatiently.

He didn't know why he was feeling such a hot tension, or why his muscles seemed to be bunching and his temper flaring.

Because he didn't think that they could do it? As much as he didn't want to think of the boy as a murderer, it seemed the most logical scenario.

He looked back at Jamie. "I'll let you know in the morning," he said, and strode out of the room.

Jenna looked at her uncle long and hard after Sam had left, then finally spoke. "I'm not so sure that telling Sam Hall who I am and what I do was the best move you might have made."

"And why not?" Jamie asked indignantly.

"Some people accept that the team gets the job done. And some people think that it's a joke. Even among the Feds," she told him.

"You can find the truth. I know that you can find who did this—you always had the knack."

"Oh, Jamie! Please, I'm not a miracle worker, either.... And, you have to be ready for whatever we do find. We don't know that Malachi didn't commit the murders yet."

"I know," he said quietly. "But, never mind that now—what would you like for dinner?"

She laughed. "Nice change of pace! *Scrod,* of course. Only in New England can you have really wonderful scrod!"

Jamie veered the conversation away from Malachi while they ate. He talked about "Haunted Happenings," an October event that brought tourism to Salem. He was a man who had his own deep and binding beliefs, but he was also fascinated by the faiths that others believed in. There were Wiccans in the city who were really Wiccans, believing in the gods and goddesses of the earth and in doing no harm to others, lest it come back threefold. And, he advised her, there were Wiccans in the city who were Wiccans because it was a very nice commercial venture in "Witch City." There were parades and balls, special events for children, theatrical programs on the tall ships at Derby Wharf and so much more.

"Now, you don't mind staying awhile, really, do you? I rather threw you into that—I mean, saying that you'd investigate," Jamie said. "And I know, too, that you're employed by the government, that you have responsibilities—"

"It's all right. A few team members are still in New York tying up some loose ends from our last case, and a few are in Virginia, outside of D.C., setting up our new offices."

He let out a contented sigh. "So you can stay."

She smiled. "Jamie, I knew from the beginning that you invited me up here for a reason. I didn't realize I'd arrive in time for it to really…begin in earnest."

He watched her oddly.

"What?"

"You always had it, you know," he said.

"Had what?"

"The sight."

Jenna was quiet at that. Her grandmother had entertained her when she had been a child with the myths and legends of Eire. She would tell a fantastic story about banshees—and then remind her that, now and again, many a tale had started at a pub. There were spirits—and then again, there were *spirits*.

It was true. Her cousin, Liam, who had become a writer, had done so discovering that the fantastic tales he could tell after a night at the pub could be put down on paper—and pay.

It was equally true that a number of people in her family had seemed to have some kind of a special sense. They could often *feel* a place, and know that violence had been committed there. They were prone to hearing the footsteps of the *ghosties* as they moved about in a place, and they could sense the presence of something that remained, even after years had gone by.

But the first time she'd *known* she had some kind of sight was when she'd been working as an R.N., and had been down in the morgue on some business.

A corpse had spoken to her. He insisted he hadn't died of natural causes, as would be assumed. He'd been helped into the great hereafter by a greedy family member.

Of course, that first time, she'd felt the speed of her heart escalate to dangerous levels. She wondered if, frequently, ghosts did not speak to their loved ones because they were afraid of giving them heart attacks—thus prematurely making ghosts of them, as well.

And, certainly, not every soul chose to walk the earth. Some remained because they felt they had unfinished business. Some remained because of the violence of their demise. Some had something that needed to be said, and some felt that their antecedents needed protecting.

"Uncle Jamie," she said, moving her fish around on the plate, "you're thinking that this is going to be a far easier thing than it is." She spoke softly, looking around. "Perhaps I do have what you call 'the sight.' It doesn't mean that I can go and see the corpse of Abraham Smith and he'll tell me who did him in. He may not have remained behind, and if he did, he may not be able to communicate. We've never had an instance where it was easy and cut-and-dried—where we just walked into a morgue and said, *Hey! Who's the guilty one?* Ghosts can help, but in many different ways."

He was watching her, listening intently. At least, with Jamie, she never had to try to pretend. Jamie told her once that he believed in the "holy ghost," and if he said so in a creed he spoke at religious services, he'd be an idiot not to believe that there was more beyond the average range of sight. Faith, he told her, was belief in what couldn't be seen. If a man had faith, he couldn't always doubt what he couldn't see. Most people had faith—even if their faith was different. A lot of different roads climbed the same hill.

He folded his napkin and set it on the table. "Jenna, I know that your team deals with what is real and tangible and out there for all to see and know. I never thought that you could come here and solve all my problems with a simple chat with the dead. It's never a simple 'How do you do, and can you answer a question for me?' But we are dealing with old stories and legends around here, true and enhanced."

"These murders aren't legends," she said.

"No. But, but the natural 'storytelling' desire is to automatically say that the kid did it, neat and tidy and a juicy, repeatable story. That he freaked out because his father was a browbeating fanatic and he figured he could say that the house was filled with devils. People

want to say this, for the newspapers at least. See what
other stories are out there, from dead men or the living.
I know that you can sort it all out."

"You do have faith in me," she murmured.

"Of course!" he said cheerfully. "Well, we'd best get
on home, huh? I have a feeling it's going to be an early
morning."

"And why is that?"

"Sam Hall is going to want me to visit his client with
him," Jamie said.

"He hasn't agreed to defend Malachi Smith yet," she
said.

Jamie grinned. "Faith, lass. I live by it!" he said
cheerfully.

It was good to be back at Uncle Jamie's house. She'd
spent a lot of time coming up here as a teenager. She
smiled, thinking of the past. She'd had local friends—
girls who had been glad to see her—and she brought
the excitement of the big city, Boston, along with her.

They'd shopped at the wonderful stores; they'd
played at being Wiccan, and it had surprised her at first
that her Catholic parents hadn't minded. They had been
amused. But they had seen the wars fought in their own
country over religion and economics and were tolerant.

Jamie's house was old, but the family had always
seemed to agree that it was a benign house. Whatever
ghosts remained, they were tolerant, as well.

Jenna went to sleep in the familiar old bedroom her
uncle had always referred to as "hers." Jamie had allowed her to have her whims: there were posters of

Gwen Stefani and No Doubt and other groups on the walls. They were a little incongruous there, since the bedroom was furnished entirely in period furniture, not from the seventeenth century, but the eighteenth century. Her bed was a four-poster; an old seafaring trunk sat at the foot of it, and a washstand with an antique ewer stood against the wall, along with an old wardrobe. To walk into the room—other than the posters and the stuffed Disney creatures on the shelves—was to walk into another time.

She lay awake a long time, what she had learned from Jamie rushing through her head. She admired her uncle and his steadfast faith; all the evidence in the world might stand against Malachi Smith, but Jamie believed in him.

When she fell asleep at last, she wasn't sure that she had done so. The room still seemed to be bathed in a gray, half light. There seemed to be movement in her room, a movement of shadows, and then they stood still at the foot of her bed, staring at her.

It was a group of women, and they were in the rather stern and drab shades of the late sixteen hundreds. Only one seemed to be in a slightly different color, and in the shadows Jenna thought it might be a dark crimson. They just stared at her, and even she, who was accustomed to meeting the dead, felt a deep unease. And then an old woman in the front lifted a hand toward her. She whispered something, and at first, Jenna couldn't make out the words. She wanted to wake up; she wanted to reach over and turn on the bedside light or just let out a scream and run into the hallway.

But then she comprehended the words the woman was trying to speak.

"Don't let the dead have died in vain."

Her throat was still tight; she was still so afraid. And, yet, she was the one who sought out those who had died.

Words came at her again.

"Don't let the blood run, don't let more blood run. Don't let *your* blood run."

Sam Hall arrived at Jamie's door at precisely eight in the morning. He was going to defend Malachi Smith, and he was going to do it pro bono.

Jenna decided that her uncle really did know how to read people.

By the time he arrived, Jenna had mused over her dream, her waking dream or her nightmare—whatever it might have been. It had been natural, certainly. The conversation all day had been about blood and murder, and her thoughts had long lingered on Salem and the city's past.

When she opened the door, dressed and ready to go as Jamie had suggested she be, Sam didn't seem surprised, though he might have been a bit irritated that they both were confident he wouldn't back away from the case.

"I'm not sure why you're coming—I have to spend time at court. I have to become the attorney of record, see what the public defender has done, see where custody lies, file motions…it could be a long day," he said. "I'm sure the public defender he hired has already made arrangements for Malachi to be seen by a court-appointed psychiatrist, and if we're going for a not-guilty plea, I have to make sure that we stall the court date as long as possible."

"I'm absolutely excellent at sitting around and waiting," Jenna assured him.

Jamie came to the door. "Let's go," he said. "Sam, thank you."

Sam grunted. "I'll drive. You two do what I say, sit when I say sit and wait as long as you have to wait."

Jamie was cheerfully agreeable.

It was a long morning, and there was a lot of paperwork to file. Since Malachi Smith was a minor with no family and still under the age of eighteen, he had become a ward of the Commonwealth of Massachusetts, and there were filings to be made with the state. None of that was difficult, not, apparently, when you were a hotshot attorney. Jamie was given a hearing and appointed Malachi's guardian. Malachi had to fire the public defender he'd been assigned and accept Sam Hall as his attorney. That was easily accomplished—Jenna waited in the car while Jamie spoke to Malachi with Sam—but then time was needed for filing all the documents Sam had prepared.

When arraigned, Malachi had not been granted bail; the crime was far too heinous. They met Evan Richardson, Sam's assistant, who had come to Salem as soon as Sam had called him and had already worked on the motions that had set the ball rolling. He would deal with more motions and more paperwork and the courts while Sam was engaged elsewhere. Jenna liked him. Just about her age, he was a pragmatic fellow from

Syracuse, New York, not embroiled in the burden of history that often came with being a New Englander.

When they finished with the legal paperwork and headed back to see Malachi with all the papers properly filed, Jamie argued the point of Malachi's incarceration with Sam.

"I can watch the young man day and night!" he told Sam.

Sam gave him a long sideways glance. "Jamie, you're forgetting something," he said.

"What's that?" Jamie demanded.

"If Malachi Smith didn't kill his family, a vicious killer remains at large."

Jenna felt a streak of cold zip up her spine.

"Someone who has now killed six people," Sam said.

Jamie was silent. She remembered her dream. Blood would flow....

"All right," Jamie said gruffly.

"And you do realize that the majority of the world will believe in Malachi's guilt. The facts point to his guilt—until we can offer more facts," Sam said.

Jamie nodded. "Yes, I see. If the killer strikes again, that will prove that Malachi is innocent, because he'll have in indisputable alibi."

"Yes. That and, if we're going to do this, no one will really have the time to babysit Malachi every moment and make sure he's safe. He's better in the psych ward for now." Sam stopped in the street, staring at Jamie. "And I have to tell you right now that if we don't discover something, and it comes to the line, I've now taken Malachi on as my client, and under any circumstance, I will defend him to the best of my ability—including changing the plea to one of insanity if I don't believe we can get reasonable doubt into the heads of the jury. You understand?"

"Of course," Jamie assured him.

Jenna did her best to stay out of the finer points of argument. She *wasn't* an attorney, and she knew full well that despite what she did know about federal law, she had no courtroom experience whatsoever.

"Let's see our client again," Sam said gruffly. He looked at Jenna and frowned as if he was still wondering just what she was doing there. But he didn't argue her presence.

Jenna didn't think that Sam was wrong to see to it that Malachi was kept in custody while they awaited trial. Jenna had expected something far worse—a long hall with bars and cells, the stench of fear and evil, and beady-eyed reprobates staring out with a desire to slit their throats, perhaps. But though Malachi was kept in isolation in a locked room with a small window box, the room was decent enough, if sparse.

It was almost like any other hospital unit. Almost. Malachi Smith was being incarcerated pending trial on murder charges. It wasn't a pleasantly painted place, nor were there any concessions to creature comforts. Jenna was grateful for her status as an R.N.; Sam Hall used her qualifications in explaining the reason for the three-person visit when he was the attorney of note.

There was a nurses' station. There was also a guard station. The guards were armed, and there was a series of doors to enter before arriving at Malachi's "decent"

room. Jenna realized that the difference between his
"room" and a cell was essentially that he had walls
around him rather than bars.

The guards were professional and courteous. They
seemed to be treating Malachi well. Extra chairs were
brought; Malachi's space included a simple cot and one
chair.

Jenna's heart immediately went out to the boy. He
was pathetically slim and small for his age; she was
certain that malnutrition had stunted his growth. He
was a couple of inches shorter than herself, while Sam
Hall and even Jamie seemed to dwarf the youth. His
eyes were huge and brown, his face as lean as his frame.
When he saw Jamie, he smiled. It was a smile filled
with hope, but it faltered quickly and he looked at the
three of them like he would begin crying in a matter of
seconds.

And he did. No sooner had Malachi walked over to
Jamie and leaned against him than great sobs started
to rack his body. Sam stood back with Jenna, waiting
for the torrent to subside.

"There, there," her uncle said, patting the boy's back.
"We're here to help you, Malachi."

Sam glanced at Jenna. For the first time, it seemed
that he was looking at her as if she could say something
that might be helpful. Well, maybe the fact that she was
a nurse *and* a *special* investigator led him to believe that
she must have empathy with others.

"I believe that the tears are for his family, honest
tears," she whispered.

"And not because he was caught?" Sam asked.

"No." She hesitated. "Though, even if he had committed the murders, the realization of his family's deaths would be wrenchingly painful."

Sam nodded, and seemed to accept her reply, especially with the caveat. She knew that he wasn't convinced yet—no matter Jamie's passion. To press forward as if she were positive as well might alienate him, and she wanted them all playing on the same side. She wasn't Jamie. She hadn't treated Malachi, and she didn't know him.

But she did step forward and put a hand on Malachi's trembling shoulder. "My uncle is right, Malachi. We're here to help you. But we need you to try very hard and tell us exactly what happened."

The boy's thin frame still clung to her uncle.

"Malachi, we need you to help us," Jenna persisted.

Finally he nodded against Jamie's shoulder and turned to look at her. He seemed like such a little kid. She tried a gentle smile and eased his hair from his forehead. He smelled of antiseptic soap and was dressed in an orange-beige pajamalike suit that resembled scrubs.

Jail attire, of course. This was a hospital division, but it was jail, nonetheless.

"Can it help?" Malachi asked quietly. "You know that, in the eyes of others, I am already condemned."

"Please, come, sit down on the bed, and we'll go through it all," Sam said. "You know that I'm going to defend you. And, remember, I'm your lawyer, so anything you say to *me* is confidential. If there is something that you want to say to me that should be kept confidential, I must speak with you alone. Now, Jamie doesn't believe that you killed your family, Malachi. And if that's true, and you want to tell us what happened, you can feel free to speak with us all here. Just remember, and this is important—I can't repeat anything. Since Jamie isn't officially your doctor right now, he could be compelled to repeat what you've said, and Jenna is Jamie's niece, and an...investigator. So if you don't wish to speak in front of them—"

"I didn't do it," Malachi blurted, drawing away from Jamie at last. His face was still tearstained, but he continued to speak earnestly and passionately. "I would never hurt them, never! I would never hurt anyone. I believe in God, and his only son, Jesus Christ—and He taught that all men should be peaceful, and seek to help their brothers. So help me, before God! I didn't do it."

As he spoke, his words so desperate and earnest, it seemed that a ray of sun burst through the barred windows.

The room was cast into an almost unearthly glow.

Then the glow faded, and Jenna wondered if it had just been the sun passing in front of an autumn cloud.

Malachi hung his head and repeated, "I didn't do it." He looked up, straight into Jenna's eyes, and said, "Thou shalt not kill. Thou shalt not kill."

3

"Malachi, do you remember me as the man who found you in the road?" Sam asked.

The boy reddened and shook his head.

"Let's sit down now and relax," Jamie said, leading Malachi to the bed. He sat the youth and smiled, then took the first chair, leaving the second and closest chair, for Sam. Jenna sat on the third.

"First, are you doing all right in here?" Sam asked pleasantly.

Malachi nodded and shrugged. "I know how to be alone," he said softly.

Compassion filled Jenna at these words. She saw a child who lived such a strict and unusual life that he saw visions of Dante's hell at home and was shunned by other children wherever he went.

"Good, good, I think this is the best place for you right now," Sam told him. "Now, Malachi, what I need you to do is really try to relax—and I know how ridiculous that sounds. But I need you to go back and try very hard to remember everything that happened the evening when I found you on the road."

"I found them," he said. "I found them." He started to tremble again; tears welled into his eyes. "My mother..."

Jenna didn't remember getting up but she found herself crouching next to him and placing an arm around his shoulders. "It's all right," she said. "Malachi, it's all right to cry. You loved them. You loved your mother very much, and she's gone. It's natural that you'd cry."

He nodded and leaned against her shoulder.

Sam waited patiently for a few minutes, and then pressed on.

"Malachi, it's important that we know where you were when it all happened. You weren't home—or were you? Were you hiding somewhere in the house?"

Malachi stared across the room, his slender face crinkling into a frown of concentration. He shook his head thoughtfully, and was silent so long that Jenna thought he wouldn't answer.

"I went to the cliff—the little cliff at the end of the road. It isn't a real park, but the kids go there all the time. It's like a park. Some of the kids just run around with Frisbees or soccer balls, and some of them go there to..." He broke off, embarrassed, and glanced at Jenna awkwardly. "You know. They go there to fool around."

She smiled at him and patted his hand. "Why do you go there, Malachi?"

"I like the sea," he said. "It's up from the wharf, and you can be alone with the wind and sea and the waves crash against the rocks there. Right at the peak, you can always feel the breeze, and it feels so good. It's like it whips through you, and it makes you all clean. Sometimes, I just sit and look out on the water. And I try to imagine what it would have been like, years ago, when the great sailing ships went to sea, and the whalers and the fishermen went out."

Every kid needed a place to dream.

She smiled at him. "Do you go there a lot?"

He nodded. He lifted his shoulders, and they fell again. "I have no friends," he said. "It's okay. I know that my family was different."

His family *was* different. In a city that made half its tourist dollars through the rather unorthodox belief in the Wiccan religion. Did people believe? Or did tourists just enjoy the edge of it all—tarot cards were fun, just as it was fun and spooky to head to Gallows Hill and wonder if the spirits of the dead rose in tearful reproach or if they indeed rose to dance with the devil. But the Smiths believed in something. Not that, but something. And with belief being so cheap, in a way, that could mark them as outcasts right off.

"Am I right to say that your family had very strict religious beliefs, Malachi? Almost like the Puritan fathers?" Sam said.

Jenna looked at him, surprised that his thoughts were running vaguely similar to her own.

Again, his face reddened. He nodded, looking down. "Father said that all the Wiccans were the same, that it was all hogwash, that there is no devil in the Wiccan belief. I don't think he really hated anyone, though. But there really was a devil—he was the horned God. People just wouldn't *say* that he was the devil. My father

didn't want to hurt anyone—it isn't our place to judge
on earth. He just said that they were all going to hell."

"Tell me what you believe, Malachi," Sam said.

"I believe in what Jesus said. That we should love our
fellow man—never hurt him." Malachi paused a minute.
"Actually, I kind of like what the witches say. You know,
that they would never hurt anyone, because whatever
harm is done to another comes back on us threefold. I
mean, I don't believe that there's a count—that doing a
bad thing to another human being means that three bad
things will happen. But I do believe in a great power,
and that we answer to that power—to God, through
Christ His son—when we depart this world. And I think
He will ask me if I was good to those around me, and
I will say, 'Father, I tried my hardest. I'm sure that I've
sinned, but I have tried to be a good person.'"

There was something so earnest about his words.
They weren't like the rhetoric of many a televangelist.
They were heartfelt and sincere.

He could be a fanatic, she told herself. *And fanatics, no matter what their religion or calling, could be
dangerous. Yes, kill in the name of God!*

But it just didn't seem that he saw killing as one of
his God's commandments.

"I do see it all a bit differently than my father did,"
Malachi added, and then tears welled in his eyes again.
"He believed—he may have been mistaken sometimes,
but he believed. He must be in Heaven now."

"Of course he is," Jenna murmured. Sam stared at
her. She stared back at him. It had been the right thing

to say, and she knew it. It didn't matter if the man's beliefs had warped his ability to be a decent father.

"Tell me what happened after you were on the cliff," Sam said.

"I—I came home," Malachi said. Jenna, sitting next to him, could feel him. He was trembling again, reliving the horror.

"And exactly what did you do?" Sam asked. His voice was smooth, easy. He wasn't attacking; he was asking.

"I walked into the parlor," he said, his voice so soft they could barely hear him. "My—my mother... She was by the hearth.... She—she was on the floor. I ran to her... I fell down on my knees. I saw...the blood, but I couldn't believe that she was dead. I held her—and the blood was all over me. And I couldn't bear the feel of it... I tried to get it off of me. I stood up and—and then I saw my father, over by the sofa... I started screaming. I raced up the stairs and found my uncle in one bedroom, and my grandmother...my grandmother, oh, God!" He cried out the last and buried his face in his hands, sobbing and wailing.

Jenna pulled him closer, murmuring soothing words. She stared at Sam as she felt Malachi's body shudder against her own.

"Do you remember anything after?" Sam asked him. "Do you remember me?"

It took a long time for Malachi to answer.

"I remember Detective Alden telling me that I was under arrest, that I had killed my parents," Malachi said dully. "I didn't kill them. I'm not crazy, and I didn't kill them. I loved them. My parents, my grandmother...my uncle. I loved them. I didn't always agree with them. But they loved me, and I loved them."

He said the words with certainty. He said the words like an innocent man. Jenna believed him.

Sam had a few more questions. She barely heard them. She sat next to Malachi Smith, trying to give him human warmth and comfort. And when it was time to go at last, she wasn't exactly sure why, but she agreed with her uncle.

Malachi Smith was not guilty.

There was something pure about him.

She had no proof, and the evidence was against him. But she believed in him.

When they left the facility, Sam Hall was quiet and grim.

And she realized that he, too, was experiencing the same feelings.

Sam sat at the desk in the den at his parents' house, idly rolling a pencil in his fingers, staring at the screen of his computer and looking at the empty notepad by his side.

He'd been surprised that Malachi Smith had now made an indelible impression on him.

He shouldn't have been so surprised, not really. From the time he had come upon the kid in the road, he'd been touched by the boy. Shaken. Not shaken. Yes… disturbed, at the least.

His client was innocent. He firmly believed it, which was good—he'd defended men when they *might* have been innocent, and when they might have been guilty as all hell.

He realized that he actually felt righteous about pursuing a nonguilty plea for Malachi. This case made no sense. He liked to believe that he could read people, and he knew all the little things to look for in a liar. Liars seldom made eye contact. They were fidgety, keeping their movements close to their own bodies. They had a tendency to touch their mouths, or their faces. The emotion in their words was often just slightly off or askew—acted out, rather than real.

The world was filled with very good liars, of course, but he'd spent a great deal of time in court, and he'd watched countless defendants, witnesses, prosecutors, judges, jurists and defense attorneys. He was good. The courtroom was actually one big stage, and often, the rest of a person's life depended on how well the ad-libbed and scripted performances were played out.

He'd been at his desk an hour now, so there should have been a list of notes on his pad. He should have been to a dozen sites on the computer. He was still staring at the screen, reliving in his mind's eye the time he had spent with Malachi Smith.

He had to shake the feeling he'd experienced with Malachi.

Sam was no longer sure what he believed in himself. He supposed that he believed in a higher power, or perhaps he wanted to believe in a higher power. No one wanted to think that their loved ones, now deceased, were nothing but decaying matter. Man had always looked to the heavens for some kind of redemption and had been inventing God around the world since the human brain had begun to recognize its own extinction.

Growing up in Salem, he'd seen everything. The old Puritanical values had died hard despite the enlightenment of man. Wiccans were finally allowed into a council of religions, but that council wasn't recognized by the hard-core fundamentalists. Less that .03 percent of the American population was Wiccan. In Salem, poll estimates suggested that there were about 4,000 Wiccans in an area of about 40,000. Ten percent.

He mused that today they might have been considered the "tree huggers."

Had someone killed the Smith family because of their fundamentalist beliefs?

He started writing on his notepad at last.

Abraham Smith, his wife, Beth. His mother, Abigail, his brother, Thomas. Killed at Lexington House. Earnest Covington, killed the previous week, three doors down. Six months earlier, Peter Andres, killed in his barn at Andover, just a hop, skip and jump away.

One in the barn with a scythe, one in a house with an ax, then four more in a house with an ax. It sounded like a sick game of Clue.

What did the victims have in common besides location? That was where he needed to start.

Sam rubbed his eyes. It had been a long day. He pushed away from his desk. He needed fresh air. He walked out of the house, locking it, perhaps purposely keeping his eyes downcast as he did so. He didn't want to think about how he'd lost himself at that moment.

Boston had been easy. Take on the high-income clientele, fight like a tiger. When a client was guilty as all hell and sure to lose in court because of absolutely damning evidence, argue out the best possible deal. Hit the high-end restaurants and bars. Indulge in a few high-end affairs and avoid commitment. Relish a victory like his last with a trip down to the sun and sand, and then start all over again.

Shallow, he told himself.

Yeah.

Once on the sidewalk, he looked back at the house. And he smiled with a sense of nostalgia. He'd thrown himself into his work and the lifestyle when his folks had died. Life wasn't fair; death really wasn't fair. He'd loved them. They'd given him everything, and they'd made him want to achieve great things because he'd wanted them to be proud.

"You'd want me on this case, wouldn't you, Dad?" he said softly. Once upon a time, he'd been filled with righteousness. He'd believed in putting away the bad guys and going to bat for the innocent and falsely accused.

Then he'd gotten to see the legal system in action. He was still convinced that this country had what was certainly the best one in the world. And yet, even the best was filled with loopholes, inept cops, inept clerks and justices who were biased even if they were charged to comprehend and follow the law. Then, of course, Congress wasn't always the best at writing laws, and God knew, a good speaker was a good speaker: attorneys themselves were certainly a major part of justice—and injustice.

And attorneys could become jaded. Had he let that happen?

Yes, definitely.

Maybe it was time to believe again.

Maybe that was the core of belief: people who had mattered and passed away living on in the hearts or souls of their loved ones. His father was no longer there to see him going to bat, pro bono, for the poor and ill-treated. It was something that would have pleased his parents.

He turned away from the house, surprised that he didn't want to be alone.

I know how to be alone, Malachi Smith had said.

Sam knew how to be alone, too. He'd been an only child. But he'd grown up surrounded by love, and his parents had welcomed other children into their home. He smiled; his mother had been concerned that he wouldn't learn how to share if she didn't make sure he learned that he just didn't get everything that he wanted.

He wondered what it had been like to be Malachi, shunned by others. And, yet, the boy seemed to have his own faith. Perhaps pounded into him by his father.

Perhaps made into something better in the lonely recesses in his mind.

Whatever demons haunted the human mind, Sam mused that everyone had them. He had his own. And he knew that right then, no matter how good he might be at it, he didn't want to be alone. And he was surprised to realize that it wasn't just Jamie he wanted to see.

It was Jenna. She was a beautiful young woman, but

that wasn't it. He was lucky. His world was filled with beautiful young women. She was different.

Yeah, right. Adam Harrison's ghost-buster-Krewe-of-Hunters different. Just what the hell had he gotten himself into?

He grinned. Whatever it was, he had feeling that she was like the flame that enticed.

Jenna was surprised to see Sam Hall standing at the door to Jamie's house.

"Hi!" she said.

"Hey," he returned.

She realized she was staring blankly at him. "Oh, I'm sorry!" she said quickly. "Come on in, Jamie is just hanging at the table going through papers while we're waiting on dinner."

"Oh. I didn't mean to interrupt," he said quickly, taking a step back. "Sorry, I should have realized that it was around that time."

"No, please, come on in—we've plenty. It's a strange kind of international goulash in the Crock-Pot, nothing at all exciting," she warned him.

Jenna realized that Jamie was standing behind her when he said, "Come on in, Counselor! Please, we'd love for you to join us."

Sam lifted a hand, as if he would back away again in a minute. "Seriously," he said, and she noted that he could have a wonderful, dimpled and sheepish smile. "I didn't mean to interrupt. I was thinking about the case, thought I should take a walk—and found that I'd walked over here."

Impulsively, she stepped forward and took his arm. "I insist," she said and smiled at him. Her mother could be one of the most iron-willed women she had ever met, but she always got her way by adding a grin. She was surprised that she was so insistent with Sam Hall, and she almost released his arm the second she grabbed it, but she had made her point.

"I've just been going over notes, trying to figure out why on earth the other two victims were murdered," Jamie said. "Come on, I'll show you what I've got."

Jenna turned and headed back through the hall to the kitchen. It was big, with the old hearth against the far wall. Jamie had built a fire against the autumn chill, and it felt good. Nothing was cooking over it, however; dinner was in the Crock-Pot.

"Why would anyone kill a grumpy old farmer in Andover?" Jamie asked, shoving a newspaper article toward Sam as both men took a seat at the table.

"Six months ago," Sam mused, taking the newspaper article. He read through it thoughtfully. He looked over at Jamie. "Peter Andres. No close relatives, but he had a second cousin living in Boston. Doesn't seem like the cousin was after money. I know of the guy—plastic surgeon, makes a mint. And it looks like the police did check out his alibi." He looked over at Jenna and Jamie. "Peter Andres was a substitute teacher. Farmer, and substitute teacher."

Jenna set the Crock-Pot on the table and pushed the newspaper back. "Make room for plates, if you don't mind," she said. "And don't suggest that Malachi killed Peter Andres because he didn't like him as a teacher!"

"Hey, I'm the defense attorney. But you can guarantee that a prosecutor will make the suggestion," Sam said.

"I'll get drinks," Jamie said, hopping up. "We'll have to see if Peter Andres worked as a substitute while Malachi was still in the school system."

"I'd bet the big bucks that he did," Sam said thoughtfully.

"Now you're being exasperating," Jenna said, opening the refrigerator door for the salad she'd tossed and setting it on the table. "It sounds as if we're trying to prove that Malachi did commit the murders."

"No," Sam argued, looking at her and hiding a smile. If he were ever in trouble, he would definitely want her in his corner. She was determined and passionate in her defense. She sincerely believed in Malachi's innocence. When he was with Malachi and heard the youth speak, he believed in him, too. When he looked at the facts, he felt that belief waver.

Jenna wasn't wavering.

"What's going to happen when we make it to trial is this—the state will make every effort to show Malachi in a bad light. They will put forth every reason he would naturally have been the one to commit the crimes. I'm debating whether or not to put Malachi on the stand, because they will try to crucify him. Then again, if he can be as convincing and articulate as he was with us, he'll be a good witness in his own defense. I don't know yet—I have to look at this from every possible angle, because that's what the prosecution is going to do. One of the things *I* have to create is reasonable doubt, and one of the best ways to do that is to think like our op-position."

"Or find the real killer," Jenna said, sitting opposite him and staring at him. "That's what you did in your last case. And, now, you have me. And, unofficially, an entire team of investigators."

He kept his eyes level with hers and hoped that his years as an attorney had made him a really damned good liar. "That's wonderful, of course."

Jenna gazed at him with cool and disdainful eyes. His acting wasn't that good. "I work with people who can find the tiniest discrepancies on film, and who can find out about any piece of information possible on a computer. They will contribute legwork, phone work, paperwork—anything you want. So your problem would be…?"

"I don't have a problem. I said, *that's wonderful,*" Sam reminded her.

"Jenna, lass, you've a starving man down here," Jamie said cheerfully.

"Smells wonderful," Sam said.

"Irish-Hungarian goulash. The very best!" Jamie said.

When the food was dished out and Jenna was seated, Sam said, "Quite frankly, it is all a lot like acting. A good attorney can act and speak and write up summa-tions that either prove a point, or leave a wide margin for doubt. And we also start out with the question, *where do we want to go?* We're going on the premise that Mala-chi Smith is innocent of murder, and, while they're not prosecuting the boy for the other murders, the state *will* have as their default assumption that the same person or persons murdered the Smiths, Peter Andres and Earnest Covington. Since they were all bloody killings committed by some kind of a sharp blade in a fairly small area, all known to the boy—it seems like a plausible assumption.

"So, we want to find the person or persons who might have actually committed the murders. That will mean investigating the victims. Of course we'll be looking at the Smith murders, but if we can also cast doubt on the police's assumption about the other two, we'll go a long way to getting them to reconsider Malachi for any of the killings. We'll question friends and whatever relatives we can find, and we also need to know if they were thought of fondly in town—or if they were thought of at all. The killings might have been random or specific, but I'd bet on specific. That means motive, and we need to find out why someone would have killed these particular people. It might have been convenience, or there might have been a more practical reason."

"I need to see the house," Jenna said.

"Why?" Sam demanded. "There's going to be a lot of blood spatter. People were killed there."

"The house itself may have clues," Jenna argued.

"Are you going to talk to the ghosts?" he asked drily.

"Maybe," she said evenly. "Sam, everything you're saying is exactly right. We do know what happened. But I need to see all the sites—we have to go to Andover and see the barn where Peter Andres was killed, and also get into the neighbor's house. But we need to start with Lexington House. You know that! You're going to defend Malachi. *You* need to know exactly what happened. And you're friends with Detective John Alden, so..."

Sam sighed. "All right. Tomorrow morning. We'll start with the house."

Lexington House. Jenna had never actually been in the old colonial building, but she had an idea of what the arrangement of rooms would be like; many such homes had been built in a similar manner. The porch led to a mudroom, and beyond that was an entry hallway. The hall stretched the length of the house, the staircase to one side. The first door to the right would lead to a parlor. Upstairs, there would be four bedrooms, two on either side of the house.

Detective John Alden led the way, ripping off the crime-scene tape and unlocking the front door for them.

As she had expected: mudroom. Work jackets hung on hooks in the small vestibule, and work boots were lined up against the wall. There was a long hallway with doors leading off to either side of the house, and a set of stairs against the left wall that led to the rooms above. They followed John Alden to the first door on the left.

Blood remained on the walls. The spray pattern was terrifying—there was so much blood. Four people, murdered here just two days ago, two of them in this room.

Two here, in the parlor. Mr. Abraham Smith and his wife.

Chalk marks on the floor designated the positions where their bodies had lain.

"You can move into the room about three feet—no farther," Alden warned.

"We appreciate your assistance in being here, John," Sam told him.

Alden was still for a minute, weighing his answer. "We do have a chief of police," he said. "And the chief wants every possible effort made on this case so that there aren't any more historic mysteries floating around out there. The murders are heinous, and they're not fancy legends—it's a seventeen-year-old boy who has been accused. I worked hard for this badge, it's something I've always wanted. And I don't want any surprises when we get to court on this one."

"Noted," Sam said. "And still appreciated."

"Just be careful where you're walking," Alden said gruffly.

Jamie took a step in to the left. Sam went to the right.

Blood. What remained of the carnage.

A table was knocked over. A pile of bloody clothing lay next to a lamp that had presumably sat upon the table. A quilt—covered in blood—had been ripped from the old sofa.

The bricks of the fireplace were dotted with stains and spray.

"Abraham Smith got it right there, in front of the fireplace. You can see where his body lay, right *there*," John Alden pointed out. "The missus was over on the floor by the sofa—looks like she dragged the quilt down and knocked over the table. She had hack marks on her arms. I think she stood up to protest, and was axed down right there. She staggered a few feet, and then died. And that pile there—that's the kid's clothes. And this room is only the beginning," he said wearily.

Jenna could barely hear him. As he spoke, she felt as if he faded away, along with the others in the room. The very color of the air distorted, taking on a gray hue. A crude straw broom appeared by the fireplace. A wire basket of wood was on the brick apron in front of the hearth. There were no lamps. Candles sat on rough wooden tables by hardwood furniture, and sconces were attached to the walls.

There was a woman in severe, puritanical dress pacing in front of the fireplace. Once she had been pretty. Her face was worn down by weather, toil and worry. Her brow was furrowed. She kept looking toward the door.

A breeze seemed to strike Jenna from the back.

She turned. The front door had burst open—two youths, one perhaps ten, another twelve, came running into the room, panicked. They rushed to their mother, hugging her one by one.

"They've declared against Rebecca Nurse," the older boy practically yelled. "Oh, Mother, it grows so frightening."

"Father says that evil must be uprooted, and that Goody Nurse is surely evil. If the girls say that she dances with the devil, she must die!" the younger boy said.

The breeze seemed to grow very chill, though it appeared that a summer sun blazed outside the gray miasma within the house. Once again, someone entered the room.

He was in breeches and boots and a white cotton shirt. His long, graying hair was parted cleanly in the middle.

He carried an ax.

Eli Lexington! Jenna thought.

He walked into the room, his hands moving on the ax as if he were testing the weight of it.

"Eli?" his wife said softly.

"Evil must die!" he roared. "Let those who dance with the devil go to the devil, and let their spawn rest in hell aside them!"

Jenna felt as if she had been kicked in the stomach. Eli Lexington walked across the room, and despite his wife's scream of protest, he brought the ax down on her shoulders, and then, wielding it again, took it viciously down upon her fallen body. The boys stared, frozen in horror. Jenna tried to close her eyes against the vision, but the image just appeared in her mind, and there was no way to hide from the horror that unfolded before her.

Eli turned on the oldest boy.

"Run!" the child yelled to his brother.

The word was cut off as the ax struck his head.

The little one had no chance to run. "Though shalt pluck out evil—*thou shalt not suffer a witch to live!*" Eli roared.

He continued to vigorously hack at his family. The last scream and moan died away. The gray air seemed to fade, and Jenna was aware that her uncle and Sam Hall were looking at her with grave concern.

She felt weak, faint, as if she would fall. She couldn't do that.

"Excuse me. I need some air," she murmured. She turned and almost stumbled. Jamie, however, was already at her side, grabbing her arm.

"Ah, lass, the scent in there is a bit overwhelming. Felt me old knees buckling, too," he said.

Reaching the porch, she sank down to sit on the step. Jamie sat beside her. While he clearly wanted to be concerned for her welfare, he was also anxious to hear about what she might have experienced.

"Jenna...Jenna...did you see? Is he innocent?"

She looked at her uncle sadly. "Uncle Jamie, I saw—but not the present, I'm afraid. I saw Eli Lexington, and he seemed to be really crazy—he believed that his wife was a witch, and that he had to kill her. And he had to kill his sons, because she had already given them to Satan, because they'd wind up in hell." She realized that she was shaking, her voice tremulous.

"Wonderful. That's really going to help us."

The deep, mocking voice came from above and behind her. Sam Hall. He'd slipped out onto the porch as well, concerned or curious.

Jenna figured it was the latter.

She stood, suddenly feeling perfectly fine. It was as if her spine had stiffened so tightly that she gained a half an inch.

"You're going to tell me that the boy was psychologically shattered by the strict deprivation of anything societal caused by his father's strange religion, and that caused him to see apparitions in the house?" Sam asked. His eyes were as flat as his words.

"No," she said equally flatly. "In my mind, Malachi

didn't do it. Excuse me. If John Alden will allow it, I want to see the rest of the house. And, quite frankly, I think we should do this separately."

Of course, *Sam* was the one who was friends with John Alden—had gone to school with him—not Jamie. And still, Jenna was convinced that if she acted with authority, she would be allowed her exploration. She'd worked against this kind of man before.

Sam shrugged. "We're here. What the hell."

Yeah, what the hell. He had written her off as a kook who liked to pretend she was a medium of some kind.

In a way, of course, it was true....

But she was part of Adam Harrison's Krewe of Hunters, and they offered so much more than Sam seemed to be able to fathom.

Well, they dealt with that belief all the time. She had to bite down and ignore his attitude, and do what she knew she could do.

She stood up and walked back into the house. Part of the stairway was blocked by crime-scene tape; a trail of blood drops ran to the upstairs.

Jenna walked into the room where Malachi's great-uncle had been killed. The blood spatter was all over the wall. A pillow was soaked in it and had turned a hardened crimson color. She held still for a minute, but felt nothing, and no images came to her mind.

She walked across the hall to the grandmother's room. The old woman had evidently been caught standing; the blood had soared far across the room in little drops, though the majority was on the floor, in the upper portion of the chalked-out figure there.

Again, she felt nothing. She knew she had to come back. With whatever "gift" she had, history seemed to be coming to her slowly. She'd gotten the seventeenth century today—she'd have to try again later to find out more recent events.

If she could...

She walked down the stairs, quiet and grim. The others were out on the porch.

"I still think you're crazy," John Alden told Sam, watching Jenna as she exited the house and joined them. "The kid is—weird. And, in his mind, he probably had good reason to kill his parents. Their brainwashing might have been some kind of mind-torture. And his prints were on the ax. That's going to go a long way in court, my friend."

"All right, John," Sam said, "his prints are on the ax. *But,* the scenario he describes could account for that. I've seen it before. Kid came home and saw the carnage in his house. He was in shock. His parents were on the floor in a pile of blood. He picked up the ax, maybe pulled it out of his mom, threw himself on his parents. He had blood all over him—he couldn't stand it. He stripped off his clothing. In shock and panic, he raced out into the night. And that's when I found him."

"Cool, you tell that to a jury, my friend," John Alden said. He cast his head to the side. "Crazy, Sam, you're plum crazy. You don't need the publicity, God knows! You're high on a winning streak. In my mind, you're going to plummet—like a crazy man."

"John, the kid needs someone," Sam told him.

John nodded. "Sure. Well, I'm not out to crucify the

boy, no matter what you might think. But I am beholden to the people here, and I have to tell you, I'm glad that one is locked up!"

"He's safe," Jenna said.

"He's safe?" Alden asked, and laughed. "Yeah, sure. Well, if that's all…?"

Sam looked at Jenna, a dry smile curling his lips. "Jenna?"

She forced a smile in return. "That's all."

"Thanks again, John," Sam said. He took Jenna's arm, leading her down the porch steps. Jamie followed, and they walked across the lawn and down to the curb and Sam's car. Jenna paused, pulling back, and looked around.

"What?" Sam asked.

"Nothing. Nothing," she said quietly.

But it *was* something. They were being watched.

She could *feel* it; she knew it.

4

Mrs. Lila Newbury was a very thin and nervous woman who sat behind her desk looking as if she wanted to jump up and move away. She fiddled with the things on her desk—a pencil, a stapler and a cup of paper clips. She seemed entirely out of place; the office had been decorated and adorned for Halloween. A carved pumpkin with a battery-powered light grinned evilly from the edge of her desk while garlands in black and orange were strewn around the windows. A paper skeleton dangled from the door, and paper images of black cats were taped here and there, along with typical autumn cornucopia. There were no witches, Sam noted, and he was sure that was because some of the school's children had to be among the ten percent of the population that was Wiccan.

Lila Newbury looked as if she had been plucked up from a sixties flower garden and thrown into it all.

Sam couldn't help but think that if this woman was the guidance counselor, many of the kids at the school would wind up like nervous terriers, running back and forth, afraid, and not even close to certain about what they wanted to do with their lives. She hadn't been there when he'd gone to the high school himself. In fact, he hadn't seen any of the teachers or office personnel he had known. Sure, he had graduated fourteen years ago; people did move on. Still, there had to be someone here he still knew. He'd look into that later.

"Mrs. Newbury?" he pressed softly. She hadn't actually agreed to see him. He'd walked in while one of the office girls had been trying to call and warn her that he was there.

"Yes, yes, I'm thinking, of course," she said.

Thinking, of course. She was thinking of a way to get rid of him.

"When this comes to court…" he warned vaguely.

"We have several hundred students here…I'm trying to recall…Malachi Smith had been pulled out of the public system some time ago. His father—God rest his soul—had decided on homeschooling."

"But I understand that was prompted by an incident at the school," Sam said.

"Yes," she admitted uneasily.

"Can you tell me what happened?" Sam asked.

"He looked at a boy…and the boy was convinced that he had some kind of power that could hurt him," she said, not looking at Sam, but toward the clock on the wall, as if the clock was going to save her if she just watched the seconds tick by long enough.

"I need to know exactly what happened," Sam said firmly, leaning forward. He was an attorney with no power as far as law enforcement went, but he was pretty sure she didn't understand the law at all and that he could bully her. "You're in danger of obstructing justice,

Mrs. Newbury. You can and will be subpoenaed, and if you commit perjury or continue to hinder an investigation into the truth, you can be prosecuted yourself."

He was glad of his reputation even though it didn't give him the power to arrest anyone. Mrs. Newbury didn't seem to know the difference.

"Teachers and counselors can't be everywhere, you know!" she said, suddenly angry. "The kid seemed to wear a target. Probably because he couldn't be riled. He was different, and trust me, Mr. Hall, children can be very cruel. They liked to throw food at him in the lunchroom. Well, one of the boys was throwing food at him and he turned and looked at the boy…"

As she continued with the familiar evil-eye story he'd heard a couple of times now, he almost couldn't wait for her to finish before he blurted out his next question: "And you believed this?"

She flushed.

She had!

"No, of course not. But we had to call the parents in, and…"

"And?"

"Well, the boy was David Yates. His father is one of our city councilmen," she said weakly.

"And he asked that Malachi Smith be expelled—and someone agreed to it?" Sam demanded, outraged.

Lila Newbury shook her head vehemently. "No! It never came to that. Abraham Smith stormed his way in here. He said that he wanted his son out of this horrible place. I helped him arrange for homeschooling." A pencil suddenly snapped in her fingers. "Look, Mr.

Hall, I did it as much for Malachi as I did for anyone. He was a sweet boy. I liked him, personally. But this is an understaffed facility, like most public venues of education. I couldn't protect him all the time. He was going to get hurt. Like I said, children can be cruel. And, as we all know, they can be lethal, as well!"

"You just said that Malachi was a sweet boy. Do *you* really believe that he could have killed anyone?" Sam asked.

She looked away. He thought that she didn't believe it herself.

But she was a woman without the strength of her own convictions. She'd never stand up for anyone if it was contrary to public opinion.

"What about Peter Andres?" Sam asked.

"What about him?" she asked nervously.

"He substituted here?"

She nodded. "And at other schools!" she said defensively.

"You know that Malachi is suspected of his murder?"

She waved a hand in the air. "Rumor, of course."

"Rumor—of course. But rumor goes a long way. Did he ever teach Malachi Smith?"

"Well, yes, of course…he was a substitute and we often called him in."

"Did they get along?"

She hesitated, and then apparently appeared to be truthful. "As a matter of fact, they got along quite well. Peter was strict, and Malachi didn't mind strict. Peter liked the boy. He said that he was 'special.' He didn't mean that in the mean way the other children did."

"Did you ever tell that to the police?"

"The police never asked me." She sighed impatiently. "Peter was killed over in Andover, what, about six months ago? Malachi was not one of our student body then."

Sam stood up. "The boy with whom the altercation took place—David Yates? Is he still in school here? He'd be…a senior, so ready to graduate next June, right?"

"Yes," she said almost inaudibly.

"Well, thank you, Mrs. Newbury. You've been a tremendous help."

She looked up at him, and her face appeared stricken. She hadn't wanted to help him at all. She managed a jerky nod.

He left her office, very afraid for the youth of the day.

Jenna had thought that there might be a For Sale sign on the farmhouse where Peter Andres had been murdered.

There was. And it was already showing signs of wear and tear. No matter how great a deal the property might be, many people would be loath to live at a place where a heinous murder had taken place. While they loved to stay at "haunted" hotels and bed-and-breakfast inns, they didn't particularly want to spend their lives in places with actual "evil" reputations.

Jenna put through a call to the Realtor. The woman who took her call seemed surprised by her interest in the property.

"You want me to show it to you?" she asked.

"Yes, please," Jenna said.

"I...uh...of course. I can meet you in, say, half an hour."

"Thank you. May I look over the grounds until you arrive?"

"Um, yes. If you wish. Look, I feel obliged to tell you that the previous owner was murdered in his barn," she said.

"I know. Thank you."

Jenna hung up quickly, glad that the woman didn't press to make sure she had a *serious* interest in the property.

She left her car on the curb and walked toward the house itself. It was a typical New England farmhouse. There was an empty paddock to the right of the house, and overgrown fields beyond. The barn was to the left rear of the house.

She felt the breeze stir as she walked toward the barn. The day couldn't have been more beautiful. The air was crisp and cool, and autumn colors seemed to hover around the property in shades of red and gold.

The doors to the barn were wide-open; she assumed a cleanup crew had been in, and that there would be no evidence of the crime remaining. Again she was proved right. The barn was clean swept. It had a lingering odor of hay and horses, but the place was spotless. She doubted that there were even spiderwebs in the eaves.

She walked into the barn. She'd had Jake Mallory perform his computer magic and get his hands on the crime-scene photos and send them through to her email, so she could close her eyes and imagine the scene. Peter Andres had died with his eyes open, a look of astonishment still on his face. His killer had used the scythe first against his throat; the victim had gripped his neck, stunned, trying to fight the flow of blood. He had gone down, and the killer had finished it all off with a few swipes to his chest. The murder hadn't taken more than a few seconds, the first strike had been so swift.

Jenna stood in the dead center of the barn and closed her eyes.

She could see Peter Andres. He had been a big man, white haired and white bearded. He had been raking autumn leaves the wind had swept into the barn.

She frowned, opening her eyes. She'd had a sense of someone so strong that she had to see if it was real or not.

She was alone in the barn.

And yet…

She'd felt as if there was someone there. Someone, or a something. There had been a figure in a cape and cowl—and some kind of a demon mask.

Halloween. It was Halloween season.

But it hadn't been Halloween when Peter Andres had been killed. And still, she was certain that she'd had a sense of such a person, looking around the barn door first, seeing Peter…

And rushing in.

The mask had been…a demon face. The figure had been dressed like a caped and cowled version of the horned demon. Satan? Malachi's father had suggested that despite the fact that the Wiccan religion had no demons, they actually did have a devil, one of their earth gods in disguise. She didn't know that much about the religion, but she knew that it was far different than the kind of imagined "witchcraft" that people had been persecuted for in the past.

She closed her eyes again. There was a rush in the air around her, a rush of movement. Peter Andres had been taken entirely by surprise. A big man, he could have defended himself.

He'd never had the chance.

He'd looked up from his work to see the figure racing toward him. He'd been confused, frowning over the evil vestige of the whirlwind hurtling into his body. He probably hadn't even noticed that the demon-thing was carrying a scythe.

She felt movement in the air. Someone was there.

She opened her eyes, backing away, instinct warning her of danger.

And ran into a little blonde woman.

"Miss Duffy? I'm sorry, I didn't mean to startle you. I'm Alison Chart, the Realtor."

Councilman Andy Yates didn't give Sam any kind of a runaround.

Sam stopped in at his office on Pickering Wharf, where, when not being a councilman, Andy Yates bought and sold period furniture and collectibles.

The young secretary in the front vestibule was a man, and he apparently recognized Sam. Sam had to be more than a decade older than the fresh-faced twenty-something sitting there, so he knew he wasn't an old acquaintance.

"Sorry for staring, Mr. Hall. I know you from the magazines." He stood to shake Sam's hand. "I'll tell Mr. Yates that you're here. Oh, sorry, I'm Greg Mason. Glad to meet you." He walked straight to the door of the inner office and tapped on it. Opening it, he announced Sam's arrival.

Andy Yates was standing when Sam entered. He was a man in his early forties, trim and in shape, with a pleasant face and a headful of sandy-brown hair. He shook Sam's hand. "I've heard you're defending Malachi Smith. I'm glad to hear it. I'm sorry for that young man. He needs to be locked up, of course, but I'm sorry for him. He didn't have much of a chance, living at Lexington House with that strange family of his."

"That's generous of you, Mr. Yates," Sam said.

"Andy, please. I'm a man of the people—or I try to be," Yates said, offering Sam a grin and a shrug. Sam could see how he made a good politician. He was self-effacing, and had slightly aging boy-next-door charm that surely stood him well. "Sit down, please. How can I help you here in our small town?" Grinning, he returned to his swivel chair behind the desk; Sam sat in the comfortably upholstered chair in front of the desk.

Sam grinned, as well. "I'm from here, actually."

"That's right. I'd forgotten. I'm actually from Marblehead."

"Beautiful place, and around the corner," Sam said.

Yates nodded. "Listen, I'm more than happy to help you—I'm just not sure how."

"Well, I'd appreciate it if you could explain to me what happened between your son, David, and Malachi Smith."

Yates sighed, looking down at his folded hands. "Well, I bet you know the basic story of the staring and the lunch tray and whatnot. But it's something I never understood—and wanted to forget. And, of course, I was worried sick about my own boy, but furious with the whole group of his friends for teasing that poor Smith kid so mercilessly."

"How badly was your son hurt?" Sam asked.

"He spent a night in the hospital, mostly precautionary. There was no major damage done, and he did it himself. He told me that Malachi gave him the evil eye, and every one of his friends agreed, of course. But I never really knew what to think.… I love my son, of course, Mr. Hall."

"Sam, since you're Andy."

"Sam," Yates said. He shook his head, as if still in bewilderment three years later. "I took David to a doctor, of course. A psychiatrist."

"Not Jamie O'Neill?" Sam asked.

"Jamie O'Neill is the best in the area, in my opinion. But my wife didn't want any kind of a conflict of interest. We took him to a Dr. Hawkins at UMass. Hawkins told us that suggestion could make people do all kinds of things. If David *believed* that Malachi Smith was giving him the evil eye, it was real in his own mind."

"You didn't harbor any ill will toward Malachi?"

Yates sniffed. "The kid? No. I blamed it on the parents. Strict—and maybe they bought into those house legends or something. You know, I tried to buy the house. Old Abraham wouldn't sell. And then I tried to forget the whole lunchroom thing. I mean, there was really nothing to be done. On the council here, we're always trying to keep a good balance going between our population of traditionalists, Wiccans, atheists—

hell, you name it. The world moves on, you know? I thought that social services should have moved in, but apparently the Smiths didn't beat the kid, they didn't do anything illegal. They were just ridiculously strict, from what I hear. No one could help Malachi. Frankly, I'm not surprised that the boy finally freaked out and lashed out on his folks."

"Yes, but you know, I assume, that the police were watching him in the cases of the farmer, Peter Andres, killed in Andover, and the neighbor, Earnest Covington, who was just killed last week."

"Well, Peter had been a substitute at his school, and, as far as I know, he was well enough liked. Maybe Malachi, in that crazy mind his parents created, thought that Peter was responsible for his misery."

"What about the neighbor?"

"Maybe he saw Malachi doing weird things, who the hell knows? Look at me—I'm no cop!" Yates chuckled. "But, look, I believe in justice, and I don't loathe you for defending him. I'm assuming you'll work on an insanity plea, and I'm sure you'll do well. Trust me, I'd hate to see him thrown into a hardened prison population, but when it comes to locking up the boy, I'm all for it. I feel sorry for him, but I don't want him loose."

Sam decided not to tell Andy Yates that Malachi Smith claimed to be innocent.

"Would you mind if I talked to your son, Andy?" he asked.

Yates laughed softly. "I wouldn't mind—but you'll have to talk to my wife. Our two kids are her life— she's a veritable barracuda when it comes to them." He paused, scratching out a number on a piece of paper. "You call her—I have to live with her!"

Sam smiled and accepted the piece of paper. He was definitely interested in meeting the boy who had beaten himself in the head because of Malachi's evil eye.

He exchanged a pleasant set of goodbyes with the councilman and dialed the number right after he left the office. Mrs. Yates hung up the minute he identified himself. He tried again. This time, she had a few words for him.

"You leave me alone! Don't you dare go near my son—you're slime, pure slime! You think you're a hot-shot, getting killers off? Well, you stay the hell away from my son. I'll have you arrested if I hear that you're within a hundred yards of him. You go to hell, Mr. Hall. You're trying to defend the devil, and you're a demon yourself for doing it! You're a crooked, money-grubbing bastard, and you will stay the hell away from my son!"

Again, the phone went dead.

Sam wasn't sure if he was amused or dismayed. He decided to start at it all from a different angle. Surely, there was someone out there who wasn't entirely biased.

He hesitated, and then put in a call to Jenna Duffy.

"What are you doing?" he asked her.

He thought that she hesitated a minute. "I came out to see the Andres home in Andover," she said.

He frowned. "Alone?" He didn't know why that worried him. It was broad daylight and, according to everyone, Peter Andres's murderer was in custody.

Did he believe that himself now? He just didn't know.

"I called the Realtor," Jenna said. "She's nice. I admitted I was looking into the case—on my uncle's behalf. She was okay with it after I explained. I'm not sure she believes she's ever going to sell the house anyway, unless she finds someone with a really morbid curiosity."

"Anything helpful? What did you see?"

"I've seen the house and the barn where he was killed. It's wiped clean," she added. "And you?"

"I was thinking of shopping and sightseeing. Actually, there's one old friend I want to stop in on—at a witchcraft shop on Essex Street. Want to come?"

"Sightseeing and shopping," she said drily. "Sure."

"I'll meet you there in thirty minutes. I'll text you the address."

"Sam! Sam Hall! I'd heard you were here!"

The words were spoken by a dark-haired young woman standing behind the counter of A Little Bit of Magic. Her pretty features were lit up, and she came walking around the sales station and threw her arms around Sam's neck and gave him a fierce hug. She pulled away quickly and gave Jenna an apologetic look. "I'm sorry. I haven't seen this boy in a long, long time! Not since the funeral."

"I haven't been back since the funeral, Cecilia," Sam said. "Do you remember Jenna Duffy? She's Jamie's niece. I think you two tortured my parents together years ago."

"Oh! Oh, of course! Jenna—I didn't recognize you at first. How could I have missed that red hair? I didn't mean that rudely—it's beautiful hair. Jenna, how are you?" Cecilia asked, overly emphatically.

"I'm good, thank you, and honestly, Cecilia, I didn't recognize you at first, either," Jenna told her. Sam had said they were going to stop in on an old friend. She hadn't realized that it was a mutual acquaintance. Cecilia Sanderson. She was a year or two older than Jenna, but Salem hadn't been a big place, and when they were young, she'd lived close to Jamie—and to Sam Hall's parents' home. Naturally, the two girls had been thrown together on those occasions when Jenna visited.

Cecilia grinned. "Well, I have changed a great deal. My real hair color is mousy-brown—for some reason, if you run a Wiccan shop, you're more alluring with very dark hair. And black clothing, of course."

"Cecilia is a Wiccan now," Sam explained.

Cecilia elbowed him. "Sam doesn't believe in anything. We're a recognized religion."

"Hey, I just question what *you* really believe!" Sam said, not offended.

Cecilia waved a hand in the air. "This is really still a small town," she said. "People talk, and judge. Most of the time, our 'traditionalists' are pretty tolerant and grateful that people love coming up here just for the Wiccan shops and curios, and so on and so on. People are more tolerant when there's money to be had."

"And," Sam said, leaning casually on the counter, "you know as well as I do that half the people who come here to open up shop are *playing* at being Wiccan."

"Better Wiccan than fanatical!" Cecilia said. "I believe in *cause no harm to others*. Some fundamentalists of other religions believe in *killing in the name of God,* Sam."

He smiled. "I'm not judging you, Cecilia. I promise. I know you're a good person."

"Yeah, yeah, yeah!" she said and laughed. "How do you like the shop?"

"It's really beautiful, so well decorated and laid out," Jenna told her. She was sincere. The windows were decorated for fall, with shimmering silk flowers and leaves, and mannequins wearing fine velvet Wiccan capes and beautiful silver jewelry. Handsome signs done in curving but legible calligraphy pointed out that herbs and jewelry were in the front, curios and books in the center section and clothing to the rear.

Cecilia smiled. "I always wanted my own shop! Well, it's almost my own. Do you remember Ivy Summers?" she asked.

"Could I forget?" Sam asked, and rolled his eyes. "She broke my Nintendo!"

Jenna laughed. "I remember Ivy, yes."

"We actually own the shop together. Ivy is at home, working the computer sales, which are fantastic. We're really pleased."

"That's great," Sam told her.

"Ah, well, not as great as being an attorney who shows up on the front page of the Huffington Post, CNN—you name it! And now, so I hear, you're defending the Smith boy!" she said, her voice curious and excited. "Give! Is it true? Sam, that whole family was whacked-out crazy, you know."

"Cecilia! Would you be judging others?" he asked.

She shrugged. "No. Yes. Well, you have to judge them. Wiccan, Judeo-Christian, whatever! The whole rest of the town thought they were all crazy."

"But there are people who think *you're* crazy," Sam reminded her. "Sorry, I don't mean you. I mean all Wiccans." He smiled broadly.

She waved a hand in the air. "Hey, yeah, well, people are people, and we don't all get along. But that's different."

"The enemy of my enemy is my friend!"

"You are exasperating!" Cecilia said. She looked at Jenna. "So…are you two dating now or something?"

"No…" Jenna said, startled and looking at Sam.

"Malachi Smith was Jamie's patient at one time," Sam explained. "She's helping me, because her uncle believes in Malachi's innocence."

Cecilia seemed puzzled. "But—it's all cut-and-dried, isn't it? Aren't you going to pursue an insanity plea or whatever?"

"I can't really talk about that," Sam said, shifting gears. "So, *you* give! Any great grudges dominating the town talk these days? Any shopkeepers stolen the customers of another? What's the rumor mill like? Any idea how the local pot and meth trade are doing?"

Cecilia looked at them both incredulously. "Wait, you think that the Smith family was murdered over drugs?"

"Probably not," Sam said. "But, hey, I thought I'd throw some stuff out there, since you talk to everyone, figured you'd know about town dynamics. Like, was Abraham Smith fighting with anybody?"

Cecilia laughed. "Anybody? How about everybody?

No one liked him much, but no one bothered with him much. His wife *never* left the house." She frowned. "Oh, there was a fellow—a councilman—who had wanted to buy the property. I think someone else wanted to buy it, too. Wiccan gossip at the bars late at night..." she explained. "I'm sorry, don't know if it's true or not, but—oh, there was something in the local paper about the councilman vying for the place."

"Councilman Yates?" Sam asked.

"Um, yes, I think so," Cecilia said. "And someone else...a magician, a medium, someone like that—oh, yes! Samantha Yeager."

"Two interested parties—for a house with that reputation?" Jenna asked, trying to refocus Cecilia's energetic talking.

"Well, of course! What a tourist attraction—the only reason that they talk about it in the paper like that," Cecilia said.

"But they can't get rid of Peter Andres's place," Jenna said. "I was just out there, and I met with the Realtor."

Cecilia shrugged, grinning broadly. "The Lexington House has a truly ghastly and grim history—the farm out in Andover had *one* bad thing happen, even if it was pretty bad. And that's recent. People like historic ghosts much more than modern ghosts. Unless, of course, it's a modern celebrity ghost. Everyone wants to stay at that Hard Rock in Florida in the room where Anna Nicole Smith died. But no one knew Peter Andres. Oh, come on, you don't need to be a psychiatrist to notice the way that people just *are!*"

"So, historically, we all know about the Lexington

family, and the Braden family after them—so the house was worth a good deal if you want to open a tourist attraction," Sam said.

"Oh, yes, of course. I think that the woman I was telling you about—Samantha Yeager—wanted the house for work. She's kind of a newcomer—okay, she's from as far away as Plymouth—but she reads tarot cards and does palm readings, sells cards, herbs and all the same stuff that we do. Yeah, yeah, I remember someone saying that *she* said it looks like the Lizzie Borden place, which is now like a B and B or something."

"People would go to her rather than someone else for the ambience of the house?" Jenna asked drily.

"Of course! I'll bet you it will be worth a mint now. Hey, the Smith kid will be able to pay you, Sam, if they sell it," Cecilia said cheerfully.

"I'm doing the work pro bono," Sam told her.

"Well, that's kind of you, to help such a nutty kid."

"I guess that's universally accepted?" Jenna asked.

They both stared at her.

"Universally, as in locally, I mean," Jenna said.

Cecilia nodded. "It's like knowing about kooks anywhere you live, you know. Everybody knew that family—although, usually we didn't give them all much thought. And, of course, in this area, Lexington House is legendary. Everyone thought it fitting that the Smiths lived there." She grinned. "And, of course, in Salem, you have all the curiosity seekers who come to see what modern witches look like! It may be 'Witch City,' but we're still the minority. I mean, we should be the *alternative* people. The Smith family made us all seem part

of the same fabric in a way...." Cecilia was thoughtful
a minute. "You know, if it weren't backward..."

"If what weren't backward?" Sam asked quickly.

"Well, I'm trying to remember. My sister just started
teaching at the high school, so all she knows is what
others say about the past, but if I remember this correctly—and you should definitely check me out, because
I'm just giving you *hearsay* or whatever—but Peter
Andres was vocal about Abraham Smith. He said that
Smith had his own money, and that he was still collecting
some kind of disability. That he was a drain on the tax-
payers, was the epitome of the worst of the system—stuff
like that. He stood up for Malachi, but he hated Abraham.
Malachi, of course, always defended his father."

"What did Abraham have to say about that?" Jenna
asked.

Cecilia shrugged. "Nothing—nothing that I know
about. But he wasn't the kind to have a drink and chat
at the bars!" she said. She smiled at them. "A lot of the
merchants around here are actually good friends, and
if we don't like each other—or don't always share the
same philosophy or vision—we still support one another. We get together to plan Halloween activities, we
work with the city and the museums. *That's* how we stay
afloat through the cold, icy winter when tourism isn't
so plentiful! So, yes, of course, we chat when we stop at
the brewery or one of the bars, and we usually do hear
what's going on around town. You know back when that
incident happened at the high school, some argued that
Andy and Cindy Yates had a crazy kid themselves, and
even some smart people said that suggestion could cause

people to do very strange things. Kind of like you can brainwash yourself. Then, the other half of the people argued on the superstitious side. There was something strange about Malachi Smith. Maybe the devil actually lived up at Lexington House and had gotten into him. But, anyway, old Abraham took his son out of school without a word, and people stopped talking about it so much."

"Until Peter Andres was murdered?" Jenna asked.

Cecilia hesitated. A group had just walked into the shop. The three women were wearing beautiful velvet capes, and Jenna had the feeling that they'd just been purchased. One of the men was dressed in similar fashion, but his hooded cape was brown wool.

"A mortar and pestle, Johnny!" one of the women said. "Ooh, in marble, how pretty—I bet I could cook up some spells with that!"

"Excuse me," Cecilia said, and walked over to the group.

Jenna could see that the newcomers seemed both fascinated and amused by the fact that they were in "Witch City." She could also see that Cecilia was accustomed to the attitude and seemed entirely unperturbed. She suggested to the woman that the mortar and pestle were also quite useful for crushing garlic and herbs.

"She's a good kid," Sam said softly.

"And a talker…but a lot of help," she replied. She couldn't help watching the man in the brown cape. There was really nothing out of the ordinary about him; people were dressed up all around the city. But his outfit reminded her of her vision—*the caped, hooded and masked person who had rushed in on Peter Andres, felling him where he stood.*

"What's the matter?" Sam asked her.

She shook her head. She wasn't ready to tell him what she'd seen. He'd mocked her at the Lexington House, and she could only imagine what he would have to say if she told him a dressed-up and horned demon had killed Peter Andres.

"It's Halloween. People like to play at being many things," she said.

"People always like to play at being many things," he told her. "I'll let Cecilia know we're leaving."

Cecilia excused herself to her customers, hugged Sam and waved to Jenna, and the two left her shop. They walked along the pedestrian street by the museums and other shops. All around them, they could hear the delighted squeals of children as they watched jugglers or paused at various stations to take part in drawing, pumpkin carving or face painting.

Jenna wasn't sure where they were going, but Sam was thoughtful.

"Assuming Malachi is innocent, what's going on is calculated," he said. "First murder a teacher, assuming that everyone would think that Malachi hated that teacher and would easily be suspected—which he was. And then a neighbor. But why the neighbor?"

"According to Cecilia, everyone hated the Smith family," Jenna said. "So, we can assume that the neighbor hated them a lot."

"So, it all looks like a series of events, with the killer, Malachi, having lost all hold on reality, and perhaps killing others before lashing out at his restrictive family. The question is…was there a real reason for the neighbor and the teacher, or were they just *there,* random victims in a plan against the family?"

"Or was there a plan, and they fit right into it?" Jenna asked.

"Well, the fact that Malachi and Peter Andres actually got on well together will help our case," Sam said.

Jenna heard him speak, but she didn't reply. She stopped walking.

Just ahead of them, moving through the crowd, was someone in a long brown cape, a monk's cape with a hood. She couldn't see the person's face and she didn't know if it was a man or a woman—or if they wore a mask or not.

She reminded herself that she had just seen a man in Cecilia's shop in such a cape.

It was Halloween season, Haunted Happenings. People would be in costumes daily, participating in all the events, and dressing up because it was fun to dress up!

The person paused—almost as if they had felt they were being watched.

He or she turned and looked back.

Jenna froze.

The person was wearing the mask.

The same mask she had seen in her vision of the murder of Peter Andres.

It was the horned devil.

5

The horned devil stared at her a long moment, and then turned.

She couldn't have begun to explain *how,* but the person in the costume knew she had recognized him.

If it was a *him.* It was impossible to tell.

Jenna found herself following the horned devil. Even as she quickened her pace, she wondered what she would say if she caught up with them.

Excuse me, but in my mind's eye, I saw you murder Peter Andres, or at least, I saw someone in the costume you're wearing....

"Hey, where are you going?" Sam called. She hadn't realized that she'd been walking so quickly until Sam had caught up with her. By the time she looked up from where Sam's arm was on her, she saw that she'd lost her target in the crowd. The horned devil had disappeared by diving through a group dressed as plums and apples and the rest of the Fruit of the Loom underwear set.

Halloween season. The season of the witch, so many thought. And in legend, the night when souls could return to earth....

And try to linger on.

But the dead weren't really returning; the living created evil.

"Jenna!" Sam said.

"I—I'm sorry," she said. "I—I thought I saw an old friend."

"Really?"

"Yes, yes, of course."

"Someone I might know?"

Jenna dead-blanked on the name of anyone she might have known in Salem.

"Just—just a girl I saw now and then. She might have been friends with Cecilia, too. I actually can't remember her name." Jenna tried not to blink, fidget, look downward or to the side, or do any of the things that automatically identified you as a liar.

"Oh," he said, looking back at her. "Well, I can't help you there."

"Oh, nothing to worry about," she said and shrugged.

Jenna realized that in her pursuit she had turned down the street toward Old Burying Point Cemetery. The cemetery contained the graves of a *Mayflower* Pilgrim, and John Hathorne, one of the witchcraft trial judges. Nathaniel Hawthorne had added the "w" to his family's name, and written many of his works, because he'd been disturbed by his ancestor's involvement in the trials. Jenna mused that it was an interesting place, and she was grateful for the historic preservation there and for the monument of benches and names that had been added just outside the gates for the tercentennial of the trial in 1992.

It was a place steeped in history and the past. A place where the dead had been interred for hundreds of years. Though tourists walked among the gravestones and sought out those of the greatest interest, Jenna could still see the hazy images of a few of the departed wandering about. Most spirits did not remain to haunt burial grounds; their business was seldom at the place where their earthly remains had been interred. Perhaps those who came just did so out of respect to others. The cemetery wasn't crowded, but she could see a man in a ship captain's jacket, a few in more puritanical dress, and a beautiful young woman in a gown that belonged in the early eighteen hundreds.

"Ah, the old burying ground," Sam said.

"I doubt if we'll find any answers here," Jenna said, turning away from graveyard itself to look at him, hoping she gave away nothing of what she saw.

"You never know. The past can usually teach us a lot. I always find people amazing—and the trials extremely interesting, as far as the legal process of the time went," Sam mused. "Those who admitted to witchcraft—dancing with the devil, whatever!—managed to save their lives. Those who denied it to the end, certain in their belief in God or just determined that they wouldn't admit to such ridiculousness, were the ones who were hanged. Or, in the case of Giles Corey, pressed to death."

"I know. I've always wondered how people managed to stay fast to such a declaration. I wonder about myself. If I believed I could be forgiven and redeemed by stating a lie—and I knew that I'd wind up being hanged if I told the truth—I'm not sure I would have stayed the truth course. But our standards have changed. We know the world is filled with beliefs, and we have to be tolerant of them now. I'm convinced that God would forgive anyone such a lie to save themselves, since their accusers were obviously so sadly mistaken in the law, religion—and witchcraft!" Jenna said.

She found herself sitting on one of the cantilevered benches, looking at the trees that seemed to whisper softly in the autumn air. She had chosen the bench that was inscribed to John Proctor.

Sam smiled, setting a foot on the bench and leaning toward her on his knee. "How wonderfully logical, Miss Duffy."

"Are you mocking me again?"

He shook his head, serious despite the charming curve of his rueful smile. "I often wonder myself how people could adhere to principle with such determination in the face of such horrible consequences. Take old John Proctor. He argued that, 'the girls will make devils of us all!' He gave his girl a good whack—hardly accepted these days, of course—and her fits stopped. She got back with the other girls, and her fits started up again, and John Proctor wound up being hanged because the girls accused him. We can never, ever forget the power of belief and the human mind!"

Then he looked around wistfully at the various graves. "Well, you're good at lying," he said suddenly, catching Jenna off guard.

Startled, she stared up at him.

"Or, not so good…" he said.

"I don't know what—"

"You know exactly what I'm talking about. Who were you just chasing?" he demanded.

"If I told you, you'd make fun of me," she said defensively.

"Try me—since I know you're lying anyway, and I'd rather you tell a truth that I might mock."

"I don't particularly enjoy being mocked," she said.

"My mind isn't that closed—there's a door in there that's slightly ajar."

"All right—I went to the murder site. The barn."

"I know that."

"I sometimes have what they call retro-cognition or postcognition," Jenna told him.

"You see the past."

She nodded. "And you're going to laugh."

"No, honestly, I'm not. I have to admit, I'm not sure that anyone really *sees* the past, but I believe that the mind is amazing, and perhaps such things as postcognition, as you say, exist because of something locked in the deep subconscious. You know an area, you've seen things, you've heard things…they come alive in the back of the mind," he said.

"Well, then, in the back of my mind, I *saw* the killer go after Peter Andres."

He stared at her a moment, then shrugged his shoulders and lifted his hands. "Well, let's hope you're right. If we know *who,* we just have to find proof and motive to back it up. You know, evidence. So who was it?"

"I don't know who."

"But you saw them."

"Whoever killed Andres did so in costume."

"In costume?" he asked, staring at her blankly. "Like in a Halloween costume? It wasn't the Halloween season when Peter Andres was killed."

"I know."

"So…what kind of a costume? I hear clown costumes are great—in horror movies, at least. There there's always your traditional white plastic mask à la the Friday the 13th movies. Or a rubber Freddy Krueger—"

She stood up. "You may be the attorney. Well, then, you have all kinds of legal research and studying to do, motions to file, arguments to plan. You know the law, Sam. I'm not so sure that you know people, or really understand much about the human soul. I think I'm better off on my own." She turned to leave, saying over her shoulder, "I'll call you when I have something tangible."

She walked away, thinking that he would call her back, that he would apologize.

He didn't.

Sam watched Jenna go, feeling a growing sense of irritation—battled by a longing to rush after her.

He steeled himself to hold still. Somehow, her crazy-good uncle had convinced him to take on the defense of a youth who had been caught with the blood of the slain all over him. Somehow, he had gotten himself into this. Jamie had always been happy to tell a tale about the gnomes, pixies, leprechauns and banshees, and how a battle of giants had created great stone steps in Ireland. His stories were fun—good drinking fare in a pub, sure to entertain.

But, now, his niece, FBI *special agent,* was telling him she could see what had happened in the past. Except that she couldn't actually *see* who had murdered the Smiths, Peter Andres or Earnest Covington. Nope, nope, just someone in costume.

A brilliant red leaf drifted down on the stone slab seat where Jenna had been sitting. He read the writing engraved there: John Proctor, hanged, August 19, 1692. Arthur Miller, in *The Crucible,* had cast the man in his early thirties, a romantic fellow who had engaged in an affair with his chief accuser, Abigail Williams—who had, in truth, been eleven at the time. There had been no affair, and the girl who had cried out first against the family had been Ann Putnam, and she had accused Elizabeth, his wife.

Sam's lips tightened grimly. Growing up in Salem, it had been impossible to miss learning about the Witch Trials, backward and forward. And also the Hollywood versions of them.

"'Thou shalt not suffer a witch to live,' Exodus, 22:18," he murmured aloud. Witches—those who had made pacts with the devil—did not exist. Wiccans didn't even believe in the devil of the New England forefathers, no matter what those like the Smiths had thought.

Jenna might well have been hanged as a witch—in the colonies. Burned if she had stumbled back to Scotland or the European continent.

Sam got up and wandered in through the gate, and over to the Hathorne grave. He wondered if the remains of the man who had been instrumental in the persecution were even vaguely in the spot anymore—the earth shifted over the years. Embalming hadn't existed here when Hathorne had died, and coffins were not made to try to stave off time. The thing of it all was that history was the greatest teacher. Nathaniel Hawthorne had been so disturbed by his family's part in the hysteria that he'd found a way to try to right the wrongs of the past on paper, not just in works such as *The Scarlet Letter* or *The House of the Seven Gables,* but in his short stories, such as "Young Goodman Brown," in which the protagonist was late getting into the woods because of his wife, Faith, who held him back before he entered the realm in which an old man, née the devil, informed him he had many friends in New England. Fear so overcame Goodman Brown that he "lost Faith." It was far too easy to believe in the evil that might be around than it was to fight against it.

The autumn breeze was rustling, and he looked around at the beauty of the leaves. He loved New England. It was home. And New Englanders, who usually accepted all their history with a grain of salt, were truly no different than people anywhere. Especially in the twenty-first century. The pace of living was frantic; the internet brought the escapades of the world closer and closer together. And people everywhere had a tendency to be influenced by the crowd around them.

Well, back in the seventeenth century, sane men were led to believe in "spectral" evidence. A witch's evil soul could leave her body and squeeze the bowels of the afflicted, pinch and scratch them. And while the modern world scoffed and laughed at such a possibility, people were still fascinated by out-of-body, near-death experiences.

And Jenna Duffy could close her eyes and see the past....

None of it mattered, he told himself. He was dealing with flesh and blood—literally. Malachi Smith had been found covered in the blood of his family.

That was evidence—hard evidence. That was the stuff he had to deal with, no esoteric comparisons of human nature over the centuries.

Sam himself had been the first to see Malachi that night. And hadn't he at first refused to acknowledge that it was blood the boy was covered in? His first impression—his unconscious—couldn't even be brought to think the boy a killer.

He imagined the questions he would ask if he'd put himself on the stand. Nothing in his testimony—sworn under oath—could possibly testify to Malachi's innocence. John Alden had found the bodies of Malachi's family; he had seen the house and the pile of Malachi's clothing.

Everything pointed to Malachi. So the trick was to find someone else who hated the boy's father, a case of *reasonable doubt*. Of course, it wasn't going to be hard to find someone like that; everyone had hated Abraham Smith.

Except, perhaps, for the old believers who had met in Beverly, at the Old Meeting House.

Sam turned and started walking toward his car. He called his assistant, Evan Richardson, back at his offices in Boston, and asked him to do research on any legal actions against the church.

It was time to head out to see the elders.

Jenna walked back through the crowd of Halloween locals and visitors—always entertaining. In Salem, some were in business attire, some were in the more day-to-day Gothic attire chosen by many of the modern Wiccans and some were in costumes of all varieties. A giant Count Chocula was walking around with a Barbie doll. A fantastic and perfectly realistic vampire was strolling the streets with two little *Toy Story 3* characters.

It was fun to walk Salem's streets. She loved the city, especially during Haunted Happenings.

All she had to do now was forget that her uncle was probably giving himself an ulcer regarding Malachi Smith's innocence, and that Sam Hall was a major-league ass.

She tried to remind herself that she and her group were often greeted that way. People found it hard to believe that other people had talents they did not, though she wasn't sure why. Jake Mallory, their computer expert, played a mean guitar, and she couldn't play to save her life. She saw ghosts. Not everyone did.

It was often difficult to believe in what couldn't be seen. And, sometimes, it was too easy to believe in it. The "witches" of Salem had been prosecuted and condemned because of "spectral" evidence. The people of the time had believed that their friends could leave their bodies—even when they were jailed and in chains!—

to pinch and torment others. Sometimes, belief could cause irreparable harm; sometimes, it was impossible to summon any at all.

Which was better?

Sam Hall was no worse than many other doubters they had come to know.

Yes, he was.

He should be getting to know her, if only a bit. There were times when they looked at each other that she was fascinated with him physically, when the light in his eyes made her think that he'd just reach out and touch her....

Frankly, that she could just about fall into his arms and explore his...mind. In all honesty, she liked his mind. He was definitely walking around with a few extra chips on his shoulders, but the concept of a pro bono case had come easily to him.

She might have been wrong to walk away in a huff. No, it had been a dignified retreat. Okay, at least a dignified huff.

She paused, wondering where Sam might be headed at that moment. She didn't want to bump into him just yet. Up until now, she'd been out to see the site where Peter Andres had been killed, and she was certain that her postcognition had given her a good first step. Whoever had killed Peter Andres had done so in costume, playing on the area's past fear of the devil as a horned demon. That made her think that the murderer was local; of course, someone could have come here and played off the past, but since the murders had been so brutal without being ritualistic, she didn't think that they were random or serial-killerish. The first two had been committed to make people believe that Malachi Smith was crazy and capable of murder; only the testimony of the grocery clerk had kept the boy from arrest.

She found a little café just off Essex, sat down and ordered coffee.

Once she'd been served, she put through a call to Jake Mallory. When he began to barrage her with questions, she promised that she would call Jackson, their team head, with a full report soon—even though the team wasn't *officially* on this case.

"Jake, I just need some information right now. Can you help me?" she asked.

"I'm at my keyboard."

"A Mr. Earnest Covington of Salem was murdered last week. Some kids said that they saw Malachi running from the house. A grocer said that was impossible unless Malachi could astral-project, since he'd been in the store buying meat at the time. I need the names of the grocer and the kids."

"Sam doesn't have that information on hand?"

"Sam is… Sam isn't into ghost investigations," she said tightly.

"Most people do mock what they don't understand—especially when we're all taught to be brave, that ghosts don't exist and there's nothing hiding under the bed," Jake reminded her.

"Will you just get me the information?" she asked.

"Call you right back," Jake said. "And be careful up there, young woman."

"Hey, I'm from Massachusetts," she told him.

"Hey, you're from Ireland."

"Okay!" she said, and laughed. "But the Commonwealth became my home. I'm okay."

"You'd better give Jackson a call soon," Jake warned her. "He tends to read the papers, you know, and he knows you're up there with your uncle, and he knows you went because Jamie asked you to, so when he starts reading about everything that's going on there right now—and Jamie's name winds up in the papers since he's the kid's guardian—he's not going to be happy that you haven't yet spoken to him about the situation."

"I'll call him now," she promised. "But this isn't official. It can't be official."

"I know. So, if you want to be able to get in there and see what you can find out, remember to play nice and disappear when you need to."

"Yes, sir," she promised. "I'll call boss man right now, while you're looking up the stories in the newspaper and wherever else you find your computer information for me."

When they hung up, Jenna realized that she'd been wandering down toward the museum. She applauded the Peabody Essex museum—the area was given a complete history there. Pirates had ranged the coast here, too; whalers had gone to sea. Pilgrims had fought off the Indians, and Massachusetts had given the country Thanksgiving Day. It wasn't all witches!

But, equally, what had happened here had helped change the future of a country. While there had been a time when superstition had reigned over the rich, the poor, the noble and the castoffs of society, the tragedy of the executions here in line with the "legal" system that convicted its victims might have been the beginning of the end for judgment without due process, heralding a true legal system in which a jury would decide on the facts, and not on hearsay or passionate words. Had there been malice involved? Surely, though many of the people had not been aware of it. It was far easier to see evil in someone if you believed that they had wronged you. But then, at the time of the Salem witchcraft trials, much worse had gone on elsewhere in the "civilized" Western worlds. Thousands had been burned in a day in Germany. The Native Americans hadn't even known that such a creature as Satan existed, but the Pilgrims' fear of Indian attack had certainly fueled *their* belief in that evil. It had been a hard world, and it was easy to blame cultural differences, death, starvation and other ill fortune on the devil.

And, of course, those who consorted with him.

She put through a call to Jackson Crow just as she had promised. Jackson listened gravely, assuring her that, at the moment, nothing big was going on; he was still in NYC and a few people were just settling into their new field offices in Arlington, Virginia, but could help her out in their limited background capacity. The Krewe of Hunters would always have her back.

"Thanks, Jackson," Jenna said. "For now, I'm just a niece visiting her uncle and serving as an 'amateur' assistant to the defense attorney, who does have the right to question the prosecution's case and witnesses."

"Well, we can always come up to enjoy Haunted

Happenings. You know, if you just want to 'show us around,'" Jackson told her.

"I've thought of that," she assured him.

"Keep me posted."

When they hung up, she drummed her fingers on the table, impatiently waiting for Jake to call her back. He did so quickly—before she had to ask for a second refill to keep her seat.

"The grocer, Milton Sedge, works at a local market, Sedge's—do you know it?"

"Yes, thanks, it's near the Lexington house."

"He works from about six in the morning until closing, every day, according to the woman who answered the phone when I called. He closes at around nine. Hard worker."

"Hey, he comes from good Puritan stock," Jenna said casually. "Did you say that I was coming by to talk with him?"

"I mentioned that someone assisting in Smith's defense would be by—I didn't give your name. She was sure that Mr. Sedge would be happy to see you. I think it's going to be dicier to talk to the boys who claimed he was seen at the cliff."

"Who are they?"

"One was Joshua Abbott. Have you heard of him?"

"No."

"The other is a kid named David Yates."

"Ah."

"Ah?"

"He's the kid who believed that Malachi Smith gave

him the evil eye," Jenna said. "His father is Andy Yates, a councilman."

"Good luck, kid," Jake said. "And, hey, be careful up there."

"People here are really good people, Jake."

He laughed. "Oh, Jenna, no doubt. But it doesn't matter where you are—people come in good, and in bad. You're trying to prove that Malachi Smith didn't commit horrible murders. If he didn't, someone else very violent did. Be careful."

"Always, Jake," she promised him.

Jenna hung up, walked back to her uncle's and got into her car. She was off to talk to Milton Sedge. While she was talking to him, she just might be able to figure out a way to get to the boys who claimed to have seen Malachi after Earnest Covington was murdered. She grinned at herself. She hadn't met them yet, but she was sure they were pretentious little liars.

People judged so easily!

The Old Meeting House was a whitewashed building a little ways down the highway.

Sam estimated that it held a couple hundred people, tops, during meetings. There were no crosses or other symbols on the outside of the structure, and a carved wooden sign announced simply, Worship With Us. All Are Welcome.

He opened a picket fence to follow the brick walk to the front door. There was nothing ornate about the columns of the single-story structure. When he opened the door, he saw that there was simply a podium at the end, with a red runner leading to it. The pews were simple hardwood, and the kneelers were wooden as well, with no cushioning.

The room was shadowed in darkness, the plain, paneled windows allowing just a few streaks of light into the simple space. Sam thought that he had entered into an empty building at first, but as he stood near the entry, blinking against the murky shadows, he heard a voice.

"Hello, and welcome."

A tall man with long gray hair, his face covered in a long beard and mustache, walked toward him. He was clad simply in a white dress shirt and ill-fitting black suit; his arms were too long for his sleeves and the pants were short.

"How do you do," Sam said, offering his hand. "I'm Sam Hall, attorney, and I'm defending Malachi Smith."

"Oh," the man said, looking at him gravely. "I'm Goodman Wilson, pastor and elder of our little congregation. How can I help you?"

"Well, frankly, I wanted to know what you thought about the whole situation. You must be aware that many people believe that your religion is unorthodox. Do you think that Abraham Smith was so strict that his son— aware of other choices in society—might have thought that he was *too* strict?"

Sam was blunt and to the point on purpose: he wanted to see Goodman Wilson's immediate reaction to such questions. He had half suspected that the pastor would immediately be on the defensive and show him the door.

He did not.

"We're not quite as fanatic as many believe," Wilson told him. He smiled. "We don't believe in idols of any kind, and nor do we drink, swear, gamble or imbibe drugs. Actually, we have a number of ex-addicts in our fold, those who need guidance to stay on the straight and narrow. We welcome them, we welcome all."

"But Abraham was a hard man, or have I been misinformed?" Sam pressed.

"Sit down, sit down," Wilson offered. "Our chairs are hard, but…"

"A hard chair is fine by me."

They sat together on the rear hard pew, staring up toward the simple podium.

"Thank you for your help," Sam said.

Wilson gave a somewhat pained smile. "We do believe in justice. Not vengeance, justice. I knew Abraham Smith, of course. I knew the family, and I knew Malachi. The boy is quite amazing, really. He has a deep and fundamental belief in God. But he wasn't among our fold."

"No?"

"We don't have music," Wilson said. "No music, no dancing. Our faith is really simple—God requires that we appreciate what he has given us. The earth, the sky, the air we breathe. We work, because society demands that we pay for our living—and that we all pay taxes too, right?"

Sam smiled. Wilson seemed to think his words very entertaining.

"Jesus believed in simplicity. He didn't need ornate clothing, and he didn't need a mansion. He taught us to love one another. He didn't sing to the masses—he spoke to them."

"And Malachi needed music?" Sam asked.

The pastor nodded gravely. "I'm afraid I can't help you if you need me to testify that the boy might have been crazy. He wasn't crazy. He was honest—he had been taught not to lie. He came to me, though he did so in confidence, and he told me that he couldn't see anything evil in the piano, and therefore, he had to leave our fold. I suggested that he think about it long and hard. I disagreed with his decision, but his deliberations were honest, thoughtful, *competent*."

"He left the church because of the piano? Because of music?" Sam said.

"That surprises you?"

"I'd have thought that it might be something more…"

Goodman Wilson laughed. "You thought we might be slaughtering goats or chickens, and the boy was appalled by blood? No. Malachi told me he couldn't comprehend a faith that didn't see God's beauty in music, and I explained the very basic nature of our beliefs. Malachi told me that he was sorry—he saw God in music. Do you have any religion in your life, Mr. Hall?"

"I believe in God, Pastor. But I don't know who among us really knows what he wants," Sam said. After what seemed to him like a respectful pause, he continued on. "Did Malachi ever offer any violence toward his family?"

"Never. In our congregation, children honor their parents. They pray, they reflect. They take the time to care for the elderly. They don't steal, and they don't fornicate. There is no bodily punishment that we offer them—just excommunication, if it comes to that. We are a family here, and that is a terrible punishment when you love your family."

"How did Abraham discipline Malachi? As a good church member, he was said to beat him for infractions, but did he?"

Goodman Wilson was quiet for a minute. Then he said, "I worried, sometimes. Not that Malachi was beaten, but…parents can speak to a child in a way that is totally demoralizing. They can make a child feel as if they can't do anything right, as if they're worthless. I believe that Abraham could be verbally abusive at times, but, Mr. Hall, I don't think that's particular to members of our church. Sadly, I've seen many a father rip a child apart, and too often, that child can grow to believe himself worthless and incapable of doing anything right."

"So, you would describe your church as a strict group, but certainly not fanatical," Sam said.

Wilson laughed. "We are different. The Mormons are seen as different, as are the Amish. But we are Christians. We do believe in God in His Heaven, and we believe, equally, that there are evil forces. We believe in sin, but as Christ stated, true remorse brings us to the forgiveness of sins. We don't seek to harm anyone else, and we don't punish those who leave the church. We are all creatures of free choice."

"All right, it's true that we all have a tendency to mistrust each other, to be suspicious of what we don't understand. You don't believe that Malachi is a killer, so I'm going to assume that Abraham Smith had enemies."

Wilson was quiet for a minute. "I'm curious that you've come here. I do read the papers, though I don't have a television. The police say that Malachi is the alleged killer of Mr. Andres of Andover and Mr. Covington, as well. What enemies would they have had that they shared with Abraham Smith?"

"That's what I'm trying to find out," Sam said.

Wilson let out a long sigh. "Do I believe that Malachi is a killer? No. Might there be something in him that I never saw? Possibly. Did Abraham have enemies? Most definitely. Only two other families with children in that area belong to our congregation, and they keep very quiet. The rest of those people…they tolerate the Wiccans in the community, thinking of them as actors, really, drawing in the tourists. They tolerate Catholic, Jewish, agnostic, atheistic, Baptist and probably Buddhist. But us? We live too simply for them. They don't understand that we honestly believe that we are judged daily, that God will come again, and that we can choose to lead pure lives, or we can choose to sin. If Abraham did have real enemies, they did not come from this church. We are of a like mind and, if anyone had a serious problem with him, they would have had a problem with all of us probably, and would have come to me."

"Did he ever seem to be afraid of anyone? Did he have comments about the murders of his neighbor, or Mr. Andres?"

Wilson shrugged. "Well, he believed that God himself determined that Peter Andres should be killed. He told me he wouldn't have been surprised to see the Grim Reaper himself or an avenging angel come down to kill Peter Andres. Then again, Peter Andres had said that Abraham was a wart not just on the community, but on the world, and that he was ruining his one and only child. I believe Andres intended to look into social services and see if he could get the boy taken away from Abraham, but to my knowledge, nothing was ever done. Andres was a big, scary man, and I'd believe more easily that *he* would have offered violence to the Smiths. But since he died first, he can hardly be suspected of Abraham's murder."

"No, of course. What about his neighbor?"

"Now, Abraham kept to himself, from what I understood. Except that he ranted and raved a lot—and yelled at Malachi loudly enough for people in the next block to hear. One of his punishments was to make the kid stand out in the cold, against the front of the house. I doubt if his neighbors liked that much—it's embarrassing to everyone to see cruelty. Of course, they lived in the Lexington House, and the house itself has a reputation. I'm sure some people believe that evil lives in the house."

"What do you believe?" Sam asked him.

"Does evil live on?" Wilson asked thoughtfully. "Evil remains, where it has always been, in the heart of man."

"Of course."

"Innocents—those who were loyal enough to risk their lives rather than tell the lie that they *had signed* the devil's book—were the ones who went to the gallows, you know, back during the witchcraft scare," Wilson said. "The trials were bizarre! Those who *admitted* to witchcraft and confessed weren't hanged. Those who clung passionately to their belief that such a lie would be against God...*they're* the ones who suffered the death penalty!"

"I know. I'm from the area," Sam said.

Wilson stood up, perhaps embarrassed at his outburst of proselytizing to a layman. "We work at the soup kitchen, helping out with the homeless," he said. "I'm enjoying our conversation, but I'm needed."

Sam stood, as well. "Thank you for your time," he said. He started toward the door.

"Mr. Hall," Wilson called.

Sam stopped and turned back.

"But, was the devil busy at work in Massachusetts in 1692? Yes. He is always busy. So, please, don't delude yourself. The devil is still alive and well and busy in Massachusetts, in the world, just as he was in 1692."

6

Little had changed at Sedge's Market since Jenna was last there. Milton Sedge ran a clean store with neat, tight aisles and five checkout lanes. Bananas and prime rib were on special. Large cardboard, handwritten signs advertised the daily deals. He had long been a holdout as far as credit cards went, but he, like the rest of the world, seemed to have succumbed to the necessity of plastic. The one thing that had changed was that.

A friendly girl at one of the registers directed Jenna to a rear office. She didn't get far, however, before she saw the man she sort of recognized as Milton Sedge himself. He was in a butcher's coat, directing an employee to clean out one of the meat cabinets. He was doing so pleasantly enough, but efficiency and survival seemed to be on his mind.

"Dates, Richard—come on! Pay attention to the dates. We never sell anything once it's past its date. That's how we compete with the big guys. Quality—and assurance!" he said firmly.

The worker was a slim youth who appeared to be

about seventeen. He nodded vigorously with his compliance. "Yes, sir, yes, sir, I'm on it!"

"Mr. Sedge?" Jenna asked.

He turned to look at her, a balding man with a large nose and massive eyebrows that seemed to be trying to compensate for the loss of hair on his head.

"Yes?" He stared at her, as if trying to decide if he knew her or not.

"Hi. I'm Jenna Duffy," she said, offering her hand.

"Do you want a job?" he asked skeptically, openly studying her.

She shook her head. "No, sir. I'm working with Sam Hill on Malachi Smith's defense."

"Oh! Well, you know I gave my statement to the police."

"Yes, sir. I know that you did. I'm just trying to hear what you have to say with my own ears and, also, to ask you, of course, if you're certain about your statement."

He nodded, distracted. An elderly woman with a cart had come next to them. "Milton, where are those bananas?" she demanded.

"Eleanor, what? You're not going senile, are you? The bananas are in the fruit section!" Sedge said, scratching his head. "Show some good old New England common sense, will you, please?"

"Milton, I'm full of good New England common sense. There are no bananas in the fruit section, and that's why I'm asking you!" the woman said, indignant.

"Richard! Will you go to the back and see that the bananas are restocked!" Sedge asked.

"Yes, sir!"

"Let's step into my office, shall we?" Sedge suggested. "It's just to the left, behind the pharmacy."

A few seconds later Jenna was seated on a foldout chair between boxes of crackers and he was behind a desk stacked high with invoices. He folded his hands on the desk.

"I've taken some guff over this, I'll have you know. But what I saw is what I saw!" Sedge said. "What is— is. And that's just the way it is."

"What do you mean, *guff?*" Jenna asked him.

He looked at her as if she had lost her mind, as well. "Guff! Guff! Grief! All kinds of misery. Folks around here believe that Malachi killed Earnest Covington, and that I'm the one who has lost my eyesight. But that boy was in this store from four to six last Saturday afternoon—the kid liked shopping, read every label on every can. I think he just liked being away from home. The cops found that guy's body at six-thirty and claimed he'd been dead for over an hour. So, if someone *is* mistaken, it's the damned doctor who showed up on the site, not me. I talked to the kid. He was a regular. He was always on a budget, so he was like Eleanor, demanding to know where the daily specials could be found. Except that Malachi Smith didn't demand. The kid was polite. Yeah, I can see where his classmates thought he was a geek. Skinny kid. Big eyes. Bad haircut. But he was *polite.* He was always stopping to get something off a top shelf for the old ladies. He waited his turn in a line. He paid with cash."

The last seemed to be the asset that truly set Malachi Smith at the top of Sedge's list.

"How do you know exactly how long he was in the store?" Jenna asked.

"I was in the front when he came in—Mrs. Mickleberry was arguing about a coupon that was good at another store—and I happened to be picking up a broken bottle of ketchup on one of the aisles about fifteen minutes later. We talked about a cut of meat about twenty minutes after that. I was working in the dairy section when he went through. I know that kid was in the store at the time they say Earnest Covington was killed. People around here want me to say otherwise, but I won't. What is—is." He sniffed. "Those kids at the school have had it out for Malachi forever."

"Which kids?" Jenna asked.

"The ones who claimed to have seen him come out of the house that day. Now, why anyone would believe that David Yates over me, I don't begin to understand. Oh, yeah. Because he's on the football team." Sedge shook his head. "Big brawny kid on the football team, and he and his pals tormented poor skinny Malachi. People need to use sense and logic. Yep, sense and logic. The Yates kid and his backfield mom are just as bad. Now, I didn't say that. You ask me—and I'm no psychiatrist—guilt started eating at that kid and in his own messed-up adolescent mind he knew he was guilty as hell of being one bastard, excuse the language. Whatever. I know what I know. My eyes are sound, and I'm not involved in any of the crazy shenanigans going on."

"Thank you, Mr. Sedge. It's wonderful that you're not letting yourself be swayed by peer pressure."

"What is—is," he repeated. "That kid might be crazy

as hell, might be a mental midget, and he might have
done anything else in the world—I couldn't argue it. But
I can tell you this and it's a fact—he didn't kill Earnest
Covington."

"Malachi claims that he's innocent, too."

"But he wasn't arrested for killing Covington, was
he?"

"He's being charged in the deaths of his family. I'm
not sure, but I believe, if the prosecutor feels he gets a
little more evidence, he also plans on adding charges,
and I know that the police believe that Malachi killed
Peter Andres and Earnest Covington, as well."

"He didn't kill Covington. And I told the cops that.
I don't know what they're thinking, not to listen to me.
Unless folks just get stuff stuck in their minds so hard
they can't see the light."

"We're truly grateful for the courage of your convictions, Mr. Sedge."

"What?"

"Thank you for sticking with the truth."

"The truth is the truth. He didn't kill Covington."
Jenna rose.

"Of course..." Sedge began, rising politely.

"Of course what?"

"Doesn't mean he didn't take an ax to his mom and
dad. Hell, if I'd been that kid, I'd have been tempted to
take an ax to that old Abraham Smith!"

"You know," John Alden told Sam, "you need to
thank God that usually, even with the mayhem that goes
on around Haunted Happenings, we're mostly a good,

law-abiding place. With Malachi in custody, I haven't
been finding bodies anywhere, and I have the time to
do this with you."

John Alden had agreed to show Sam around Earnest
Covington's house. They stood just outside, and Sam
waited for John to let him in and give him whatever
instructions he might feel obligated as a detective to
give.

"You're a true gem, John, and a great believer in
justice," Sam said.

"Actually, you know, the cops usually work with the
prosecutors," John reminded him.

"Ah, but, first and foremost, you are a great believer
in justice, and therefore agree that the defense has the
right to question witnesses and investigate when a client
makes a plea of not guilty. You wouldn't want to get
caught up in any red tape, and you like to keep an eye
on me."

The policeman sighed. "Earnest Covington was a
widower, lived alone, but he ordered out a lot, so it
was actually a kid from the Pizza Palace who found
him. The door was ajar so the kid just came in and saw
Covington on the floor, right in front of the hearth. The
chalk marks are still there—as is the blood spatter,"
John said, his mouth growing tight.

Covington's house was built in much the same style
as the Lexington House: front and back entries, parlors
to either side of the entrance, and a narrow stairway that
led to several rooms above. There was an attic as well,
but according to the police report, it didn't appear that
the house had been ransacked in any way. Just as in the

murder of Peter Andres, it appeared that the killer came with but one thing in mind—murder.

"The pizza kid found the door ajar?" Sam asked.

"Yep, just like I said."

"Did your crime-scene people find anything that indicated that the killer had jimmied the lock in any way?" Sam asked.

"No," John said. He sighed again. "And before you ask, there were so many fingerprints on the door that the lab is still working on sorting them all out."

"So what made you suspect Malachi Smith?" Sam demanded.

John's eyes narrowed and he offered Sam a grim smile. "Because we already suspected him in the case of Peter Andres."

"But why? From everything that I've heard, Malachi liked the teacher. And Peter Andres liked Malachi well enough—he hated Abraham Smith."

"There'd been trouble, bad blood with Malachi," John said. "God knows, maybe at one time, Jamie O'Neill might have been able to help him. I know that O'Neill kept trying—despite the system that gave the kid back to his parents without interference—and he might have had some luck with him. But, come on—the kids were terrified of him."

"John, he was like the runt of the litter—picked on."

"And, sometimes, Sam, when kids pick on another kid, there's a good reason. Oh, come on, you know that the signs of a serial killer can be seen at a young age. Sickos who throw rocks at dogs and kill kittens."

Sam stared at John. "And did anyone ever report that Malachi Smith killed a kitten?"

"Not actually."

"Not *actually?*" Sam demanded.

"Kids talk."

"Do you know of a kitten that was killed?"

John opened his mouth, arched his eyebrows and then closed his mouth again. "No."

"John, you persecuted that kid because of hearsay."

"No, Sam, you weren't here. Something really happened to the Yates kid—David. He was in agony. Whether Malachi Smith just has something about him that threatened the other kids or not, he's strange."

"I don't think you can be tried for murder just for being strange," Sam said.

"And I should ignore all the warning signs—not to mention the fact that the kid was covered in his family's blood—and fail to make an arrest? He hasn't been charged with the murder of Earnest Covington or that of Peter Andres. He was a person of interest, that's all. And in the Covington case, Yates and his friend said that they saw him coming from Earnest Covington's house."

"And Milton Sedge said that the kid was in his store."

"I just said that he'd only been a person of interest," John told him.

Sam let out a long breath and knew that he needed to maintain control. John Alden was legally obligated to give him certain information vital to the case, but he didn't have to go out of his way to be helpful. He couldn't push the man too far; he was already basically questioning his police work.

"I'm sorry, John. If he was brought into court on the Covington murder, I'd rip the prosecution to shreds in a matter of minute. These days, I have to prove reasonable doubt, and in a he-said-he-said situation, I'd sure as hell have doubt."

"Sam, you saw him the night I arrested him. What would you have done?"

"Arrested him," Sam admitted after a long pause.

"I don't judge. I'm not on the bench, and I won't be on the jury," the policeman said. "I try to maintain the law. I'm not out for Malachi Smith. Prove to me the kid is innocent, and I'll be the first to tear apart the world trying to get at the truth. But right now, he looks like our man."

Sam nodded. "Of course. And thank you, John."

John nodded back.

"So, the killer came in by the door—without forcing it—and apparently came right at Earnest Covington, sliced him to death and left," Sam said.

John nodded, watching him. Sam walked back to the front door, halfway closed it, pushed it open and walked into the hall. He looked to the right and left, and headed in toward the hearth in the parlor to the left. Earnest Covington must have been standing by his hearth. On the mantel, Sam saw that he kept a kept a metal receptacle for mail. Possibly he was looking through his bills when his killer entered. Sam took a closer look. There was a letter in the bin that looked as if it had been almost shoved back in, a letter postmarked

Sydney, Australia. The sender was an Earnest Covington, Jr. Through the envelope, he could see the outline of photographs; Covington might not have owned a computer or a cell phone.

Blood spattered the cheap Rembrandt knockoff on the wall above the mantel. The floor in front of the mantel was still soaked with a dark stain.

"There's one thing I should tell you," John said.

"What's that?"

"Another reason Malachi Smith came to mind—around here, folks aren't great at locking their doors. Earnest Covington almost never did, according to his neighbors. He told them he didn't have anything worth anything, and if some poor fellow walked in, he was welcome to take what he could."

"Why did that make you think of Malachi?"

"Malachi lives in the neighborhood and he would have known that."

"Was he supposed to have bad blood with Earnest Covington?"

"Not the kid—the old man. Covington was pretty vocal about the fact that he thought Abraham Smith should sell the house...and get out of the neighborhood. But, to be honest, I never heard about anything negative happening between Malachi and Covington—in fact, once, when Covington fell on an icy step, Malachi came over, dialed 911 and stayed with him until help came."

"That really suggests murder," Sam said quietly.

John shrugged. "Maybe the old man—Abraham Smith—killed his enemies, and his son freaked out and killed his father and family when he found out.

You know, religious duty and all. Now, there's a rational theory for you."

"A rational theory—just as rational as someone else having committed all the murders," Sam said.

John watched from the doorway. "Reasonable doubt—maybe you could prove that if Malachi had been charged with Covington's murder. But reasonable doubt on his family when we found him bathed in blood? Sam Hall, you have a hell of an uphill road ahead of you!"

Sam suddenly wished that Jenna was with him. He wasn't sure that he believed in "postcognition," but he wasn't getting a thing himself. It all seemed too simple.

"Mind if I walk around the house?" he asked.

"Knock yourself out. Covington has one son, lives in Australia. He's a single father, twin two-year-olds. We've been keeping him informed on the investigation through Skype online. I'm sure if you think it will help solve the mystery of his father's murder, he'll be all for an explanation. You just promise me one thing, Sam Hall."

"What's that?"

"If we prove that Malachi Smith killed these people, and you do wind up defending him with the excuse that he's crazy as all hell, you don't demand that he be let out on the streets in a year!"

"I promise you, the actual murderer will be locked away for a long, long time," Sam said with final authority.

Jenna saw John Alden's police car on the street. Crime-scene tape hung from the door and the door itself was ajar. She hesitated before touching the knob.

"Hello?" she called.

John Alden came and opened the door for her. "Miss Duffy. What a surprise. Only it's not a surprise—right? Sam probably just called you."

"True," she said.

"He's upstairs. Come on in. Though why he called you, I don't really know. You don't seem to react well at a crime scene, and I'm damned glad. That makes you nicely human."

He meant to be nice. She smiled. "I'm okay."

"And you're FBI, eh?"

She laughed. "Tougher than I look, I guess."

"But you must get lots of blood and guts," John said.

"I do, but—"

"No, no, sorry for being abrasive. You're right—when it stops bothering us, we need to get the hell out of law enforcement."

Jenna heard footsteps coming down the stairs and then Sam's voice. "Jenna! You're here." He glanced at John. "We happened to talk. She was in the area."

"Of course," said the cop.

Sam grinned at him. He looked at Jenna again. His expression was grave and yet, he seemed relieved. Maybe he'd been afraid she would refuse to come, after the way they had parted. He had almost called her a charlatan.

"Jenna, here's what I know, what I suspect. Earnest Covington was known to leave his door open. He wasn't afraid of thieves. So, he either left his door open and the killer walked in—and caught him in front of the hearth—or he let his killer in, they came into the parlor together, and then the killer struck. I've a hunch it was the former rather than the latter. I think that Earnest Covington was just about to go through his mail, something he probably wouldn't be doing with company. Plus, the first letter in the mail grate is from his son. There's a picture in it, and he might have been about to admire his grandsons."

Jenna looked at him and nodded. "Makes sense. I'm going to just take a look around, too, then."

"Makes sense," Sam replied, and began a conversation with the policeman that seemed more like a smokescreen for her than anything real.

She walked back to the door to let her mind encompass what had taken place, while she tried to let her heart imagine Earnest Covington. She closed her eyes and had an impression of an older man—the perfect grandfather figure. He'd had white hair, he'd been lean and weathered, a man who had worked through his prime, and was still fierce in his thoughts and opinions. His life was somewhat lonely, but he didn't mind—his wife was gone, and he wanted no other. He lived to tell the occasional visitor what Salem had been like before they'd gone modern-day witch crazy, before they'd become so commercial and when the House of the Seven Gables hadn't been blocked from view by a dozen gift shops hawking witch T-shirts.

As she thought these things, it seemed that a shadowy haze slipped over her, and the house. She had a sense of coming home and leaving the door open. Who would want his old stuff? The sofa with the upholstery that was all lumpy, or the TV that barely worked and certainly wasn't attached to any newfangled gadgets. He walked into the living room, having just been for a stroll down the street. He smiled, thinking of the letter his son had sent. Wretched boy, falling in love with a foreigner, and heading off with her to Australia. It was with a heavy heart that he thought of the daughter-in-law he'd met at the wedding but never seen again. She'd died in a flash from a virus that no one had been able to stop. So now, of course, his son was still in Australia, but Earnest hoped that he'd come home soon enough, when the boys were a little bit older and his in-laws learned to live with their loss. For now, he had the pictures that Andrew sent, like these new ones....

He hadn't really heard the door open; he just became aware that someone was with him.

He'd been puzzled at first; in fact, he had laughed.

"If you're looking to do something creepy at the old Lexington House, it's down the street at the end of the block," he said, not unwarmly.

The costumed intruder just stared at him.

"Private residence!" Earnest said, growing aggravated. He'd seen similar costumes before. It was like something out of the old days when the Puritan ministers tried to scare their flocks with pictures of an evil, horned and tailed devil. Of course, this person didn't really have a tail. He was wearing a cloak, with a hood, the horns stuck out from the hood. The mask was red and black—of course, the devil was red, like a fierce, burning fire—or black, in the way that a heart could be black, and the costume was damned creepy and scary.

"Hey!" he said. "My house—I don't remember inviting you in!"

The person stood very still for a moment—almost as if he was confused, or uncertain.

Then, the figure drew its hands from beneath the folds of the cape.

Earnest was briefly aware of a shining blade.

He barely had time to throw his hands up to protect his face....

And all to no avail.

He was aware of a crunch as the ax hit his skull; he was even aware of the warm spray of blood that sailed around him, oddly beautiful. Red like the devil himself....

He hit the floor.

And knew he was dying.

"Jenna!"

She gave herself a shake, mentally and physically, and refocused. Sam was standing in front of her; his hands were on her shoulders. His eyes, gray and sharp, were hard upon hers.

She knew that John Alden was standing right behind him.

She wasn't going to say anything in front of the man who already thought she was a squeamish crackpot, especially not in front of John, who had yet to judge her as such.

"Yes, I've pictured it as you said, Sam," she said simply, "and I believe that you're right. I think that Earnest Covington came in and left his door open. I think he might have been anticipating the pleasure of looking at the pictures again. The killer just walked right in and killed him."

Sam nodded. He turned to John Alden. "Thanks, John. I'm not trying to let killers loose on the streets, I swear. I appreciate your helping see to it that the defense has all the facts."

"Well, I don't want the prosecution losing on a technicality—as in the defense not having everything it's legally due," John said. He looked at Sam. "Hey, come on, I'm not a mean or horrible man! I feel sorry for the kid. But I feel even sorrier for Peter Andres and Earnest Covington.... And the Smith family, of course."

The last was definitely added as an afterthought, Jenna was certain.

"All right then, we'll get out of your way, John," Sam said.

"I drove you here," John reminded him.

"I have a car," Jenna said quickly.

"All right. Keep me posted if you need anything else," John said.

"Will do," Sam told him.

He opened the door for Jenna, nudging it with his elbow. They walked outside.

"The car is down the street, at the grass by the cliffside park," Jenna said.

He nodded, walking alongside her. They passed Lexington House and both of them paused. Crimescene tape still roped off the entire property. Fierce signs warned the curious off: arrests would be made for trespassing and interference.

"Covington's house is seriously just a block away," Jenna murmured.

"Yep."

"Well, you won't have a problem in court as far as the Covington killing is concerned—if Malachi is charged."

"Oh?" he asked her.

"I went to see the grocer. He's convincing. Sedge swears up and down that he saw Malachi several times during the hours when the M.E. says that Covington was killed."

"Well, that's great. You, uh, just decided to interview him?"

She looked at him. He wasn't angry; he was slightly amused.

"I have a feeling that my people skills may be better than yours, at times," she said.

He nodded and took her elbow. Even by the light of day, Lexington House had a depressing facade, and it seemed that the windows were horrible eyes with evil intent—watching out for the unwary.

Sam had drawn his eyes from the house. "So?" he asked.

"So?" she repeated.

"What did you really see?" he asked her.

She groaned. "I'm not talking to you about any-thing—*just the facts, man.*"

"Actually, please. I'm sorry. Tell me what you really saw, felt…or imagined in your mind."

Imagined in your mind. Was that his way of saying that he was interested in her visions revealed?

She stopped walking again and stared at him. "I saw

that the killer wore a costume again. I'm not sure that
either of these two men knew, even as they died, who
did it. The costume could just be some kind of a logical
choice because it is Salem, where people are known to
have a deep and profound belief in both God and the
devil, or the person really believes that they need to
dress up as something to get away with murder. Right
now, though, in either case, with Haunted Happenings
going on, who in the world is going to really notice
anyone in costume?"

She expected him to groan and say that, of course,
even if she might have some kind of special ESP—it
wasn't telling them a thing.

He didn't. He looked at her, as if perplexed. "*Now*
Haunted Happenings is going on. *Now* you might not
notice someone in a costume. Peter Andres was killed
six months ago."

"True," Jenna admitted.

They reached her car and the park at the cliff. He
didn't get in but walked past it and started up the path
that led to the cliff. It wasn't a high cliff, but rather a
rise created from the jagged granite that was the solid
base of so much of the area.

There were scattered trees, creating a copse here and
there, to the northern portion of the little park. Where
the ground leveled at the top of the rise, there was a
walkway to the edge, which overlooked the water. Sam
followed the path, and Jenna followed Sam.

White waves crashed with a fury in the autumn wind
that rushed around them, stronger here, or so it seemed,

than when they'd been down on the sidewalk by the neighborhood of old houses.

Sam stood staring out over the water.

"I used to come here myself," he said, looking out. "It was always a great place to come and work out whatever adolescent problems I was having." He turned to look at her. "Malachi said he was here when his family was murdered. I can imagine him coming here often. Somehow, being here makes you realize that your problems aren't so great, there's a vast world out there and we're only a small part of it. I always loved the way the ocean seems angry here. I don't remember ever coming when the waves weren't white capped, and the crash of the sea against stone wasn't loud and passionate."

"It's a beautiful little area," Jenna agreed.

He pointed to the trees. "Kids come here to neck. And smoke pot."

She laughed. "Did you come here to smoke and neck?"

He grinned. "Sure. I was a kid once. Believe it or not."

"Actually, I even vaguely remember."

He studied her. "You would have been accused of witchcraft, back in the day, you know."

"Possibly," she said. "I like to think I would have kept the concept of seeing or feeling the past to myself. But thank God I don't have to as much in this century."

He sat down on the grass by the cliff. Puzzled, she joined him. "Of course, if you'd been one of the magistrates, Sam Hall, you would have laughed the whole

thing out of existence, since you don't believe in anything."

"I never said that I don't believe in anything," he
said, plucking a blade of grass from the ground and
running it through his fingers. He looked at her. "The
law was quite different then, you know. We've come
a long way. The colony was English. And the entire
Christian world believed in witchcraft. It was a way to
cast and apportion blame. To explain the unexplainable.
I don't know why, but I keep thinking that there is some
kind of answer in this that has to do with the past. The
thing is, witchcraft was illegal and punishable by death
back then. If you commit murder in death penalty states
nowadays, you may be executed for the crime. It's the
law. A judge is legally and morally responsible to hand
out sentences that conform to the law. Now, we have
the concepts of legal and illegal searches, individual
rights and so on. The people of 1692 weren't protected
that way—they seldom had any kind of representation.
When I decided to go into the law, I would pretend that
I had been Rebecca Nurse's defense attorney. If I'd been
there, of course, she wouldn't have hanged."

"I'm sure she'd appreciate that," Jenna said, smiling.

He grinned in turn.

"Salem and Salem Village were in turmoil. The Puritans might have adhered to strict teaching, but they
weren't above wanting to make money. At the time,
the Porters and the Putnams and others—even though
some of the families were actually intermarried—were
having all kinds of land disputes. They'd been around
for many years, so I'd say a good part of the population

was related in one way or another. But, hey, it's hard to imagine, but true, that in royal and noble families brothers and nephews killed one another over a crown. So, it's not so hard to believe that they let bitterness carry them away here. Whether or not they really knew it, the people were probably letting their anger with each other prejudice their belief in what was happening. Hey, if you're really mad at someone, it's easier to think ill of them. And I think about kids—maybe they weren't malicious, maybe they even believed part of what they were saying—you tell a lie often enough and it becomes real in your own mind."

"One of the first women accused was Sarah Bishop," Jenna said. "She was supposedly disagreeable, and her husband's children from a previous marriage also wanted property she owned. They say, too, that she wore a scarlet bodice—not very Puritan of her!—and had drinking parties. She'd been accused before, so she was an easy target."

"One of the first people hanged," Sam said. "She wouldn't confess to being a witch."

"And Malachi will not confess to being a murderer," Jenna said.

Sam nodded. "He's an easy target, too," he said softly. "And I'm willing to bet he's being targeted for a reason. It looks like all evidence is against him—just as, to the Puritans, it looked as if there was solid evidence against those they executed. And Giles Corey— pressed to death because he wouldn't make a plea. The old bastard didn't intend to let anyone get a hold of his property, and by the legal system, not giving a plea protected his property."

"I'd have let them have my property," Jenna said. "Life is so much better."

Sam laughed. "Me, too, probably. But by the law, if he didn't plead, he couldn't be tried, and because he wasn't tried, he died in full possession of his property. And to force someone to make a plea so that they could be tried, they were pressed. Giles Corey was an old buzzard—he testified against his own wife. But he endured two days of pain—his tongue bulged out and the sheriff had to put it back in his mouth with his cane, and the old man still endured. 'More weight!' is all that he ever said, according to the records, and witnesses were horrified. What happened, of course, wasn't caused by any one person, but belief mingling with old grievances and the social structure and laws of the day. The thing is, we've come far, but we'll never get past being human. Malachi isn't accepted in society. Good people will easily believe he could be a killer. I have to prove reasonable doubt, and that's going to be hard. He wasn't arrested for murdering Peter Andres or Earnest Covington; he was arrested for the murders of his family. I have all kinds of motions filed, but since he wasn't legally accused of the other murders, I most probably won't be able to use the fact that he was seen elsewhere when Earnest Covington was murdered. It depends on how all the motions filed sit with the judge. I have to prove reasonable doubt in those murders, and since he was covered in their blood..."

"His explanation is reasonable," Jenna pointed out.

Sam stood and offered a hand down to her. "Bridget Bishop wasn't really hanged for what she did. She was hanged for who she was."

"You believe that Malachi is facing the same fate?" she asked.

"Yes. But with one big difference."

"The law has become more equitable?" Jenna asked.

Sam grinned. "No," he said. "He has me." She was startled when he touched her cheek in something that was almost a tender gesture.

"And," he added, "he has you."

7

Sam joined them again that night at dinner, but it wasn't much of a social occasion. He spent half of his time on the phone with his assistant in Boston, discussing the paperwork he wanted done. During the meal, he talked earnestly with Jamie, wanting to know more about the boy's psychological makeup. Jenna spent most of the evening listening, and realizing that the more she watched Sam, the more she was drawn to him. She hated to admit the fact—even to herself, or especially to herself—that there was something about the testosterone-filled energy he exuded that was seducing her.

Sam mentioned that he was going to visit Malachi in his hospital-slash-jail cell tomorrow, and then head to his office to deal with some of the massive amounts of paperwork that seemed to go with every sneeze. It had to be done—it was the major part of the game of law. Jamie was going to accompany him and spend time with Malachi.

"The law these days is demanding," Sam began. "But ultimately it's a good thing. The witchcrafts trials couldn't have existed today, but we learned a lot about 'hearsay' evidence because of the injustices of the past. And, thank God, there's no longer such a thing as 'spectral' evidence. But, the paperwork! I really want to talk to the Yates kid, but his mother has threatened me with every lawsuit in the book if I go near him. I'm going to have to have help on that. And I'd also like to have an interview with Samantha Yeager, find out what, if anything, her connection to the Smiths was. But I have to head into Boston and the office for a few hours. You should probably come with us," Sam told Jenna.

"I'm afraid I would be worthless helping you with legal paperwork," she told him.

He frowned. "You could spend the time with Malachi and see if there was something else in his mind that might help us, something we haven't discovered yet."

"Jamie is his friend, and has been his doctor," Jenna pointed out. "I can get more done here."

He arched a brow. "Jenna—"

"Maybe I can get near David Yates," she said.

That brought a frown. "It could be dangerous for you to be here," Sam said, looking at Jamie as if for help, but not wanting to give away what happened yesterday.

"I'm a Federal agent," Jenna reminded him. "And that's not going to change. I can handle myself around dangerous people. But, besides that, no one is going to attack me. The killer would know that the second something happened while Malachi was in custody, the whole concept that he was a maniacal killer driven to acts of extreme violence because of some strict fundamentalist upbringing would be in the trash, and the hunt would be on again. I'll be fine. I'll be more help-ful here."

Sam wagged a finger at her. "You need to be care-ful."

"I always am," she assured him.

"Jamie?" Sam asked.

"Sam, she just looks really sweet. There's little as tough as an Irishwoman," Jamie confirmed.

She looked at her uncle, not sure whether to appre-ciate his support, or tell him that she wasn't exactly a sumo wrestler. But she did want to explore on her own, and even though it seemed that Sam wasn't scoffing her "sight" in the way he had been, she knew that he had difficulty believing in any kind of ESP.

"See? Tougher than nails," Jenna said. She smiled, liking the way Sam was looking at her. It was nice to feel that he came with the instinct to protect, even if she didn't feel that she needed to be protected. Certainly not in broad daylight, and not when the streets were filled with people.

Then again, she had to admit, protection wasn't ex-actly what she wanted when she looked at him.…

Not good.

"All right," Sam said, "but you need to stay out of trouble."

"What kind of trouble could I possibly get into?"

"Legal trouble, too," Sam said gruffly.

"Seriously, there's nothing for you to worry about. The killer honestly can't act at all. We've agreed we're not dealing with an all-out psycho who's acting willy-nilly, but with someone possessing very specific, material motives. So, you see, in the devious little plot—whatever it might be—that's going on, I couldn't possibly be safer."

Soon after, she walked Sam to the door. She found him hesitating as he said good-night; he looked at her awkwardly, which seemed odd—he was so totally a man of the world. She couldn't imagine that he had ever been awkward in a social situation.

But they weren't exactly in a social situation.

He started to say something, and then didn't. Then he touched her cheek again, and his fingers seemed to linger just a minute.

"Be careful, kid, really," he said, and his voice was gruff.

She smiled at him. "In my experience, honestly, a ghost never killed anyone."

She hesitated. "The scariest unknown in the world is the human mind," she continued on. "But in that, a ghost is no scarier than a dog, really. But any kind of suggestion is like hypnotism. People have claimed that all kinds of things have 'made them do it.' A dog, video games, television, the movies, ghosts—or the devil. I'm not afraid of ghosts. I can be very leery and careful of people, but I won't do anything that could remotely be considered dangerous, okay?"

He nodded. He stood there another minute, looking at her, and she was surprised that, although he no longer touched her, she could feel warmth emanating from him that almost reached out and stroked the length of her body. Heat rushed through her, and it was very hard to maintain her even eye contact with him, to give nothing away of the sudden longing that rushed through her.

Was it him?

Was it wishful thinking?

She wasn't without self-confidence, but she knew his type.

Type? she mocked herself. *Wasn't that judging unfairly?*

He was wealthy; he was a powerful man, and he had the kind of steadfast assurance that was sensual in itself. He drew attention when he walked into a room. Men admired him, and women fantasized about him.

Which, of course, she was doing right then.

And women would easily come, and just as easily go, out of his life.

"Good night," he said somewhere in the middle of her internal monologue. And then he was gone.

That night, she felt something on her bed. And again, despite her assurances about ghosts to Sam, despite her beliefs, she felt an odd sensation of fear. She wanted to reach for the light. She wanted to run out of the house.

There was an old woman sitting at her bedside. A very sad-looking old woman.

For an insane moment she thought that the ghost, apparition or figment of her imagination was going to say something incredibly grave and overused, such as "The truth is out there!"

But the figure simply stared at her with dignity, and then spoke softly. "You must save the innocents. Let not the blood of the innocent be shed."

And then, Jenna felt a stirring of the air, and something that seemed cold and warm at the same time touch her cheek.

An old woman's gentle touch.

"Let not your blood be spilled—for the devil lives, he lives in all of us. Sometimes his name is Envy, and sometimes it is Greed. Let not the blood be spilled...."

It was everything she could do not to scream.

The vision faded into the night.

Jenna leaped from her bed and hurried into the kitchen. As she knew, Jamie always had a bottle of good Irish whiskey on hand.

She found the bottle and gulped down a burning shot.

And then she took another. She noted that the darkness of night was just beginning to break. Morning was coming. Sleep, just a few hours, brought on by the relaxing quality of the alcohol, would be great just about now.

At his office, Sam thanked God for the competency of Evan Richardson, legal assistant extraordinaire. Sam inspected the paperwork on the motions filed. The prosecution would fight many of his motions regarding what could and could not be brought into evidence. In defense of his client, Sam would make court appearances himself, but Evan was exceptional at keeping the legal paperwork moving at an expert rate. Since they were not going for an insanity plea, Sam had planned to deny the prosecution's request for their expert psychiatrist's opinion on Malachi's mental stability.

"But what if you *do* have to switch over to a mental competency plea?" Evan asked worriedly.

Sam smiled. "At that point, we'll allow them their expert. Not now."

"All right. Are we moving to keep allegations regarding the other murders out?" Evan asked.

Sam shook his head. "No, because we have a discrepancy on that. If the prosecution wants to bring up the other murders—which I don't believe they're willing to risk at this time—we have witnesses that will cast the shadow of doubt, affecting their entire case."

"Well, all right," Evan said. He chewed on the nib of his pencil. "Sam, you're taking a huge risk here, you know."

"If it comes down to it, I won't risk sending my client to prison. We'll plead insanity," Sam assured him.

Evan still looked glum.

"Cheer up, I'm not going down in an earthquake. I can win this, man. I won't take you off a cliff with me."

Evan still didn't look convinced. Actually, he looked like a young man whose older mentor had gone entirely senile.

Sam had to wonder if he was crazy himself.

When Jenna walked into A Little Bit of Magic that morning, both Cecilia and Ivy were working. After allowing her to get reacquainted with Ivy, following Ivy's massive, enthusiastic hug greeting, Cecilia finally asked the question it looked like she was dying to ask.

"Hey, how's it going with Malachi?"

"Slowly," Jenna admitted.

The shop was busy, but both the owners seemed to have the ability to have a conversation and keep an eye on their clientele, as well. Ivy hadn't gone with the completely black look as Cecilia had done; her hair was still a shaggy mix of brown and blond, colors that complemented her hazel eyes.

"Well, if you are trying to prove his innocence, that's going to be hard," Ivy said, making it obvious that the two women had discussed the situation.

"Actually," Jenna told them, "I came to ask you two a few questions about Wicca."

The warmth left Ivy's eyes. "If you're trying to say that this is the result of witchcraft—"

"No, no, no! Not at all," Jenna assured them quickly. "I know that—"

"Our beliefs aren't so different!" Ivy said. "All gods and goddesses are part of the Source, and the source is like the one god of Christianity and Judaism and Islam. Catholics see saints—we see other gods and goddesses. Praying in itself is important, as is the goodness that we are supposed to practice in everyday life."

"I know, I know—honestly, I know," Jenna assured them. "But we all know that other people—in any time—can twist and contort what is supposed to be good and pure into other things, or try to make it appear that what is good—isn't."

They both stared at her blankly.

"There is a horned demon, right?" Jenna asked.

Ivy shook her head. "No demons. And no devils."

"Ivy, there is a horned *god,*" Cecilia reminded her. "But he isn't *evil.* He isn't a devil. He is one of the oldest of gods. Many believe that his image has been drawn on walls by cavemen. He is…"

"He is the connection between us and the earth, the wind, the sky, the greenery," Ivy finished, as though reading a pamphlet.

"Ah, but when you talk about people *contorting* things, he could easily be contorted," Cecilia told her. "He is often connected with images of the Green Man, and he is seen sitting with immense arms, embracing the heavens and earth, with a very erect phallus. He is the cycle, fertility, birth and the sexuality that is essential for rebirth.

"And," Cecilia added, "though as far as I can tell none of the Witch Trial victims was a pagan, I can see how the prim and so-called proper people of the day would try to make him into a devil or a demon. Oh, he's considered the god of the underworld, so I suppose, in Christianity, that would make him the god of hell. You know—he is represented with cloven hoofs and horns and all that." She shivered. "People were so…easily scared!"

Jenna smiled and agreed. "Well, there were Indian raids, babies died, there was so little light…and they'd been killing one another for decades and decades over religion on the Continent by the time the Pilgrims came here."

"Why are you asking all this?" Cecilia asked curiously.

Jenna wasn't about to explain to them that she'd seen one, in postcognition—murdering people. "I've seen one running around," she said.

Ivy groaned. "Yeah, yeah! And you'll see witches
with warts on their noses, too. It's Halloween. A holiday for one and all."

"Hey, now, tolerance is what we need, and it's what
we're all about," Cecilia reminded her.

"Oh, yeah, and if I ran around dressed like Jesus
Christ or the Virgin Mary, people wouldn't be pissed
at me?" Ivy demanded.

Cecilia sighed. Before she could speak again, a
woman walked politely up to them, excused herself,
and asked about her psychic reading with Merlin.

"I'm sure he'll be right out," Ivy assured the woman.
"Merlin is excellent at keeping his appointment times,
but he's very thorough. I know you'll enjoy your time
with him, and that he'll be tremendously enlightening."

As she spoke, the man Jenna assumed to be Merlin
came out of the curtained-off area in the back, followed
by a young woman who seemed to be glowing.

She had certainly enjoyed her reading.

The man came toward them. He had long, curling
brown hair, and was wearing a cape covered in stars
and moons against a deep blue velvet background.

As he came even closer, Jenna realized she knew
him and smiled. "Tommy! Tommy Wainscott!"

He smiled as well and walked forward, giving her a
hug and whispering, "Merlin, please, if you will, Irish!"

Tommy had gone to school with Cecilia and Ivy.
They'd all been friends. On her many visits to Salem,
he'd liked to tease Jenna a lot about the color of her hair.

"Merlin!" she said quickly.

"Merlin," Ivy said, a dry edge to her voice. "Your next appointment is waiting."

"I'd heard you were here," Tommy said, brown eyes dancing as he looked at her. "Will I get to see you?"

"Sure," Jenna said.

"Gotta go now! Business is good, but there's competition in town," he told her. He turned, thoughtfully rather than dramatically, to the young woman who was his next appointment. "If you will, please?" He indicated the back.

Jenna smiled. "So Tommy is a medium now?"

"He's very good," Ivy said.

"I believe you," Jenna assured her.

"He can stand against any of them," Cecilia said. "Even the new blood with the big boobs."

"Who's the new blood with the big boobs?"

"Samantha," Cecilia said.

"Oh? Samantha Yeager—who wanted to buy the old Lexington place?" Jenna asked.

"The one and only," Ivy said.

"She's working at a shop down at the end of Essex Street. It's right next to Winona's Wine Bar. I think her people come in on the *spirited* side to begin with. Also, she gets lots of men who wouldn't step foot in with a medium if their lives depended on it otherwise…"

"Ah. I'm curious about her," Jenna said. "Maybe I'll go for a reading."

"Merlin is much better!" Cecilia assured her.

"Much!" Ivy added.

Ivy frowned. "You're not into a different—lifestyle these days, are you? I mean, it's absolutely fine with us. We love our friends no matter what their religion or whatever, including sexual likes."

Jenna smiled. "No, no lifestyle change. Just curiosity."

"She's investigating stuff for the Lexington House murders, silly," Cecilia reminded her. "But, hey, we're curious as all get-out about Samantha, too! You've got to come back and tell us all about it."

"Will do," Jenna promised.

She left the shop and walked along the pedestrian mall. Haunted Happenings remained wonderfully in full swing. She noted a row of small buckets and saw that the town fathers had figured out how to have kids bob for apples in a more sanitary fashion than when she'd been a kid. One mouth in a tub—and then it was washed and refilled. The bobbing-for-apples crew—attired in pirate gear—was busy.

A medieval group had set up to sing and play a bit farther down, and one shop front boasted The Best Haunted House In All New England.

Still farther along, a busy group had children doing mock gravestone rubbings.

There was something for everyone.

At last she came to a shop where a large sign advertised Madam Sam, the Best Reading In All New England!

Not in Salem—just like the haunted house, she was the best in all New England!

She noted the wine bar next door and smiled.

Bells chimed when she opened the door to the shop. Like the other merchants, the store was enjoying the busy trade of Haunted Happenings. Men and women in and out of costume looked at beautiful dolls, herbs, gris-gris bags, magical stones, jewelry and clothing.

Jenna approached the counter and asked about a reading with Madam Sam.

"Well, you're in luck!" the girl behind the desk with black pigtails and a huge nose ring told her. "A lady just became faint, and had to go back to her hotel. We're otherwise booked all day, so you are lucky, lucky, lucky!"

"How lucky indeed," Jenna murmured. "The woman is all right?"

"What?"

"The lady who was faint—she was all right?"

The girl waved a hand in the air. "Oh, her husband just took her back to her room. It's the Fates! You're the one who should have the reading!" she said happily. "Come along—we have to adhere to a schedule, of course. You're ever *so* lucky!"

Jenna followed the woman to the back and a setup that was similar to that at A Little Bit of Magic.

The clerk opened a heavy damask drapery for her and led her into the small cubicle where the medium was working.

Madam Sam was a beautiful woman. She was wearing a low-cut gypsy-style dress, and her hair was ink-black, long and sleek as it fell down her back. Her eyes were so blue they were almost violet, but Jenna could see, even by the dim light that added atmosphere to the cubicle, that the color had been enhanced with contact lenses. She wore very heavy makeup, especially around her eyes, adding to her look of the sexy gypsy reader.

She wore a live boa constrictor around her neck; the animal somehow seemed to increase the size of her breasts and enhance her sensual mystique. There was something about her that seemed familiar, but Jenna couldn't quite put her finger on it.

"Ah," Madam Sam said softly. "Welcome. How curious that you have come to me for a reading!"

She didn't offer Jenna a hand but instead indicated a chair in front of her table, which held a crystal ball and a large tarot deck.

Jenna said. "You know me? Have we met?"

Madam Sam—or Samantha Yeager—laughed, a low, throaty and melodious sound. "Of course I know you. Your name is Jenna Duffy, and you're attached to that delightfully devilish rogue, Sam Hall, and you're here to investigate the recent horrors that have occurred in Salem. Have we met? No, never, I'm afraid."

"Very good," Jenna told her. "I mean, we haven't met, but you do know exactly who I am."

"Oh, yes, and you work for the FBI," Madam Sam said.

"Okay…"

"Aye, yes, well, my other powers may be questionable, but I do read the local papers very well," Samantha said, grinning. "You didn't have to pay for a reading to speak with me." Her voice had changed; it was tinged with amusement, and the sound was down-to-earth.

"I've wanted to talk to you. And with all the business going on with Haunted Happenings, I thought I should seize this opportunity."

"Talk away. We have fifteen minutes," Sam told her.

The boa stretched out toward Jenna.

"Nefertiti won't hurt you," Samantha assured her quickly.

"I'm not afraid of snakes," Jenna told her.

"Good old Saint Patrick got them all out of Ireland, eh?"

"Doesn't she scare away costumers?"

Samantha shrugged. "Some, maybe. But I think she attracts more than she loses. It's all showmanship, really."

"So you're not a medium?"

"What's a medium, really? I talk to people, I try to understand them. I don't tell them that money is going to fall into their laps, or that they will find true love. What I do is try to draw out what is troubling them, and show them the directions they might take. I don't have any kind of a degree in psychology but, really, reading people is simple as long as you listen."

Jenna laughed softly. "Some might call that being a fraud," she warned.

"And some might call it making a living. I'm sure that some call you a fraud."

"Oh, definitely," Jenna said, chuckling some more.

Samantha picked up the tarot cards and shuffled them. "Not the tarot cards—they come up as they come up, and a reader is supposed to interpret them. I've studied the tarot and all the ways that the cards might be interpreted. So, shall we read the cards? Cut, please, and we'll use the Celtic Cross layout."

Jenna cut the cards and Samantha began to lay them out.

"So, what did you want to know?" she asked.

"You wanted to buy the Lexington House."

"Yes, I did. I still want to buy it."

"And you made an offer to Abraham Smith?"

"A very generous one."

"But he turned you down."

"Flat." Samantha looked up at her. She was smiling. "And you want to know if I killed the old man and his family—except for the crazy kid—to get my hands on the house?"

"More or less," Jenna admitted.

Samantha kept looking at her, still amused. "Nope," she said.

"You think that Malachi Smith is crazy?"

"As a loon!"

"So, do you think that he killed Peter Andres and Earnest Covington, too?"

"Yup."

"Even though the grocer swears he saw Malachi in his shop?"

Samantha laid out cards before answering her, and then looked at her again. She sighed. "I'm not a cop or investigator or whatever, but I understand that the poor kid is truly a pathetic creature and I can also understand that you feel sorry for him. But you have to feel sorry for the dead people, too, the victims. Why kill Peter Andres? He was a farmer who substituted at the schools now and then. And Earnest Covington? He was harmless. You had to be crazy to have killed either of them, that's all I can imagine. Oh, dear!" she said suddenly, looking down.

Jenna wasn't really familiar with tarot cards, but she saw that the horned god—or, according to the cards, the devil—had come up in the middle. She tried to recall what she did know of the tarot.... The card known as the devil was really a half god, half devil, and he represented what was in all men, and the fact that they had to choose to be slaves to the evil within, or to slip out of the chains that bound them.

Samantha looked at her and smiled. "Well, seems you have a few options ahead of you. Give in to decadence, or hold the line of morality. If it were me—I'd sleep with the man!"

Samantha had been intuitive enough on that one!

"It could mean, too, that there's both evil and goodness around me," Jenna said.

"Oh, it could, but how boring! And look, you have the Fool over here—ah, yes, so, moralistically, you are looking at others. How rude of you! Your Fool looks down upon the Devil, yet sees no evil in himself. And there—you have the hanged man. At least it seems you are progressing and realizing the foolishness of judging what you see as evil in others. Sex, perhaps. Is that it?" She looked curiously at Jenna.

Jenna didn't answer. She tapped another card. "Death, of course, means change?"

Samantha laughed. "Or death! Oh, come, I'm sorry. Yes, it signifies change. But, without kidding you or just being bitchy—really, forgive me—the layout of these cards is almost..."

"Almost what?"

"A warning that if you judge others and pursue them,

you will die." The look she gave Jenna was perplexing. "You seem like you're really nice. Yes, I'm a fraud, but...maybe you need to be careful. You have the Devil, followed by Death."

Suddenly, the cards seemed to leap from the table and fly across the room. Both women jumped back in their chairs.

And then they stared at each other accusingly.

"I swear, I didn't do that!" Samantha breathed, and the look she gave Jenna seemed both stunned and fearful.

"I didn't do it," Jenna said.

Samantha waved a hand in the air. "You've asked your questions. Go, will you?"

"I have another question," Jenna told her, rising.

"What?" Samantha asked crossly.

"Where were you when the Smiths were killed?"

"That's easy. I was right here—ask the clerk!"

"And what about Earnest Covington?"

"I was probably right here!" Samantha said, growing agitated as she started picking up her cards.

"And Peter Andres?"

Samantha stopped and stared at her. "How the hell would I know? That was six months ago! I had barely gotten to town. Look, please, this is how I make a living."

"Sure. Thanks," Jenna said. She slipped out from the curtained cubicle and walked to the counter to pay for her reading. She wasn't sure what she thought about Samantha Yeager. She was a woman who knew showmanship and how to use her assets. She knew it was all a game, as well. And yet…

She started looking at the jewelry in the glass case at the checkout counter and drew the young clerk with the huge nose ring into conversation. When they had chatted about the marvels of Madam Sam and Haunted Happenings, Jenna asked her, "And Madam Sam has been working here since the Haunted Happenings began?"

"Oh, yes."

"Huh. How sad that none of the mediums in Salem thought to warn Abraham Smith that he and his family were about to be murdered," Jenna said, shaking her head with sorrow and leaving the shop.

"Malachi, we know that when Earnest Covington was killed, the grocer, Mr. Sedge, saw you in his store," Sam said.

"Yes."

"But David Yates and his friend claim they saw you coming out of Mr. Covington's house," Sam reminded him. "Are they still angry with you? Is that why? David believed, you know, that you had mind control over him and made him hurt himself."

Malachi had been tenderly cradling the acoustic guitar Jamie had just bought for him. The guitar was a modest piece of equipment, to be sure, but Jamie had been certain that it would make the time pass for the boy. He had strummed a few strings and listened in awe. And then, of course, he wanted to play with it.

But now he paused, frowning and concerned. "I don't understand. I don't understand what happened at all. I had just gotten my tray. I saw David Yates and I knew he would try to knock it out of my hand or walk over and spit in my food. I was only looking at him to try and figure out the best way to back away from him. He stared back at me and started screaming—and then he started beating himself in the head. And he begged me to stop! A bunch of his friends stared at him, and then at me, and then they came after me—and I ran. I almost flew like a bird, I was so afraid. The school was in an uproar, and the cops came, but the kids had to admit that I hadn't touched him."

"You were never anywhere near him," Sam mused.

"Had you ever threatened David Yates?" Jamie asked gently.

Malachi looked at Jamie with such confusion that Jamie might have been the one considered to be mad. "Me? Threaten him? Never. Dr. Jamie, sir, look at me. And look at David Yates. He could rip me to shreds in a minute. And it's not like I don't know how to take a beating, and I know, God help me, that you turn the other cheek, but…no. No. I never threatened David Yates."

"Was he acting?" Sam asked. The boys would have all been young teenagers at the time, all about fourteen. Still very impressionable. If they heard talk around town about Malachi's family, they might believe what they heard.

"No, sir. I don't believe he was acting. He almost broke his own nose. And he was bawling. Tough guys like David aren't supposed to cry, I don't think," Malachi said. He paused, looking at the guitar again, forget-

ting Sam and Jamie for a minute. "I cried. I cried so
hard it hurt. But crying doesn't ease the pain when you
lose somebody. It's just something that happens, and
you can't really stop it."

"It's okay, Malachi," Jamie said. "President Lincoln
was known to cry. He couldn't show tears to the country, but he cried when he lost his children, and he cried
when he knew how many men were dying in the war.
Men do cry."

Malachi nodded. "Yes, sir," he said softly.

Sam knew that he had to find out more about David
Yates, but he had been threatened, and though he wasn't
afraid of threats, he wasn't going to lose a case over his
own mistakes.

Jenna.

He thought grimly that he was really going to have
to depend on her.

He looked at Jamie. It was time that they headed
back.

They rose. Jamie gave Malachi a warm hug, promis-
ing him that they'd return.

Malachi shook Sam's hand.

They could hear him playing the guitar even as the
door closed behind them.

"Well?" Jamie asked.

"Let's get back to Salem," Sam told him. "Have you
talked to Jenna?"

"No. Do you want me to call her?"

Sam hesitated, surprised that he was afraid of sound-
ing eager. "We're headed back. We can see if she wants
to meet us somewhere for dinner."

Jamie pulled out his cell and dialed. Sam waited.

"She's not answering," he said.

"Oh, well, we can call again on the way," Sam said. He didn't know why, but the missed call made him anxious.

And he didn't know that he was driving far too fast until Jamie said, "Salem has been there hundreds of years—I think it will wait for us. And Massachusetts, as you should know, can be fierce on speeding tickets."

"Try Jenna again," Sam said, easing off on the gas pedal.

He thought that, when she didn't answer a second time, even Jamie looked concerned.

He decided to screw the thought of a speeding ticket.

Hitting the pedestrian area again, Jenna met insanity.

A group was coming from the wine bar, having imbibed quite a bit, and they were in a good mood as they tried to entice her to join them. Since one was in a clown outfit, she tried to escape by being equally jocular while assuring them she had to meet someone.

Escaping, she hurried around and up the hill toward the cemetery.

She looked at her phone and realized she had missed a call. Jamie. He'd call back; they were probably heading home.

Dusk was starting to fall. Tourists were leaving and the gate was due to be locked. She passed the graves, and tried not to note the air of history that hung there, that whisper of darkness that seemed to carry the shadows of the deceased. It wouldn't be long before they came to close the gates, but she wandered into the cemetery and walked along the graves, aware of those around her, and respecting them with her silence. She noted the graves of little children, and she felt the pain of long-gone parents, laying their tiny babes to rest.

She walked along the stone wall to the rear of the cemetery and was startled to see a man in Puritan apparel in front of her, his features grim.

"The devil! The horned devil—he is real, and he is coming for you!" he warned her.

She blinked, not sure if she was seeing the past or the present, the image had become so very real and solid.

And then she turned.

In the place where a huge oak had grown right through the stones of the deceased, she saw something. Shadow.

Not shadow. It was far darker than the hazy figures of the dead.

It was real.

A lithe figure in a cape and cowl, wearing the mask of the horned god, stood in the cemetery.

It saw her as she saw it.

Like the grim reaper, it wielded a scythe.

And it started striding swiftly across the graves and the dead to reach her.

Jenna looked around—it was just dusk, for God's sake! There were still people about.

They just weren't in the graveyard.

She could hear laughter from the street below. There were still plenty of people around; she didn't think that they had closed the doors to the wax museum, or the museum or shops across from it—there would be people leaving those businesses, people casually walking the streets.

This was insane. The creature coming toward her with a scythe couldn't be serious. It had to be someone she knew, trying to give her a scare, or a college kid....

But it wasn't. And she knew it. This was the same figure she had seen walking in the pedestrian mall, the same figure that in her visions brutally murdered Peter Andres and then Earnest Covington.

As it came toward her, it suddenly began to swing the scythe, backward and forward, low along the ground, just as if it were mowing down long grass or stalks of corn.

The scythe made a whipping sound through the air, louder and louder the closer it came.

8

When they neared Jamie's house, Sam had Jamie put a call through to Jenna again. Still no answer.

Jamie swore, an unusual and colorful event. "By all the damnable banshees of the night! Why isn't that girl answering her phone?"

"I'll let you out. I'll keep looking," Sam said. "Call me if she's in the house."

Jamie got out of the car. "Aye, and if she's not, I'll start around the common and the blocks around the Hawthorne."

Sam let Jamie out and tried cruising around on Church Street. There was no sign of her, but Essex Street was blocked off to everything but pedestrian traffic. As he tried to maneuver the streets, the going got difficult. Horrific murders might have recently taken place in Salem, but to the tourists flocking the area, the situation was in hand. The killer had been caught.

And, of course, they were tourists. They wouldn't be likely targets of a maniac who'd only killed locals in his own realm thus far. Just as the mob had never really threatened the average Joe on the streets of Chicago or New York, visitors could allow themselves to feel safe.

Indians, pirates, crones, vampires and princesses walked into the streets against the lights, and he had to drive slowly and carefully.

His phone rang: Jamie.

"She's not at the house."

"All right. I'm parking. I can crawl faster than I can move in the car."

"She wouldn't have left the historic area."

"Is she armed?" Sam asked Jamie.

"I...don't know," Jamie said.

"All right. We'll keep up."

He swore to himself—far less colorfully than Jamie. He parked at the next opening. A tow-away zone. Screw the car.

He exited and headed for Essex Street, wishing he'd made her give him an agenda, his heart pumping harder with every passing second.

Jenna figured she couldn't jump over the wall—at the rear of the cemetery it was a huge drop down to the street below.

It occurred to her that she could confront her attacker. But the light from the streets flashing off the honed blade convinced her that she didn't have what was needed for such a thing.

She should have carried her gun. After the team had been made official—proving themselves in New Orleans and learning that they could be a viable force together—they'd gone through the regular route of Federal training. She was good with a gun. She'd been careful here, not carrying it, because she didn't want the police complaining to her superiors. Plus she wasn't entirely used to having it on her yet.

Not such a good plan, despite the finest of intentions....

The creature kept coming.

Keeping her eye on it, Jenna began a snakelike movement toward her right and the back of the museum that bordered the graveyard, using the cemetery's overgrown trees as a protection against the creature.

True panic gripped her when she heard the scythe being swung through the air, high this time. She felt it whizz by her, and then she heard a strange, hollow sound as it smacked against a headstone.

Riddled with relief, she paused.

Plastic. The damned thing was plastic!

She turned and stood her ground, staring at the *horned god* for a minute. The figure was close, and she could now see that she was taller than the creature by a good two or three inches.

She smiled.

It looked at her, and turned to run.

Jenna wasn't about to let this fool go. She sprinted after it, glad for the training she'd been compelled to complete, it having taught her how to run well over uneven surfaces like the jagged line of standing and broken gravestones within the cemetery.

The masked figure turned back once and saw that she was almost upon it.

Jenna heard a yelp of panic.

They were nearly back to the middle of the cemetery when she made a dive and tackled the creature.

"Ouch! Stop it! You're hurting me!"

Jenna eased off and pulled the horned god mask off over his head. She looked down in the hazy light, and saw the least likely of assailants.

It was a kid. She estimated the boy to be thirteen or fourteen, a young teenager. He had a freckled face, and sandy red hair, a spattering of acne and a look of sheer terror in his brown eyes.

"What did you think you were doing?" Jenna demanded.

"Aw, come on, I was playing with you. A little scare for Halloween!"

Jenna stood and reached down a hand. The kid stood, and looked quickly to the side as if he was ready to bolt again.

"Oh, no, no, no! Who are you, what are you doing and who set you up to do this?" she demanded.

He made the slightest turn; she gripped his wrist in an iron vise.

"Ow!" the kid wailed.

"You're not going anywhere. I'm getting the police."

A look of petrified alarm came to his face. "No, please! Please—please, please don't do that."

"Then you'd better start talking."

She fumbled in her pocket for her phone. It wasn't there. Cursing, she tried not to let on that it was going to be difficult to carry out her threat.

The graveyard was empty now except for the two of them—and the hazy shadows that gathered around, anxious for excitement in their endless days and nights. Jenna kept her attention focused on the boy.

"You know who I am, don't you?" she asked.

He looked away.

"Don't you?" she demanded, her fingers tightening again around his wrist.

"Yeah," he said dully. "You're that whacked-out FBI lady who talks to ghosts—and who wants to let a crazy killer out on the streets!"

She gritted her teeth. "No one is going to let a crazy killer out on the streets. But you, young man, are an idiot. You're right. I am FBI. What if I'd been armed? I might have taken a shot at you!"

"It's plastic!" he protested.

"You meant to scare me. If you'd scared me enough, plastic or no, I wouldn't have known, and I might have shot you. It's a damned good imitation of the real thing."

He was silent, his cheeks red. "Look, I'm sorry!" he pleaded.

"Who are you?" She'd thought at first that it might be the bitter David Yates, or his comrade in accusation, Joshua Abbott. But this kid was too young to be either. Those two had to be seventeen now.

"My mom will probably kill me," he murmured.

"Your name and your mom's name, or I call the police. And I want to know *why* you're doing this."

"Marty—Martin Keller. And…I just did it because I hear them talking. All the adults in town are talking about you and that Mr. Hall. They're all angry. They say the cops have a killer and Mr. Hall is such a hotshot attorney he wants to prove that a crazy kid is innocent just because he can. He doesn't care if they let Malachi out on the streets, because he lives in Boston. And the rest of us will all be hacked up in our beds."

Jenna took a deep breath. "What made you choose this costume?" she asked, somewhat calmer.

He lowered his head. "We had it at the school for years. Every year, they do a play—about the witchcraft trials, you know? And about the city now, and how we all have to learn to like each other, whether we're Jewish or witches or whatever. Nobody uses it after the first of the year. Nobody cares about it. I was going to put it back, honest, just as soon as Halloween is over."

"And that's it? The costume was convenient?"

"It is a scary costume. Please—scary, huh?"

"What else?" Jenna asked.

He looked away again.

She shook his arm. "I can and will call the police!" she warned. *Well, she would—when she found her phone.*

He let out a long sigh of surrender and aggravation. "Okay, I wanted to be a big shot. I wanted to tell the kids at school that I'd made you pass out or something."

"How long have you been chasing me?"

He looked puzzled. "What do you mean—how long?"

"How many days?"

His frown of confusion deepened. "Just…just now. I saw when you left that shop—I followed you after that, and barely no one was in the cemetery, and…I just meant to scare you and disappear, that's it, I swear it!"

"How long have you had the costume?"

He shook his head. "I just slipped it out of the drama

room today, honest. I told the kids what I was going to do. You can ask—they just finished their like once-a-year cleanup thing yesterday. I wouldn't have taken it before then. I'da been caught."

She stared at him long and hard. He was starting to shake.

She was glad that he was afraid of her. He might be a couple of inches shorter, but she wondered how she'd make out in a brawl with him. He was an adolescent starting to gain broad shoulders and a frame.

"Are you on the football team?" she asked him.

"Uh, yeah—junior varsity."

"So you were trying to impress the seniors, huh?"

He squirmed.

"Like David Yates and Joshua Abbott."

"Hey, that kid hurt David Yates. He really hurt him!" Marty protested.

"And you'd be big man on the field if you scared the FBI agent, huh?"

He lowered his head. "Please don't get me in trouble. Please."

"You are in trouble. Give me the costume. Get out of it."

"Here? In the cemetery?"

"You bet. Now. It's not getting out of my sight. It's a cape and cowl, kid. You've got to have something on beneath it."

"Boxers and a T-shirt."

"Then you're going home in boxers and a T-shirt."

"What are you going to do?" he asked, his voice almost a whisper.

"Find out if what you're telling me is the truth. And I'm going to have this costume inspected."

"For what?"

"For blood, Marty, for blood," she said.

"But—"

"If it's clean, I'll see that it gets back where it's supposed to be without anyone knowing. And if I find out that you've told me the truth, then this whole event will be our little secret.

"But, Marty, if this was ever used to hurt anyone, there won't be anything I can do about telling the truth."

"I didn't hurt anyone!" he protested, sliding out of the cape and handing it to her. At least, he was wearing decent boxers. On a beach, he might have looked ready for a swim.

"Jenna!"

She whirled around at the sound of her name. *Sam's voice. And there was a hint of panic in it, of relief—and of anger.*

Marty was going to use it as a chance to bolt. With her free hand, she caught his wrist again.

Sam leaped the little fence from the street side of the cemetery and came striding in.

"What the hell...?"

He looked as if he wanted to pull her into his arms. And shake her.

He eyed her hold on Marty, the costume in her hands.

"Marty wanted to scare me," she said.

Sam seemed to tower over the boy. His shoulders were far broader, and he just had that look of *Sam—*

authoritative and something like a well-tailored and groomed bulldozer.

"I'm sorry!"

She thought that Marty would cry any minute.

"We'll call the police," Sam said, reaching for his phone.

"No," Jenna said softly. "We've already been through this. Marty and I have an agreement. I'm going to get this costume to our lab, and find out if there is anything on it. Marty has apologized to me. He just borrowed the costume from the drama department today because he's heard how much we're loathed for what we're doing, Sam. Seems that most people believe that Malachi is guilty, and they want us to stop doing what we're doing."

Sam stared at Marty. "Why *this* costume?"

"Because," Marty said, his voice filled with exasperation and fear. "It was *there*. Every kid in town knows it. It's just a creepy costume and mask from our school events!" he said.

Marty was shaking. Jenna was certain that he was repeating what he had heard the adults around him say over and over.

She almost felt sorry for him. And she was surprised when Sam spoke sternly but evenly.

"Marty, think about it. What if Malachi is just *different*? If he's just a skinny kid who is super religious because that's the way he was raised. What if he didn't do it?"

"But—but he did do it," Marty said.

"How do you know? How do you know that for a fact?"

"I've seen the TV. Hey, I know they all thought that he killed old man Andres—and that Covington guy, too," Marty said. "And then his crazy dad—hey, we don't even blame him for killing his crazy dad, but he could kill us!"

"We know that he didn't kill Mr. Covington," Sam said flatly.

Marty shook his head. "No, no—David and Josh, they said that he killed Covington."

"Marty, David Yates is afraid of Malachi. Don't you think that he might make up a story—or that maybe he even thought that he saw Malachi?"

Marty's eyes darted from Sam to Jenna. "He—he's afraid of him for a good reason!"

"Oh, come on, Marty! You're a smart kid. You don't believe in the 'evil eye,' do you?" Sam asked him.

Marty was confused and still very scared. "I—I...I don't know...."

"Let him go for now," Jenna said softly. "Marty needs to learn that everything he hears isn't true. Come on, Sam. Let's let him go."

"How am I going to explain going home in my underwear?" Marty asked.

"How were you going to explain going home in a stolen costume?" Sam asked him in return.

Marty looked at them both. Jenna was no longer holding him.

He turned and ran.

They watched him for a moment, and then Sam

turned to Jenna. She thought for a minute that he was going to put his hands on her and shake her. He looked as if he wanted to do that, but with supreme effort refrained.

"Why the hell didn't you answer your phone?" he demanded. "I thought that something serious had happened to you. Your uncle is in a panic. Your uncle!"

Without another word, he pulled out his own phone. He dialed Jamie, staring at Jenna.

"Found her."

She could hear Jamie's reply. "Where?"

"In the cemetery."

"What?"

"She's fine, Jamie. We'll see you soon."

"Why didn't she answer her phone?"

"Because I lost it!" Jenna said loudly. "And I think probably in here—probably against the back wall."

"Did you hear that, Jamie?" Sam asked.

"Aye. I'll meet you at the new barbecue. It's two blocks from the graveyard. Lost her phone! Eh, my heart's not old enough for all this fibrillatin'!"

Sam pocketed his phone, staring at her. "You did just cost us about ten years of life, you know."

"Sam, I dropped my phone. It's in here somewhere. I have to find it."

"Jenna, it's almost dark."

"I'll find it."

"Retrace your steps."

She nodded, and explained where she'd been, not explaining exactly why. They split up by about twenty feet, trying to cover more ground.

"You should never be alone," he called to her.

"Oh, please, Sam! It was a kid trying to scare me, and I handled it."

Night was on them; the only light came from the street, and she wondered herself if she had a prayer in hell of finding her phone.

"You could ask the ghosts for help!" he called.

"Maybe I will!"

She was surprised when she felt a soft touch on her arm.

It was a young woman. She had large eyes and soft flyaway hair, and she couldn't have been more than twenty years old when she had passed away. She managed a gentle smile and led the way.

Jenna found her phone against the back wall.

"Found it!" she called to Sam.

"That's a miracle!" he told her.

"Oh, well, you know, a ghost helped me!" she called cheerfully. "Of course, if we were smarter, we could have just had you call it...."

He came to her and took her arm. She wished she didn't get such a feeling of heat every time he touched her. She hoped her cheeks didn't redden, or if they did, that the shadows of the night hid her reaction.

"Let's get out of here," he said huskily.

"Sam, I want to get this costume to a lab right away. If we can find a twenty-four-hour FedEx or post office—"

"Want to head to Boston?" he asked drily. "You know, the Massachusetts police aren't the Feds, but they are pretty damned good."

"Sam, I'd have to explain that in my mind's eye, I *see* someone dressed like this killing people. And I'd have to explain how I got it."

"Legalese, Miss Duffy. I can work it out with John Alden. He's a good guy."

"Sam, we may be letting loose of a piece of evidence—"

He sighed. "And you have no jurisdiction here at the moment. You weren't invited in. If the costume goes to an FBI lab and something is found, I might wind up with a chain of evidence issue in court, or a judge could find some other reason to have it thrown out. We'll just head to the station and call John."

As he spoke, they heard the single *wong* of a siren. They had reached the low wall to the street; suddenly, a flashlight blazed into their faces.

"Graveyard is closed! Gate locked. What are you two doing in there?" An officer, his face shielded in the shadows cast by the glare of the light, demanded.

"Sorry! We were just leaving," Sam said.

"What's that you've got?" the officer demanded.

"It's just a costume," Jenna offered.

"It's a serious offense here to tamper with the graves! To vandalize!" the officer said angrily.

"We weren't vandalizing!" Jenna protested indignantly.

"Look, hey, the gates were locked when we were in here!" Sam said.

"Bad enough dealing with kids and whackos during the season, but it's worse when wiseass adults are playing around in the cemetery!" he said.

Sam looked at Jenna. "Okay," he told the officer. "Take us in."

"Take you in?" the officer was surprised. "I wasn't arresting you—I was giving you a serious warning. You're to come here to learn and have a good time and not destroy what is historic and can never be replaced."

"I know," Sam said. "And you're doing a great job. Go ahead and bring us in, though. I'll call Detective Alden while we're on the way. He might just be sitting down to his supper."

John arrived right after Sam and Jenna had been seated in his office, in the middle of her call to Jamie. He was perplexed as to why it was so important to have the costume brought to the lab.

Jenna leaned forward to speak to John Alden, but Sam thought they were going to be in much better shape if he did the speaking.

"John, bear with me on this. You're a good guy. You're really one of the good guys. And I know that you find it hard to believe that the evidence before your eyes is telling you the wrong story. I have a theory, and it may be crazy, but hear me out. No matter that you're only charging the boy for some of the murders, you think the same person killed everyone, and I agree with you. You believe it was Malachi Smith. I don't. And it's not just because I'm defending him in court. I don't believe the kid did it. You're a cop, and yes, you work with the prosecutor. But prosecutors don't want to prosecute the wrong person. No officer of the court wants to be responsible for a miscarriage of justice. That's what we're looking for here, John, justice."

"Why this costume?" John asked, willing to listen to them but undeniably confused.

"The kid wearing it—?" He paused, looking at Jenna.

"Martin Keller," she said. Her voice was tight, her jaw set. She wasn't happy with him. But they were playing on the same side in a precarious game, and she had to see that.

"Martin Keller 'borrowed' the costume from the drama room. He was using it to scare Jenna. I believe that our killer is dressing up when he or she sets out to commit murder. It may be slim, but there is a possibility that the person is dressing up not just in a similar costume, but one borrowed from the drama department."

"He or she? You think it might be a woman?" John said. "This much violence perpetuated by a woman is pretty rare."

"I didn't say it was a woman," Sam said. "I don't know. But, yes, look back. In the Tate/LaBianca murders, Manson's stable of idol-worshipping followers were mainly women, and they were capable of extreme brutality. Karla Homolka seduced the victims when she and her husband went on a killing rage—she was responsible for the rape and murder of her own sister."

"So, you do think it's a woman?" John asked.

"No, John, honestly, I don't know yet. I'm just pointing out the fact that even if statistically men have committed more murders with this kind of violence, it's more than possible that a woman *could* be responsible," Sam said. He waved a hand in the air. "At this point,

John, what I'm trying to explain is this: wear a costume, and you're someone else. Wear a costume, and you can walk around unnoticed. Or even, wear a costume, and it might mean something specifically to you."

"You think they were ritual killings?" John asked.

Sam lowered his head, fighting the frustration. "I know that a kid in this costume tried to scare Jenna tonight. I know it comes from the school's drama department. I believe someone is wearing a costume like this—an encompassing costume, one to hide identity—to commit the killings. Please—hey, Jenna wanted to take this to the FBI."

John stared at Jenna. "The FBI has *not* been invited in."

Jenna stood, irritated. "Would it be such a bad thing? No one wants to take over. Obviously, we respect the Massachusetts police. No one wants to take charge of the investigation. But if you have help, please use it! Use us! The world is working on lower budgets. Why not charge a Federal lab? But Sam said that you were a good and honest cop and we could keep a chain of evidence. If you think we're just being silly, then please, give the damned thing back to me!"

Sam noted that John just stared at Jenna for a moment, his jaw fallen. Then he smiled and looked at Sam.

"I'll get the costume to the lab. I don't want a miscarriage of justice, Sam. I just can't believe that someone else has done all this. The kid was covered in blood. Covered. In. Blood. But I won't have it be said you were denied anything in the right to defend your client." He pointed at Sam. "You two chose not to call the police, and the costume is in your hands. So as long as we're being 'unofficial' about everything, you see to it that school is afforded a new costume. And I'll see to that Martin Keller is—"

Jenna started to move forward again. Sam stood to block her.

"No, John, please. Meeting the kid was a good lesson for both of us. We know what a lot of the local people are feeling. Let's not say anything until we know about the costume. I don't want to make it so no one in Salem will speak to us by having a kid arrested for a prank."

"If by a bizarre chance something is found…"

"Of course. It would be remiss if you were not to become involved all way through Martin Keller, his parents and the school. Thanks, John."

He herded Jenna out, and then remembered he didn't have his car. "Um, John, a ride to my car, if possible?"

The same officer who had come upon them at the cemetery drove them to Sam's car.

It wasn't there.

"Tow zone, Mr. Hall, I'm afraid," the officer pointed out. "You won't be able to pick it up until tomorrow. I'm afraid you'll have to pay that fine, too."

Sam was ready to explode. He didn't give a damn about the fine, but he did love his car. It made coming and going the distance so much easier.

It was a material object, he reminded himself.

Yeah, but it was *his* material object. He'd always loved cars. He'd mowed lawns for his car, painted, hauled trash, worked hard. He couldn't help it; he just really loved cars. He spent a lot of time in his car; it was a place he often spent a lot of time just thinking and calculating his arguments.

"I can drop you somewhere else," the officer told him.

"You can drop me at the foot of Essex," Jenna told the officer. "I think that Sam is just going to stand here and stare at the spot where his car used to be."

She got back into the police car. Sam shook his head. "Right. I'm going to stand here." He tapped on the hood. "Go."

He watched as the car drove away, and then he kicked the ground. Damn it. He'd been frantic over her, and now, because of it, his car had been *towed.*

She lost her phone in the cemetery while accosting the kid who had tried to scare her. What the hell was she doing in the cemetery again—communing with her ghosts? And she was flipping pissed off at him because he'd stopped her from speaking so that he could get a rational argument through to John Alden.

But she was safe. That was worth a car being towed. Well, of course. Logical and ethical. Human life was always the most precious commodity. When life was gone, it could not be returned.

It was more than that.

Tense and angry, he walked back toward his own house. He didn't find the streets all that charming at the moment; partygoers were out, dispersed among families, just trying to find a place for dinner before settling back into their bed-and-breakfast inns or hotel rooms for the night. There were endless balls in Salem as Halloween approached. Some private, some sponsored by the Wiccans, some sponsored by frat houses and sororities. It was true that every manner of costume known to man could be seen in the city.

As he walked, he turned back to look at a rowdy crowd of fraternity boys. They were all dressed up as Greek heroes.

A Warrior Princess Xena was following in their wake; she must have been freezing her...*assets* off. The night had definitely grown chill.

He frowned suddenly, stopping dead in his tracks. Just behind Xena Warrior Princess was someone else who didn't belong in the crowd of Greeks.

Someone in a Celtic costume—that of the horned god, or the goat god. He started walking toward the group. The warrior princess cried out as she was pushed by the horned god, falling over and only just being saved from a hard meeting with the pavement because Sam was there in time to catch her.

"Rude asshole!" one of the Greeks called out. "Thanks—" he began to say to Sam, but Sam was already moving through the crowd.

He saw the horned god, and he took flight after it once again. The horned god turned and saw him, and slipped back into a crowd of princes, princesses, a frog and one Freddy Krueger. Bert and Ernie and the Count from Sesame Street took up most of the sidewalk.

By the time he made his way through the cartoon menagerie, the horned god was gone.

He stood, puzzled. It was a common costume, especially in Salem. At one time, surely, the Christian church had mistaken the Celtic goat god or horned god for the devil, and thus the creature of decadence had become something like evil incarnate.

Pictures of the horned god adorned many of the museums dedicated to explaining what might have happened to cause the Salem Witch Trials.

So why run? Why run away in the costume because Sam had seen him?

Because Jenna was right?

Feeling uneasy, still angry, angrier with himself because he'd allowed himself to get caught up in it all and angrier still because...

She did something to him. It wasn't like the simple burst of hormones, wanting a beautiful woman. That would be too easy. True, he thought. *Men could be ruled far more easily from below the belt. But that was easy, simple. I want you; do you want me, too? His life had been gifted, too many appetites easily achieved.*

This...this was a different kind of hunger. Not the kind that was easily appeased, and not the kind that he could walk away from and...

He didn't like it.

Sam Hall. Oh, yeah, the clever one. Sometimes you'd need to intimidate—investigate. Become a P.I. Size mattered, psychologically, face-to-face with someone in a courtroom. Remember to go to the gym. Join the defense—remember to win.

Fall for a red-haired Irish lass and...

"Ah, yes," he said softly aloud. "Burn in hell!"

He reached his house. Inside he shed his trench coat and stripped haphazardly as he headed into the shower.

Cold first, cold as ice, and then hot, the kind of water to knead the tension out of his muscles.

It worked on his muscles, not on his mind.

Death. Death was what you couldn't take back. You could argue, you could rail. You couldn't win against death.

He'd learned that.

And then, tonight, when she hadn't answered her phone...

FBI agent. Competent. Trained.

Competent, trained people, veteran cops and marshals and soldiers all fell when they were ambushed, unadvised, unwary.

He heard his doorbell ring as he turned off the water. Frowning, he slipped into his terry robe and padded barefoot to his bedroom. He kept his Smith & Wesson in the drawer next to his bed. With all that was going on, if someone was ringing his bell at night, he was going to the door armed.

He looked through the peephole and felt all the tension he had just tried to ease from his body slam right back into it with a searing sensation of heat.

9

As she stood on her toes to see if she could actually look in the peephole, Jenna saw that it darkened. Sam had come to the door.

It swung open. He stood there, still damp from the shower, wrapped in his robe, feet bare, a rigid and wary look on his face and a gun in his hand.

"Hey, I come in peace!" she told him.

"I doubt that," he said drily, turning from her. "If you're coming in, lock the door behind you."

He'd headed off toward one of the rooms to the right side of the stairway. Jenna walked into the foyer and stood uncomfortably, then turned and locked the front door.

Had she come in peace?

Not really.

Why had she come?

She didn't have to answer her inner turmoil; he reappeared, the gun now gone. Her heart was fluttering and she couldn't seem to breathe correctly, and worst of all, it felt as if there were a burning sensation that stirred in the center of her core and shot down her thighs.

Disgraceful, good God! Sex, desire, they were all human instincts, and all kept under control in a civilized society, and...

"So, what do you want?" he asked flatly.

What do I want?

The dead blunt question took her by surprise. She was disappointed that she couldn't quite lay it on the line.

You.

"You're a jerk," she said.

Good beginning.

"This couldn't have waited until tomorrow?"

"No."

She walked over to him and shoved him on the chest. "No, it can't. You almost put your arm down my throat to make sure that I didn't speak this afternoon. What? You were afraid that I would just sit there and blurt out to the repressed New England cop that I see and speak to ghosts and that I can also relive certain experiences sometimes by being somewhere?"

"Were you?" he asked.

She laid her hand against her own breast. "I am a Federal officer, Sam Hall, with all the rights that go with that title, and I did all the running, jumping, history, science and arms training that went along with becoming official. I worked hard, and I'm real."

"You just see ghosts," he said.

"Hasn't anything in your life been anything other than a Jaguar? Oh, probably a tailored suit!" she mocked. "Guess what? You can't take them with you. You, me, everyone dies, Sam. And sometimes there's a pain, a loss, something that can't quite let you go. And you know what? Those left behind are here because of their hearts and their souls, things you can't see in the living. Good God, I'd never expect you to see them in the dead! You see nothing that isn't completely tangible, nothing that makes the rest of us human! And, for your information, Mr. High-and-Mighty bring-in-the-big-money Hall, I've done a hell of a lot more toward finding out the truth in this case than you have. And—" she came toward him again, poking a single finger at his chest "—you mark my words, the killer was wearing a horned god costume!"

He caught her by the shoulders then, his hands not rough, but something of force about him as he backed her against the wall. "You listen! You came to me to defend a kid covered in a blood—the kind of evidence that leaves the prosecution dancing in the streets. You can't begin to imagine all the motions that had to be filed, and you still can't imagine what it's going to be like to find the right jury, and most of all, how dare you? I don't speak to the dead—dead is dead and gone, and therefore, no! They don't answer questions for me, not in a court of law. I believe the last time that was tried innocent people were killed for 'witchcraft.' And if you're so brilliant and precious and understand the psyche of everyone living and dead, why the hell haven't you just asked Abraham Smith who the hell it was who murdered him?"

She stared back at him, speechless for a minute.

"Yeah, right," he said softly.

She shook her head. "It doesn't work like that. It's

not dial-a-ghost and connect to the right spirit. No, no…
but we're close to the truth and I know it. I know what I
have seen, I know what I've learned, and it all has to do
with that damned costume, and the fact that people still
don't understand their neighbors, after all these years.
We still don't see each other clearly. We can't tolerate,
we can't forgive strangeness…but it's there, and we are
close and…"

"And we're just about going to have to pray that
someone runs into the middle of the common and
screams, 'Hey, I'm guilty!'"

"Sam—" Jenna began.

"Shut up!" he cried.

"What?"

"Shut up!"

"You shut up!"

"I'm trying to!" he shouted.

She stared at him, stunned. And then she noted the
look in his eyes, and he was suddenly close against her
and she could feel the damp fire of the length of him,
and she opened her mouth to speak but she couldn't.

"I didn't want you to try to explain anything to John
tonight, that's true. But I was behind you. Whether I
believe or understand or not, I was behind you. And
you're not really angry with me."

"The hell I'm not."

"That's not why you're here."

"Why am I here?"

He lowered his head and found her mouth. His lips
captured hers, and his kiss was firm and coercive, his
mouth forming over hers with a liquid fire, desire seem-

ing to burn in the very way that he touched her. She felt the incredible vitality and supple strength of the length of him as he pressed her there against the wall, and she was grateful for the wall, thinking that, for her, it had been far too long since she had let herself even begin to feel such sensation.

His tongue moved into her mouth, again strong and coercive and seductive, and she was even more grateful that he pinned her there. This was what she had wanted, yes, but she hadn't imagined that she would feel so deliriously weak, and so at a disadvantage. He was a good lover, she thought, because he was a practiced lover; she had seen from the beginning that he moved with a confidence and ease that meant he would hold everything an alpha male held, power unto himself, the physical arrogance that was undeniably attractive. She felt like an inexperienced teen again, unsure and uncertain, and afraid she was far out of her league.

His lips broke from hers, and his mouth remained just inches away, but she could see his eyes again, and she was stunned that they seemed to be a clear gray, hiding nothing, offering something that might have been honesty and even humility.

"Is this why you came?" he asked hoarsely. "Because, dear Lord, I think I might have simply burned to a cinder, longing for you and not knowing how to even begin to ask."

She nodded, not trusting her voice, and felt the brush of the back of his fingers on her cheek. She was astonished to see that his fingers trembled.

She moved against him, burying her face against his

chest, then lifting her head and finding his mouth again. She felt his arms around her, lifting her more tightly against him, and through clothing and terry, she could feel the rise of his sex, he was so instantly aroused. She slipped her hands beneath the terry of the robe, fumbled at the belt, and drew more flush against him. He backed away, and together they pulled off her sweater, and she realized then that his clothing was strewn about. She looked at him, puzzled for a moment.

"Cold shower when you left me!" he told her.

And she found that she could laugh, and crashed into his arms again. It seemed that they couldn't kiss enough at first, delirious wet kisses that seemed both too much and somehow necessary between them, and then he began to half lead and half carry her into the bedroom on the side of the house, and they fell together onto the large canopy bed there. Jenna got one boot off before he pulled her back down, and she let the other go. Their mouths met again, and his lips trailed to her throat and her shoulders while his fingers eased around to her bra strap. She ran her hands down the length of his naked back, trembling and hungry and yet wanting every minute, every sensation that led to the pent-up desire she'd been so eager to suppress. His hands and mouth covered her flesh, and he was amazingly giving in all that he did, as if he were fascinated beyond measure by every aspect of her skin, every inch....

She touched him as he touched her, running her hands down his midriff, taking it farther, wrapping her fingers around his erection and bringing a gasp from his lips. "Not fair, I was half-naked already," he whispered, rising above her. For a moment she caught the silver-gray glint of his eyes in the shadows cast into the darkened room by the hallway light, and she was mesmerized by the dusky shade of the room that seemed to envelop them in some kind of ridiculously magical realm. Could she be so abandoned in bright light? She didn't know, but she reached out, taking him to her when he moved down to kiss her lips again and then inch down the length of her body, kissing, caressing and stroking while he found the waistband to her jeans and shimmied the denim down her body and, at last, rid her of her last boot, the last vestige of clothing.

And then he rose above her, looking down at her again. He lowered himself, lacing his fingers with hers, and eased himself into her, pausing, and then moving, and moving again, more deeply and deeply, until it seemed that his trust shot through to her heart, and her body—core and limbs—became electric in themselves. She moved against him, arms around him, legs entwined around his back, and she marveled at the miracle of sensation and sensuality and sex, because it was magic, and she'd left the world behind, wanting nothing but the touch, scent and taste of him, and the writhing, undulating, wet, slick movement between them.

She climaxed with a desperation that left her body drained. She felt him expulse, felt his arms around her tighten, and she felt his weight, and then the way he eased down beside her, and brought her back into his arms again. The drumbeat of their hearts seemed ridiculously loud in the room, and the bed's comforter seemed cool, and still her body seemed to be on fire.

And for a moment, she winced inwardly. It was sex, just sex.

But she *liked* him so much; she didn't want to...

She did. She was fascinated by the way he moved, and the way he thought, and the tone of his voice, and his little idiosyncrasies, the way he paced and put his hands in his pockets, thought out his words and didn't think out his words....

For a moment, she must have eased away.

He pulled her back, his voice husky. "Come here, Red."

"Oh, please! Don't call me Red."

"Okay, come here, Irish."

"Don't call me Irish."

"Is it bad to be Irish?"

"Of course not!"

"Then...?"

"Okay, you come on over here, Puritan!"

"Ouch, ooh. That one does hurt!"

"Well?"

He rolled up on an elbow to look at her. "Jenna. Come here, please, Jenna. Please, don't think about leaving me yet. I'm begging you."

She eased back against him. "I wasn't leaving," she said. "Not now."

"You should just stay. I can call Jamie—"

She rose out of his arms onto her elbow and stared down at him. "You're going to call my uncle and tell him that I'm staying the night?"

"Better than have him worry."

"He was almost a priest!"

"Exactly. Almost a priest. The key word there is *almost*."

"But—"

"Jamie is human, Jenna."

She laughed and lay back down by him. He pulled her against him. "He's my uncle," she said.

"And I'm sure he knows that you grew up."

"Still…"

"Okay, okay, I'll take you home. He'll think we're assuming that he's either stupid or entirely blind himself."

"That won't work," Jenna told him.

He laughed.

"I really can't stay long. Of course, we could be discussing the case, should be discussing the case—"

"No, definitely not. Not now, not here!" he whispered, and pulled her against him again.

This time, he was achingly, deliciously slow, teasing and tormenting, and she struggled to do so in return. When they were spent at last, she collapsed next him, ridiculously glad to know him so well and so thoroughly. She wasn't sure where it could lead, and she couldn't allow herself to care. It was now, and it was still magic, and she'd never regret having come here, because somehow, on this night, no matter what aspects of philosophy and life divided them, they were one for those few hours.

They lay there entwined as seconds ticked by. Then, rather than Jenna, it was Sam who rose, and after a minute, he returned to stand in the doorway. She couldn't help thinking that he was something like an indifferent Adonis, unaware of himself. She wondered if he had any idea of just how perfect he might be; in his world, his tailored clothing was his mask.

"We're all set," he said.

"What?" She leaped out of the bed. "All set for what?"

"I called Jamie—"

"And you asked him if I could stay the night?"

"No, I said you were here, safe, with me, and I was about to walk you back, and he said that we should both just get some sleep and he'd see us in the morning."

"Just like that?" Jenna asked.

"I swear, God as my witness," he said.

"I'm not sure you believe in God," she said.

He stood there a moment. "I do believe in…something. A greater power. I believe in life, and all that goes with it. I even believe in people, and that love itself is one of the greatest powers on the earth. The things I've seen done when love is real are remarkable. And, anyway, on all that, I swear, it was Jamie's idea that you stay."

He walked to her, taking her into his arms.

"I'm hungry," he told her.

"Yes," she murmured.

"No, I mean, I'm really starving, although, of course…all my creature desires seem to be calling to me at once."

She laughed and stepped away. "Got another robe?"

There wasn't much in the house despite their attempts to concoct something substantial from the meager pickings. Sam found a takeout menu from a pizza restaurant that delivered as late as two in the morning, so they sent out for pizzas. There was enough for a salad, which they had just managed to finish putting together when the pizza arrived. They sat at the kitchen table with a bottle of sauvignon and their food, and Jenna found that she couldn't help but bring up the case again.

"I feel we have the answer, as if we're looking right at it," she said.

"So far, we know that a number of people like to dress up as the horned god, and that they probably do so because the teaching facilities use that likeness to show why the Puritans were easily led to believe that Celtic religions and paganism *did* have a devil. And since the Puritans were busy getting rid of Calvinism— by *any* means necessary—and were supposed to be the most amazing fundamentalists, they could be convinced easily enough that there was a devil, and, at first, that those who weren't good churchgoers might easily dance with the devil. Midwives and healers were always the first suspects."

Jenna drummed her fingers on the table. "Yes, but Rebecca Nurse was accused by the girls, and she did hang, and she was an extremely noble woman."

"Ah!" he said, waving his fork at her. "There were two main families who held the money in the town at the time—they didn't seem to be against money. It was the Porters and the Putnam family. Okay, they were a little messed up and inbred by then, but it seemed that each section of the families had to side with one of the families. The Putnams were throwing out the accusations—Rebecca Nurse was on the Porter side.

"It all started with Tituba, the slave from Barbados, telling tales. Tituba was different."

"As Malachi is different."

"Yes, but I guarantee you, John Alden—and many other fine people in this city—are not going to let people run around crying, *Witch!*"

Jenna shook her head. "No, but we saw tonight that children listen to their parents. Okay, maybe not when the parents want them to, but they definitely listen to adult conversation. The Smith family was disliked. Many people felt sorry for Malachi—they hated his father. But the family itself was hated. So, that made Malachi different. Then there was the incident with David Yates. Okay, logically—and yes, I believe this—David was afraid in his own mind and hit himself in the head. Sam, that was like the girls twitching and crawling around the floor and speaking in so-called tongues. They were afraid. Tituba told the girls stories. David had been cruel to Malachi, and he'd heard that the family was fanatical."

"I agree. It's a sound correlation. But here's the thing. I believe, and if you're right about the murderer wearing a costume, the murders were well planned, as well. And if that's the case, they were well planned to make it look like Malachi was the murderer. *That* doesn't go along with hysteria," Sam said.

"Maybe it's all a combination of both," Jenna suggested.

"And the past," Sam said thoughtfully. He smiled at

Jenna across the table. "Somebody wanted something, so they were using prejudices that were already there to accomplish what they wanted."

"But who—and what do they want?" Jenna asked thoughtfully.

"The diamond answer," Sam said. He looked at her. "Somehow, now, you have to get to see David Yates, and I have to find a way to talk to Joshua Abbott. We have to get them apart."

"All right. Oh! Oh!"

"What? What?"

Jenna grinned. "I'm sorry—I forgot to tell you. I went and had my tarot cards read yesterday."

"Okay?"

"I went by A Little Bit of Magic. I spoke to Ivy and Cecilia, and saw another old friend, now known as Merlin. Anyway, they said he had competition—Madam Sam. Who is Samantha Yeager."

"She gave you a reading?"

"Yes, but she already knew who I was."

"Really—why bother with the reading? And what did she say?"

"She said that she didn't kill anybody over a house, basically. She's interesting. And she had an alibi—as far as killing the Smith family, anyway. The clerk verified that she had been giving tarot readings when they were killed."

"I should meet her," Sam said.

"Yes, you should. She's interesting. I mean, very theatrical. But she admits it's all an act. I think she's entirely different when she's not being Madam Sam."

"Well, then, I'll go and have a tarot card reading." He paused a moment, looking at her before speaking softly. "Then I think that we have to go back to the murder house again."

"Lexington House?" Jenna asked. She felt as if her skin crawled with the thought of it. She wasn't afraid of the house, she told herself. The house was a shell.

A shell that had witnessed terrible cruelty and violence.

"If you can," he said. He set his hand on hers. "Jenna, I don't want you to do anything that hurts you in any way. I still don't know what I believe, but you were practically bleach-white the last time we were in there, and…"

"It's what I do," she told him. "And I'll be all right."

"You're certain?"

"Of course. You'll be there, too."

He stood up, finishing the last swig of his wine. "We do need to get some sleep," he said, setting down his glass and reaching for her hand.

"Are we going to sleep?" she asked him.

He grinned. "Eventually."

Jenna was startled awake by the very loud ringing of her phone.

She groped blindly for it, remembered her handbag was in the foyer where she had dropped it, and bolted from the bed.

Sam was already up. He had showered and was dressed, and she could smell the delicious aroma of freshly brewed coffee.

He handed it to her as she came dashing out.

"Wow, I do like the way you look in the morning!" he teased.

She gave him a warning glance, dived into the bag and found her phone.

She answered with a quick, "Duffy!"

"Jenna."

It was Angela Hawkins, Jenna's team member, and one of her favorite people in the world. Angela had been a cop before joining the unit, and though she was a slim, blue-eyed blonde, she really was tough as nails. She was also wonderful at making contact with whatever spirits might remain behind.

"Angela! Hey, how are you? Is everything all right? Oh, please, I hope we don't have to be somewhere right now—"

"No, no. Jackson thought we should come up. Unofficially, of course. So, we're just here for Haunted Happenings."

"Here?" Jenna said.

"We're at your uncle's house—Jackson, Will and I."

"Oh! You're in Salem already."

"Yes. Actually, Will has a permit—we're sending him out to perform magic in the street and he can see what passes by—we're going to put him just outside one of the museums on the pedestrian walkway. Anyway, should we come to you?"

"No! Ah, no," Jenna said, glancing at Sam, who had poured her coffee and brought it to where she stood. "No, fifteen minutes, we'll be there. Sam and I."

"Take your time. Jamie is filling us in."

She hung up, feeling panicked, and then laughed.

"Is that hysteria? What's going on?" Sam asked.

"Jackson, Angela and Will are here. Part of my team."

"Jackson Crow—the behavior guy. The profiler."

"Angela and Will, too. She was a cop in Virginia... and Will was an entertainer, from Trinidad, originally—fascinating guy. He works with film and sound and all that. He's going to do surveillance down by the shops and museums on the pedestrian walk, pretend to be a street performer doing magic."

She was afraid for a minute that he was going to be angry—afraid that his rapport with John Alden would be destroyed if the FBI showed up.

"Brilliant," he said. "A worker who can see a zillion tourists, of course, but also get to know all the people in the area—shopkeepers, guides, Puritan and Witch Trial actors and actresses."

"*Brilliant?* You're sure?" she asked.

He nodded. "I liked your speech to John Alden the other day. We will happily use what we can get."

"But what about John? Will he become defensive?" Jenna asked.

"I don't know. We'll see. Hey—they're here, right? And it's a free country. They don't have to have police cooperation to be here and look around a tourist city as private citizens."

She let out a sigh of relief and took a long swallow of coffee. "A shower. I've got to get into the shower... my clothes! I need both boots, oh, hell...."

"There's a shower in the back of the bedroom, in the

bath, extra toothbrushes and stuff like that in the cabinet above the sink, and…" he said, caught her arm before she could tear off and kissed her lips quickly. "Don't panic. Sex is older than the hills, you know."

"No, I'm not panicked. I've just got to move!"

He laughed as she hurried away.

Twenty minutes later, Sam and Jenna had walked the short distance to Jamie's house.

Since he'd met Jenna, Sam had found himself intrigued to meet Jackson Crow. The man was about his own height and build with exceptional features that told of a Native American background. Angela was a slim, stunning blonde with grave eyes, and Will Chan was tall with a fascinating mix of cultures, predominately Asian, visible in his features, as well. They seemed relaxed and easy, but ready to hear everything they could about the case.

"We'll be discreet," Jackson assured Sam. "No problems with the locals. We can just be your legs or eyes as needed—you can't be everywhere at once. And we can send any questions straight to Jake Mallory. He can find out about any human being in the world, and he can do it legally. Most of the time. I believe."

Will had given Jenna an affectionate kiss on the cheek, as had the others, when they had met. Sam was surprised to realize that he felt a twinge of jealousy—this was a team that was tight and supportive. He was accustomed these days to doing most of his own work in his head, arguing out plans and actions by himself, despite the fact that Evan Richardson was such a great assistant. He'd come up in the world; sometimes he missed the early days when he'd been in the D.A.'s office himself and he'd sat in a pool with others, all searching out legal histories and planning stratagem. Not to mention the larger group—being friends with the cops instead of being considered a thorn in their sides, as a defense attorney often was.

"Excuse me, I start right away," Will said, rising and shaking Sam's hand. "I have my cell, and it's on buzz." He hesitated. "I'm trying to get in for a guest performance at the school. We'll see how that goes."

"Maybe I can help with that," Sam said. He hadn't told Jenna, of course, but he believed her angry speech about law enforcement being open to whatever help there was might have given John Alden a twinge. Maybe John even believed—just a little—that he wasn't in the right. Or, at least, that Sam's involvement—and Jenna's—could only help to prove Malachi's guilt. And if he couldn't pull this one off, he knew who could. "Jamie!" he said. "Don't you still take cases from the school?"

"I do. But I'm assuming that I'm not particularly loved there at the moment," he said. "They all know how I feel about Malachi—that he's being railroaded."

"Yes, but most people are basically decent, even when they're swayed by a common concept," Sam said. "I think you should go in first."

Jamie nodded.

"All right. I'm heading out," Will said and left them.

Jackson asked Sam, "What about getting back into Lexington House?"

"I'll talk to John Alden. He's the lead detective on the case."

"All right, what can we do?" Jackson asked.

Sam went over everything that he and Jenna had discussed the night before. Jackson listened attentively. "I have to ask this—do you honestly believe that the young man is innocent?"

"Absolutely," Sam said.

"I believe in him and, Jackson, when you meet him, you'll believe in him, too," Jenna said. "There's something…I don't know. He's special. And I don't mean that in any kind of a negative way. His belief is so strong. And antiviolent."

"I think," Sam said, "that Andy Yates would definitely be someone to get to know better. He was interested in purchasing the house, *and* it's his son who was involved in the altercation or whatever with Malachi. I still want to talk to his son, David Yates—and the friend, Joshua Abbott—who agreed that they'd seen Malachi rush out of Earnest Covington's house. Their statements directly contradict those of the grocer."

"I spoke with the grocer," Jenna said. "And he's adamant about what he saw."

"So the boys are lying," Jackson said.

"At the moment I've got them on hold, but this has to change now. However, Andy Yates's wife threatened me not to get near the boy," Sam said. "As the defense attorney I do have the right to speak with the witnesses. I've been trying to think of a way around that. I'd rather not walk in pulling out the official card, just yet."

"Yeah, and we can't compromise the case in any

way," Jackson said thoughtfully. "But it's not compromising the case if it's the law."

"It *is* the law, and I can argue the issue—but only if the prosecution is calling him in. If David Yates is going to be a witness, I can get a court order for the kid to talk to me," Sam said. "I was hoping *not* to force the issue, since people talk more easily when they're not forced to do so. And then there's this—so far, Malachi has only been accused of the murders of his family. If the prosecutor doesn't press further charges and doesn't intend on bringing further charges against Malachi and bring David Yates into court, I won't have any standing. But, still, I'm hoping I could sway them to drop the prosecution if they can see the other two murders were done by someone other than Malachi. I think that should work."

"The kids are always hanging out at the cliff park-that's-not-really-a-park," Jenna said. "Maybe I can show Angela the view, and we can hope the boys wind up there."

"All right," Sam said. "You two try the cliff after school. I'll take Jackson with me. I'll introduce him to Councilman Yates, then we'll take a ride over to Beverly. I still think someone at the church Abraham Smith was attending might know something."

"You're forgetting something," Jenna told him.

"What's that?" Sam asked.

"Samantha Yeager."

"Ah, yes, well, we definitely need to have our cards read!" Jackson said.

After they discussed arrangements to get Sam's car

and get everyone where they needed to be, Sam noticed Jenna seemed to be getting a touch antsy. "What are you going to do before you go to the cliffs?" he asked her suspiciously.

She arched a brow to him. "Ghost hunt!" she said.

"Ghost hunt," he said. "Just like that—ghost hunt. I thought you told me that it wasn't anything like dial-a-ghost?"

"It's not. That's why it's *hunting,*" Jenna said. "Sam, we're looking at similar crimes in the same place, different times. It might be good to see what we can find that attunes us to a similar energy. Trust me, please, on this."

Jamie had already headed for the door. Jackson followed him and Sam started to do the same. Instead, he headed back. "Be careful," he told Jenna. "Please, be careful."

"Hey. FBI agents here, albeit on the weird side!" Angela said cheerfully. "But, just so you know, I was a cop in some tough areas of Virginia."

He nodded.

"And, honest, I'm capable," Jenna said, smiling at him.

He hesitated, longing to walk over and kiss her good-bye. He didn't quite know how she was feeling about them, at least in front of her team, so he refrained.

He took a step closer to the two women instead and asked softly, "Jackson?"

"We refer to him as Mr. Logic," Angela said. "He has some intuition, but remember, at one time, he was one of the best profilers in the country."

"Since it seems you're looking more the he-man, man's man variety!" Jenna teased.

Sam went ahead and walked on out of the house.

Ghost hunting....

What the hell had happened since that night he'd found the blood-drenched kid in the road?

He thought of the night gone by. Of Jenna.

Whatever it was, he wanted it to keep happening.

10

"So, tell me, did you know him before?" Angela demanded, grinning as she turned to look at Jenna, who was doing the driving.

"Yes. No. Not really. I vaguely remember meeting him when I was young. His mom was a doll. She had Sam, no other children, but I imagine she would have liked to have had a daughter, too. She'd kind of babysit area girls, let us have slumber parties and all at her house, so I saw him there. I think, once before, he yelled at me and I called him a jerk." She grinned. "He's still a jerk."

"But *your* jerk now, I take it?" Angela asked.

"No."

"Hmm, I could have sworn... I mean, you were at his house when we got here? Still fairly early in the day... And he's certainly impressive. Size alone. I mean height and shoulder breadth, of course..."

"Well, yeah, definitely he's attractive. I was attracted, and I fought it for a while because of the circumstances, but then I started thinking about moments, and that we really only get *moments* out of life...but anyway, he's a high-powered attorney in Boston—who really laughs at the idea that we actually communicate with ghosts—and I love what we do. I think it's important. I think we've saved lives. And I don't particularly care what kind of car I drive, and I grew up in a household that believed in magic, and…he's a hard-core New Englander. Practical all the way."

"Jackson is practical all the way," Angela pointed out.

"True—but Jackson has also had his own experiences, so if he's not as intuitive, he still knows for a fact that there is more out there. And I'm not trying to *date* Jackson."

"So, in your mind, you're looking at a dead end," Angela said.

"Seriously, where could it go?"

Angela laughed. "You'll never know if you don't look through the forest paths at the end of the road. Whatever. I'll try to stay out of it. So!" she said, her voice denoting that she was changing the subject. "I've been here before, and I've done all the touristy things in the center of town. What could we do that lies beyond?"

"What is now Danvers was once Salem Village," Jenna said. "Rebecca Nurse lived out there—and her homestead is out there and, actually, it all started out there."

"Let's take a ride," Angela suggested. "I'd like to reacquaint myself with all this, get a feel for it. Wasn't Rebecca Nurse supposed to have been a really good person? But was caught up in it really quickly?"

"She was associated with the wrong family, or that's

the way historians see it. Just because the founders were Puritans didn't mean they were saintly or that they lacked human emotions—like envy, greed and so on. It wasn't just that. Remember, these people believed that the devil was very real, and they allowed their fears to take them on a roller-coaster ride."

"And that's what you feel is happening again?"

"In a way—think about it! Your neighbors have been brutally murdered. That's damned scary."

"Driving through Salem, even in the early hours, it didn't appear that people were terribly concerned—they were out in droves already, and half of them dressed up for Halloween!"

"Because they feel safe—Malachi is being held without bond. The devil is locked away."

"But we're looking at modern America. It's not like people stay indoors at every fright, even without all that," Angela pointed out.

"Yes, and it's a city and area like any other—except that it has a tremendous history that we do take with us into modern America. We learned from the Salem Witch Trials. What I'm saying is that there's no way yet to prove that Malachi isn't guilty—the evidence, the solid evidence, points to him," Jenna said. "I'm just saying that because his family was so different, it was very easy for people to accept the fact that he could be an ax murderer. And I also think that we're looking at what is human and what has been human since the people first began walking around. Why do the sane commit murder? Passion, greed, anger, love—avarice and envy."

"And you're sure you don't believe this just because you can't accept that Malachi Smith might be guilty?" Angela asked.

"You need to meet him. Once you meet him, you'll understand. I know that you will."

She hesitated. "Being emotionally sensitive is a gift we share all share, isn't it?"

"Let's hope," Angela said.

They reached the homestead and it was barren and empty, field stretching out in either direction, the house sitting forlorn in the colors of autumn.

"Damn! I forgot, it's only open by appointment except for Saturday and Sunday once it reaches this time of year," Jenna said.

"Let's call for an appointment," Angela suggested.

"They'll probably say no."

"We won't know until we try."

Jenna pulled out her phone and dialed the number on the sign. To her surprise, the friendly woman at the other end of the line agreed to meet them. While they waited, they stood outside the car and looked on at the structure.

"She must have been a truly sympathetic character," Angela commented.

"They deemed her innocent at first, but the girls put on another show, and she was questioned again. She was mostly deaf, and didn't answer the questions quickly enough, or misinterpreted or something, and she was then condemned. I'm still in awe that their faith was so strong that they wouldn't tell a lie to save their lives— those who confessed were saved through prayer, I guess.

They paid the bill for being held—for their room and board, and for their shackles—and those who didn't die in prison were eventually freed. I'd always imagined jail cells or a prison such as we see today, when I was a kid. But they were kept together, and their beds were mats on the floor. A number of the victims died while they were being held."

Looking across the expanse of property that surrounded the homestead, Jenna suddenly frowned. She pointed. "There's someone there."

"Where?"

"By the house!"

"I don't see…" Angela said.

"The person is gone—she walked around the side."

"Why would someone be sneaking around the Rebecca Nurse Homestead?" Angela asked.

"Good question," Jenna murmured.

A car drove up behind them. A woman exited the car and waved to them. "Hi! You're lucky, I happen to be available. I'm Sandy Halloran, nice to meet you."

Jenna and Angela both thanked her profusely for coming out and, before they went farther, made a large donation to the upkeep.

Jenna had been here several times before, but it had been long ago. It never failed to tug at her heartstrings to think of a woman who had lived and worked in the heat and bitter cold of New England, who had endured childbirth many times, only to die at the end of a rope.

Angela was fascinated by the homestead, by the sparse furniture, by the hard life lived by seventeenth-century farmers. She listened gravely while their eager guide described Salem Village at the time, the families that constituted it and how family matters and money played into everything. "A lot of people suggested that mold in the wheat might have caused the girls to have hallucinations," Sandy told them. "I never bought into that theory. Why would only the girls be affected? I think that they started a lie, and perhaps they played it out so well that they believed it themselves. None of us will really know now, will we?"

Angela and Sandy seemed to be having a good conversation so Jenna slipped outside, walked around the house and looked toward the western side of the property, and the graveyard. She remembered that the old section of the graveyard was closest to the old cart road; it was most probable that Rebecca Nurse's family had taken her body and brought it home, secretly, of course. Witches were not to lie among consecrated graves, and any of the victims who received a proper burial received it because the love of a family member was stronger than the fear of repercussion.

Rebecca Nurse, however, most probably would not tarry in the graveyard. She had been a wife and mother.

Jenna turned back to the house and paused. Made of mist now, and yet clearly there before her, stood the spirit of an old woman. Her dress was severe, fastened to her throat, with only a white collar against the dark blue of her bodice. A cap covered her graying hair; she was wrinkled and withered, but she had beautiful blue-gray eyes that carried centuries of wisdom. She made a hand motion and started toward the graveyard, so Jenna followed.

Certainly, there was no telling where Rebecca Nurse was really buried. In later times, the family had erected a stone to her memory. The remains of George Jacobs, Sr., another victim of the trials, had been unearthed on the Jacobs property in the 1950s and laid to rest here with great ceremony during the tercentennial. Jenna wondered if the spirit of Rebecca wanted her to honor him here as well, but she didn't head toward the memorial. She walked instead toward a patch of ground that was devoid of memorial markers, even the fieldstones that denoted the resting places of so many family members.

Fog swelled through the pines that surrounded the graveyard, and for a moment, Jenna felt as if she'd been whisked back in time and that she and the old woman who had met such a cruel demise stood in a place entirely removed from all others.

"What are you trying to tell me?" Jenna whispered.

"Look to the young, and those who would be innocent, for they only learn from the voices around them," the woman said, her voice like the rattling of tree limbs stripped bare of their leaves. "Babes so quickly learn that lies often serve to please, and so they learn to lie. They know not the tragedy of their words. John Proctor whipped his girl, and she had no fits. She found the others, and those who would watch and applaud, and she began again, and yet, I think, I believe, not with malice, yet with fear that what she began to believe was what she must."

"Even now, you forgive," Jenna said. She felt like crying for all those wronged. She didn't believe that she could have ever known such courage. She reached out toward the specter.

But the old woman seemed impatient. "Children! They know not what they say. They know not what they say."

The trees seemed to shake with the sudden burst of an autumn wind. The fog stirred and rolled and seemed to lift, and when it did, the image of the old woman was gone.

Jenna stood alone in the graveyard, wondering if she was indeed sane and gifted, or if she created what she saw in her mind. It was always so real, and then so completely *vanished.*

She realized then that either the spirit of the long-deceased woman—or the spirit she created in her mind—hadn't been talking about the past.

They had yet to interview the boys.

And, she believed, especially after the words of the ghost, the boys were the key.

Angela and Sandy emerged from the house, talking animatedly. Jenna realized that Angela would want to see the graveyard, and she was suddenly eager to leave it herself. She wanted to get to the cliff-side spit of land where kids—old and young—hung out. She told herself that they might not come at all—not David and Joshua, anyway—but she was anxious to try there.

"Sandy is an amazing tour guide," Angela said. "I've so enjoyed discussing the history with her. We're going to tour the graveyard—"

Jenna quickly stepped forward to take Sandy's hand and pump it. "Perhaps another day! Sandy, you were so kind, so wonderful! I know we'll be back. Soon. Angela, I just realized that we might miss that appointment. We've got to go…quickly. Now."

"Appointment?" Angela said. "Oh, yes, of course, how could I forget? Sandy, thank you very much."

"There's really so much more to see here. They built what must be an almost perfect reproduction of the Old Meeting House in Salem Village. This is really where it all began. There are other houses—"

"Thank you! We will see them!" Jenna assured her. Grabbing Angela's hand, she dragged her back across the property to her car.

"All right," Angela said, once they were seated. "What's going on?"

"We have to get to the cliff side by the Lexington House."

"Yes, we were planning that, but school's not even out yet."

"It will be."

"So…"

"I saw Rebecca Nurse."

"I see."

"She was a victim of injustice, Angela. I thought I was just listening to her talk about the past—about the girls. But she was trying to help me now. I think an old man from the era was trying to help me at the graveyard in Salem the other night…someone who saw the injustice, and saw that lies created more lies, and people began to believe them, even those who weren't really involved. Angela, good people were involved all those years ago. This is totally different, we're living in a different world, and yet, it can all play out the same. People believe what seems to be obvious. And kids are all too easily caught up in playacting. And if you do it long enough, in your mind, it becomes the truth!"

It cost more than three hundred dollars to get his car back, and though he'd given himself a few stern lectures on being materialistic, Sam was grateful that his beloved Jaguar hadn't been scratched or dented.

"Nice ride," Jackson commented.

"I do a lot of driving," Sam said. He saw that Jackson was grinning. "Okay, hell, yeah, I like my car!"

He told Jackson about his previous meeting with the elder, Goodman Wilson. Jackson listened and said, "He really called himself *Goodman* Wilson?"

"Yeah."

"Reverting to Pilgrim days, so it seems."

"He's very honest about the fact that they're a fundamentalist church. No singing, drinking, dancing… and certainly no worship of false idols. But I believed him when he said that their teachings were about peace and that they were strictly nonviolent."

"So why did everyone hate Abraham Smith and his family so much?" Jackson asked.

"I think it is human nature to hate what you don't understand. I think that the church tends to be isolated, and that the members keep to themselves. And, probably, what the people knew came from Malachi, who was in the school system. Oh, and Abraham did rail a lot, apparently, about the people who deserved to go to hell—Peter Andres among them. But, since Abraham and Peter are both dead, I don't think that Abraham killed Peter." He hesitated, glancing over at Jackson. "Jenna is convinced that the killer dresses up as the Celtic horned god and goes in while in costume and then kills. Says she's *seen* it in visions."

"What do you think?" Jackson asked him.

Sam shrugged. He had just met the man beside him, but he knew that Jackson Crow had acquired an exceptional reputation with the bureau before joining Adam Harrison's special unit.

"I can't say that she's wrong. I don't know. It would be an easy way to come and go during Halloween—apparently, it's a popular costume—but Peter Andres was murdered six months ago. Back then they had no more reason to go after Malachi Smith than anyone else."

"I thought you said that Abraham Smith hated Peter Andres—wouldn't the police have questioned Abraham?"

"I'm sure they would have gone after him if they could have," Sam said. "Eyewitnesses put him on his own property in Salem while Peter Andres was killed in Andover. Malachi loved to go to the cliff by his house, but he had no corroborating witnesses to vouch he was there when his family was killed. Even if he'd been seen there by any of the other youths in town, I sincerely doubt they would have spoken up for him."

They reached the Old Meeting House in Beverly.

As they exited the car, Jackson said, "Thank God."

"Thank God?"

Jackson looked at him. "That I wasn't born a Puritan!"

Sam smiled as they headed toward the door of the church. As it had been before, it was open. They stepped in, and shadows seemed to surround them.

"Goodman Wilson?" Sam called.

A man rose from the front pew. He turned to them.

"Ah, Mr. Hall. You're back."

"With a friend, Goodman Wilson. This is Jackson Crow," Sam said.

"How do you do, sir?" Jackson said.

Goodman Wilson lowered his head. "Welcome to our church."

"Thank you."

"So," Wilson said to Sam. "You are still going in circles, hoping that eventually you will go around and around so long, you'll stumble upon what you're seeking?"

Sam smiled. "Something like that."

"It sounds like the mysteries of faith, in a way. I wish you God's blessing on your quest. I don't know what I can tell you that I didn't say before."

"Well, different day's job, different memories. I was chatting with Sam here and thought, 'How could he *really* know all his members?' I mean, what about those who have left the church?" Jackson asked.

"Our congregation is small. I know my members. They are peaceful. I don't know that anyone would go after the Smith family." Then Wilson asked in turn, "And if, by some wild chance, someone murdered *for* Abraham Smith, why would they murder him after?"

They were good questions, Sam knew. "All right, but you also said that Malachi was a fine boy with a great faith—he just loved music. But many people think he's a killer. Would it be easier if you just gave us a list of your members?"

Goodman Wilson once again smiled tolerantly. "Now, you know I will do no such thing. Only a subpoena or warrant can compel me to, and even then it would be under immense protest."

"I thought you might want to help us, since it was one of your members and his family last killed," Sam said.

"In any way that I could, morally within my own heart, I would do so. But my members are not compelled to tell their neighbors or coworkers that they are members of this church. Faith is silent. It's in the heart. We are not evangelists. Those who truly seek the Divine Truth will find us."

"You know that I'm Malachi's attorney. Is all of your stalling because he was *not* a member of your church any longer?" Sam asked directly.

"You will have to bring the law against me," Goodman Wilson said. "I'm sorry. Now, I'm sure you will do so, and we will speak again. I am at prayer, so I will bid you good day."

"Thank you," Jackson said.

When they exited the church, Sam said, "The old bastard!"

"He expects you back."

"Yes, but I'll have to get a judge to give me a warrant…and he knows I'll do it, so he's just stalling for time."

"Do you want to take care of that now?"

"I'll call my assistant," Sam said. "I still plan on seeing the councilman and, of course, we have to go have our tarot cards read."

"Ah, yes," Jackson said. "Nothing like a good tarot card reading."

When Jenna parked the car, Angela got out and stared at Lexington House. She shivered.

"Very creepy place. Why would anyone want to buy it?"

"Despite or because of the tremendous history of the area, it's a great commercial venture as far as the tourist industry goes."

"I'd like to get into the house," Angela said. "What did you see in it?"

"Murder—but murder from the 1690s, I'm afraid," Jenna told her. She hesitated. "Sam actually suggested we go back in, too."

"We could sneak in?" Angela suggested.

Jenna shook her head. "No, Sam has a good relationship with the lead detective. John will let us back in, but I want to ask him. We're probably looking at a court date for Malachi, and we don't want to jeopardize the relationship."

"Of course not," Angela said. She shivered again. "The evil in men's hearts can linger, we do know that."

"Yes, but that would make Malachi the one who was exposed to evil and, Angela, I swear that boy is not evil. He's almost holy!"

"Where's the cliff?"

"Right down the street."

They left the sidewalk and hurried across the grassy plateau that led to the dirt-and-pebble path that led up to the cliff. When they reached the top, Angela looked around and studied the trees and the open area, and the rise that led straight to the water. They could hear the crashing of the waves.

Angela walked over to the area where the hard New England granite jutted out over the sea. "Beautiful," she murmured.

"Yes—I think everyone local must come here at some time. It *is* beautiful."

Angela turned to her. "But I don't think we should be standing here."

Jenna laughed. "We should hide in the trees?"

"Not hide, just sit. So that we're not seen immediately, don't scare anyone off."

They walked over to the barren oaks and sat beneath them. It was chilly. The autumn breeze turned to wind on the cliff, and Jenna lifted the cowl of her sweater higher around her neck. "We could sit and freeze here for a while," she said apologetically.

"So we could—we've done worse!"

But they didn't have to wait long. In a few minutes, a group of three youths came walking up the path.

They were big kids—most of them at least six feet. *The school's football team,* Jenna thought.

"Who's got it?" one of them asked. He was a good-looking kid with stylish brown hair and a handsome, angular face.

Jenna frowned, studying him. She'd seen him before. He'd been at the common on the day she had first arrived, when the younger children had gotten in trouble for reciting the rhyme.

"Jonathan, there," said the boy who had followed directly behind the first. Jenna was pretty sure she had seen him as well that day.

"Well, let's light it up!" the first boy said.

Angela cleared her throat and rose, and the three boys started, staring at her. They seemed so surprised to see her that they didn't run.

"Hey," Angela said, striding over to them with a wide smile. "Sorry, guys. Just wanted you to notice us before…well, you know. Before you pulled your cigarettes out."

Jenna rose, as well.

"Uh, hey," the first boy said, looking from one of them to the other.

Jenna stepped forward and offered her hand to the brown-haired youth who had led the trio. "Hi. I'm Jenna Duffy. This is my friend, Angela."

"Jenna was showing me the place. She used to come here when she was young."

The three were on the defensive, and they now looked as if they wanted to bolt, but they weren't going to.

"I know who you are," the brown-haired youth said. "You're Jamie O'Neill's niece, and you're trying to get Malachi off when he's a bloody murderer."

Jenna kept an even smile. "And I know who you are, I believe. You're David Yates."

He stiffened. He looked across at the other boys. "Yeah, I am. *What of it?*"

"I don't want to get anyone off—who's guilty," Jenna

said. "I thought that you could help us understand what happened. We're just trying to understand what has really gone on, that's all."

"Malachi isn't just nuts—he's dangerous!" the second boy said.

"Joshua Abbott, I presume?" Jenna said.

He flushed and looked uncomfortable.

The third boy, Jonathan, backed away from them all. "I'm not even here!" he said. He turned and fled.

"Asswipe!" David Yates called after him, and turned back to Jenna and Angela. He flushed suddenly, maybe due to his choice of language in front of two female strangers.

"Here's the truth—Malachi is dangerous. And there's something really not right about him, I mean, really evil. I think that the ghost of old man Lexington got into him—for real. He gave me the evil eye. I don't care what the fu—what the psychiatrist tried to tell me. I know the evil eye when I see it. He *made* me hurt myself. I'm not kidding you. I'm lucky I didn't run into the little prick up here—he might have made me jump off the cliff."

"Thank God you were just in a lunchroom," Angela said.

"Yes," Jenna agreed. They were a good fifty feet from the cliff now; she intended to make sure that they stayed that way. Though these boys were still kids, they were also almost men.

"But now I've got another question for you. I talked to Mr. Sedge at the grocery store, and he absolutely swears that Malachi was in the store on the day that Earnest Covington was killed. But you and Josh swear that you saw him running out of Mr. Covington's house."

"We did!" Joshua said with conviction.

"You saw him? Malachi Smith. For certain?" Jenna demanded.

Joshua lowered his gaze and his eyes shot downward to the left—and toward David.

"Yeah, yeah, I saw him."

He was lying. She needed to get to him. The boys needed to be interviewed separately, just as Sam had said.

"I saw him. You're damned right, I saw him!" David said angrily.

"You bet, he was there. David saw him. I saw him," Joshua said.

"And what the fu—what the hell? The cops found him covered in his old man's blood," David exclaimed. "Say the bastard is crazy and get him locked up that way, but, lady, do us all a favor and make sure that monster is locked away for good."

"So Mr. Sedge is lying," Angela said. "Why would he lie for Malachi Smith?"

"Who the hell knows? I know my mom says the grocer is a crazy old bastard, too. He might think that Malachi was there, and he probably was—the day before."

"Did she say all that about Mr. Sedge before or after he swore he saw Malachi?" Jenna asked pleasantly.

She saw a touch of color come to David's handsome face. "He's old and senile, that's what he is. He doesn't even remember where he puts stuff or what's on sale," the manchild said. "And my father is councilman here, you know. Best friends with the mayor, and he knows the head of the cops and all that. I can't help it if Mr. Sedge is going into Alzheimer's. I don't know."

"So," Jenna said, "in a court of law, facing charges of perjury and jail sentences if you were lying, you two would both swear that you saw Malachi Smith come running out of Earnest Covington's house?"

There was the briefest hesitation before David said, "We aren't going to court, lady. It's not going to happen. They aren't charging Malachi with that murder—just the murder of his family. They figure that's all cut-and-dried because Malachi was found in the road in all that blood."

"Naked," Joshua added with a snicker.

"Well, they just may charge him with Earnest Covington's murder. I know that the cops are planning to do so. And with the two of you swearing that you saw him, well, they may take a chance and add that to the existing charges. Why not? That would help get him locked away for good, which, of course, is exactly what you both want, right?" Jenna asked.

They looked at her in stony silence.

"Let's get out of here, David," Joshua suggested.

"Yeah. Ladies, it's been great, but we gotta go," David said.

"Hey, no, you two smoke your...cigarettes," Jenna said. "We'll go. Oh, but you should think about this. If the police do charge Malachi with Covington's murder, you will have to go to court. And you'll have to swear an oath that you saw Malachi. And Mr. Sedge will be there, ready to swear that he saw Malachi, too. And that could leave the defense with a chance to prove that since someone else obviously killed Covington, someone else might well have killed the Smith family, and that Malachi is telling the truth. You've already admitted to being near Covington's place…as a *witness,* or so you say."

She smiled. "Nice to meet you. And thank you so much for your help."

Angela smiled as well and walked past the two.

Jenna followed.

She knew that the two boys watched them all the way down the cliff. She also got the distinct impression that they would have liked to push them over it.

11

"You're back. With reinforcements!" Andy Yates said, smiling as he shook Sam's hand and then Jackson's.

"Jackson Crow," Sam said, by way of introduction. He didn't attempt to explain who he was. "We're still beating the same path."

"You do know," Yates told them, "if I had thought of anything, I would have called you. I think that Malachi Smith is guilty as all hell, but if I were to find out something to the contrary, I would consider it my civic and my moral duty to tell you so."

"Thank you, Councilman, I believe that," Sam said easily.

"We just had a few more questions about the property issue," Jackson said.

"Ask away. My life is public record," Yates said. He indicated chairs in front of his desk for the two to take while he walked around to sit behind the desk himself. "I told you, I made a generous offer for the property, and I was refused."

"You aren't a Wiccan, are you, sir?" Jackson asked.

Yates smiled. "Me? No. I'm Anglican. Well, I try to

be. Can't say I make church every Sunday, though we try. My wife, Cindy, she thinks it's good for the kids."

Jackson laughed easily. "Yes, my parents wanted me in church, too. And she's right—growing up with a belief system is good for kids. At least, I think it is. When you hit eighteen to twenty-one, you can decide where you're going in life, but it's good to have a start learning that life does come with a moral code."

"Exactly," Yates said. He frowned. "What would my being a Wiccan or not being a Wiccan have to do with the property?"

"You were going to open a bed-and-breakfast, right?" Sam asked.

"Sure. I thought it would be great. A bed-and-breakfast in a haunted house. You know, when the season is right, people love spooky old places like that with history. Well, old history. I don't know what it would be like now. I mean, before, the murders were all in the distant past." He looked at Sam and shrugged. "Actually, I'm undecided on that thought. It could be worth even more now—people can love the gruesome, you know."

"Do you know the other interested party?" Jackson asked.

"Pardon?" Yates said.

"Samantha Yeager—she wanted to buy the property, too," Sam said.

"Oh, yeah, well, sure. When she moved in, she came to some town hall meetings." He shrugged. "Impressive woman. Have you met her?"

"Not yet," Sam said. "But I plan to."

Andy Yates laughed. "Well, then, I imagine you're going for a tarot card reading. She's awfully busy these days."

"I guess that's what we'll be doing," Sam said, smiling.

"You think that she killed the Smiths? And Earnest Covington and Peter Andres?" Yates said, his smile still animated.

"We don't think anything, really," Sam said. "It's starting to look like I don't really have anywhere to go."

"Why is that? Oh, yeah, *I* think Malachi Smith did it, but we are a somewhat transient community. Some maniac could have come in and hung around and moved on," Yates said.

"There you go—room for doubt," Jackson said, looking at Sam.

"I don't know if that's really room for doubt—Malachi Smith was caught red-handed. Or *red-bodied,* the way I hear it. I'm just surprised that you seem to be giving up so easily, Sam Hall. I mean, you are his *defense attorney,*" Yates pointed out.

"I'm not giving up," Sam said, smiling.

"But we are investigating with research into the method and manner of the killings. These were crimes of passion, the way I see it," Jackson said. "Overkill. Yes, those who are psychotic can practice overkill, but that usually comes with some form of torture. I think these crimes were perpetuated by someone with a real grudge."

Yates groaned. "I see, I see, I see. And I'm supposed to have a grudge because of my son. Well, I don't. David is doing extremely well. His grades are high, and he's being scouted for a football scholarship by a number of major colleges. I don't bear a grudge. Why should I? Malachi was taken out of school. That was that. I knew Peter Andres, of course. He was a substitute. All that poor guy did was try to help Malachi. I knew Earnest Covington. He came to meetings, too. He supported me. I'd have no reason in the world to hurt either of them—much less want to hurt either of them in a 'crime of passion,' as you say. And I suggest that you do meet Samantha Yeager. You'll feel pretty ridiculous if you are thinking that she might have swept into town, killed Peter Andres, and waited around to kill Earnest Covington and then the Smith family. I'm afraid if you're looking for someone with a grudge, you do have nowhere to go. And, sadly—and I mean that—that just leaves Malachi Smith hitting a breaking point and going crazy and on a murder streak. Not sure I blame the kid, but it's a tragedy that Andres and Covington had to die along with the Smith family."

"You feel nothing for them?" Jackson asked quietly.

Yates sighed and leaned across his desk very slowly. "Yes, I feel for them. But they created the monster, didn't they?"

"Bratty little liars!" Angela exclaimed as Jenna revved the motor.

"Well, bratty, yes. Little, no," Jenna said.

"They wouldn't have dared try anything!" Angela said, her eyes flashing. "Or, if they had tried it, they would have been surprised. We've had some pretty good training."

"Yeah, so have they—on the football field!" Jenna said with a laugh.

"You're not armed. And neither am I…but still, we're Federal agents," Angela reminded her.

"I know. I was thinking that last night when the kid came at me in the cemetery. I'm glad I realized he was a little punk. Still, maybe it was a good thing I'm not armed—what if I had panicked and shot the kid?"

"You wouldn't have.…" Angela assured her. "So, where now?"

"I thought I'd park the car and we'd see what was going on in the center of it all."

Angela groaned. "The men are going for tarot card readings. You're not going to make me get one, too, are you?"

"No. I thought we'd see how Will is doing with his street entertainment."

When they drove back to her uncle's house and she parked the car, Jenna noted that Jamie wasn't back yet.

"I wonder where he went. School has been out for a while, and he went in early," Jenna said to Angela.

"Call him."

She was relieved when Jamie answered the phone right away. "You'll not believe this, lass, but I've got myself a new patient!"

"Really?" Jenna asked.

"Um. And his name is Martin Keller."

"The kid from the graveyard last night!"

"The same. Apparently, his mother was deeply concerned about the fact that he came home in his under-wear last night."

Jenna laughed. "Well, have you learned anything?"

"Ah! Patient confidentiality, I'm afraid. Suffice it that I tell you that a kid in his situation would be truly sorry about a little fiasco like you experienced last night. I think the fact that he'd have to see me would definitely make one such child repentant! I'll see you all later then. I've just slipped out between meetings with…a patient…and the talk I must now have with that patient's mother."

"Go, uncle!" Jenna said, and hung up. She repeated the conversation to Angela, who smiled. "Well, it is interesting to listen to the mouths of babes!"

"That's what Rebecca Nurse told me this morning. It's the kids we have to get to—and I'm not going to feel guilty trying to question children, because it's the adults who have gotten to them!" Jenna said.

They walked down to the pedestrian way. Once again, Haunted Happenings was in full swing. Stilt walkers in various costumes were posing for pictures and teasing the young and old alike. A troupe of per-formers was putting on a pirate skit.

Down toward the center they saw Will, resplendent in a sweeping velvet cape and top hat, and with a group of children sitting before him as he made multicolored light leap from a crystal ball and then dart about over their heads.

"He is a master of light and illusion!" Angela said.

"And knowing the difference between the real and the illusion," Jenna added.

When Will saw the two of them watching him, he didn't miss a beat in his trick as he motioned for them to stay. Jenna nodded, and they waited. He completed his act with a final sizzle of light in vibrant colors above the crystal ball, and then he bowed to the applause and promised he'd be back in a minute, when he'd present them with a little bit of the old "Trinidadian" fantasy, magic and illusion.

The crowd before them dispersed. Will swept off his hat and cape and hurried toward the two of them. "Wine bar right there—let's slip in. I could do with a nice Cabernet!"

The establishment was as crowded as the rest of the area, but Will had apparently formed a bond with the young woman at the hostess stand and they were quickly brought to a small, intimate booth in the back. They were served quickly.

"You have news? Or you just wanted a glass of wine?" Jenna teased.

"Two things," Will said. "Not fifteen minutes ago, I saw the head of that church old Abraham Smith attended. Goodman Wilson."

"What? How did you know it was him?" Jenna asked.

"Oh, ye of little faith!" Will said in mock horror. "Jake. You'd asked Jake to delve into things. He pulled up everything you asked for, and then some, gave us all a nice thick dossier."

"So, the churchman was here, in the middle of all this?" Jenna asked, surprised. "No liquor, no dancing, no singing…wouldn't that include no bobbing for apples?"

Will shrugged. "Maybe it doesn't relate to young children. He came and he looked around for a long while. Finally, he approached a group of children who had apparently come down as a school group."

"And?" Angela asked.

"He bent down to talk to one of the little girls."

"What did he say?" Jenna demanded.

"I don't know, I couldn't hear."

"Oh," Jenna said, sitting back in disappointment.

"Ah, but it brings us to the second thing I have to tell you," Will said.

"So tell us!" Angela said.

"Well, one of the mothers recognized Goodman Wilson, too. She came over like a bat out of hell, and grabbed the little girl."

"I guess no one likes an unusual church," Angela said.

"I did hear what the woman said to him," Will said. He lifted a hand before either of them could prod him. "She told him to get away from the children, that he had created Malachi Smith and caused everyone to die, and that his church was pure evil."

"What did he do?" Angela asked.

"He just stood very straight and spoke to her calmly. He said that God loved everyone, and that Jesus taught us all to seek peace and to turn the other cheek. Then he walked away."

"And that was it?" Jenna asked.

"Well, it was it as far as Goodman Wilson was concerned." He smiled, waiting this time for one of them to ask him what else had happened.

"Will, damn it," Jenna said.

"Okay, okay—another mother came running up to the pretty blonde woman. She set a hand on her shoulder and said, 'Cindy! Cindy, please, please, don't let all this upset you so much.' And then the blonde—Cindy *Yates,* I figure, started crying, and she said, 'It's that man. It's that awful man. He was trying to get near the children, and he creates killers. I wouldn't be surprised if the wretched old bastard had *helped* Malachi Smith do all those killings.'"

"We are booked. Well, Madam Sam is booked. She's the best, I'm afraid," the ring-nosed girl at the counter told Sam and Jackson without much conviction.

"Oh, please, see if there isn't something," Sam begged, leaning on the counter and flashing her his best smile.

She smiled uncertainly in return. "Well…I don't think I can get you both in."

"You go. I can try again tomorrow," Jackson said, letting out a feigned sigh of complete disappointment.

"No, I mean, really. I should have her on a break when her current client comes out, but you ask so nicely…I can slip you in," the girl said.

"That is really good of you. Thank you, thank you," Sam said.

She smiled and walked toward the back. Sam followed her.

"Just wait here. When the curtain opens, you can go on in."

Sam waited as told. In a few minutes, a twenty-

something-year-old heavy-metal rocker type man with
jelled black hair, head-to-toe tattoos, earrings, lip ring
and giant lobe rings came out looking as if he had just
reached nirvana.

Sam walked on in.

"Madam Sam" *was* something.

She was sexy.

She *reeked* overt sexuality; in fact, he assumed that
a good portion of her "clientele" had to be pubescent
males. Her breasts nearly heaved out of her peasant
blouse. Her eyes were ringed darker than a raccoon's,
and her boa constrictor seemed pleasantly entrenched
with its head centered in her cleavage.

Sam sat down in front of her. She studied him for a
moment and smiled. It was the kind of smile that made
him imagine she might have a forked tongue of her own.

"I'm Sam, too," he told her.

"Give me your palm," she said.

He did so. She let out a soft sigh.

"What is it? What's wrong?" he asked.

"Well, I see here that your life is…about to change
drastically. You've enjoyed the adoration and admira-
tion of friends and strangers alike…but, ah! There's
just a twist and jiggle in the lifeline. You're about to
do something that will make you the laughingstock of
millions!"

She looked into his eyes. He smiled. "I'm flattered.
You know who I am."

"And you know who I am. Now just ask your questions. I saw your girlfriend yesterday. You're going to

ask the same questions, and I'm going to give you the same answers."

He smiled. He wondered if he would have corrected her about Jenna if he'd been the one to come in the day before. He doubted it. He'd known then what he wanted; he just hadn't known if he'd get it or not. He wasn't at all sure that one night constituted a relationship, but he knew that he was sure praying like hell for a second night like the one before.

"Actually, I'm not going to ask you questions. I just wanted to meet you. I'd been by to see Andy Yates, and he said that I'd be impressed. I am."

"And now *I'm* flattered," she said. "So—you no longer think that I've gone crazy and run amok and gone about town killing people?"

"All I've tried to do from the start is ascertain the truth."

"The truth was handed to you on a silver platter on your drive into town," she said. "Is that why you decided to take on the case? You just like a challenge? Or do you actually feel that sorry for the poor, demented kid?"

"I'm a sucker, I guess, for kids covered in blood."

"Well, I honestly wish you luck."

"Just curious—what do you think will happen now? The kid will probably have to sell the house. Should I see to it that he starts a bidding war between you and Andy Yates?"

Samantha Yeager took no offense at all. She stroked the back of his hand and seemed to stretch like a feral cat. "Oh, you are a naughty boy, thinking that Andy Yates or I might want to capitalize on this!"

"But you will, won't you?"

She shrugged. "Maybe. Frankly, I don't know if I even want the place anymore. It's a long way down the road, the way I see it. I mean, the kid has a fantastic attorney, doesn't he? Maybe you'll still get him off."

Sam stood. "Maybe I will. Who knows? Thanks for your time."

"Oh, well, you'll be paying for it," she said.

He started out the curtain. She called him back.

"Hey, handsome."

He turned.

She smiled and leaned forward, crushing her breasts together and pushing the boa's head from its perch. "If Red gets boring, give me a call."

He came back in and leaned toward her, heedless of the boa. "I'll do that," he said. "But you know what they say about the Irish, and especially those with red hair. Tempers—and other things—run hot. But, hey, thanks for the invite."

He smiled, reached into his pocket and produced one of his cards. He slipped it under the boa and into her cleavage.

"Nice touch," she purred.

"Call me, will you, if you think of anything?"

"I can think of many things."

Sam smiled again, turned and walked out. He paid his bill at the counter, slipping the clerk an extra ten for getting him in.

She rewarded him with a look of absolute adoration.

"Madam Sam" must have been raking it in, while the clerk just got to work.

Jackson was no longer in the store. Sam went out into the street to look for him, and at that moment his phone rang.

"I found a few strays," Jackson's voice told him. "Come on down to the wine bar. Jenna and Angela are here. I'm thinking it's time to compare notes."

"On my way," Sam said, hanging up and heading the few doors down.

Will had gone back to put on another show for the appreciative audience enjoying Haunted Happenings. When Sam arrived, he squeezed in next to Angela.

Jenna couldn't help but rue the fact that she was positioned between Angela and Jackson.

Getting ridiculous! she warned herself.

"How was your reading?" Jackson asked.

"Interesting. I'm going to crash and burn," Sam said cheerfully.

"She knew who you were, right?" Jenna asked.

"Oh, yes. Well, shall we compare notes?"

"Here?" Angela asked.

Sam shrugged. "We're going to be lucky to hear one another over the music."

It was true. The booths were dark and velvet covered, and each was a little intimate enclave unto itself. Jackson had already updated them on what he and Sam had done during the day. Jenna and Angela told them about their day, as well. Jenna chose to omit trying to explain that she'd had an encounter with the spirit of

Rebecca Nurse, and Angela followed her lead. But she was adamant when she said that the boys were lying.

"It seems," Jenna said, "that David Yates is primarily the one saying that he saw Malachi coming out of Earnest Covington's house. I think that Joshua is just saying it because he believes David. If David says it—it must be true. Sam, he did all the evasive things that someone does when they're lying—and then he became belligerent. He more or less threatened us with his father, the mayor...you name it."

"And what did you do?"

"Well, I didn't threaten him back. I did mention perjury, and that it was likely that he would wind up in court, and that an adult would contradict his testimony with passion and credibility."

"Ah, well, then, let's see if that brings about a response of any kind," Sam said.

Jenna lowered her head, trying to repeat everything that Will had told them.

"Now, that's really interesting," Sam said. He looked at Jackson. "What do you think? Could Goodman Wilson be involved?"

Jackson shook his head. "I haven't met the boy yet. But if he's as faithful to his beliefs as you all say, he wouldn't lie, even for the pastor who kicked him out for loving music. And I do find that fascinating. And oddly charming. I don't know. I really think that if Goodman Wilson is involved, it's on his own."

"But not impossible," Sam said.

"Hey, profilers aren't perfect. But if you ask me...I don't see it being Wilson."

"So, why do you think that Cindy Yates is so hateful toward him?" Jenna asked.

"She believes that Malachi Smith wronged her precious baby," Jackson said. "And if Malachi harmed her child, he did it because of the teachings of his father—and his pastor. Actually, we should ask her."

"She's hung up on me," Sam said.

"Maybe there's a way.... Odd. Her husband is so open," Jackson said.

"Oh!" Jenna said, and told Sam and Jackson that her uncle had taken on a new patient—Marty Keller. "Technically, I'm not telling you this. And technically, of course, I don't know myself. After he came home in his underwear, his parents decided that he had to see someone since it was obvious he must be having mental problems."

Sam smiled at her. "Well, that's good. Keeps Jamie in the loop. I haven't heard back yet from John Alden about the tests on the costume."

"Perhaps you could call him," Angela suggested.

"I can...."

"And when you do," Angela asked, "can you ask him if we can get back into Lexington House?"

Sam looked around the table. Jenna saw that Jackson and Angela didn't flinch.

Sam nodded. "Yes, of course. I'll ask him about that, too. He may be tired of me and he may say no. I had the right to get in there, but...I've been in."

"He's an old friend, right?" Angela said. "And I know *you* can get him to let us in."

"We'll get in," Sam said. He sounded weary. "I hope

it can help. So far, Goodman Wilson claims he has a congregation that will give him an alibi for the murders. Jenna talked with Madam Samantha Yeager's clerk, and we know that she was working the night the Smith family was killed. Yates will have a pack of alibis… there has to be something missing."

"The boys," Angela murmured. "I know for sure that they are liars."

"We'll find out where they were," Sam said grimly. "Hey, do they have food in this place?"

"Cheese and crackers," Angela informed him.

He groaned.

"We need to move on," Jackson said.

Will was still in the street. He took a minute to confer with Jackson, but he wanted to stay on a while. He'd head back to Jamie's house when he packed up for the night.

Jenna called her uncle, but he'd already made it back home and was going to go to bed, so she, Sam, Jackson and Angela made their way through the costumed crowd—garish, silly, horrific and beautiful—to an Italian restaurant off Essex.

They hadn't eaten since that morning, and they weren't particularly talkative when the food came. When they had finished and stepped back outside, Sam said, "I guess it's time to call it quits for the night."

Angela yawned. "Especially if we're going to get into the Lexington House in the morning."

With that prompting, Sam excused himself to put through his call to John Alden.

They could all hear John Alden groan at the other

end. Nothing had come back yet from the lab regarding the school's horned god costume; he reproached Sam, reminding him that he would have called right away if it had.

His groan was louder when they asked about Lexington House.

But in the end, John agreed that they could all go in the next morning. Apparently he had a few words for John about making sure the FBI agents knew that they hadn't been *asked* in; Sam assured John that they all knew that very well and appreciated the courtesy extended to them.

"Let's head back," Sam said.

Angela and Jackson strolled ahead. The revelry of the night had not abated, even though schoolchildren were no longer—sanitarily—bobbing for apples.

Jackson stopped walking. "You know, we all just dumped our stuff at your uncle's house. He doesn't mind, does he? I mean, do you have enough room, or should we have found an inn?"

"No, no, there's plenty of room," Jenna said.

"Especially since Jenna can move on over to my house—just a block down," Sam said.

"Oh, no!" Angela protested. "We wouldn't dream of putting you out, Jenna."

"Hey!" Jackson said.

"But, really—" Angela began.

Jackson groaned, pulling her to him. "My darling, use a few of your investigative skills. Jenna wants to stay at Sam's, and Sam very much wants Jenna to stay at his place."

"Oh, of course! I know, of course. I mean, I don't *know*. I mean, oh, Lord! Shutting up now!"

"I think Jenna wants to stay," Sam said, looking down into her eyes.

"Well, it's the only right thing to do, really, isn't it?" she asked.

In another block, they broke apart for Jackson and Angela to head to Jamie's house, and Sam and Jenna to return to his.

When they stepped into his house, she started to say something about Samantha Yeager. He didn't let her.

He pulled her into his arms.

"But—"

"No more case tonight," he said softly.

His mouth found hers and his hand was on her clothing.

She felt his fingers on her bare skin.

And she agreed.

Jenna wasn't usually a dreamer. And of all nights for her to dream, it shouldn't have been that night, while she lay curled against Sam's naked flesh, held in his arms.

But she did dream.

She was standing on the walkway to the Lexington House. The dormered windows stared at her like giant dark eyes. The wind had picked up, and she could feel an icy salt chill to it. As she stood there, despite the wind, a mist of fog seemed to settle and grow darker and darker, silver mist at first, and then gray…and darker gray.

The house itself…could hold evil.

But…

Malachi Smith seemed so filled with light.

Malachi wasn't there. Someone else was. Something that had come, or something that had remained.

She had to go into the house. The answers were there, somewhere, in the house.

She started up the path. A figure began to form in the mist.

It was that of a woman.

The old, worn woman who still had eyes of gentle watery blue.

Rebecca Nurse. Gentle, pious. Good.

Trying to stop her.

The specter of Rebecca Nurse held her hand up. "No," she said. "No—for the lies will rip you apart."

"How will I know the lies, if I don't find the truth?"

"The children…they have fits. They listen to what they hear."

Jenna started to open her mouth to ask the specter more; she wasn't able to do so. The dark eyes of the house suddenly seemed to explode, and liquid spilled from the dormered eyes, and then the eaves, and the door frame.

Liquid rushing out to encompass her.

And the liquid was blood.

12

Sam awoke with a strange sense of comfort, especially considering the fact that he was the kind to wake with every detail of his current case lined up in his mind.

Then, of course, he realized he was draped in silky female flesh, and the thought was enough to achieve instant arousal. But he kept himself still, not wanting to wake her. He watched the sunset color of her hair splay over her shoulder and curl down her back; he felt the fall of her leg over his own and saw that her eyes remained closed, her breathing deep and even. He was tempted to pull her closer, as he had in the night when she'd suddenly wakened and felt like ice.

It was nothing of course; she'd smiled and assured him that she woke easily, especially in old houses where things creaked and moaned and always seemed to go bump in the night.

He'd told her that he knew how to make her forget bumps and creaks in the night, though he wasn't sure at all about moans, which, of course, had made her moan and laugh. But she'd been glad to accept his kiss and roll into his arms and forget whatever had plagued her in the wonder of new love or sexual fascination or whatever she had found in him.

He heard the second hand on the beside clock ticking, and he remained still, and for the life of him, he couldn't remember the last time he'd remained with a woman overnight, or brought her home and thought about breakfast in the morning. His last partner had been in South Beach, a bikini-clad blonde he'd met in one of the hotel clubs that brought the dancing out to the sand on Miami Beach. No thoughts of the future on either side. She was a bonds attorney from Ohio on vacation. And when she had propositioned him, she had assured him, "Half the women and all of the men are here just looking to get laid. Hey, it's like breathing, you know."

Like breathing...

In a way, yes, it was like breathing. But he felt something of awe that Jenna was there now, that the morning light was trickling in, catching the red of her hair and making it seem that a warm and surreal glow emanated from her and encompassed her. And he wondered what it would be like to wake every morning feeling like that, knowing the life and breath and vibrant beauty of such a woman beside him. So, high-powered, cutthroat Boston attorney meets Federal ghost buster/civil-servant, willing to put her life on the line for others, and working hard with a team of ghost busters/civil-servants who seem to have formed a working bond that extended into the kind of friendship that would bring them all to one another's aid, and still have enough left over for those others they ran into along the way.

His mom and dad would have loved that the girl they had known had become the woman now beside him.

Maybe that was something he shouldn't mention. He wouldn't want her thinking he'd brought her home again so that the ghosts of his family might approve!

He winced; he still wasn't sure about *ghosts*. He knew that Jenna and the Krewe of Hunters seemed to have something—an ability to see beyond what was obvious. But he still wondered what tricks the mind could play, and if there wasn't something in the psyche that triggered a memory, or if they had all somehow tapped into that vast percentage of the brain that scientists knew humankind had yet to figure out how to utilize.

She stirred against him. Her eyes opened, as green as an endless field, and when she smiled at him, he forgot all thought. He didn't whisper a word; he kissed her, and he made love to her, and she made love in turn.

Like breathing.

In this case, he thought, *if you didn't breathe, you died.*

Jenna saw John Alden's car as they drove up and parked on the sidewalk outside Lexington House. She looked again at the way the house stood, just up on its little rise, and she thought of the dream that had plagued her in the night.

It was one of the fall days in New England that warned of the approaching winter. The sky was gray and overcast, and even on the rise before the Lexington

House, they could feel the chill breeze that ripped the coastline of Massachusetts.

She thought of how she often shook her head at the Puritans who had come to Massachusetts, seeking religious freedom but refusing to grant it to others. She thought of the people who had allowed the witchcraft scare to take root, and then she reminded herself that it had been a different time—in Europe, thousands upon thousands had been hanged or burned at the stake for doctrinal differences between versions of *one* religion.

She found herself thinking of those Pilgrims who had come and died in the first harsh winter, and that perhaps they'd needed to be stubborn and rigid stock to have ever made their home in the wilds of the new colony, where the wind was as rugged as granite rocks and as brutal as the winter's ice.

Lexington House stood there as it had for centuries, weathered and worn and holding the secrets not so much of humanity and the past, but of the madness that could enter any man's mind when he was brought to it—or when the feral instinct of the animal that remained in man brought about those emotions that were far from fine: fear, greed, envy, hatred and anger.

Sam looked at her, frowning. "You're sure you want to go in again? I can just show the place to Jackson and Angela."

"I have to go in again," she told him.

She smiled. She loved the way he looked at her. The first day, his eyes had been filled with so much mockery. Now they showed concern.

"I want to go in again," she amended.

The door opened as if it were a great, greedy maw, ready to suck them in. John Alden walked out onto the porch.

"Hey, you coming in, or what?" he called out to them.

They crossed the street to the lawn and walked up the steps. Sam made the introductions, and John Alden peered at Angela and Jackson suspiciously.

But Angela turned on the charm, pumping John's hand and telling him how grateful they were to be allowed to assist Sam, and whatever John might have felt about any intrusion, he apparently decided to let go.

"Glad you made it before we brought the cleaning crew in." He winced apologetically. "Even here, even in fall, we've got to get 'em in when there's this much blood, or the pests come on into the house, and the rats multiply and head on out to the whole neighborhood. We've got to move on a real cleanup. We've had the crime lab out. Prosecution has seen the place and defense has seen the place. Anyway, come on in, I can give you about a half an hour. Watch where you step, and what you touch." He looked at Sam.

They stepped into the house, entering the foyer together. Jenna found herself drawn back to the parlor and held back when Jackson and Angela started upstairs with John. Sam stood in the hallway, watching her.

She looked around the room and then closed her eyes for a moment. When she opened them, it seemed that an opaque quality had fallen over everything, as if she floated in a soaring motion back, and looked on from a distance. She was there, and she wasn't there. She was watching from a strange distance that couldn't be tallied by space but by time.

A woman moved about the room. Her hair was brown and graying and tucked back in a severe knot at her nape. She dusted and straightened up. She was doing so when a young man came to the door. He leaned against the door frame, looking in. His face was lean and well shaped; his eyes were dark and should have been appealing, but they had a hollow and bitter look to them.

The woman didn't look up. "Soup in the kitchen, though you're not deserving."

"Mother, I hope not," the young man said. He was in a long, straight coat, vest and suspenders. The woman was in a long, flowered gown with a high neck. "Who the hell is deserving of week-old soup."

"You're a lazy, no-good lie-about," the woman said. "And the soup is fine. Fine for a lad who grew to be worthless."

"Like my sister? My sister, who dresses in twenty-year-old clothing, mends and darns socks and grows old since no man of substance will have her?" he asked softly.

The woman looked at him. "You're a greedy one, as well as a worthless one. Would that I'd never had such ingrates fall from my womb!"

"Would that you never had," he agreed. He straightened where he stood. His hands had been behind his back. He drew them forward, displaying the ax he held and hefted as he spoke. "Would that we'd never lived in this godforsaken house. Would that we'd had actual warmth in winter, that Father had allowed fires to burn, or that his heart had been open to more than a passion for hoarding at the expense of all else. Would that I'd not spent my days in the attic, imagining the insanity of Eli Lexington hacking his family to little bits and pieces."

The woman looked over at him, frowning. "*You're* actually going to cut wood."

"No, Mother," he said softly. "I'm not going to cut wood."

She didn't start to scream until he walked toward her. Then, it was too late. His first strike was high and overhead and filled with passion and rage, and cleaved her skull so that her face seemed to fall apart in a burst of blood.

And then he struck again and again. And when she lay dead, the young man sat down on the sofa, covered in her blood, and he waited. And in time, a tall man in a cap and shabby tweed coat walked in and made it into the parlor, where he saw the woman on the floor and his son drenched in blood.

He started to shout; the young man, who had been all but immobile, leaped to his feet, and this time, the ax hit its target first in the throat, and the only sounds that were heard other than the sickening crunch of the ax were those of a man choking...until those sounds came no more, and the man lay dead on the floor, and the smell of blood was stringent and horrible on the air. The man with the ax just stood there. Then the door burst open and a young woman came rushing in. She might have been pretty, beautiful even. But her face was far too thin; she appeared tired and worn, like a faded rose.

At the doorway, she surveyed the scene in horror.

"I had to, Isabelle. I had to," her brother said.

"And we must move, and quickly now. Your clothes! We have to get rid of your clothing, and we must get away so that we were elsewhere when this thing happened. Come, Nathan, come. Oh, dear brother, what have you done?"

The young man started to laugh.

"Oh, Lexington, he loved his wife,
So much he kept her near,
Close as his sons, dear as his life;
He chopped her up;
He axed them, too,
and then he kept them here.
Duck, duck, wife!
Duck, duck, life!
You're it! Oh, Isabelle! Now, I'm it!"

"Nathan! Come! Now. Touch nothing, we'll go out the back, to the cliff...I'll get you new clothing...we'll sink what you're wearing, Father's fishing weights are in the back...we must move quickly! Oh, dear baby brother, what have you done?"

"They can hang me, Isabelle. They can hang me. Better death than the life we were living!"

"Come!" Isabelle urged, and at last, he seemed able to move.

Jenna stood frozen, the scent of the blood almost overwhelming her. The image of bits and pieces and flecks of flesh all around her was horrifying, and she felt as if her knees were composed of nothing but water.

The mist receded. She felt as if she was whisked back in time, and then thought she was going to fall....

She didn't. Sam was holding her, looking down into her eyes with grave concern.

"I'm getting you out of here. I don't give a damn what you say."

He half lifted her and strode, carrying and dragging her, out to the hallway, the foyer and then outside.

He set her down on the porch, and sat beside her.

"Jenna?"

She took a deep breath. Out here, the blood of the distant past and the more recent past was all washed away by the breeze that came in from the water, cleansing the sins of time.

She was no longer dizzy. She managed a weak smile and set her hand on his.

"I'm okay, Sam."

"I know, I know. It's what you do. Maybe it comes at too high a price."

Her smile steadied; he hadn't even asked her yet what she had seen.

"No, because, as you can see, I'm fine now. I just wish..."

"What?"

"I can't seem to bring my vision to the right century."

"What do you mean?"

"I saw the Braden family. They weren't nice people, Sam. I mean, of course, no one out there *deserves* to be murdered, but I believe that the parents were pretty horrible to their children. The son did do it. And his sister knew, but she was the one who helped him get out of the house and clean up, and she probably swore for him at the trial that he wasn't in the house when it happened."

Before Sam could answer, they heard footsteps on the stair. John Alden came out to the porch and looked curiously at Sam and Jenna. "You done?"

"Yes, thanks, John," Sam said.

"Almost!" Jenna said. She jumped back to her feet.

Sam caught her hand. "Don't do this to yourself," he said softly.

She looked down and saw something dark and disturbed in his eyes. She couldn't allow him to stop her.

"I have to go back in, Sam. I have to try," she said, and walked back into the parlor. She stared about the room. She closed her eyes and thought about the recent past. She tried to imagine the more current murders—and a figure in a costume that resembled that of the horned god coming in to commit murder. She waited and she opened her eyes.

But the mist wouldn't come.

She saw the chalk markings and the blood stains, just like anyone else would.

And she saw no more.

Jackson and Angela came and stood in the hallway for a moment, and then came into the parlor. Angela stood very still while Jackson looked at the chalk marks and the blood spray and moved carefully about the room, as if he tried to imagine exactly how the killings had taken place.

Sam stood in the doorway, his expression stony.

Jackson looked over at him and, behind him, at John

Alden, who stood just a foot or so behind Sam. "Thank you," he said.

"You're ready?" John asked.

"Yes, thank you," Jackson repeated.

They all exited the house. Jenna and her group waited while John locked the house and replaced the crime-scene tape.

When John joined them on the lawn, Sam asked him, "What about the lab report on the costume?"

"Hopefully, I'll get it back today."

"As soon as possible would be great," Sam said.

"Sam, damn it, you know that I can't give it priority. It's a costume you took off a kid, and it may or may not have anything to do with anything."

"I know, John, thanks," Sam said. "Still, sooner would be better."

"Damn it, Sam. I'm doing my best here, huh? And that's good, considering I'm starting to think you're almost as crazy as the kid."

"Ah, but think of it this way. When we get to court, you'll have done your job backward and forward, the prosecution will love you if all this investigation's nothing and just proves the case against him is as airtight as you say," Sam told him.

Muttering, John waved to the others and headed down to his car.

When he was gone, Jackson looked at Jenna. "Well?"

She shook her head. "I can tell you about Eli Lexington and the Braden family, but I've gotten nothing on Abraham Smith. Angela?"

"I saw a little girl, and I believe she died of typhoid

sometime in the eighteenth century," Angela said apologetically.

Sam stared at them both.

"I've got some work to do," he said. "Alibis. We have to start cracking alibis."

"We can give Jake a call, and he can do a lot of computer and phone work, at least with the members of the Old Meeting House."

"Contact him for me, will you, then? I have legal papers…I'll leave you all at Jamie's house. I'll be in contact soon."

He was leaving her though, and just as she felt like someone literally reached into her chest and squeezed her heart.

"Good idea," she said lightly. "We'll get going on a chart, trying to trace the movements of everyone involved."

Sam agreed and drove them to Jamie's house. He seemed to step on the gas when he drove away.

Sam sat at his desk, trying to work. He scribbled out scenarios for the courtroom, assuming he wasn't able to prove that Malachi Smith was covered in blood because he'd loved his parents. He scribbled out a dramatic scene in which they had discovered enough evidence to at least prove that there might have been another killer, and he imagined his voice ringing in the courtroom as he introduced the facts that might save his client. Of course, the prosecution would fight him tooth and nail, and…

He stood, stretching, and he knew that he was here,

alone, because his emotions, so constantly logical and controlled, were in the midst of absolute turmoil.

He'd imagined earlier that he woke up every morning to have silken red hair sweeping over his naked flesh, and the warmth and beauty of an exquisite figure draped around his. Those green eyes of hers would open, and sometimes they'd be lazy, and sometimes frantic, and sometimes he would just leave her sleeping because work was a reality of life, and, of course, they both loved their work....

But it wasn't imagination to relive the way Jenna had looked while "envisioning" the past, be it real, or a product of the recesses of her mind.

He sat at his desk again and buried his head in his hands, tearing his fingers through his hair.

He had to think about the case. The case.

As he sat there, he felt a gentle touch on his head.

He spun around, thinking that, somehow, though he'd locked the door, Jenna had slipped in.

He was alone. Completely alone.

His own imagination was going wild with everything that was happening.

"Hey! Is anyone here?" he demanded.

His voice echoed in the empty house.

He cursed at himself. Crazy. He had to concentrate.

He flipped a page on his notepad.

Samantha Yeager: Clerk swears she was working when Smith family killed.

"Goodman" Wilson: says congregation will attest to his presence. Jake Mallory, agent, doing computer search for members and phone work.

Councilman Andy Yates: appears open and honest, denies nothing. Good suspect, since his son involved in altercation.

The boys, David Yates and Joshua Abbott: Liars. No known alibis for any of the occasions.

He hesitated and pulled out his phone and put a call through to Andy Yates's office. An answering machine informed him that it was Saturday, and that "Councilman Yates is devoting his weekend to his family. We hope you are enjoying yours, as well. Happy Halloween!"

He hung up.

He wanted to know where those boys had been. Maybe not Joshua. According to Jenna and Angela, Joshua seemed the kind of friend who would go along with whatever David Yates said. David Yates—the boy who had been the victim of the "evil eye." A big kid now, a football hero. But did he really have what it would have taken to pull off the murders? Enough sense for a costume, enough rage to plot out a way for Malachi to be blamed? He was only seventeen.

Lots of heinous murders had been committed by seventeen-year-olds; he knew that well enough. Malachi was seventeen. Ah, but Malachi was supposed to be crazy.

His phone rang, and he answered absently. "Hall."

There was a brief hesitation. "Sam, it's John. John Alden."

He looked at his phone, surprised Alden had felt the need to give his last name.

"Yeah, John—did you get the results back?"

Again, there was a brief hesitation. "Yeah," Alden said thickly. "They found trace amounts of blood on that costume you pulled off the kid. Trace. The costume had been washed, and might have been dry-cleaned, as well. We're still working on it, but…I'll call you back in a couple of hours. They're trying to see if it it's a match with the blood from the crime scenes now."

At the house, Jackson put a call through to Jake Mallory, who had remained at their new offices in Virginia. He was glad that Ashley, Jake's fiancée, was up from her family plantation in Louisiana to be there with him, or else he'd have been manning the ship alone, since Whitney Tremont, the last of their sextet, was in Jamaica on her honeymoon.

The Krewe sat together at the dining room, talking on speakerphone.

"You want me to find and talk to all the members of a congregation when we don't have the pastor's agreement to let out a list of the members?" Jake's voice positively boomed through the phone.

"I believe that Sam is getting a warrant for the records, but it's Saturday, and that could take time," Jenna said. "And it's just possible that a judge might block us, too."

"You want me to do this legally, right?" Jake said.

"Not really, but yes—we're talking about a court case here, so everything has to be obtained legally. Not, of course, that I'd ever want you to do anything illegal," Jackson said.

"Right…well, I can pull up public records and newspaper clippings and dig around the best I can. What do you want exactly?"

Jackson explained that they wanted to know exactly where Pastor Goodman Wilson had been at the times of the murders, and anything any of the members might have to say in reference to any of the players involved. "And dig up anything else you can on Councilman Andy Yates, his family and a woman named Samantha Yeager, medium," Jackson added.

"Gee—that's it?" Jake said, laughing. "You got it."

Just as Jake disconnected, they heard commotion at the door and Jenna quickly stood up, heading toward it. Uncle Jamie had just come home.

She looked at him expectantly.

"I can't betray—"

"Jamie, tell us what you can."

"Well, *this* is public knowledge: Martin Keller is at the police station with his parents. They found traces of blood on the costume. Even though they've been highly compromised, the horned god mask itself came through—there was enough in a crease in the mask to make a one-out-of-millions match to Peter Andres. The costume and mask, it seems, *were* worn by the killer when Peter Andres was murdered."

Sam sat across from John Alden. Marty Keller was in another room with his mother, waiting for the police to come question him.

"What I want to know is, what in God's name made you have me research that costume?" John demanded.

Sam arched a brow, thinking quickly. He leaned forward, as if the question were obvious. "John, the kid came at Jenna in the cemetery in that costume."

"Yeah—and he might have just been a bratty kid, out to scare anyone."

"He might have been, but since everyone knows that Jenna is working with me, it seemed completely logical that there was a reason for the kid to try to scare her. It was a hunch, John. You know—hell, you wouldn't be a detective worth your salt at all if you didn't work off a hunch now and then!"

John stared at him. He let out a sigh. "All right, you can't come in, but I'll let you listen in when we question the boy."

Sam stood behind the one-way glass, looking in. Marty Keller's mother had apparently been crying. She still brought a tissue to her eyes now and then. She'd arranged for an attorney, and when Marty started to answer a question, his mother slapped his hand and told him he had to first consult the attorney, a white-haired man who looked deeply concerned.

But the attorney nodded to Marty.

"I swear! I just took that costume after the drama inventory. I swear, Mom, it's the truth. I—I wanted to help out in some way. I know that everybody is all upset 'cause the pretty FBI lady is helping that guy who wants to get Malachi Smith freed, and everybody is afraid of Malachi Smith. I thought if I could just scare her enough, she'd go away!" Marty Keller's voice was tremulous; he'd been crying, too. "And she's a liar—that lady, she's a liar! She said she wouldn't call the cops if I just told her about the costume."

"She didn't call the cops," John Alden told him. "But we found blood on that costume, Marty. The blood of a man who was *your* substitute teacher at times. She didn't call the cops on you—and this isn't a matter of a mere prank any longer."

Tears streamed down the boy's face.

"Stop badgering him!" his mother cried.

John shot her a look. "Who else uses those costumes, Marty? And I'm warning you—I'd better find out that there was an inventory done before you took the costume—and who's to say that you didn't take it before?"

"Detective, you are badgering my client," the attorney said. "And unless you have specific charges—"

"Would you *like* me to charge him right now with the murder of Peter Andres?" John asked.

"Please!" Marty's mother begged. "Please, no—please check out his story." She gasped suddenly. "I can prove that Marty didn't kill Peter Andres. I remember the day. It was that Saturday in April—I saw the news first from the dentist's office. Marty was having a root canal that day. Who knew? Who knew!" she cried with relief. "I was so angry that he hadn't taken better care of his teeth…but it's true! You can call the dentist, Dr. Waverly Johnson—he's in Swampscott. Call his dental assistant! Call them all. Marty is innocent of murder!" Her eyes narrowed. "It was that Malachi Smith!" she said firmly. "You have him in custody. There is no reason for you to badger my boy!"

John Alden looked frustrated. "You sit tight," he said.

He left the interrogation room and walked over to Sam. "Well?"

"Well, I say it's time to find out what's going on at that school. Malachi Smith wasn't going there anymore. He'd have been noticed if he'd tried to get into the school during opening hours, and it's locked up at night now, isn't it?"

"Sam, you're a pain in my ass."

"I know. So, when are you starting at the school?"

John let out a sigh. "I'm going to have a man keep the place under lockdown until Monday. Monday morning, we'll go in before the teachers and the students, talk to the drama coach, the wardrobe mistress, and every kid in the school. You happy?"

"As a lark," Sam assured him.

"Pain in my ass!" John repeated.

Sam started out. "Justice, John, justice. She's a wicked mistress for us all!"

Milton Sedge was in his office when Mabel, his last clerk on duty, knocked on his door. "Milton, it's after seven. I saw to it that Harry restocked the shelves for the morning, and I'm going home, okay?"

Milton looked up. "You bet, Mabel. You go on home."

"Have a nice Sunday, Milton."

"You, too, Mabel." Milton was still a big believer in closing on Sundays. The rest of the world had apparently forgotten that it was a day of rest, but he'd be damned if he would. He worked the place himself, worked it hard. But Sunday was his church day, and he liked church. He had lost his wife, Sheila, some years ago, and Sunday he got to see his grandkids.

"You come on out and lock the door. I got the lights off, but you never know—some wandering visiting Halloween fool might just walk in here anyway."

"You bet, Mabel, I'll be right out."

"Night then."

"Night."

Milton added his last list of figures into his computer and rose. He left his office and headed past the pharmacy area and down the middle aisle, heading straight to the bolt at the front door. There was an alarm there, too, but it hadn't worked in a while. He was pretty sure that just the idea that the alarm was there was enough to ward off most would-be thieves. He never kept money in the place, or not much, anyway. The deposit was made every day at five, precisely.

As he walked toward the door, he paused. He listened, hearing a strange rustling sound from the canned goods aisle.

He walked around, but there was no one there.

Curious, he looked around a bit more and caught sight of something in the middle of one of the big overheard mirrors. What appeared to be a big lump sat on the floor, right around the corner, in the breakfast section.

The lump moved.

Milton groaned.

Well, Mabel had warned him. Or maybe the prankster or wino had been in the store and she hadn't seen him when she'd left.

"Hey, come on—we're closed!" Milton said.

The shadow rose. Milton could see it in the mirror. *Halloween prankster!* he thought with sheer irritation. And on a Saturday night, right when he'd been looking forward to his Sunday!

The person was wearing some ridiculous goat mask. Or a devil mask. Hard to tell which. The thing had creases and lines and horns.

"Buddy, we're closed! Come on, now—don't make me call the cops!"

But the creature whisked around again, heading into the canned goods.

Milton pulled his cell phone from his pocket.

"Last chance. I'm calling the police!"

He started to hear a rumbling just as he reached an aisle where a giant stack of gallon-sized tins of olive oil had been aligned.

He paused, frowning.

Then his heart began to race and his instincts warned him to back up—quickly.

He couldn't move quickly enough.

The first can caught him right in the forehead, and he saw stars. His legs went weak and he fell to his knees.

The next can broke his nose.

And then he wasn't sure what happened. One hit his shoulder, one his head again, and then he was aware of one coming straight for his eyes as he blinked and tried to look up.

He didn't feel anything after that.

He wasn't aware when another twenty cans fell on

top of him, halfway burying him. One burst open, and olive oil spilled over his bruised body.

He was aware when the shadow, the creature, the goat or horned devil, came walking around the aisle.

The creature didn't touch him.

It looked, stepped around him and hurried out of the store. On the street, the horned god swiftly joined a group of costumed revelers and blended into the crowd.

13

"There's a party tonight," Sam said. No *hi, what are you doing, what's going on, good to talk to you, so glad you answered....*

"A party?" Jenna said. "Um, are you inviting us?" she asked.

"Of course. It's important, I think, that we all go. You got a costume? It's a costume party," he explained. "Actually, it's being put on as a charity event by Ivy and Cecilia's coven—the Coven of Light. The ticket sales benefit the children's hospital. It's all for a really good cause."

"And that's why we're going?" Jenna asked.

"It never hurts when you can aid in a good cause," Sam said over the phone.

"When—where?"

"It's in the ballroom of one of the new hotels down by the wharf—not far from the House of the Seven Gables. I'll pick you all up in an hour."

"An hour! But—we *don't* have costumes."

"Just run down to the shops across from the Peabody Essex Museum. There are three or four right there that sell all kinds of things. All right, I'll get you in an hour and a half."

She hung up and walked back to the parlor where Jamie was talking to Angela and Jackson. "We're going to a costume party. We have to get costumes. Quickly."

"Oh, no. I've lived here way too long," Jamie said. "I'm opting out of this. I'll be here. If you need me for anything, just give me a call."

"We really have to get costumes?" Angela asked.

"Yes, and quickly, let's run!"

Most of what they were able to find so close to Halloween and on such quick notice were Wiccan capes and Goth clothing. Jackson went with a simple black mask and black cloak. Angela found a cat costume, and Jenna decided that she'd try a modern Goth outfit with a ribbon corset and long velvet skirt and a shimmering purple hooded cloak. The clerk seemed deliriously pleased that they made their selections and paid so quickly.

They ran back to the house and dressed, Jenna using Jamie's room, since she'd given her own to Angela and Jackson.

Jamie tapped on the door just as she was finishing up. She opened the door and he offered her an affectionate but flattering long whistle.

"Thanks. Maybe I should get a nose ring."

"Ah, nose rings, in my opinion, are dangerous," Jamie said. "You never know when someone might decide to lead you around by one. Seriously, lass, you're looking great! I just wanted to tell you to be careful out there tonight."

"Jamie, I'm always careful. I'll be with Jackson and Angela—and Sam, of course."

"Ah, yes, Sam," he said, studying her with a twinkle in his eye.

"Jamie, I—"

"Lass, you owe me no explanations. You're all grown-up now, you know."

"Yes, I know, but…this is probably just circumstances—we're being thrown together. And I don't think that…I don't think that Sam is capable of really believing in me, or even beginning to understand me."

Jamie laughed. "Ah, well, that's to be seen, isn't it? Sometimes we're far too hard on the ken of those around us."

She laughed. "Well, I'm not sure I understand him, then. How about that?" she asked.

He smiled and took a moment. "Sam Hall is a far better man than I think he ever knew. Maybe he's discovering it now himself. Anyway, he's here."

"Oh!"

She gave her uncle a kiss on the forehead and hurried out. Sam, Jackson and Angela were waiting for her. Sam, like Jackson, had gone for simplicity. He was wearing a black poet's shirt and black jeans beneath a black cape.

He stared at her a moment, then he smiled. "Wow," he murmured.

"Thanks. You're pretty wow, too."

"Jenna," Jackson broke in. "Sam was just telling me that the police verified Marty Keller's alibi for the day that Peter Andres was killed, so even with the trace evidence of Peter Andres's blood on the costume, he's probably clean. But what a good find you made."

Jenna looked at Sam. He was still studying her. "You were right," he said. "About the costume, I mean."

She nodded, not sure of what to say. "So?"

"The school will be under guard until Monday morning," Sam said. "Then, the cops will go in and try to find out more about the costume. Thing is—access. Almost eight hundred kids might have had access. Not to mention teachers and parents."

"We'll have to wait till Monday," she said.

Sam nodded.

"So, we're scoping the local scene?" Jackson said.

"There should be quite an array of characters at the party," Sam said. "Councilman Yates and his wife make appearances. Seniors from the various schools are tacitly admitted. I guess it's kind of a rite of passage. We won't see anyone from the Old Meeting House, but we should see Wiccans, every other belief held in the area, performers—and mediums, such as Madam Samantha Yeager."

"Sounds good," Jackson said. "Let's head out."

The new hotel was modern and beautiful. The entry was grand, and a red velvet runner led to the ballroom. A large sign over the double-door entry read, Blessed Be! Welcome One and All!

Beneath the giant sign was one in smaller print. *Frankenstein's monster and werewolves enter. Princes and princesses. Leprechauns, blobs, vampires, faeries, do come in! No crones, no hags, no warted beings on* broomsticks. *Only beautiful, modern Wiccan dress al-lowed!*

"What if I'd wanted to be Maleficent, from the Disney movie?" Angela whispered.

"You'd be cool," Sam said, grinning. "She was a fairy!"

"Oh! You made it!" came a loud voice.

Jenna didn't realize at first that the wood nymph in the colorful eye mask who hugged her at the door was Cecilia.

"Of course. Thank you so much for having us. Oh, Cecilia, meet my friends, please!" Jenna said, and performed the introductions.

Cecilia laughed. "Hey, Sam gave us a very nice do-nation over the price of the tickets. And it *is* for a good cause. The area covens get together to donate their time, decorating expertise and money to put this on. All the revenue goes to the children's hospital."

"That's wonderful," Jenna assured her.

"Go in! Eat, drink, be merry and dance like a maniac!"

They went in. Jackson and Sam went for drinks with colorful names such as *Wiccan's Brew, Bloody Mary and Lew, Hallowine, All Souls-Tinis* and *Salem-hattans.*

"Look!" Angela said suddenly.

Jenna turned. There, not ten feet away, was a party-goer dressed as the horned god.

She started toward the being, but Angela tugged at her arm. "And over there!"

In the other direction, there was another horned god. This one, however, was busy drinking, and his mask was pushed back. He was a man of about forty, with a friendly smile and a lot of laughter in his crinkled face as he chatted with the pretty belly dancer before him.

"Two more over there," Angela said glumly.

"Wish we could just strip them all and have their costumes tested, too!" Jenna said.

Jackson and Sam returned. Sam handed her a glass. "Wiccan's Brew."

"What's in it?"

"Bourbon, cranberry, Sprite, if I got it right. Liked the color," he said and shrugged. "Should have been called *Witch's Brew*. You know, don't you, that they would have hanged you? Witchcraft, magic, *were* illegal. I'm not sure how I would have defended you. *If* they had allowed for the accused to hire defense, of course."

"I have never danced with the devil," she told him.

He smiled. She waited. "I just needed some time," he said.

She nodded.

"And what did time do for you?"

"It made me know for certain that I didn't want to sleep alone tonight."

Jenna lowered her head, trying not to laugh. "I have a feeling there are dozens of women in this room who would keep you from that fate," she told him. "Including the snake charmer over here. Madam Samantha Yeager is here. With her boa constrictor."

"I draw the line at snakes in bed."

"I'll bet she'd give it up for you."

"I just don't think that you'd want to let her in," he teased.

"And would you?"

"Nope, nope, don't think so. Not in this lifetime, that's for sure."

"Ah, so do we have more lifetimes?"

He grew serious. "I believe that we do have something. The soul. Heart and soul. Whatever makes us unique. Whatever that is about me—nope, nope, still no. Just not my type. I love redheads. Especially when they have just a trace of an old accent."

Jenna started to speak, but the band abruptly stopped playing and the microphone gave out a sudden loud shriek. "Ouch!" the speaker said.

He was dressed as a Native American, and looked good in the outfit. It was Councilman Yates.

"Welcome, one and all. The good sisters and brothers of the Coven of Light have allowed me to address you all. First, welcome, and thank you all for coming out for this wonderful ball, and for supporting our children in their need!"

His words were met by applause and shouts of approval.

"Secondly, we know that the area has been deeply concerned by some horrible things happening, and despite the fact that they have a suspect in custody, an investigation is still ongoing. I want to warn you all to be smart and practical—well, I mean as far as your personal safety goes! With the cops—be open and honest. Give them everything that they need. We've come a long, long way! We don't give in to superstition, and we don't condemn a man until he's been proven guilty beyond a shadow of a doubt. That said, I know you're all still going to whisper about recent developments, but while you're doing that, be helpful and be careful. And that's all I have to say, except, Blessed Be!"

The audience responded with applause and the band started up. Dancers drifted to the floor again. Jenna took a long swallow of her drink, which wasn't half-bad.

"So, they're all whispering. We'll hear what they have to say," Sam said, nodding to Jackson. The two, apparently, had found an instant and easy rapport.

"I'll drift toward horned god number one," Angela said.

"Think we'll make it to all twenty of them?" Jackson asked.

Jenna adjusted the lace and black velvet eye mask she was wearing and drifted casually toward the stage. She'd noted that Councilman Yates had come down from the stage and was speaking to an outstandingly beautiful peacock.

He kissed her, and by moving a shade to her left, Jenna could see the peacock's face. As she had expected, it was Councilman Yates's wife, Cindy, the same woman she had seen on the playground the first day she had arrived chastising the children.

The same woman who seemed to hate Pastor Goodman Wilson so much. The mother of David Yates.

She decided to move closer.

"Why were you so late?" she heard Yates ask his wife.

"Me? Where were you when I was trying to get *our* daughter settled with the babysitter?"

"Cindy, you know I have responsibilities."

"To everyone but your family!" Cindy replied.

She must have noticed Jenna near them because she looked right at her, frowned and turned away. Yates watched her go, letting out a weary sigh.

Jenna started to move on.

The microphone screeched again. The band stopped playing, the lights blinked and a spotlight shone on the dance floor.

Couples cleared off.

And a scantily clad snake charmer appeared.

Samantha Yeager.

She was stunning with her long black hair, ribbed abs, and jeweled harem costume. She wore a gold snake crown around her forehead and held her boa high and undulated like the snake as she moved through the crowd. She swayed and sashayed with lithe talent, and a hush fell over the crowd.

She went from man to man, but she'd also draw women out onto the floor and try to entice them to dance with her.

At the end, she found Sam. She reached out with a free hand, touched his face and drew her hand down the length of his body before doing a sleek fall to the ground.

"Madam Samantha! See her for all your *mystic needs!*" the lead singer from the band cried out.

"It wasn't my idea!"

Jenna turned to see that Ivy, lips pursed, was at her side. She looked at Jenna and grimaced. "She paid a lot for that performance."

"Well, she's getting a lot of applause. It will prove to be the ball of the season, I'm sure."

"Slutty twit!" Ivy said, and, shaking her head, walked back toward the door, ready to welcome any latecomers.

Jenna was ready for another Wiccan's Brew. As she headed over to one of the bars, Madam Samantha—in all her half-naked glory—cut in front of her. "Ah! Jenna Duffy. It's not a party until the cops…er, Feds show up."

"Incredible performance," Jenna said. "Where's your snake?"

"Oh, back in the cage…this is a lot of stimulation for a snake, you know."

"I'm sure your snake is used to stimulation."

"Food, sex, good wine…slinky pets!" Samantha said to her. "Oh, you're not angry, are you? Your man is a stud, you know."

"Why would I be angry?"

Samantha laughed. "Oh, honey! You can't be that naive. Maybe he's got the hots for you, but I'm sure I got a nice rise out him."

Jenna was glad that the way the woman said the words actually and naturally made her laugh. She probably couldn't have said or done anything more insulting, and she knew it because Samantha's face turned a mottled shade or red.

"Sure," Jenna said. "Excuse me, I was heading for the drink line. Can I get you anything?"

"Yeah. Yeah. You can get out of town. All you're doing is hurting a lot of good people!"

"Noted. Now may I pass?"

"You going to *make* me move?" Samantha asked.

Jenna sighed. "I am a Fed, Miss Yeager. Lots of training under my belt," she said softly.

Samantha moved. But as Jenna walked by, she warned, "You should get out of the *state*. You need to be careful. Whatever training you might have had, you're not infallible. You could get hurt. I saw your cards, Agent Duffy. Actually, you could get *dead*."

"Are you threatening me?" Jenna turned and asked.

"I would never! I'm telling you what I saw in your cards!"

Jenna continued toward the drink line. She was stunned when her way was blocked again.

Not by Samantha.

By a peacock.

Cindy Yates stared at her with teary eyes behind her jeweled mask. She seemed to be trembling with rage.

"How dare you? How *dare* you!" she demanded. "How dare you accost my son!"

"Mrs. Yates, I was at the cliff, showing the area to a friend of mine. Your son came to the cliff when I was already there."

Cindy Yates continued to stare at her, shaking and looking more like a rooster at the moment.

"That boy *is* the devil. That boy could kill us all. You stop trying to hurt our children. You stop what you're doing—you—you—"

Jenna waited, certain she was going to hear another threat.

"You—you're the cruelest, meanest person in the world!" Cindy said.

Then she didn't threaten. She hauled back and slapped Jenna across the face with a startling strength.

Jenna was instantly aware of movement in the crowd. She knew that her group had rallied around her. She felt Sam at her back, as protective as a giant alpha wolf.

She lifted a hand quickly. "I'm so sorry, Mrs. Yates," she said softly, and she stepped around the woman. Whoever had witnessed the exchange began to huddle together and whisper, but Jenna knew that she had avoided a real scene—or a brawl!

Sam caught her arm. She saw the gray of his eyes beneath his mask. "Are you all right?" he asked anxiously.

"My cheek is stinging, but another Wiccan's Brew will fix that," she assured him.

He slipped his arm through hers and led her to the drink line. "Well, we did want to get the lay of the land."

Angela and Jackson were behind them in the line, as if they'd tacitly decided there would be no more divide and conquer; they would close ranks.

"So, Wiccan's Brews, four, please," Sam told the bartender. She looked at Jenna a moment, and then smiled.

"Welcome to Salem," the bartender said. "Glad to have you here—all of you. Welcome. I mean, come on! We are the original Patriots, too!"

They thanked her and took their drinks. Ivy and Cecilia went up to the microphone the next time the music stopped. They thanked everyone and offered a special surprise performance.

Jenna was startled to see Will, elegantly attired, take

the stage. She glanced at Sam, and she realized that he had planned the performance.

"Sneaky like the wolf!" she whispered to him.

"Hey, thought he should garner a nice audience this way."

Will went through the beginning of his performance with lights and prisms, and then, to her surprise, a light went through the audience and settled on her. "Ah, we have an ancient Celtic queen to join us! Miss, if you'd come to the stage...?"

She wasn't sure what he was up to, but Sam quickly escorted her to the stage. She'd halfway expected the crowd to boo, but apparently everyone didn't hate them; she received the appropriate applause as Will welcomed her as his assistant.

"All are welcome here, but we are here due to the benevolence of the Coven of Light. So, we have our Celtic queen of old here, and she'll crown the two who have brought about this wonderful, giving occasion. Because we know, in modern Salem, that Wiccans believe that all souls have the right to do as they will, as long as they harm no others. No two show greater kindness of spirit than our true queens from A Little Bit of Magic—Ivy and Cecilia!"

Will handed her two beautifully wrought gold crowns surrounded with ivy leaves and flowers. He cast his hand out, and rays of light fell over the two women. Blushing, they headed for the stage. They had obviously not known about this part of the entertainment.

"This is really great of you, Will," Jenna whispered. "But what are you doing? What am I doing?"

"Trust me!" Will said briefly.

Ivy and Cecilia were escorted to the stage, where they stammered and flushed some more and thanked everyone who had helped them.

"And now, they shall be crowned true queens of the ball!" Will announced. "But! Every queen must have a king, and it's our beautiful Celtic goddess of old who will help find the proper kings for our queens! Goddess!" he said, looking at Jenna.

She arched a brow.

"Just turn around and lift your hands!" Will whispered.

When she followed his instructions, rays of light started shooting through the audience and landing upon the men in the crowd. Somehow, Will managed to find all those wearing the horned god costumes; there were a few vampires and werewolves thrown in, apparently for good measure.

The audience was laughing and applauding.

The costumed guests could do little but oblige, coming to the stage. Will was determined that each man would unmask, and she would choose the appropriate kings through their answers.

The first two horned gods were from out of town; the second two were women, giggling schoolteachers from Idaho. Will said that they had every right to be kings, but if they were kings, they'd still be called queens. The crowd laughed some more.

A vampire and a werewolf followed. The vampire, too, was a woman.

Three more horned gods came up. One was from

Boston, one from Ipswich, and one was down from Gloucester.

They went through more and more horned gods.

Jenna didn't recognize any of them or their names.

Until the end.

The last horned god had tried to slip away, but the good-natured crowd pushed him forward.

He was unmasked.

This horned god she knew.

It was Joshua Abbott, best friend of David Yates. Jenna decided that she definitely had to name him as one of the kings. The other honor went to Jason Middleton from Gloucester, since she'd suspected that Ivy had been flirting with him earlier.

There was laughter and applause. And finally, Jenna was released from the stage. Sam was there, watching over her, arms across his chest as he surveyed everyone around her.

He stepped forward as an Indian—Councilman Yates—approached her. She could see that Sam was going to bar his way.

He did. Andy Yates stopped and stared at him.

"My God, I just heard what my wife did. I am so, so sorry."

"It's all right, she's upset," Jenna said.

Yates looked at Sam, shaking his head. "She—she's so fragile. Honestly, I'm so sorry. She went home, you won't be bothered again."

"Councilman, it's all right," Sam said. "We understand."

Yates shook his head. "I meant what I said. People

should help you. But, you know, of course, everyone heard that there was blood found on a costume that boy had worn to try to scare you all away. It's reopened the whole thing for everyone." He paused. "Look, we're good people, we really are. Ordinary people—maybe better than others, because we do have a history of what lies and hatred can do. But be careful. Please, be careful!"

Jenna nodded. "Thank you."

He nodded to Sam. "Really. I'm so sorry your evening was spoiled."

"It's not spoiled. We were about to dance," Sam said.

"Yes, yes, of course," Andy Yates said, hurrying on.

"Were we really about to dance?" Jenna asked Sam.

"Hell, yes. It's a slow number. I'm kind of a tall guy, and I look ridiculous when I try to gyrate—trust me. It's an ugly picture."

She was happy to go out on the dance floor with him, and shocked to hear the number end with an announcement that it was after two in the morning, time for all kings, queens, princes, princesses and frogs to head on out. They ended with the song "Closing Time," and everyone started heading out.

As they drove from the hotel, Jackson said, "A very interesting evening. Of course, Jenna, you did have to get slapped, but now we've seen that Cindy Yates really is pretty much a basket case."

"I heard her talking earlier—I don't think she believes her husband did enough when David received the so-called evil eye," Jenna said.

"The question is—could her disappointment in him

for his failure to defend his son have caused him to commit murder, to prove he's a good enough father?" Angela said.

"I've got to admit—I'm frustrated that it's another day until we get into the school," Sam said. "I think it's really interesting that Joshua Abbott decided to come tonight as the horned god."

"A show of defiance or of strength?" Jackson asked.

"Oh, the little weasel wouldn't have taken off his mask if Will hadn't forced the issue!" Jenna said.

"But Will did indeed force it," Sam said, smiling. "Good man!"

"My team is the best," Jackson said gruffly.

Sam stopped at Jamie's house. Jenna felt Sam's hand on her arm. "Come back with me. Please."

"Reconvene in the morning? Around ten?" he asked the others.

They agreed and said good-night.

Jenna and Sam drove in silence the rest of the way to his house. Inside, Jenna doffed her cape and let out an oath of exasperation. "Corsets! The hardest damned thing in the world to get off."

"Ah, yes, but I'm happy to be of assistance." He came to her, met her eyes and spun her around to work at the ribbons that tied the corset. "Have to say, good outfit."

"Glad you liked it."

"It was the best in the room."

"Aw. You're just saying that."

"Nope."

The corset fell to the floor and she turned in his

arms, reached up, lifted his mask and tossed it down, as well. He let the cloak fall.

"I must say, we are messy."

"Hey! We pick up in the morning."

The back of his fingers brushed over her collarbone and her breasts, and he said, "Now, it's really becoming the best outfit."

"Ah? Better than the bits of fabric covering Madam Samantha Yeager?"

"Did she bother you?" Sam asked, grinning.

"No, it might have been the other way around."

"Oh?"

"I think she was really angry. I insulted her."

"How?"

"She said that even if you were with me, you were a man, and when she slinked against you, she was sure you got an erection."

He laughed. "Oh?"

Jenna shrugged.

He grinned, sweeping her off the ground and heading into the bedroom. He plopped her down on the bed and lay beside her.

He played with the catch on her velvet skirt. "Actually," he said, his smile deepening, "I think that woman could shrivel the old horned god himself."

"Mmm," she murmured, tugging at his jeans.

He eased them off, lay half on top of Jenna and repeated, "Mmm. And that's a fact. Know what does give me an erection?" he asked.

"What?" she whispered.

"The sound of your voice."

"I think I can handle that."

"Good," he said softly, touching her cheek.

"No. I mean, I think that I can physically handle that," she told him. She reached out for him, touching far more than his cheek.

He moaned, pulling her to him. They kissed, and she moved down on him, and they made love until light began to break, just drifting through the windows in whispers of luminescence.

When Jenna slept, she slept deeply, basking in the comfort of the heat that emanated from his body. She didn't dream.

They woke up to the loud sound of his bedside phone ringing.

The sound was strident, as if the plastic piece of equipment knew it was about to report something shattering.

Sam rolled over and answered.

Jenna watched the grim expression that tightened his jaw.

"I'll be down there. Thanks," he said tersely.

"What?" Jenna whispered.

"I have a dead witness," he told her.

14

A crowd had gathered around Sedge's grocery store.

Police tape, of course, prevented onlookers from coming too close. An emergency vehicle stood near the front door, helping the police create a shield to stop the curious from looking in.

John Alden, after conferring with one of the medical examiners, looked up to see that Sam was there with Jenna at his side.

He walked over to them and lifted the tape.

"It's not what you think—you can see for yourself. And this is a courtesy, just so that you don't get conspiracy theories running around in your mind," John asked.

"How do you know what I'm thinking?" Sam asked in reply.

"You're thinking the old guy was murdered, that he was being shut up just in case the D.A.'s office decided to charge Malachi with the Earnest Covington murder. But Milton Sedge wasn't murdered," John said.

"Okay. Then how did he die? Heart attack? What happened?" Sam asked. It was just too damned convenient that Sedge—the one voice to stand against the boys who claimed to have seen what they hadn't—was dead.

"Damnedest thing—well, he was an old coot, you know. And I couldn't believe it myself at first, but he was done in by olive oil."

If John Alden weren't so grimly serious, Sam would have been tempted to laugh. As it was, he couldn't speak for a moment.

"Excuse me?" Jenna finally said.

"Bad shelving, and being in the wrong place at the wrong time," John explained. "He was having a special on those gallon tins of olive oil. Extra-extra-virgin olive oil. We have a large Italian community up here, you know.... Sometime this week, they'd done up a display with tin on top of tin. He must have jounced against the stack, and the tins and the shelf and everything came down. I just talked to the medical examiner—he received a lot of good head wounds, but it is possible that his old ticker stopped when all those gallons upon gallons crashed down on him. They're heavy as hell, especially for an oldtimer like Sedge—test them yourselves one of these days."

"I've held a gallon of olive oil, John," Sam said.

"Well, then you imagine dozens of those suckers coming down on you," John said.

Sam glanced to the side. A group of Sedge's employees had gathered there. They were sobbing softly, from some of his cashiers—nearing retirement themselves— to his younger stock and bag boys and girls.

He walked over to the crowd. "I'm so sorry," he said.

One woman let out a loud wail and fell into his arms. She took him by surprise, but he put his arms around her to pat her gently on the back. "So sorry," he said again. "There, there," he said ineffectually, but it seemed to help.

The woman tried to compose herself. "It was all my fault!" she wailed.

"Mabel!" another of the elderly cashiers protested. "Honey, it was not your fault. Mr. Sedge wanted that display, and he told everyone exactly how he wanted it set up."

"No, no…" Mabel moaned. "I left. I left. I walked to the back and said that it was all closed up and I was leaving. And I told him to come lock the door. I should have waited. We should have left together!"

Sam kept trying to console the woman, but he felt a new spark of anger and suspicion. He held Mabel at arm's length. "Mabel, you're saying that you left him alone in the store, with the door open?"

"Oh!" She started to sob again.

"No, no, Mabel, this wasn't your fault!" he said quickly and lifted her chin. "Was the store empty when you left?"

She frowned, looking at him. "Well, yes. I mean, well, yes, I think so. I did the call over the announcement system. I asked everyone to check out, and announced that we were closing. I turned off the lights—except, of course, we have the safety lights. And the lights were still on back in the office, but it gets kind of dark in here—shadowy, at least. Oh, that's it! He didn't see that he was going to run into the display. Oh! Oh, no, it could have been a child. But the shelving was behind the tins…" She broke down in tears again.

"There, there," Sam said.

Jenna had come to stand quietly beside him. He looked at her helplessly.

She slipped in, putting her arms around the woman. "Mabel, none of this is your fault, and you get that out of your head."

"He missed his wife, honey," another woman said hopefully. "At least he's with her now."

"Yes, that's true, that's true.…" Mabel agreed, but then she sobbed again. "But he loved his kids and his grandkids!"

"But he's with his wife, and he probably missed her terribly," Jenna said.

Jenna managed to get Mabel into the arms of another of the women.

She grabbed Sam's sleeve. "I want to see the body," she told him.

He frowned, staring at her.

"Sam, I'm an R.N. Not a pathologist or anything, but I've been around an emergency room a time or two. I want to take a look at the body." She looked up at him with her green eyes earnest and clear.

He nodded, caught her hand and made his way to John Alden.

"You really want to allay my suspicions—and those of anyone else, should questions arise, which you know they will," Sam said. He added, "Please."

John started to let out a sigh of exasperation, but then he looked at Jenna, and he seemed to hesitate, perhaps remembering the fact that she'd brought in the horned god costume that yielded results.

He groaned. "What? What? What now?"

"I'd like to see him, please," she said.

John scowled. "The medical examiner has cleared us to have the body taken to the morgue."

"I'll only need a minute or two," Jenna said.

"What now, what now?" John demanded.

"What now—you're a good cop. And, of course, that doesn't mean that you have to agree to do any favors for me. But, come on, John. You don't want me having to question you later, or say that you were willing to accept the obvious with no question."

"Pain, *royal pain,* in my ass," John told him.

"But I'm right sometimes," Sam said.

"You got two minutes. And be careful—hell, I don't want either of you dead or crippled by olive oil."

Then John called to the officers who were holding the line at the door. "Let them in!"

Inside, techs were still marking off positions. It was obvious, though, that the rush had been to attempt to save a man's life, not preserve the scene. Towels had hastily been spread on the floor to keep emergency help from sliding into mayhem themselves, and the offending cans had been tossed everywhere.

But a path had been cleared to the body, and Sam watched as Jenna carefully made her way to Sedge's bloodied and crumpled form.

"Excuse me?" the medical examiner, who had been writing on a chart, asked with a frown.

"Alden's permission, Doctor," Sam said. The M.E. lifted an eyebrow, but he didn't protest.

"We'll be taking him out in just a minute," the doctor said.

"There will be an autopsy," Sam said.

"Of course. Accidental death," the M.E. assured him. "And that didn't take a medical opinion. Just look at what happened here. Of course, that's not official. As you said, certainly, there will be an autopsy."

Jenna didn't touch the dead man. She went down on her knees, heedless of the conditions around her, and studied the injuries. As she looked down, she felt a strange ripple down her spine. She looked up.

And the dead man was there, looking down at her and at his broken body, incredible sadness in his eyes. He looked from his mangled form to her eyes, and he formed a single word with his ghostly lips.

"Murder!"

Jenna looked back to the corpse. Then, true to her word, she was up in a minute. She smiled her thanks to the M.E. and the techs that had paused to watch her.

"R.N.," she said weakly.

"Honey, he's way past that!" one of the techs said.

"Yes, I can see that," Jenna assured the woman.

She walked to Sam, nodding, and they headed back out.

John Alden was right in front, still trying to soothe the crowd while writing in his notebook.

"See—death by olive oil," he said, and there was no humor in his voice.

"Yes, definitely, the tins killed him," Jenna said.

"There was no sign of a heart attack, although, of course, I'm not an M.E."

"No, you're not," John said firmly. "But why do you say that?"

She arched her eyebrows, playing for time as she sorted out what she had seen in her mind. She wasn't going to tell John Alden that the dead man's corpse had been standing over his earthly remains.

"Well, on the one hand, there were deep contusions and lacerations on his head. It would be like being beaten to death," she said. "And, in my mind, his coloring—I'd expect different coloring from a heart attack. What time are they estimating time of death? I'm going to say early last evening."

John stared at her, perplexed.

"Well?" Sam asked.

"Yeah, on cursory inspection, that's what the M.E. believes. He must have had the accident when he was closing up," John said.

"Who found him?" Sam asked. "The store is closed on Sundays."

"His son came when his dad wasn't at church. We've sent him on home. He has to tell his wife and kids. And…it wasn't good for him to be hanging around here," John said, sympathy in his voice. "Now, I called you. I let you see the situation—and the body. Can I get back to work?"

"Yes. Thanks, John," Sam said, pausing before adding, "Oh, and, hey, by the way, if it's an accidental death, why are you here? I thought you only worked homicide."

Alden hesitated, looking at him. He sighed. "With the mess going on in Salem, naturally I'm going to be called to the site of any accidental death. And Sedge's son called it in as a homicide. Since he might have been called as a witness in the one of the current murder cases, I decided I was going to stick with it and investigate it thoroughly. Happy?"

"You bet I am," Sam said. "Thanks."

"Thanks," Jenna added as Sam set his hand on her back, leading her from the crowd. Local stations were setting up cameras. Sam saw that a cable channel was already live and he knew from experience each one of them was hoping for a sensational scene. If it bleeds, it leads. But if it wasn't sensational, it wasn't national.

Jamie, Jackson and Angela were once again around the kitchen table at Jamie's house; they'd been watching the news. Jenna told them what had happened at the store.

She was surprised when Sam's fist hit the table. He didn't seem to give in to frustration frequently. "He was murdered. *Death* by olive oil. Like hell—it was *murder* by olive oil. Someone was in that store, and someone beat him to death with those cans."

"Coincidence?" Jamie asked.

"I don't believe in coincidence. Especially not when it's this convenient," Sam said.

"I don't believe in coincidence, either," Jackson agreed and began firing off questions that Sam answered wearily. No, the door hadn't been locked. One of his longtime clerks had been the last to see him. No,

Jenna was damned sure that he hadn't died of a heart attack when the tins had started to fall. He'd been discovered by his son, who had called it in as a homicide.

Jackson's phone rang as they were sitting there. Seeing it was Jake, he put the phone on speaker.

"Interesting news that might not have been easy to find, *unless, of course,* you thought to look in all the right places," Jake told them.

"Quit gloating and tell us what you've got," Jenna said.

"First, I found—public record, Jackson—articles for the Old Meeting House when it was founded, and when it was designated a house of worship. They requested more tax exemptions and conscientious objector status for some members, and a petition that was signed by most of the membership. Now, who *didn't* sign, that I don't know. That was something I had to dig for, so I'm thinking most of them signed it, assuming it was a private petition. I've emailed the list to all of you—including you, Sam. Your contact info was easy enough to find."

"Thanks," Sam said glumly.

"No problem," Jake said cheerfully. "And here, children, is something that you should know."

"Spit it out, Jake!" Jenna warned.

"Be nice, Miss Duffy! All right, your two prospective buyers are in business together."

"What?" Sam said, staring at Jenna with disbelief.

"Oh, yeah. There's a lot of 'doing business as' going on in both of their lives, but Andy Yates and Samantha Yeager are in business together. One of his company's companies is called Magic Madam. In any other state, it might have been a cleaning service—I think Magic Madam and Her Gals *is* the name of a cleaning corporation somewhere in Georgia. Sorry, never mind. Anyway, seems like the money to start up came from Yates. He's the investor and she's the workforce."

"Well, Andy Yates did say that he knew her and that she was an impressive woman," Sam said drily.

"Well, she is impressive—I'm just not sure what her impression is!" Angela said.

"Ah, think about it," Sam said. "With the right guy… you never know."

Jackson glanced at him. "You mean someone with a repressed home life and a wife who's kind of a delicate flower but longs to be supermom and probably has no time for her husband?"

"Yep. Exactly what I was thinking," Sam said.

"Jake, you're brilliant!" Jenna said.

"I'm even more brilliant. I looked up the school's football team. And I can tell you this. On the afternoon that Peter Andres was killed, Councilman Yates and his son were at one of the school's major football matches—in Revere. There's a newspaper picture of the councilman with his arm around his son after the school won against Lynn, Mass. I tried all the timing—the kid was in the game all day, and the whole team, along with Dad, celebrated at a restaurant in Peabody that evening. That accounts for daddy Yates, baby boy Yates and even Joshua Abbott for at least ten hours, and, according to the medical report, Peter Andres was killed between two in the afternoon and six in the evening."

Jenna looked at Sam, who appeared frustrated. "Thanks, Jake, you're still brilliant, you know, despite that."

"Well, thank you there, Miss Duffy. I'm still on the list of members belonging to the Old Meeting House."

"Jake," Sam said, "what I'd like you to find out is if you can cross-reference members with people who have children in the school. We'll be heading there tomorrow when the police go in to question the kids and drama department."

"I'll be on it. Should have more answers for you later in the day."

When they hung up, Sam glanced around. "I wish he was my researcher."

Jenna smiled. "Jake's the best," she said. Her mind, however, was reeling with what the researcher had told them. She didn't want to share her suspicion yet, not until she had done a little sleuthing on her own. With Sam, despite the fact that he seemed to have accepted her and the others, she wanted facts. "So, Sam Hall, Esquire, where do we go from here?"

Sam drummed his fingers on the table. "I say it's time to pay another visit to Madam Samantha. The clerk said that she was working during the Covington murder and the Smith family murders. I still want to talk to her again. Obviously she knows much more than she's shared so far. We could try to catch up with the councilman, but it's Sunday, and I bet Mrs. Yates won't let him let any of us near him at this point. That leaves Madam Samantha."

"I could go to church," Angela suggested.

They all looked at her.

"Well," she said. "No one knows me yet at the Old Meeting House. If it's a fundamentalist group, I'm willing to bet that they meet all day."

"I can go with Angela," Jenna said. She didn't really want to go, but she wanted to make sure that Sam didn't rope her into going with him. She needed to do what she wanted to do on her own, at first. She had a hunch, and if her hunch was right, the crime-scene photos might prove it.

"No, too many people know that you're working with me. None of the church members would have seen Angela yet, so she could go," Sam said. "Except, of course, I think you've all had your pictures in national magazines at one time or another."

"If they recognize me, they'll kick me out," Angela said.

"All right. Angela, you head to church," Jackson said.

"What about Joshua Abbott?" Jenna asked. "He was one of the people wearing the horned god costume at the ball last night."

"We'll get to Joshua tomorrow at school," Sam said.

"You could try to speak with him today—his mother never threatened you," Jenna pointed out.

"Ouch!" Sam said. "All right, I can try to get that in today, too. If not, I'll have John Alden make sure he breaks up the two—David Yates and Joshua Abbott— tomorrow. Even if we're considering them cleared, they know something. Call it a hunch."

"A *hunch,* huh?" Jackson said, smiling. "Just mess-

ing with you. I can do my part and try to get to the rest
of the Abbott family."

"I'd like to speak with Milton Sedge's son," Sam
said. "But I don't want to intrude so immediately on
his grief, especially since none of us can do so now in
an official capacity. This evening, maybe. John Alden
isn't going to give me any help with that. He's convinced
it was an accident that killed Milton Sedge. But I don't
want to sit around, either, and with what we know now,
I think that Madam Samantha could answer a few more
questions." He looked at Jackson. "Madam Samantha
definitely has a bold edge to her, and she seems to like
to taunt men. Jackson, you and I will go to see if we
can't get in for more readings." He grinned at Jenna.
"No offense—you're not her type."

"No offense taken," Jenna assured him, relieved. She
hesitated.

"Madam Samantha, Joshua Abbott—and Sedge's
son," Jackson said.

"Sam, do you have the police photos taken at all the
murders?"

He shook his head. "Just the Smith family crime
scene."

"Then I think I'll pay a visit to the police station. Can
you call John Alden for me? At his level, he's probably
typically off on Sundays—probably rushing home after
having been called in this morning."

Sam groaned. "If you want the photos, I should go
with you."

"Maybe it's best if I just go," Jenna said. She smiled.
"John Alden is a good guy, like you said. I think he'll

help me. You call, I'll talk. I have a hunch. I just want to see something. I'll go to the station, see the photos, and then I'll just hang around on the street and watch Will's form of magic. We can meet up there."

The bored clerk still liked Sam. She probably knew exactly who he was by then, but she still seemed to like him.

And she still turned him down.

"You know, we're in full swing here these days," she noted. "Halloween is just two days away. You've got to understand. Madam Samantha is in the highest demand. She's doubled her rates for these last few days, and we're still turning people away. I can't possible slip you in today."

"She must come out to breathe.… Maybe I could take her for lunch, coffee, drinks…something?" he asked hopefully.

"And I haven't had a chance for a reading at all," Jackson said.

"No. No, no and no—and I'm so, so sorry!" the girl said. "Look, I do readings too, you know."

Sam was thinking quickly of something courteous and politic to say in return when a client in Gothic attire came out from behind the curtain. Madam Samantha followed, stopping dead when she saw Sam and Jackson.

"I was just telling them how busy you were," the clerk said.

Madam Samantha smiled slowly. She pointed at Sam. "You. You, come with me."

"Go get her, buddy," Jackson whispered lightly to Sam. "I'll talk to the charming clerk for a bit and see if I can't still verify our tarot reader's whereabouts, see if there was any way she might have slipped out during the murders."

Sam followed the sultry "psychic" to the back. He was curious that she had decided to see him. She knew who he was, and she had to know he was trying to trip her up. What the hell was it that gave her so much confidence?

They went back to her curtained area. She took her seat behind her table with its crystal ball and tarot deck. She indicated the chair in front of the table.

"Getting tired of Red already?" she asked him.

"Maybe," he said. "I'm just trying to figure you out."

She lifted her hands and offered him one of her overtly sexual smiles. "What's to figure out, Mr. Hall? I'm an open book. You want to accuse me of murder because it's always the sexually unabashed and brassy woman who turns out to be the murderer. Come now, Mr. Hall, you're a renowned attorney! You know the world doesn't work that way. I was here, right here. I have a dozen witnesses to testify that I was working when the Smith family was killed. What? Do you think you're in Salem and you can use *spectral* evidence? My astral self went out and committed murder while I was here, in the flesh, with a dozen clients?"

"No," Sam said. "I believe that you didn't kill the Smith family."

"Then?"

"I want to know about your partnership with Andy Yates."

She lowered her eyes and smiled slowly. "Hmm. Yes, well, someone dug deep to find out about that."

"Business agreements like that are public record," Sam reminded her.

"Yes, but…never mind. We weren't trying to hide assets from the government or anything. Yates just wanted it all…well, he's a *councilman*."

Sam leaned forward. "You're the talent, I take it."

"I think you know that."

"And he's the money."

"He does do well," she said.

"But you both tried to buy the Lexington House. Wasn't that a conflict of interest?"

She shrugged. "One of us might have gotten it."

Sam frowned, leaning back. "So why would Councilman Yates loan you money? Were you having an affair with him?"

She smiled. "Well, you see, that's none of your business." She rose, walking around the table and leaning against it so that her legs were pressed against him. "I should just tell you to go to hell. I obviously am innocent of the Smith murders, and the police have a kid in custody who was covered in blood. But I do like you. I like your scent, and I like your size, and I even like your face, Mr. Hall. Still, I *am* getting bored of all this." She leaned forward, hands on her knees, pressing her cleavage tight. "Next time you call me, it had better be to get laid, or I'm not going to talk to you again."

She stood. "Now get out."

Sam smiled and rose. "Madam Samantha, you're right about one thing."

"You really do want to get laid by someone who offers real excitement?" she asked.

"I'm a good attorney. I'll find a way to bring you into the courtroom."

"Really? But you don't have a witness anymore, do you? Poor Mr. Sedge was found dead today in a pool of olive oil!"

"I can see your concern."

"I've been here, working. You know that yourself." Her anger had returned to her face with a vengeance.

"Before I was an attorney, in law school, I went and got my private investigator's license, and I know a lot about breaking alibis," he said pleasantly.

"Call me when you want to sleep with me, honey. You don't even need to buy dinner," she said, and winked.

"Oh, honestly, I don't think that will be the case," he said pleasantly, and he walked back out to the main shop room.

Jackson was leaning over the counter, smiling as he chatted with the clerk. He arched an eyebrow at Sam. Sam thanked the clerk and paid his bill for Madam Samantha's time.

He and Jackson walked out of the shop.

"The place does have a back door," Jackson informed him. "But Madam Samantha was fully booked with clients when the murders occurred at Lexington House."

"And when Earnest Covington was killed?"

"Not quite as packed, but still here."

As they stood on the street, he noted a couple walking by hand in hand. They were both dressed as vampires—she was beautiful, and he was handsome. They made a cute couple; the costumes were exactly alike, except that his had pants and hers had a long black skirt.

It struck him that many people loved masks and costumes because they were able to *be* different people by wearing them. And, in fact, people could be *each other*.

"Jackson, what if…what if there were two people involved?" Sam asked. "Such as two people who were having an affair? That would explain the costume. If the killer was seen in costume, and the plan was to commit several murders, it would be natural to suspect that it was the same person. A costume takes away an identity. That's what we've been going on all along. But what if there were two people involved—maybe two people who were having an affair?"

"I can't believe I'm doing this," John Alden told Jenna. "I mean, I can't believe it. You're Sam's friend, Jamie's niece…and damned good-looking, but still, I can't believe I'm doing this!" he said.

Jenna laughed. "You're doing it because you're a good officer of the law, John."

"What do you think you're going to get from the crime-scene photos? You've seen the blood spray, so you know the murders were vicious and horrible."

Jenna nodded. "I know. I've never seen the victims in situ."

"Tell Sam I don't think I'm going to answer the phone

anymore when he calls," John said, sliding open a desk drawer.

"I will not, because it's not true," Jenna said.

John groaned. "I love Salem. I love my home. I love the Wiccans, the shops, the people who shake their heads at the Wiccans and still appreciate all the tourism they bring in. I love the historians, who also shake their heads at the Wiccans, except for those who are themselves Wiccans. I haven't had my badge that long, and I've explained that the chief wants this investigated and properly so. I want this to be solved, and over."

Jenna smiled at him. "See? And that's why you're helping me," she assured him.

He laid out a number of folders, pulling the photos from them.

"I told you—they're a gruesome sight."

"Yes," Jenna said. The photos depicted tremendous carnage. She had to study them carefully. And she thought that she found what she was looking for—even though she hadn't actually known what she was looking for when she started out. But if all their suspects had an alibi for one of the murders, it seemed now that she might have discovered why.

"John, look at the ones of Peter Andres."

"Yeah?"

"It's not as much overkill."

"What are you talking about? He's hacked to pieces."

"Hacked—just to make sure he's dead. Now, look at the photos of Earnest Covington."

"Yeah?"

"He's— Well, he's far worse."

"The killer was escalating. Isn't that the kind of thing you all preach about at the FBI? Or in your behavioral units?"

"Yes, sometimes. But I don't think that it's true in this case."

"You're losing me completely."

"I think we're looking at two different killers," Jenna said.

John's thick eyebrows shot up. "Two killers," he repeated. He nodded grimly. "People thought they saw old man Smith when Peter Andres was killed, but eyewitness accounts are remarkably unreliable. Everyone knew that Smith hated Peter Andres—Andres wanted Malachi taken away from his parents. Andres believed that living with Abraham Smith was like living with an abusive parent, even if Smith didn't technically beat the kid."

"I wasn't really suggesting that Abraham Smith killed Peter Andres.…" Jenna said.

"But it's possible. He had motive. And he certainly owned an ax!"

"You didn't find an ax at the murder scene, did you?"

John scowled. "You'd know if we had. Right, right, the bloody ax was at the Smith house. Andres was a scythe. Maybe Abraham Smith killed Peter Andres— and his son knew it and just went crazier and crazier because Peter Andres was his one hope, his one salvation…and his father had killed him."

"As far as I understand, several witnesses saw Abraham Smith on the day Peter Andres was killed," Jenna said. "And, as you said, and as I believe, people are basically decent. It's the odd man out who usually causes death and mayhem. And if Malachi Smith was going crazy with fury against his father, why kill Earnest Covington first?"

"Maybe Earnest saw the kid getting ready to kill his folks," John suggested.

"No, that didn't happen," Jenna said, thinking about her experience in the Covington house.

John wagged a finger at her. "And how do you know that, Jenna? A ghost told you so?"

"John, be rational," she said, not about to share the workings of her inner mind with him. John Alden certainly had to know something about her official work and their team, but she'd never tried to explain to him that she could see ghosts. "Covington couldn't have possibly seen Malachi—or anyone—from inside that parlor of his. And if he'd been outside, Malachi would have attacked him there, right? Besides, Earnest Covington's door was open. He had just gone back in his house and was killed while thinking about his son. The evidence shows that."

"The evidence in your mind!" John said.

"We know that the costume worn by Peter Andres's killer came from the drama department at the school," Jenna reminded him.

"Abraham Smith could have gotten a hold of it."

"I doubt it! He would have been reported at the school—he, as in any member of the Smith family. Malachi Smith was out of school then, and pretty much so despised," Jenna reminded him.

"I'm not buying your explanation," John said.

"Well, Abraham and Malachi as both being murderers doesn't makes sense to me." Jenna stood. "John, I know I'm pushing it, but could we get copies of these photos?"

"I'll think about it," he told her. "Sam has already been shown photos regarding the Smith family. Malachi hasn't been charged in the other murders yet, and I don't know if Sam will pursue warrants and subpoenas on the other murders yet—he doesn't have an eyewitness to support him anymore."

She leaned on the desk. "There's the horned god costume, John. He'll pursue the whole thing. I know he will."

John groaned. "I'll think about it—until a warrant comes or I decide! Damn, but you can tell you're Jamie O'Neill's relation—cuter, but a damned bulldog. Please, let me have the rest of my Sunday? God's day of rest, you know?"

15

Angela Hawkins sat among a crowd of about one hundred at the Old Meeting House. Pastor Goodman Wilson was at the pulpit, preaching. She surveyed the congregation. The pastor's flock looked like ordinary people, but, as a group, they were a bit different than most congregations she'd been a part of before. Here, the dress was conservative, down to the last person. There were no short skirts among the women, and certainly no plunging necklines. The men wore suits beneath their coats, button-down shirts and ties. Church wasn't exactly formal, but it was conservative and proper.

The service had been going on for some time when she arrived, but an usher at the door, open and friendly, had guided her in.

Goodman Wilson was preaching about tolerance.

So far, nothing that she heard suggested anything ominous or particularly different from what she might hear in a sermon at a more commonplace church.

"My friends," Goodman Wilson went on, "we are all here because we choose to be here. The world offers so many subversions. Satan does remain at the door. I say this, because Satan stands at the doors to our souls. We all know that he doesn't really play out there in the woods, trying to seduce the unwary to dance naked with him!"

That brought about a spate of laughter, which, it seemed, the pastor had intended.

"Our community is facing a time of trial again. We are often ostracized because our devotion is so deep, and because we see perpetual invitations to sin in those things others often see as innocent. But, my friends, we stand fast in our faith. We do not consider that we rise above others. We only know in our hearts where we want to go. While we practice tolerance—patience with our fellow man, though our fellow man often has no patience for us—we must also realize that we are part of this community. Jesus Christ suffered the mockery and cruelty of others so that we might learn to live our lives with His help to free us from sin. I am asking all of you to open yourselves up to the mockery of others. A terrible injustice is being done now. Though it will open you up to the mockery of others, I'm asking that any who can help in the matter of the deaths of our brother Abraham Smith and his loved ones, look deep into your hearts, and open your hearts, souls and even your lives to those who are so desperately investigating the truth in this matter. My friends, my brothers, my sisters, I don't ask that you act in haste—I ask that you search your own souls. I don't believe that anyone in the Smith family was a murderer. I believe that those investigating the case can use all the help they can get."

Angela stared at the pastor.

He had just baldly asked his congregation to step forward.

"Go in the peace and goodness of our Almighty God!" Goodman Wilson said. "May God's blessing follow you as you leave this place of worship, and may you do His work in all things. Peace be with you."

With that, the service was over and Angela stood. A number of people eyed her, but most of them shook her hand and welcomed her to the church and asked her to return.

She was surprised when Goodman Wilson approached her after the service, but she thought that the pastor would probably welcome any newcomer.

"Ah, welcome—Miss Hawkins," Goodman Wilson said.

She smiled. "You know who I am. Was that sermon for my benefit?"

"No, Miss Hawkins, it was not. It was written last night as I sat at my desk and pondered all that was going on."

"Do you think that any members of your congregation truly know something?"

He hesitated. Angela saw that he was looking toward the door. She turned, and saw a woman hurrying out with a young teen and a little girl with blond hair.

"Can I tell you that for a fact? No. But I do have members who have seen their children tormented by other children for their religious affiliations. If any of them does have information, I hope that my words will help them see what is right," Wilson said.

"That's kind of you," she said.

"No. That's what my God dictates I do, Miss Hawkins." He bowed to her slightly. "Good day, Miss Hawkins. I wish you Godspeed in your quest."

He walked away from her. Angela hurried out. She saw that the woman with the teen boy and small girl were getting into a car.

She made a mental note of the plate number, hurried to her car and wrote down the number. Then she put a call through to Jake Mallory.

Sam and Jackson had just stepped from the shop when Jackson paused to answer his phone. "It's Will," he said briefly to Sam.

From where they stood, Sam could actually look over the heads of the crowds to see Will's "magic" tent and the area before it where a number of people, young and old, in costume and not, were already gathering for the next performance. Will, inside the tent area, had his back to them as they talked.

"Thanks," Jackson said briefly.

"What?" Sam asked.

"The two boys—Joshua Abbott and David Yates— are there. Seated toward the back in a group that's getting ready to watch the next show."

"Then we'll watch, too," Sam said.

The boys were in football uniforms. They might have just left a practice, since their white-and-blue uniforms were grass stained.

Sam and Jackson walked over to stand at the back of the crowd while Will turned around and welcomed his audience, challenging them to determine what was magic and what was science, and what lay in the magic of the mind.

Quite a showman, Sam thought.

Will's act that day was all about light and music. He knew that the beat of the music caused some of the jumping of the light, but he was still amazed at Will's ability at sleight of hand, because he was definitely maneuvering some of his performance so that he could keep an eye on the crowd's reaction, but he was doing it with an amazing ability.

He made the image of a brilliant fairy that seemed to be composed of colored light appear before one little girl, and when he closed his hand around it, he thrilled her by turning the image into a plastic toy and giving it to her.

He repeated the performance, creating a small football and handing it to David Yates, and then creating a toy horned god—and presenting it to Joshua Abbott.

Before Abbott could respond, Will hurried on, creating his finale—a large snow globe with a beautiful dancing fairy and presenting it to one of the young women sitting in the first row. He was greeted with thunderous applause, and those who had been sitting rose to move on, though some stayed, eager for the next show.

Sam watched as the two boys in their football uniforms stood and walked toward Will. David Yates was angry. Joshua followed behind him. "Hey, hey you— what the hell was that all about?" David demanded of Will. Both boys moved in on him.

Sam had the feeling that Will knew how to take care

of himself, but he and Jackson seemed to decide simultaneously that it was time to step in.

"What's going on here?" Sam asked.

David Yates swung around. Joshua Abbott backed away about half a foot—a telling gesture. On his own, Abbott would crack.

David stared at Sam, knowing who he was. The boys were big, but Sam and Jackson were bigger by a few inches. He could see in the boy's eyes the recognition that he wouldn't intimidate either of these men.

"This freak is playing with our minds. And you— you're just ripping apart the community. You know who did it all!" David Yates told him. "You know who did it all, and you want to prove that you're such a hotshot attorney, you can make someone innocent look guilty. He—this freak!" David paused to point at Will, who just grinned. "I'll bet he's one of you! He tried to pick on Josh last night just because he was wearing the horned god costume. *Tons* of people wear that costume and you know it! And now he's handing him horned god toys, and if you don't lay off of us, my father is going to come at you!"

"Is he?" Sam asked. "Your father seems like a true law-abiding citizen. I think he'll be more measured in his response than you're being." He looked at Joshua Abbott. "So why did you wear that costume last night? You had to know that we picked up Marty Keller trying to scare my colleague in the horned god costume from the school—*and* that it had Peter Andres's blood on it."

Joshua Abbott looked at David and didn't speak.

"It's just a costume that everybody wears around here!" David said.

"You know what I think?" Sam said pleasantly. "Joshua, I think you wore that costume because David goaded you into it."

Joshua Abbott turned red. "No, uh, no! It was my choice. I wore it because I wanted to. Hey, the freak is in custody."

"Yes, and, of course, you know Milton Sedge is dead," Jackson said quietly.

Sam thought that the confusion that briefly touched David Yates's face was real.

"It was an accident!" he said. "He died in an accident!"

"Maybe," Sam said.

"Maybe not," Jackson added.

"Ah, come on, what the hell is the matter with you guys? You're wicked idiots!" David said. But he swallowed quickly. "You just want to make something out of nothing—'cause that kid is crazy. And he's cruel."

"That's right," Sam said. "He gave you the 'evil eye.' You need him to be crazy—and a homicidal maniac—to make sure you never look like an imaginative young idiot yourself, for beating your own head with a lunch tray."

David Yates turned red. "He gave me the evil eye—I swear it! Hey, you don't put yourself in the hospital and having to see a shrink on purpose!"

"I never suggested that you did it on purpose—I do believe you did it to yourself. So does your dad," Sam told him.

"My dad is a pansy-ass!" David said, apparently before thinking. He winced. "Stop it, please, stop all this!" It was an honest plea.

"I'll stop—when you two stop lying," Sam said. "I will get you in court. And if you're caught perjuring yourselves, you will face the law yourselves. Think about that. And—" he grinned, looking up at Will, who had been watching the exchange with his arms folded over his chest "—next time a magician gives you something, just say thanks!"

He turned to leave the boys to think over the encounter.

Jackson followed him.

"Well?" Sam asked him. "How did I do?"

"They're scared," Jackson said.

"They should be. I get the feeling that…all right, well, they are lying. Now, is it just because they want Malachi locked away? Or is it because they're afraid for someone else?"

Jenna was just leaving the station when her phone rang. Angela was on the line, very excited.

"Hey! I think I might know what was going on when Goodman Wilson approached that little girl. Sorry—remember what Will told us about Cindy Yates yelling at Goodman Wilson when he approached the little girl?"

"Yes. What? What happened at church?" Angela asked her.

"Goodman Wilson gave a sermon today—asking his people to go and talk to the police if they knew anything! Anyway, I watched a woman leave with two kids so I got her plate number. Jake ran it down for me. And the boy—the teen—goes to school with David Yates and Joshua Abbott. I think the little girl that Goodman Wilson approached was the daughter…and, since Cindy Yates went after him like a tiger, I'm assuming that the family has been keeping their churchgoing activities a secret. I've got an address. You want it? I'm still hanging around by the church, but I can go if you want."

"No, no, I'm just leaving the station. I'll go. Who am I going to see? What's the family name?"

"Parents, Michael and Alice Newbury. Teenage son—*seventeen*-year-old son, Michael, Jr. Little girl, Annie, seven. You'll find them just off Chestnut Street—I'll text you the exact address."

"Thanks, Angela!"

"Oh, and I just spoke with Jackson and Sam. They're going to go and see Mr. Sedge's son. After, we'll all meet at the wine bar."

"All right, see you soon."

Jenna hung up and a few seconds later, her phone buzzed, the address coming through. Checking it twice, she got in her car.

As she drove, she mulled over just how she was going to approach the family. All thoughts went out of her head when she drove up to park on the curve across the street from the modest home. The Newbury family was in the front yard. The teenage son, still lanky but growing tall, was tossing a football to his little sister while the parents looked on from their porch.

The father, Michael, saw Jenna and said something to his wife.

He walked forward as she approached. "Well," he said quietly. "You found us quickly. Did Goodman Wilson tell you where to come?"

Alice Newbury rose as well and came forward as Jenna answered honestly, "No, sir. My colleague saw your wife. We traced your license plate."

Michael Newbury nodded, looking at his wife. "Just as well. We should have spoken before. I'm not sure what good it will do, but we should have spoken before."

The kids had stopped tossing the ball.

"What's wrong?" the little girl asked her brother.

"Nothing, Annie, nothing," Michael, Jr., said to her. "You go play with your dolls for a little bit. We can run around the yard again in a minute. I think that the lady wants to talk to me."

"May we get you something, miss?" Alice asked. "We don't drink spirits, but I can get you some hot coffee or cocoa."

"I'm fine, thank you."

"Well, come to the porch," Michael said.

Alice looked around, as if afraid their neighbors would see them talking to Jenna.

"Alice, we all need to admit the truth, and Goodman Wilson has taught us that it doesn't matter what path a man takes to God, he can be a decent man. Our neighbors are good people."

She smiled at her husband. Jenna found herself thinking that while their beliefs might be strict, they were together in those beliefs and had a strong bond.

"Thank you," she said.

"It's Michael, Jr., you want to talk to. We'd just be hearsay," Michael told her.

Michael, Jr., took a wicker chair across from Jenna on the porch. He glanced at his father. "I can't really say anything that will help you a lot—I mean that, I really *can't*. I would if I could."

"Please, just let me know what has, clearly, been bothering you. You never know what will help an investigator in a situation like this and what won't," Jenna tried to reassure him.

The young man looked at his parents again and then at her. "We don't lie about our affiliation with the church," he said. "We just don't talk about it. We all went to the same schools for years, and we saw quickly that a lot of the kids really liked to tease and torment Malachi, so...well, I just tried to avoid being teased and tormented, you know?"

"I understand," Jenna said. "So, what do you know?"

"I don't *know* anything, except that David Yates has been the big man on the school ground since we were kids. And Joshua Abbott has been sidekick for years. If David says something, Joshua repeats it. If David wants to do something, Joshua will do it."

Jenna nodded. "Yes, I've met them together, and I get that impression."

Michael, Jr., seemed to have gained his own confidence, knowing that his parents were behind him. "David has talked about Malachi for a long time—since the evil eye incident. But it seemed that he got even worse after Mr. Andres was killed. He told everyone that the Smiths had killed Peter Andres because 'that old freak hated Andres.' And he said that Malachi secretly hated him, too. And, well, everyone is kind of afraid of David Yates, so they all believe what he says. Anyway, then David and Joshua both said that they saw Malachi coming out of Mr. Covington's house the day that he was killed, and I know the police talked to him and his folks, but the grocer—Mr. Sedge—said that he'd swear before God and the angels and all the saints that he knew damned well that Malachi hadn't done it."

"Yes, we know that," Jenna said.

Once again, Michael, Jr., appeared uncomfortable, and he looked over at his parents.

"Michael?" Jenna said softly.

"Well, Mr. Sedge was already saying it, so...well, I was in the grocery that day, too. And I saw Malachi in there. I can't swear how long he was there, but I know that I saw him talking to Mr. Sedge, and I talked to him myself. He'd left the church, but we all understood why, and we just kind of hoped that he'd return...."

They had another witness! But the witness they'd once had was dead!

"That's the way of our church, Miss Duffy," Michael, Sr., said. "We don't condemn those who leave. We just hope that they'll return."

Jenna nodded. "I understand." She stood. "Michael, for now, please, don't say this to anyone else."

Alice Newbury stood in fear. "You—you think this could put our boy in danger?"

"I just think that you should remain silent for now. I won't tell anyone who will let it out of our realm of investigation, and you should just keep quiet, too," Jenna told them.

Michael, Sr., looked at his wife. "She's saying yes, Alice. Mr. Sedge is dead. Accident, my foot. We'll keep silent, Miss Duffy. Just as you say."

"I'm always silent at school," Michael, Jr., told her gravely.

"That's a wise move," Jenna told him.

"Oh, the kids would never hurt me. I just don't want to be accused of giving any of them the evil eye."

"Were you there when it happened?" Jenna asked him.

He nodded.

"And what did you think?"

He hesitated and shrugged. "I think David might have believed that's what happened. But I know that he'd gotten called down a few days before—actually, by Mr. Andres. Mr. Andres really berated him for being so mean to Malachi. And Mr. Andres…well, he had a way of yelling at kids—well, not really yelling—but of making you feel *really* bad about what you did wrong. You know, he just had the right words, I guess. And that's what he did with David Yates. So, maybe, when it happened, David was feeling guilty?"

"Maybe," Jenna agreed.

Michael, Jr., smiled at her. "I feel bad for him, really. I know he uses his dad's influence all the time to be kind of like a big man, but I think he believes sometimes that his dad doesn't help him enough. You know, he probably just wants more attention from the guy."

"Michael, you seem to be wise beyond your years," Jenna said, and he flushed.

She thanked them again, shaking hands with the three of them. "If anyone asks me, I'll just say that I was doing a routine interview, that you were polite and cooperative but couldn't offer anything of consequence."

"Thank you," Michael, Sr., told her.

Jenna hurried to her car, anxious to see the others.

Sam and Jackson stood at the door to the Sedge home. Sam carried a large basket with a smoked ham and an array of sides for the family; he and Jackson had decided that bearing food was the right thing to do—and that it was their way in, as well.

An attractive woman in her thirties, her expression drawn and her eyes tearstained, opened the door. She appeared to expect people but frowned when she saw them, not recognizing them as neighbors she knew.

"Our deepest condolences," Sam said.

"Thank you," she said, accepting their offering. "I assume you're friends of my husband, Ricky? I mean, forgive me, I don't know you."

"We were actually affiliated with Milton," Sam said. "And I know that it's a horrible time, but..."

Her eyes widened suddenly. "You're the attorney!"

"Sam Hall, yes," he admitted, expecting the door to slam in his face.

It didn't.

"My husband will want to see you," she said, staring at Jackson.

"My colleague, Jackson Crow," Sam explained quickly.

She nodded and opened the door wider. "Please come in. Neighbors are here—and my mom is out back with the kids—but Ricky is in his office. I'll show you right in."

Ricky Sedge was behind his desk in his den, a small room with shelves that held books and trophies and pictures—family pictures. Sam winced inside, wishing he didn't have to cause the man more pain. It was evident that his had been a close-knit family; most of the pictures were family shots, many of Milton Sedge holding two little boys, many with Sedge and his wife, and several of various weddings, two older couples with the next generation of Sedges.

Ricky Sedge had been sitting there, squeezing an exercise ball with a vengeance when they walked in.

He stood, surprised, and looked at his wife.

"This is the attorney, Mr. Hall, Ricky. And his associate, Mr. Crow. I thought that you'd want to talk to them."

He stood and, to Sam's surprise, he seemed pleased to see him. He was glad. He'd half suspected that even if Sedge believed that his father had been murdered, he'd want to blame Sam. He was the one pursuing the case others thought was sewn up, after all.

"Finally! Someone who might believe me!" Ricky Sedge said, indicating a couple of small chairs in the room. "Sorry, sorry, about the space. It's kind of a full house...Margery is dealing with all those trying to help. People don't realize that sometimes you've got to be alone. Although, I guess it's good to keep the kids occupied—they loved their Papa Milty."

Sam and Jackson took seats.

"Mr. Sedge—" Jackson began.

"Call me Ricky, please. Every time I hear *Mr. Sedge,* I see my father."

"Ricky," Sam said quietly. "I understand you found your father."

"I found him. Yes. I made a mess in all the olive oil, trying to revive him. But, of course, he was cold as ice," Ricky said.

"And you called it in as a homicide," Jackson said.

Ricky Sedge hesitated a minute. "You know, sure, it looks like an accident. Unless you knew my father. He was a careful, honest, really good man. He would have *never* allowed those tins to be set up in a display that would have just fallen down on its own. When I say that to anyone else, they just want to pat my back and tell me that time will heal my wounds. And that the store was fairly dark, so accidents can happen, especially to the elderly. But my dad was in good shape, and he had great eyesight. Said he couldn't read a menu anymore without his glasses, but he could spot a bird in the sky a mile away. He didn't just walk into those tins of olive oil. Someone was in that store. Thing is, the police don't believe me—they just want to pat me on the back, too."

"What about a security tape?" Sam asked.

Ricky groaned. "Dad didn't have a security camera. He said that if someone needed groceries that badly, then they were probably hungry. The clerks knew all the neighborhood kids, and they knew how to catch the petty little gum-stealers. Dad ran a real family business." He leaned forward, studying both men. "Can you make someone pay attention? Dad was the only one who was going to swear that Malachi Smith didn't kill Earnest Covington. He was killed because he'd be willing to swear that up and down in a court of law!"

Sam let out a breath. "That's what I believe, too," he said. "And I'm so sorry."

Ricky Sedge lowered his head for a moment. Then he looked Sam in the eyes. "You don't have to be sorry. My dad believed in honesty and justice, and he wouldn't have changed what he had to say, no matter what. You didn't kill him. But if you want to help, find out who did. Make the police realize that he was *murdered,* and find out who did. Make sure that they do face justice. That's what I want! That's what my family needs. Don't let my father have died in vain for doing the right thing."

Jenna looked into the wine bar, but none of the others had arrived. She went back out into the pedestrian throughway and decided that she'd catch Will's magic show and see how he was doing.

Will had a little girl with him up on his impromptu stage. He was pulling quarters out of her ear and delighting the crowd.

He caught her eye. She frowned as she saw him jerk his head to the left.

Looking over at the edge of the crowd, she saw that he was indicating someone who was slowly drifting away from the scene.

Someone wearing the horned god costume.

She nodded to Will in acknowledgment.

The horned god moved away, toward the road. She waited. He moved again, and she followed.

After a couple of blocks, he headed down a side street, toward the graveyard.

She followed.

When she reached the area, she cursed silently. She'd lost track of her quarry.

Dusk was coming, but the gate hadn't been locked yet. Jenna walked into the cemetery. In the misted light, she closed her eyes against the souls who seemed to hover around the graves, some aware of one another and chatting quietly, and one following a tourist from stone to stone, tugging at her sweater now and then and laughing delightedly when she looked around to see who was touching her.

Jenna wandered toward the area near the rear of the wax museum, reading stones as she went along. Some were very sad, so many having died at such a young age.

She felt something behind her back and whirled around. It wasn't a person; no one wearing a horned god outfit.

It was the same older man who had warned her away before, the ghost who had wanted her to know that she was being stalked. Of course, she was being stalked by the boy, Marty Keller, but the ghost hadn't known that.

"Go! Go!" he told her.

He lifted a thin arm, pointing toward the huge tree that had grown right through the centuries-old graves. "Hurry!"

But as he spoke, a figure emerged from the tree—a figure in the horned god costume.

He was wielding an ax. He hefted it in his hands.

Another kid trying to scare her?

There were still others in the cemetery, but they were more toward the memorial benches.

"Put it down!" she said angrily. "I'm calling the police!" She reached into her bag for her cell phone.

The horned god immediately charged, ax swinging.

Just like in her visions.

16

"I can't imagine why she's not here yet," Angela said, taking a seat at the wine bar. "I talked to her quite some time ago. She was visiting the members of the church, but she should have been back by now."

Sam frowned, wondering why he felt such an instant jab of fear. He dialed Jenna's number, and he was rewarded with her answering machine.

"What if the church members…"

"No, no!" Angela said. "A mom went home with two kids. I saw her, Sam, and I don't know how to explain it, but no—they wouldn't have hurt her!"

Sam wasn't sure that he believed that at all. He stood and looked at Angela and Jackson. "Sorry, you wait here for her. Angela, give me that address. I'm going over."

"All right. We'll call you, and you call us if you hear from her. I honestly believe she'll be right along," Angela said.

"Go on, can't hurt," Jackson said.

Sam headed out into the street. Immediately, he saw Will performing, and Will, seeing him, looked concerned. "That way!" he said, working the words and a nod strategically into his act. "That's magic," Will cried to the crowd. "I say that way—and you look that way while I'm going the other!" Sam didn't wait to see more. Will had indicated the road down to the cemetery by having him reverse his gaze.

He started out at a walk, then began to run. As he neared the graveyard, he heard screams.

People were hurrying out of the graveyard; he saw that a number of them had pulled out cell phones and seemed to be called the police.

He stopped one woman. "What's happening? What's going on?"

"There's some maniac in there with an ax! He's after a woman. Oh, God, I hope the police get here fast enough!"

Sam let her go and tore into the cemetery himself. He rushed through the wide-open gate and looked across the expanse of graves and grass.

And saw the horned god, and the ax. Jenna was desperately dodging and ducking his every swing of the blade.

And then she rushed him, making Sam's heart nearly stop.

Knocking the figure down, she rolled herself off him to get away.

But the horned god was back up, staggering, reaching for his head.

Sam took advantage, letting out a loud roar as he raced for the figure. Crashing into him, he took the demon back down, sending the ax flying to the side, cracking the man's head against a tombstone and falling in front of it. Sam stood quickly, crying out. "Jenna!"

"I'm here, I'm fine," she said, hurrying to his side.

The horned god was still down, unconscious. Sam bent down and stripped the mask off his head. They both stared down in puzzlement. It was a man, a grown man. And it was someone Sam had never seen before.

"Do you know him?" he asked Jenna.

"No!"

By then, they could hear the police sirens. They stood a few feet from the man, waiting. Sam wasn't surprised to see that John Alden was leading the pack of officers who came rushing into the cemetery. If John had heard the word about a situation in the cemetery from the dispatch office, he would have been the first on the scene.

"I should have suspected you two!" he said, walking up, pulling out his phone and telling the paramedics to move in. He bent down by the body, feeling for a pulse. "Still breathing. Wait, I did suspect you two. What the hell...?"

"Hey, I was just walking in the cemetery, and he came after me. With that ax!" Jenna said, pointing.

"And he meant business. I saw it," Sam said.

"And—?"

"And I tackled him, right after Jenna rushed him, and if she hadn't known something about defense, she'd be bleeding to death right now!" Sam said angrily.

"All right, all right," John said, feeling in the man's pocket for a wallet or ID. "Nothing, of course," he said with disgust. "Let the paramedics through!" he called to his men. "We've got a live one here—and we *need* him alive!"

He looked at Sam and Jenna and sighed. "All right. Your attacker is out cold. Let the doctors do what they can for him. They'll call me as soon as he can be questioned. You know the drill—it's time for the paperwork."

Before they left the cemetery, Sam called Jackson, to let the others know what was happening and that Jenna was all right. Jackson said that they'd head to Jamie's and wait for them there.

The paperwork was tedious but didn't take as long as it might have. The horned god ax-wielder in the cemetery hadn't come to. Apparently the shot to his head was quite severe, and the man was in a coma. His prints, though, were taken at the hospital and run through the police system, so before they left, John Alden came and reported to Sam.

"His name is Gary Stillman. Does that mean anything to you?" he asked them both.

They shook their heads.

"He's in the system for misdemeanors in Boston. Seems he has a crack habit, too. That's expensive. But he wasn't really out to rob you, was he?" John asked Jenna.

"Nope. Definitely there to kill," she said flatly.

John scratched his head. "I don't know what the hell is going on here. He didn't kill the Smith family, that's for sure. He was being held in Boston on drug charges the night that the Smiths were killed."

"Gun for hire. We need to track a money trail on him," Sam said.

"I told you, he wasn't the Smith family killer. He was being held on drug charges," John said.

"Yeah, and you're hedging. Come on, John. Like you said, crack is an expensive habit. He was hired to kill Jenna. And you really know, somewhere inside, that no accident killed Milton Sedge. There's a killer loose here, because you've got the wrong suspect behind bars."

John stared at him. "Don't you dare tell me I don't know how to do my job, Sam!"

"I'm not!" Sam argued. "You were right to arrest Malachi—he was covered in blood. It's my job to prove he didn't do it."

John waved a hand in the air. "Get out of here. Ever since you drove in, my life has been a nightmare!"

"I'll see you at the school in the morning," Sam said.

John gritted his teeth. "Yeah, yeah, first thing in the morning!"

An officer dropped them at Jamie's house. Jamie hugged his niece fiercely, berating her for walking into danger.

Jenna hugged him fiercely in return.

"You'd have been in trouble if Sam hadn't happened upon you!" Jamie told her.

Angela and Jackson kept discreetly silent.

Sam found that he had to step up to the plate. "Actually, Jenna does know what she's doing, Jamie. She was holding her own."

Jamie looked disgruntled. Jenna shot Sam a glance that held a speculative, wry smile.

"Uncle Jamie, I'm not quitting my job."

"Well, you all need to stop—this is getting too dangerous!" he protested.

"Uncle Jamie," Jenna said quietly, "*living* is dangerous. I love what I do. It's important. And more people might die if we don't get to the bottom of this. It's always better to face danger head-on when you have to fight it."

Jamie opened and closed his mouth several times. "I'll get the stew," he said at last, then gruffly added, "You set the table for me, eh, lass?"

"I'll help, too!" Angela said, jumping to her feet.

They compiled the information they had all garnered during the day. Sam listened gravely to Jenna as she explained what she was certain the crime-scene photos told her. "It wasn't as if I could say, 'Oh, the person who did was left-handed or right-handed' or anything like that. But it appeared that the Andres murder was just something to be accomplished, while the Covington murder showed a greater violence, and the Smith family was—well, pure rage. And, yes, I know, escalating violence is often part of the profile of a serial killer, but, in this instance, I can't help but think there are distinct two killers."

She looked at Sam expectantly.

"I thought that myself today," he told her.

They both looked at Jackson, who nodded.

"So, we think that Andy Yates and Samantha Yeager are having an affair—and that they're making sure that they each have an alibi for murder?" Angela clarified, a statement more than a question.

"It is a theory," Sam said.

"A good one," Jenna said. "I know that Michael Newbury, Jr., believes that David Yates has been disappointed in his father, that he believes his father hasn't stood up for him enough. What better way to prove your love than kill the family of and incarcerate the boy who supposedly gave David the evil eye?"

"Why the others?" Angela mused.

"Peter Andres—because he chastised David Yates," Sam said.

"What about Earnest Covington?" Jamie asked. "What did he do to anyone?"

"In that instance, I believe that he was just there, collateral damage. He was in the community. The trail for finding out who had killed Peter Andres was growing cold. Bring it close to the Smith home—and have a son who will swear that he saw Malachi come out of the house—and you have a good fall guy. I think that the Earnest Covington murder was a setup, and when that didn't work, the family had to go. And Earnest Covington was such an easy mark. He lived alone. He never locked his door," Sam said.

"And the man in the graveyard tonight?" Jamie demanded.

Sam sighed. "Even John Alden will be looking for a trail on that. But," he told Jackson, "you should get your computer whiz on it. I have a feeling that we're not going to find out that any huge checks have been written. We need to look for alternate indications of money transfer."

"Murder for hire is expensive," Angela said.

Sam's lips formed into a white line. "Expensive? That's relative. Apparently, the guy from the cemetery was on crack. The kind that will make you do just about anything for money."

"But what was it going to achieve?" Angela asked.

"Jenna's death?" Sam stared at Jenna and let out a soft sigh. "I don't know if our killers know what you all do, with ghosts and spirits and all that…but I do think that the killer is afraid of her. He or she—or *they*— believe that she can see more than most people, some-how."

Of course, when they eventually went to bed, they didn't sleep, not right away. Jenna wondered if her own brush with the edge of an ax had made her more appre-ciative of living that night.

She and Sam made love until exhausted, and as they lay together she wondered what he was thinking.

"Thanks, by the way," she murmured.

"For?"

"Helping me out with Jamie."

He was silent, and she wondered if her time with him was ending soon. Sad, for in such a short time she had realized that he was what she wanted desperately. Sam was the reason she'd never been serious before— she'd been looking for someone just like him, with his eccentricities, and his sense of honor and ethics. She cared far too deeply. He had what she needed in a man, and she was falling in love, even with his arrogance.

Sam rolled over to look at her. His eyes were deep and serious.

"Do you still think I'm a jerk?" he asked.

"Sometimes," she said, threading her fingers through his hair, smiling.

"Good. Because sometimes I still find you scary as hell."

"Because I see ghosts and have postcognition?"

"Because…because I thought I was going to die tonight when I believed you might have been struck by an ax."

"You're always out there on the front line," she said.

"I'm an attorney."

"Oh, now…that's the truth, and not the truth. Last I heard, you defended a man who was entangled with the mob."

"The son of a mobster, and he was innocent. That's different.… I don't know if I can bear being with you," he said.

"It's all right," she told him.

"No, it's not. Because I don't know if I can bear *not* being with you."

She rolled into his arms. He held her against him. "On this one, though, will you give in to me? Will you promise not to try to slip into the school? Call it silly, I have this weird premonition about tomorrow. I want you safe."

"I won't slip into the school tomorrow," she told him.

She felt guilty, because she had no intention of telling him what she really was going to do. But they were going in circles. And she thought that she knew the way to end it.

"This is even crazier," he murmured, rising above her.

"What?"

"I think I'm falling in love with you," he said.

She pulled him down to her. "I like crazy," she assured him.

John Alden was true to his word; he was at the school, which had been in lockdown over the weekend. When Sam and Jackson arrived in the morning, the wardrobe mistress—the drama coach—swore up and down that Martin Keller had been telling the truth about the inventory, but other than that, she couldn't vouch for what might have happened with the costume earlier.

Some of the parents were at the school; although the boys that Sam really wanted questioned were the seventeen-year-olds, he had nothing against the parents being present.

Joshua Abbott was brought in to speak with John, Sam and Jackson alone—without David Yates there to tell him what to say or give him leading gestures. Just when they were about to begin, Joshua's father, Ben, arrived.

Sam thought that he'd be belligerent, angry that his son was being questioned. But Ben Abbott was just the opposite.

"Damn it, Joshua! This is serious. Perjury. You follow that Yates kid around like a puppy, but you straighten out right now. You want to go to college? You want a football scholarship—you want a life? You're not in any pact with David Yates. You're just a kid, and he's just a kid, and the two of you might wind up with jail time. *Tell the truth!*"

Joshua looked at his father miserably and lowered his head.

"Did you see Malachi Smith leave Earnest Covington's house the day he was murdered?" Sam asked quietly.

"The truth!" Ben Abbott repeated.

"Yes," Joshua said. Then he looked up. "I mean—I didn't actually see him, but David did. And David wouldn't say that he saw him if he didn't. He said that people might not believe him if someone else didn't say the same thing. And then…then I had to stick to it because…because I'd said it, and I couldn't turn on David and…Dad! Dad, I'm sorry. But David wouldn't lie to me—we're friends."

With that, John, Sam and Jackson thanked Joshua for his honesty and stepped out of the room. "John, listen to me, please, and I know that this is hard. I honestly believe that Councilman Yates and Samantha Yeager conspired to commit these murders," Sam said once the door had closed.

John stared at him as if he'd lost his mind. Sam spoke quickly, with Jackson's help, explaining that it was his belief that Samantha Yeager had engaged in an affair with Andy Yates. On her part, it was sheer greed. She wanted Lexington House. Andy Yates had watched what he thought was his son's terrible suffering; he had to right a wrong.

"You're crazy!" John said, looking at him.

"John, help us out here, please. Half the parents are

here. Can you get Andy Yates to come down? If we can
all talk to him with his son present…?"

John sighed. "All right. I'll get him down here."

"You want to what?" Angela demanded.

"I want to get back into Lexington House," Jenna
repeated.

"Oh, Jenna, I don't know if that's necessary. Why
don't we wait and see what happens at the school today?
When they actually get to the kids…"

"No. Angela, I've been twice. The first time, I saw
Eli Lexington kill his family. The second time, I saw
the day that the Braden son killed his parents. My cog-
nitive self might be working in a time pattern. If I can
get back in there one more time…"

"Maybe you're right. But, still—"

"If we wait, Sam will have to call John again, and
what I'll probably get won't actually be proof, just
an idea of the direction we should take to find proof.
They're about to go in with cleaning crews. We've got
to go now—before they do that," Jenna said.

"I'm still uneasy about it. The killers are out there.
They hired people to look for you, for God's sake."

"And they wouldn't dare do it again, not so quickly,"
Jenna said.

While Angela drummed her fingers on the table,
Jenna's phone rang. It was Sam.

"Joshua Abbott's dad came in and gave it to him,
and he admitted he'd been lying," he told her.

"That's a start."

"It gets better. John is bringing Councilman Yates

in, saying that he wants him present when David is questioned. You never know what happens when you get that kind of dichotomy going. We could get somewhere today."

"That's great!" Jenna told him. "Keep us posted."

"Will do," he said, and hung up.

"No one is going to be out to get me," Jenna assured Angela. "They're bringing Councilman Yates to the school."

Angela nodded. "Maybe the ghosts will talk to me, too, today.…" She groaned and rolled her eyes. "We're going to go under the police tape, huh?"

"We'll put it back, just the way it was. No one will ever know."

"Where's Jamie?" Angela whispered.

"He went back in to spend some time with Malachi. Angela, I feel that I have to do this."

"All right," Angela agreed. "Then…let's go."

Jenna drove. As they pulled out of Jamie's driveway and headed down the street, Angela frowned and looked into the rearview mirror.

"There's a car following us," she said.

"Oh?"

"Nope, never mind. It was just a woman, I think, on her cell phone and following too close. The car turned off. We're good."

Jenna was careful to park a few blocks down on the street. As they exited the car, Angela said, "If I head to the cliff area—the park-not-really-a-park—I can easily see Lexington House. I'm thinking that I should keep an eye out and warn you if someone does come. And then, after you've taken a try at reading the place, I can go in, because I want to see if there are ghosts in there who will talk to me." She smiled apologetically. "We both know that ghosts are as strange and moody as— well, as they were when they were living. And sometimes, they'll feel an affinity with one person and not another. You can keep watch and I'll go in if you don't get anything."

"Ah! Now there's a plan," Jenna said.

In front of Lexington House, they split, moving quickly. Jenna looked around; the neighboring houses were few, and she was pretty sure that the workday had already begun for most people in the area.

She didn't try to slink into the house, but went straight up the walkway, slipped under the tape and jimmied the lock open.

FBI training was helpful in many ways, she thought.

She entered the foyer. She started to head into the parlor but changed her mind. In the parlor, too many events had occurred. She walked up the stairs. If she stood in one of the rooms where Malachi's great-uncle and grandmother had been killed, she might get more.

She chose the left bedroom, and as she stood there, she felt the opaque mist start to form before her eyes, the thing that told her she was about to see.

She gripped the bedpost and waited for the scene to start to unfold.

And it did.

She saw an old woman. She might have been out of the past; she wore a nightcap and a long white night-gown, one that buttoned to her throat. But she wasn't from the distant past. There was a digital alarm clock by her bed, and she checked it to make sure that it was set for six the following morning.

Then she lay down, and reached into her bedside table for her Bible.

Smiling, deep into the comfort of her mattress and her covers, she began to read.

Jenna felt something by her side. She turned, and there it was, the specter of the horned god, bearing an ax.

An ax that already dripped blood.

The old woman looked up. Confusion tinged her rheumy eyes at first.

And then she started to scream. A silent scream, because she couldn't quite draw breath.

And then the horned god was upon her, the first swing catching her in the center of her breast....

Something seemed to happen then. The opaque image faded; she could see it, but more as a backdrop to something else.

And there was something else there.

Another image, standing at the side of the bed.

"Rebecca?" Jenna breathed. She was facing a ghost, or a spirit, a gentle, benign spirit. And the woman was speaking to her.

"The children, the children hear the words of their elders. Leave! Leave now!"

Jenna hadn't come unarmed this time. She started to reach beneath her jacket from her weapon.

And that's when the entire world seemed to come down on her head, and she whirled only quickly enough to see who had come upon her.

The horned god, once again....

* * *

Andy Yates and his son were seated in uncomfortable chairs; Jackson had purposely found those that had uneven legs for reasons of interrogation strategy. The light was made as bright as possible, and John Alden faced the table while Jackson and Sam took chairs at each end.

"I don't understand," Andy Yates said, bewildered. "A costume was taken from this school and used when Peter Andres was killed? And so you're questioning all the students—not just David, right?"

"That's right, Mr. Yates," John Alden said.

"We were at a football game when Andres was killed," he said. "I know you can check that out—you've probably checked that out. So—"

"So, we also know that David has lied to us," Sam interrupted.

Andy frowned, looking at his son.

"I didn't lie!" David said.

"Your friend, Joshua, admitted that he didn't see Malachi Smith on the day that Earnest Covington was killed," Jackson said.

"What?" David protested. "Joshua wouldn't say that."

"He did," John Alden said. They'd agreed to keep the questions coming from around the table. Like uncomfortable chairs, question being shot from all directions helped confuse a person who was lying.

"Wait! What does the costume used when Andres was killed have to do with the day Covington was killed?" Yates demanded.

"You see, we're not looking for one killer. We believe

there were *two,* working in unison to make sure they could provide alibis for the murders," Sam said.

"Wait, wait," Andy Yates protested. "You think that—"

"Yes, Mr. Yates. We think your boy might be guilty," Jackson said.

"We think he's in a conspiracy with someone else," John Alden said.

David gasped. "Me! I didn't murder anyone!"

"But you lied!" Sam told him.

"I didn't kill anyone!"

"But you did lie!" his father said, looking at his son with a sick expression.

"I lied to protect you!" David Yates said.

"Me!" Yates sounded astounded.

"I saw—I saw—" David said.

"You saw *what?*"

"I saw… I thought it was you…heading into the costume shop after the play last spring. You and mom were there, and then you weren't, and I thought you just went to speak to the drama teacher, ask her why I didn't have a better role."

"I never!" Andy protested, staring at his son.

"Mr. Yates, are you having an affair with your *business* partner, Samantha Yeager?" John demanded. "You hated Malachi Smith. You blamed him for every problem your son ever had."

"You blamed him for the stigma of having to see a shrink," Jackson said.

"And you'd have done anything for Samantha Yeager!" Sam said.

"Wait—*what?* No! No!" Andy protested. "We were in business, yes, and if Abraham Smith had agreed to sell the place, we would have opened it together. Yes, yes! That's true. But I—I wasn't sleeping with her. I swear it."

"You hired a hit man to kill Jenna Duffy just last night!" Sam said.

"No, no! That wasn't me—it wasn't me—" Andy Yates's protest broke off in a moment of pained silence.

"Dad—" David Yates began.

"Shut up! Shut up!" Yates said. "I want a lawyer. We won't say another word until we get a lawyer."

Sam looked at Yates, the way he pulled back, and suddenly he knew. They'd been wrong. They'd been close, but they'd been wrong.

He jerked out of his chair and headed into the hallway. He hadn't wanted Jenna here today; somehow, he'd just felt she was in danger. He'd been worried sick last night.

But she should be at Jamie's house—safe. Unless someone called on her.

He dialed quickly. The phone rang and rang, and her voice mail came on. He tried calling Angela, but got her voice mail, too.

Jackson came out to the hallway.

By the time he tried Jamie's house phone, Sam was already running out of the school. He reached his car, and he didn't know where he was going. Jackson slid in beside him. He started to jerk the car into gear, and stopped.

There was an old woman standing in front of him. An old woman in costume. Hell, it was Halloween.

"Get out of the way, get out of the way, get out of the way—"

"Who are you talking to? Where are you going?" Jackson demanded.

"The woman! That old hag in the road. Jackson, get her out of the way before I run her down!"

"There's no one—" Jackson said. "What does she look like?"

"Old. Dressed to the throat. In a cap—what are you talking about? She's right there!"

"No. She's just there for you. Start the car. She'll move."

"What?"

"Tell me again, who does she look like?"

"An old Puritan woman!" Sam exploded. "Damn you, Jackson, no one is answering a phone. *I can't reach either Angela or Jenna.* And it's not Andy Yates who's a killer—it's his *wife!*"

"Drive!" Jackson said. "And follow her—she's here to lead you."

"To what?"

"Life for the innocent."

Jenna came to slowly and saw a horned god hovering over her. She tried to move, but couldn't. She realized that she'd been tied to the sofa downstairs, that she was lying in the chalk outline that denoted the place Abraham Smith had been killed.

"Why couldn't you have let well enough be?" the

horned god asked her. "I never wanted to hurt you...I didn't want more dead."

"Shut up, Cindy!" someone behind her said. Jenna knew the voice.

It was that of Samantha Yeager.

"Why? We both came in from the back," Cindy Yates said, impatient. She pulled off the mask of the horned god and looked at Jenna, serious anxiety in her eyes. "He really is evil, you know. Malachi Smith is evil. His father was evil. This house makes everyone in it evil, you have to understand that."

"Cindy, come on!" Samantha said. She was wearing the horned god's cape, like Cindy, but she hadn't bothered with a mask. "Get a grip! We need to get this over with. I have to get back to the shop or I won't have an alibi."

"Well, we're not going to chop her up," Cindy said. "It has to be an accident."

"It won't be an accident. My partner's on the cliff right now, watching the house," Jenna said. Her head hurt. Her mouth seemed to be working only with great effort.

Samantha Yeager chuckled and leaned over her. "No, honey, she's not watching anything right now."

"You better pray that you didn't kill Angela," Jenna said, trying to keep calm. Except that she had panicked at first and jerked against her binding.

It was loose. And they hadn't bothered to tie her legs.

"If you hurt her, you'll have to watch out for Jackson Crow. He's part Native American, you know. He learned all sorts of unique tortures from his father's family," she said.

"She's bluffing, the wicked little bitch!" Samantha said, hunkering down beside her. She lifted a strand of Jenna's hair. "But your ol' Indian pal won't have to be upset—your friend will be okay. I got her with a slingshot from the woods—I was ready from the minute Cindy saw you on the move and called me. Slingshot! I'm good at it, by the way. Like I am with so many things..."

"Like making men think that you want them?" Jenna suggested, carefully inching around in the ties that bound her.

She'd hit pay dirt. She eased back.

"It's only fair," Cindy said.

"What's only fair?" Jenna asked.

"Oh, my husband! My fine, upstanding husband!" she said. "Our son is attacked, and what does he do? He sends him for psychiatric care! A real man would have gone to battle for his child! He would have done something about Abraham and Malachi Smith existing in the same world as our David. He should have done something. But, no! He looked at *my boy,* my beautiful, strong, handsome boy, and said that he needed help! *What kind of a father does that?*" she demanded. "And then, oh, he's such a smarmy bastard! He meets Samantha, and what the hell does he do? He comes on to her! He brought her into our house, introduced her to me and my children, and then came on to her. He's such a fool."

"A fool with money," Samantha murmured.

"If he weren't," Cindy said, her eyes narrowing, "I'd have been out of that house by now. And then you come into town and start sleeping with that sleazy lawyer! Bringing your hotshot FBI friends. And when I challenge you, what does my smarmy bastard of a husband do? He yells at me! He yells at me for slapping you, you bitch!"

As if suddenly realizing that her husband wasn't around to yell at her now, she slapped Jenna. Hard. And then again and again. The blows were stinging, but Jenna used the time to work harder at the ropes binding her.

"Stop it!" Samantha warned her. "We have to figure out exactly how to make this look like an accident."

"Like you did with Milton Sedge?" Jenna asked, running her tongue over her lips and tasting blood.

"That was me," Cindy said proudly. "Samantha did in Mr. Andres—with my compliments, of course—and I took care of the rest. They deserved to die! The Smiths deserved to die! They were horrible people. Don't you understand? They were evil!"

"Cindy!" Samantha pleaded.

"Does it matter what we tell her now?" Cindy asked softly.

"What about Earnest Covington? How the hell could you butcher him like that?"

"I had to! Don't you understand? I had to. They had to lock up Malachi!"

"Cindy! Stop it, please. Come on, and move! I've got to get her head cracked in and then leave her at the foot of the stairs. You wanted to talk to her—to explain.

You've done it. We've got to get rid of her *now,* Cindy. Come away!"

Cindy started to rise. It might be Jenna's last chance.

Jenna knew that she couldn't tear free from the bonds holding her, but she might be able to use her legs to help her get free. She jerked up with all her might, chair still strapped to her back and arms, desperately finding her balance in split seconds. She had no choice of weapon or flexibility: she head-bashed Cindy, causing her to cry out and fall back.

"Oh, screw this!" Samantha cried, and she reached for the old lamp on the table and started to bring it down on Jenna's head.

Jenna threw herself down and managed to avoid the first crash by tumbling awkwardly away. Her head was still ringing; it felt like it was a thousand pounds itself, and the wood chair slats and rope hurt her skin.

"Cindy, help!" Samantha raged.

Cindy staggered to her feet.

Samantha picked up one of the heavy candlesticks from the mantel.

She raced toward Jenna; Jenna ducked the blow.

Cindy came up behind her with the remnants of the lamp, striking her hard. She willed herself not to feel the pain. She still had no weapon but the force of her own body.

She threw herself on Cindy, taking her down.

Samantha reached for Jenna, grasping a handful of her hair and viciously pulling her up. She rammed Samantha, but Cindy rose.

And Jenna realized that her strength was failing. She

fell to her knees, hunched over, the chair covering her somewhat.

But she didn't want to die....

"He's here!" she exclaimed suddenly. "Abraham Smith is here...and all those who have died at the hands of others. They're all here, watching you!"

Jenna had wanted the exclamation to spook the women, but she found that she wasn't actually lying— the ghosts of the deceased had gathered in the room to watch them.

As if sensing something herself, Cindy stood still in fear, shaking. "Where, where?"

"Nowhere!" Samantha cried. "Help me, Cindy."

She had retrieved the candlestick and went at Jenna again.

"Abraham, no!" Jenna called, seeing that the ghost was going to do his best to trip Samantha. "Let the law punish them, and it will be years and years..."

"Stop it!" Samantha shrieked. But coming forward, she tripped and landed inches from Jenna, who pivoted on her knees to hit the woman with the legs of her chair. "Cindy, help, she'll kill me!"

Cindy cried out herself, lifting the coffee table, ready to hurl it at Jenna.

But, before she could, a whirlwind rushed into the room.

It was Sam. He put his arms around Cindy and threw her to the ground, the table landing with a loud crash. At that moment, Jenna became aware of the sound of sirens coming closer. Samantha rose one more time to come after her.

Jenna felt lightness in her head, and she knew she was going to faint, with darkness and stars bursting before her eyes.

But Sam ran in her direction, and his arm snaked around Samantha before she could strike. He lifted her off her feet, swinging her around to crash land on top of Cindy.

"I always knew you wanted to touch me, honey," Samantha said, dazed.

Then Jenna saw no more. The stars in front of her eyes burst, and then became blackness.

Waking up, Jenna felt a bit as if she were on display. There were so many people staring at her.

A doctor in a white uniform and a stethoscope in his hand. A concerned nurse in a pert white hat. Uncle Jamie, Jackson, Angela, Will, John Alden—and Sam.

Sam was seated by her side on the bed, holding her hand. His gray eyes were so misted with concern that it seemed her heart ached, rather than her head.

"Ah, you're back with us again," the doctor said. "Well, that was a pretty good wallop you got on your head, and I know you're an R.N., Miss Duffy, but you're staying right here tonight, you understand. You should know that a good concussion is definitely something to watch."

"Don't you be worrying!" Jamie said. "The lass will be staying right here, till you say that it's fine for her to leave."

"Ditto," Sam said sternly, squeezing her hand.

"May we have just a minute?" John Alden asked.

"A minute!" the doctor said sternly.

"I'm not leaving at all," Sam said. He looked at the doctor. "I'll be good, I swear. I'm just going to sit here and make sure she doesn't try to get up."

"All right, but not too much stimulation—the rest of you out of here in two minutes!" the doctor said firmly.

When he was gone, John Alden said, "Jenna, I just want to say—well, I just want to say that the women are both locked up, and—" he paused, shaking his head with a smile and looking at Jamie "—and the prosecutor has already gone in to see that the charges against Malachi Smith are dropped. Of course, now he has to press charges against Samantha Yeager and Cindy Yates, and you will be called to testify in court, and God knows, Sam may be defending them—"

"No," Sam said. "Sam won't be defending them."

"Who knew?" Jamie said quietly. "Who knew that a woman like Cindy could go quite so crazy over the perceived injury done a child?"

"Well, we did think that maybe Andy Yates was that furious," he reminded her. "We didn't think that a mother would resort to that kind of violence. That's still the way of the world—we don't like to think that the female of *our* species can be so violent and diabolical. And I sure didn't suspect that the affair was with *Cindy Yates,* not Andy," Jackson said apologetically.

"Oh, my God, Angela!" Jenna tried to sit up to address her friend.

"No!" the word was a cacophony from the entire group, and Sam gently pushed her back down.

"I'm fine—absolutely fine," Angela told her. "I'm

embarrassed, frankly. I was armed and everything. The rock came from the trees the minute I turned to watch the house. But, honestly, I was already getting up when Jackson came rushing over for me. So much for my intelligent stakeout."

"They would have just gotten us both inside," Jenna said.

"Maybe," Angela said. "And maybe not."

"Listen," Jackson said, "our two minutes are up. We can go through all of it later—when you're up to it. Come on, everyone out. Jenna, you get your rest, and don't you dare try to get up again."

"Wait!" Jenna said. She looked at her uncle. "How is Malachi?"

Jamie smiled. "Malachi is just fine. We had a long talk on the phone, and I'll go and pick him up when I leave here. I'm making arrangements for him to do his senior year at a boarding school in New Hampshire— one that has an extensive music department. He wants to pursue a career in music. He has the guitar now, and while I'm getting him situated, he'll have the piano at my house. We'll see his name in the newspapers again, I'll warrant. In the entertainment section. He's going to make it. He'll have support now, and belief. Music, he told me, is his gift from God. Who knows? Maybe he'll become the singing priest! A nun made it that way, once!"

Jenna nodded and leaned back, smiling.

Jamie kissed her cheek, then Angela and Jackson. Apparently, John Alden would have felt left out if he hadn't, so he did, as well.

She caught his hand. "Thanks for being a good cop, John," she said.

"I didn't want to believe any of you," he said. "Me. The man who should have learned the most from the past."

"You're an exceptionally good cop because you were willing to be honest and not blindly insist that you were right. You're a good cop because you pursued justice, not ego," she told him.

He grinned, kissed her cheek again and left.

And she was alone with Sam.

"Wait until you're well," he told her, moving closer and holding her fingers tenderly. "Such a brat, still! You were supposed to be at the house."

"I never said I wouldn't go to Lexington House," she told him.

"Brat. Omission is as good as a lie."

She smiled, not looking at him. "I'm just grateful that you came. I learned something, of course. Anyone can be taken by surprise. I'm pretty good, but... Cindy might have been the one to commit the most vicious murders, but Samantha is one mean opponent! How the hell did you find us?" she demanded.

"I figured it out when David and Andy Yates were together," he said. "I knew where they were—but I didn't know where Samantha and Cindy were. I tried calling you. You didn't answer."

"But—did you just figure I would have gone to Lexington House?" she asked.

He lowered his head. "No," he answered after a minute.

"Oh?"

"Someone showed me the way. I think she's a friend of yours."

"Oh? Who?"

"Rebecca Nurse."

She stared at him in astonishment. "I—I thought she was just an old woman in the way, but Jackson didn't see her. He said that she was there for me...and to follow her. And I did." He was thoughtful. "She knew how easy it was for even good, sane people to believe what others said, I believe. Maybe—maybe she stays, making sure that others don't follow the same route—making sure that history matters."

Jenna could barely believe what he was saying—and that he meant the words, earnestly.

"She kept telling me that children listened to their parents. And they did; David Yates knew that his mother loathed the Smiths. He knew, too, that his father wanted them out of the area. And I think he was terrified that his father *was* a murderer, and he had to keep saying what he did so that nothing happened to his family."

"That boy is going to need a lot of help," Sam said thoughtfully.

"And what about Malachi?"

"I think your uncle is going to become his guardian. He was already saying that he wanted to get him down to New York or out West, maybe. He wants to put him in a good music school."

"Actually, he needs to meet Jake."

"Jake, Jake! I don't want to hear about this Jake."

Jenna tried not to laugh; laughing did still hurt.

"Jake has got a gorgeous fiancée, so not to worry. But he's an incredible musician. I think he and Malachi really must meet."

"In Virginia?"

"Yes, Jake is in Virginia now."

He raised the hand he was holding in both of his, and kissed her fingers.

"I've actually been thinking that Virginia, the capital region, is really a phenomenal place for a truly renowned attorney to set up shop. Think of the graft! Think of the slimy politicians! Think of the masses, where crime just happens. I am considering looking into it. That is, if you think I should?"

He could push her back down if he chose, but she had to rise for a minute. She held on to his shoulders and kissed his lips.

"I don't think that I could bear it if you didn't," she told him.

Epilogue

They let Jenna out on Halloween morning.

She was delighted, but while the city was going crazy with talk and newspaper articles and the news on television, the last thing any of them wanted to do was join in the crowd.

Still, Jenna wasn't ready to leave Salem. She and Sam spent the night at Jamie's house, dispensing candy during the early hours, and just enjoying each other's company the night through.

The next day, Sam was the one who wanted to get an appointment to see the Rebecca Nurse homestead.

They arrived right at dusk, and he headed straight to the graveyard with Jenna at his side.

At first they saw nothing.

And then they saw her as the mist fell with the coming twilight. She said nothing; she smiled at them and vanished into the fog. Sam knelt by her memorial marker and placed a spray of daisies there.

"Thank you," he said softly.

He rose then, and took Jenna's hand.

"Virginia, eh? So I get to meet Jake?"

"And his fiancée, Ashley. And Whitney and her new husband. And—"

"Adam Harrison?" he asked.

"Of course."

"And I get to wake up every morning with you?" he asked softly.

"Yes. Well, every morning unless we're on a case. Sometimes—"

"Sometimes, *I'll* be on a case!" he reminded her.

"Yes, but you know—"

"Shut up while we're both ahead. Kiss me," he said. She did.

And while she kissed him, she thought she saw a number of the ghosts of Salem and Salem Village swirling vaguely in the mist. Looking on.

Smiling.

* * * * *

In my quest for regional food and drink, I asked my Massachusetts friends and family what they considered to be *the* Massachusetts traditional choice for imbibing. They all looked at me strangely and said, "Well, Sam Adams beer, of course!"

So…beer drinkers, there you have it. Sam Adams!

But long ago, another drink was quite popular, and is becoming so again: a good rum punch. This was begun by the hearty seafarers who came to the New England shores, fishermen, whalers, pirates and more. There are many variations, of course, but rum was the drink of the New World, and it was allotted to seamen. To stretch it out, improve taste and perhaps keep from falling overboard, seamen began to add things to rum. Sugar, because sugar is sweet. Fruit, because fruit is sweet—and keeps those at sea clear of the dreaded scourge of scurvy!

RUM PUNCH

Single serving.

Ingredients

1 shot Captain Morgan rum (Arrrrgh. Get your pirate going.)
1 shot light rum. (Bacardi, or even a flavored Bacardi. Your choice—there are so many out there!)
2 oz orange juice
2 oz grapefruit juice
1 tsp sugar (Dieting? Sugar substitute works fine, and may help…a wee bit!)
Splash of 7Up or other lemon/lime soft drink

Directions

(Variations include adding a touch of grenadine instead of sugar, adding orange or other fruit-flavored liqueur, or making your own mixture of rums, as in, say, Bacardi light, dark and flavored.)

Mix ingredients with ice. Sugar-frost a cocktail glass and serve straight up, or serve on the rocks.

For a crowd, use a large punch bowl, a half bottle of dark rum, a half bottle of light rum, a half gallon of orange juice, a half gallon of grapefruit juice, one bottle of 7Up (or other), ten tablespoons sugar, a touch of grenadine and add fruit slices to the bowl.

Drink!

Ah, New England winters! They're brutal at best. Staying warm is a challenge, and throughout history, our hearty Yankee friends have learned the secrets of thawing themselves out. New England clam chowder is one of the delicious delicacies they have shared with the nation and is one of the tastiest and heartiest soups to be found. Great to make and enjoy before a roaring fire.

NEW ENGLAND CLAM CHOWDER

Serves 6.

Ingredients

3 tbsp butter (or substitute, if you choose; salt-free is fine)
1 medium onion, finely diced
2 celery stalks, sliced into 1/4-inch pieces
3 tbsp all-purpose flour
2 cups chicken stock (Are you an almost-vegetarian who eats fish? Use vegetable stock)
2 cans chopped clams in juice
1 cup heavy cream
1 lb potatoes, cut into 1/2-inch cubes (Tip: buy potatoes that would taste delicious in baked form)
1 bay leaf
Salt and pepper to taste

Directions

Using a large pot, heat the butter without burning or scalding over a medium-high heat. Add the onions and celery and sauté. Carefully add in the flour and stir for consistency. Add the stock and the juice from the cans of chopped clams. When the mixture is thoroughly combined, add the potatoes and the bay leaves. Keep stirring while you bring the mixture to a simmer, and then heat on a lower temperature for about twenty minutes. Add the clams and salt and pepper to taste, and cook for another two to five minutes, keeping the clams firm. Add an extra touch with homemade croutons! Take an old baguette, French or Italian bread, and cube the pieces. Sauté in two tablespoons of butter, substitute or olive oil. Add seasoning to taste, such as garlic powder, pepper and salt. When they are crispy and dry, serve on the soup.

Garnish with a sprig of fresh parsley, or…serve in a bread bowl!

My personal favorite dish when I arrive in New England is baked scrod. Start out with fresh fish! Or purchase filets from a company known for expert freezing.

BAKED SCROD

Serves 4. (To serve 6 or 8, add a quarter or a half to all ingredients)

Ingredients

4 scrod fillets
2 tbsp lemon juice
1 ½ cups white wine
Salt and pepper to taste
¾ cup melted butter (reserve half)
1 ½ cups dried breadcrumbs

Directions

Preheat the oven to 350°F—very important when baking fish!

Butter a baking dish. Make sure scrod can be laid out by piece with space. Add the fish, the lemon juice and the wine. Add salt and pepper to taste. (Substitute salt is fine!) Use a quarter cup of the melted butter to set a fine drizzle on the fish.

Bake for approximately 20 minutes; no under- or over-cooked fish. The fish should be flaky, yet still moist.

Turn the oven on to broil. Dust the breadcrumbs evenly over the fish, and then add the remaining butter evenly over the fish filets. Broil for another few minutes, just to brown the breadcrumbs to a delicious toastiness.

Serve with your choice of rice, potatoes or pasta, and a veggie, such as asparagus or broccoli.